To renew, find us online at:
https://capitadiscovery.co.uk/bromley

Please note: Items from the adult library may also accrue overdue charges when borrowed on children's tickets.

If you liked
One More Night and *Tempting the Enemy*
why not try

Reawakened by Rachael Stewart
Fast Lane by Margot Radcliffe

Also by Caitlin Crews

Filthy Rich Billionaires

Teach Me
Take Me
Tempt Me

Hotel Temptation

Unleashed
Undone
Untamed

Summer Seductions

The Pleasure Contract
Just One More Night

Also by JC Harroway

Billionaire Bedmates

Bound to You

The Pleasure Pact

Bad Business
Bad Reputation
Bad Mistake

Billionaire Bachelors

Forbidden to Want
Forbidden to Taste
Forbidden to Touch

Discover more at millsandboon.co.uk

JUST ONE MORE NIGHT

CAITLIN CREWS

TEMPTING THE ENEMY

JC HARROWAY

MILLS & BOON

First Published in Great Britain 2021
by Mills & Boon, an imprint of HarperCollins*Publishers*
1 London Bridge Street, London, SE1 9GF

Just One More Night © 2021 Caitlin Crews

Tempting the Enemy © 2021 JC Harroway

ISBN: 978-0-263-29797-3

MIX
Paper from
responsible sources
FSC® C007454

Printed and bound in Spain
by CPI, Barcelona

JUST ONE MORE NIGHT

CAITLIN CREWS

MILLS & BOON

To all the DARE editors who worked so hard on these books, and to all my fellow authors who told such brilliant stories in the first place. It's been such a pleasure to be a part of this line!

And to my readers, thank you so much for going on these dark, delicious adventures with me. It's been an absolute delight!

CHAPTER ONE

INDIANA MARCH, CALLED INDY by her loved ones and much filthier things by her lovers, landed in Prague on a gorgeous June afternoon, ready to face her destiny.

It had been two years since one night in Budapest had changed everything.

Two years since she had made a promise before flying standby back to New York, where she'd moved in with her far less free-spirited older sister—who never would have gone to Budapest in the first place and wouldn't have gotten into the trouble Indy had no matter where she went.

Bristol was the *good* March sister.

She had recently gotten her doctorate after a lifetime of endless, serious, and committed studying. Indy, on the other hand, was committed to having fun. And while she was at it, living up— or down—to everyone's expectations of the other March sister.

Not *bad,* she liked to say. But *better.*

Especially because when she said things like that, and vamped it up, it made her sister roll her eyes. And then laugh in spite of herself.

Indy and Bristol had settled on these designations for themselves when they'd still been little girls in small-town Ohio. And all these years later, Indy still thought she'd made the better choice. She'd decided school was boring in roughly the fourth grade and had decreed that she had better things to do, leaving Bristol to study away to her heart's content while she danced and partied and ran around just being silly, because she could.

Bristol would probably be off studying right this minute—because there were apparently *post*-doctorates for people who felt the one PhD wasn't enough—if it weren't for the little summer adventure Indy had sent her sister off on. *An opportunity to discover the parts of you that aren't all about your mind, at last,* Indy had told her—but that was another story.

Indy smiled at the notion of studious, killjoy Bristol getting her freak on out there as her plane taxied toward the gate, bouncing a little on the tarmac. She couldn't wait to see if her big sister finally loosened up a bit—and couldn't really imagine what a *loosened up* Bristol would look like. As the plane came to a rocking stop at the gate, she gathered up the small carry-on that was all she'd brought with her and held it on her lap, watching as all around her, people leapt to their feet and started dragging much heavier bags out of the overhead bins.

It always looked so unpleasant. And then the reward for all those heavy bags was that you then had to lug them around with you. Where was the fun in that?

Indy never troubled with much baggage, figurative or literal. After college she'd backpacked around for a couple of years, but never with one of those massive packs that some people toted across the planet that made them look like unfortunate tortoises. Their packs were always seventeen times their body weight, the better to mark them to all and sundry as a tourist, and barely fit in the narrow, often cobbled streets that they were always trundling along in. Not to mention, they might as well have worn neon signs inviting any predators to take a swing their way.

No thanks, she thought now, though she smiled nicely enough at the woman next to her and her two enormous, overstuffed suitcases.

That wasn't how Indy operated. She was less about neon signs that weighed her down and more about going with the flow. And she'd never had an issue with predators.

Well. She stood up from her seat when she could

finally step out into the aisle and considered. That wasn't *entirely* true, was it?

Indy had made up no itinerary, back in her world-traveling backpacker days or even today. Because *itineraries* were boring. They nailed you down to a time and a place and a *schedule* and Indy was all about never, ever being boring, nailed down to anything, or, God forbid, the kind of person who couldn't grab a drink without consulting seventeen sticker-laden planners and her phone's calendar app. She'd watched Bristol—whose whole life was about schedules and responsibility and tedious meetings about any number of inane things—whittle away her life in tiny little recorded increments on hundreds of planner pages, but Indy had never wanted any part of that kind of nonsense. She had barely made it through college. Not because she was dumb, but because there were always so many more delicious things to do than study. Or sit in a yawn-worthy lecture. Or write dreary essays that were never about the things that interested her.

Those being, in no particular order: life. Sex. Fun.

Indy wanted to squeeze every last bit of the good stuff out of every single day, then roll herself around in it until it became who she was. On a cellular level. What else could possibly be the point?

Sadly, that was not, it turned out, the kind of

mission statement the average employer liked to see on a résumé. Or the average landlord liked to hear about when rent was due, so it was a good thing for Indy that Bristol was always so dependable.

Still, Indy never had too much trouble finding work. Or getting laid, for that matter, and the two often twisted together in ways she was sure she could probably hashtag about—if she weren't too busy living to live tweet. She didn't have any particular airs and was perfectly happy to take a waitressing job here or a temp job there. Just as she was happy to roll under one man in the morning and ride a different one that night. Jobs and men were an endlessly renewable resource, in her experience. There were always, always more when a girl was game for whatever came her way.

Her sister and her perfectly lovely parents back in Ohio did not understand Indy's approach to life—and only Bristol knew the more salacious details, thank you. All her parents knew was that Indy *had trouble settling down.*

Her mother thought she needed a man. Indy had to bite her tongue every Christmas to keep from saying things like, *don't worry, Mom, I've had many.* She didn't think that would shock the unflappable Margie March. Nothing could, in her experience. But it would open up her personal life to conversation, and Indy always figured that was a bad idea all around.

Particularly these past two years when, she could admit, her usual carefree, hedonistic attitude had become something a good deal more…manic.

It was true. She'd had something to prove, hadn't she?

Indy shivered a bit in the cab that drove her from the airport down into the old city. Prague spread out before her like a fairytale, but not the kind of fairytale that warmed the hearts of wannabe Disney princesses. Bristol had been the one who loved those happy ever afters when they'd been girls. She'd always longed for the Prince Charmings and the perfect kisses.

But Indy had been far more intrigued by the Big, Bad Wolf. She'd seen no reason for Little Red Riding Hood to waste her time swinging an axe or even getting a passing huntsman to do the same on her behalf.

Not when there were so many other things to do in the dark.

She shivered again, even though it was warm in the cab. The truth was, Indy had been aching like this since she'd left Budapest. It had only gotten worse over time. Her nipples were always so tight they hurt. Her pussy was always *so* wet. Sometimes she could simply clench her thighs together and make her clit throb, or even get herself off sometimes, but none of it was enough.

None of it was near enough.

No matter how many cocks she rode or took deep in her mouth, none of it had made her feel the way today did. Just here, sitting in a taxi, was already hotter and better than all the sex she'd had since she'd left Budapest.

Combined.

Because today she got to keep her promise.

Indy didn't let herself imagine, even for a moment, that he wouldn't be here.

He would. She was sure he would.

He had to be.

His instructions had been simple and clear two years ago. He'd given her the address, a time, and a key. The same key she could feel tucked between her breasts now, because she'd hung it from a chain when she'd gotten back to New York. The key she'd never taken off, no matter who she was fucking or what other adventures she might have had since.

Sometimes she'd gotten off more to the memories the key kicked up in her than whatever—or whoever—she'd been doing. She wrapped her hand around the key on its chain now and sighed a little, feeling her whole body hum in anticipation.

She'd never been one for waiting. But she'd waited for this. Some days she'd been sure the waiting might kill her—but it hadn't. And now here she was. Alive after all.

The waiting was finally over.

Or almost over. Indy had a few hours before the agreed-upon meeting time, so she didn't go to the address she'd been given. She had the taxi drop her off on the cobbled street ringing Prague's Old Town Square and dodged armadas of tourists as she walked around the looming statue of the fifteenth-century martyr that dominated it. She peered up at the great Gothic church that always made her sigh a little and got a glimpse of the famous Astronomical Clock over the inevitable crowd waiting for its next show.

It felt good to walk. The last time she'd been in Prague she'd been so exhausted after far too much clubbing in Berlin that she'd hardly been able to feel her own feet, much less fully register where she was. She knew she should have been jet-lagged today, but she wasn't. Or if she was, it was buried so far beneath her excitement and the adrenaline of finally being here that it didn't affect her at all. She hadn't slept on the overnight flight from New York to Zurich. She hadn't nodded off in the Zurich airport where she'd caught her connection. And she'd been good and wired on the plane into Prague.

When she sat down at a table in the crowded,

open-air café, she waited for a wave of weariness to take her over.

But it didn't come.

She was *amped*.

Indy settled back in her café chair and blew on her coffee when it arrived. She was hardly able to believe it was only a matter of hours now. She checked her phone. Less than two hours.

And she could still remember that night in Budapest far too clearly. As if it had happened last night instead of two years back.

Indy had been with some friends she'd hooked up with in Croatia. She'd been two solid years into her world traveler phase and hadn't seen any end in sight, at that point. These particular friends were the sort she picked up wherever she went. A hostel here, a club there—there were always like-minded people about. Always another party, always another adventure. A new city, a new face, a new story to tell. Indy hadn't been able to come up with a single good reason why she would ever return to what waited for her back in the States.

That being the hum-drum little lives that all her friends lived in the various places they'd settled down. Nine-to-five desk jobs, paycheck to paycheck, dreary cubicles, and boring conversations about *the property ladder.*

None of that was any fun at all.

You need to make some real decisions about

your life, her father had told her after her college graduation, which everybody liked to say had been a skin-of-the-teeth kind of deal for the not-so-good March sister. *Serious decisions.*

Indy had felt that she was full up on *serious*. She had taken a fifth year to get her degree and might have taken a sixth if she hadn't been so deeply bored by the whole thing. Still, she'd paid her way—meaning there had been no letting anybody down if she made academic decisions that didn't suit them, like failing a class because she'd forgotten to attend it, or accidentally going off to a music festival instead of taking her exams.

Disappointing them, sure. But not actually letting them down or spending their money. Indy had some standards, thank you. And she had never felt the need to let her father know *how* she'd paid her way through college. Or why it was she had such a robust savings account come graduation.

There were things a father didn't need to know.

I know what I want to do with my life, she had told him, wrinkling up her nose in his direction as they'd sat down by the river near her childhood home, fishing.

Or in Indy's case, pretending to fish while doing what she did best. Lounging.

Okay, what she did second-best.

Nothing *is not a good answer,* Bill March had replied. He'd shot her a look she knew well, filled as it was with laughter, love, and that particular gleam that made her think, sometimes, that her father knew exactly how free-spirited she really was.

I'm going to live, *Dad*, she had said. *Deep and hard and wild. Isn't that what you're supposed to do with a life?*

Everybody's hard and wild until it's time to pay taxes, her father had said with his typical calm midwestern practicality.

I'm going to be just fine, she had told him, smiling wide. *I promise.*

And she had been.

She had taken a certain delight in sending her raciest photos to her sister, because Bristol was so easily scandalized. Indy had sent postcards to her parents from every new place she went. London to Bali to Perth to Rio and back again. She'd worked when she needed money, went on marvelous adventures as the spirit took her, and followed her pussy wherever it wanted to go.

The club in Budapest had been one of the underground ones she'd developed a taste for over time, on all continents. She loved the inherent mystery of these pop-up events. A warehouse or a field somewhere, often in a sketchy part of town to make the whole thing feel more edgy and exciting. There was never any possibility of planning for these things, there was only waiting for the text to come and then racing off—no matter her state of inebriation—to dance and howl and party until the sun came up.

That was why a wise woman didn't have a plan. All the good stuff happened outside those lines.

The night in question had been like all the other nights in all the other cities and fields and beaches she'd discovered on her travels. The DJ had been particularly good and Indy had lost her friends somewhere in the crowd, but that was never something she worried about. She liked to let the universe take a hand in such things. She would either find them again or she wouldn't, but her experience, everywhere, was that there were always new friends to be made.

You have a low bar for what you call friendship, Bristol had told her. More than once.

Or you have a ridiculously high one, Indy would retort. *You can make a friend, Bristol. It's not a lifetime commitment unless you want it to be. It also won't kill you.*

Bristol, as ever, had remained unconvinced. And also lonely, by Indy's reckoning, though she would die before she admitted it.

But Bristol hadn't been on Indy's mind that night in Budapest. She'd danced and danced. At some point she'd decided she needed a little bit of fresh air after all that dancing and she'd wound her way through the crowd, buzzing along nicely on the music and the beat she could feel deep inside her.

Indy had slipped out the side of the warehouse, and never knew, later, what made her wander away from the groups of people doing the same thing she was. Either taking a breath from the party inside or carrying on their own festivities out in the summer dark. She'd wandered away from the clusters of them, half wondering if she could see the stars in this part of Budapest. If she got away from those party lights and all the lit-up cell phone screens. If she'd had another motivation, she couldn't remember it.

She hadn't known what she was walking into until it was too late.

Scary men arguing in a dark alley. A gun in her face.

Then Indy on her knees on the pavement, hard, her heart pounding so wildly it had made her feel ill.

In that moment, she'd been certain that every warning she'd ever been given was about to come true. With a vengeance. Every dire prediction anyone had made about the way she lived, the way she *was*, was about to happen to her after all.

You don't think before you act, her sister had said a thousand times.

I hate to think of you getting yourself into trou-

ble, her mother had said more than once, *and all because your head is always in the clouds.*

And her father had frowned at her, the day he had dropped her off at the airport. Looking far more serious than he usually did. *The world isn't a magical place just because you want it to be, honey. Be smart out there.*

Indy had not been smart. She had been the opposite of smart, in fact, and had reveled in how little care she'd taken because it made for a better experience and then a better story to tell. And she had known, then, that she was going to pay for that in some out-of-the-way alley where no one would ever find her if they left her for dead.

Assuming they left her.

But that wasn't what happened.

She shuddered now, her hands cupped around her coffee. Far away from Budapest in a crowded café in lovely, fairytale Prague, two years later.

Still, Indy shuddered, because she could remember too well her first sight of him. That face of his, so beautiful it was cruel as he'd stared down at her in disbelief. She'd noticed that *face*, like the blade of a hatchet, piercing and inevitable. She'd had the impression of a tall, well-built, dark-haired man, but he'd had the eyes of a poet, intense and yet almost dreamy as he'd gazed at her there on her knees.

Their eyes had met down the length of the gun he'd held, pointed directly at her forehead.

And she'd had no doubt whatsoever that he knew how to use it.

He asked her something in a language she didn't understand. Hungarian, she'd thought, which would make sense as she had been in Hungary. Indy had shaken her head, almost smiling in an out-of-body sort of way, because at least if she was going to meet a brutal end it would be at the hands of a man who looked like an angel.

A fallen one. And fallen hard.

That he was dangerous, brutal and powerful at once, would have been obvious even if he wasn't holding a gun. Right in her face.

Even with those too-blue eyes.

What are you doing here? he had asked her in English, after trying a couple of other languages and getting nothing. His accent had made the words seem like liquid, swirling around her and washing through her. A new, potent heat.

I have no idea, she had replied, honestly.

And for a long moment, possibly a lifetime, she had been aware only of him. That look on his overwhelming face. That gaze of his that made her want to cry. The electric *something* that arced between them, even with concrete digging into her bare knees and her hands in the air.

For that little while, nothing else existed.

Nothing.

He had muttered something she'd understood was profane, even if she hadn't understood it.

And then everything got fast.

Indy remembered it like a blur, though she knew that each action had been precise. Surgical.

He had looked at her. She'd seen something in his gaze, something that had made her breath catch.

Something that had gone through her like an earthquake.

Then he had turned and taken down the other three men standing there with him. She had hardly had time to gasp, to shake, to react. She'd thought of poetry again, all of it lethal, as he'd spun around with blistering speed and laid all three men out flat.

Two kicks, one punch.

Like he was an action star.

Come, he'd said to her when they were all slumped on the ground. *You cannot be here.*

He'd reached down to pull her up to her feet with a possessive grip on her arm.

And Indy had gone willingly.

More than willingly. Because he'd saved her, that she'd had no doubt—even though it hadn't been clear if he was one of the things he'd saved her from.

But there was something about his grip on her

arm. The way he'd moved them both out of that alley. Quickly, but with that same liquid grace she'd already seen used with lethal intent on his friends.

It had occurred to her then that she ought to have been more scared than she was. As scared as she'd been when she'd first understood what was happening to her. As scared as she'd been before she'd actually caught his gaze and everything had…shifted.

If you're just going to kill me in a different location, she'd said as he led her away from the alley, *I have to tell you that it will be very disappointing.*

They'd made it out into the street by then. She could hear the pumping sound of the club she'd so foolishly wandered away from, though she couldn't see it. Had she wandered into the alley from the other side? And yet Indy hadn't really cared, because there had been a streetlight and she could *really* see him then.

He was built like a weapon far deadlier than any old hatchet. His beautiful eyes were breathtakingly blue, and he had a set of lips that should have made him a courtesan—and might have made him pretty if his face wasn't drawn in such harsh, male lines. She'd thought she would happily pay the whole of her life savings, and then some, to have that mouth between her legs.

But those were the only two soft things on his body.

Everything else was muscle. Thick and honed at once, so that he fairly hummed with power. With threat.

She remembered thinking how odd it was that she had been with so many men and had always happily explored all the various ways they used their power. Physical and intellectual alike, but nothing like this. Like him.

This man was darkness personified and his body showed it.

Indy had noticed a tattoo rising from the neck of his T-shirt, the same T-shirt that strained to contain his biceps. The same T-shirt that seemed unequal to the task of his hard, ridged abdomen. He wore dark jeans and the kind of dress shoes men wore on this side of the Atlantic because trainers were frowned upon for nightlife purposes in so many European countries.

She had been fully aware that he had that gun tucked in the small of his back. But looking at him, not only did she also know that his hands were weapons all by themselves—not to mention the feet that she'd seen in action with her own eyes—but that he likely had other things stashed around on his body, as well.

His profession seemed pretty clear.

I'm not going to kill you, he had said in that

accented voice of his that lit the night on fire, low and gravely with that impossible blue gaze behind it.

Or maybe the fire was only in her, making her wet and hot and something too close to desperate.

When she had never been desperate in her life.

She had tipped her head slightly to one side as she regarded him. *You sound surprised.*

I should have killed you the moment I saw you. His voice was matter-of-fact, suggesting that roaming about *killing people* was an ordinary occurrence for him, and yet his hand was still on her arm and she'd felt the heat of his grip. And she still hadn't been afraid. *That's what happens when foolish girls stumble into business meetings in the wrong part of town. Would anyone have missed you?*

Not tonight. Why had she said that? She might as well have knelt right down again and invited him to use that gun of his. Worse yet, she had kept talking. It was something about that faintly arrested look on his face, like he didn't understand what he was doing, either. It was that grip on her arm. It was her certain knowledge that something had *happened* between them in that alley. *Eventually, people back home would miss me, but they wouldn't know where to look. Most people think I'm still in Croatia.*

He had gripped her arm harder, though not hard

enough to hurt. He'd pulled her closer to him then, his poet's eyes blazing with a distinctly unpoetic fire as he'd gazed down at her—and she still hadn't been afraid.

She'd been *exhilarated*.

I fucked up my life for you, he'd gritted out at her. *I don't ever fuck up my life. For anyone. The kind of life I have, fuck it up too much and you lose it*.

Indy hadn't understood anything that was happening. All she'd known was that it was happening to both of them—and it was as intense as it was impossible.

They should never have met. She should already have been a statistic.

None of this should have been happening, but she'd been wearing red and he was clearly a wolf and somehow, it had all made sense. She had felt the sense of it everywhere, like fate.

Indy had reached up with her fingers and spread them over those beautiful lips of his.

Careful, he'd warned her.

But Indy had only smiled. *Too late*, she'd said.

Then she'd surged up on her toes and kissed him, like the dark little fairytale she'd always wanted to come true at last.

CHAPTER TWO

SITTING IN THIS bustling café in Prague all this time later, Indy could not only remember how it had felt to kiss him like that.

She could feel it still.

Kissing him on that deserted street in Budapest had been foolhardy at best. She'd had two years to question her behavior, and she had. Oh, she had.

But she couldn't regret it.

Kissing him had been like nothing she'd ever experienced before.

It was a shock—and it was no fairytale.

Because he'd kissed her back and there was nothing least bit tame about him. His lips alone were a revelation. He didn't use his hands to hold her head in place, because he'd managed to do that with his mouth alone.

And Indy had *ignited*.

She'd melted into him so that her nipples, already so hard and so greedy, were crushed against that stone chest of his.

He'd angled his jaw and thrust his tongue against hers and she'd come from that alone in a shimmering, shuddering rush.

He'd torn his mouth from hers, muttering filthy-sounding curses in languages she couldn't identify.

Damn you, he said then, his English sounding tame in comparison.

She knew, somehow, that he wasn't cursing her. Not specifically.

Then he'd picked her up, swinging her into his arms while she still had all those delicious waves of pleasure moving through her. She had only been half-aware at that point. He'd carried her down the street to a dark and gleaming SUV waiting at the curb and then he'd climbed inside, pulling her over his lap as he went.

I'm surprised you can park here, she'd murmured while he tossed his gun in the glove box, because she'd been loopy and her clit had still been pulsing and she felt like maybe what had actually happened was that she had died. That this had all been some kind of extended death scene in her head. It was the only thing that made sense. *I'm surprised no one stole this while you were off... doing whatever you do.*

She'd been straddling him and that had meant she could look down into that astonishingly beautiful face of his and see it when something like amusement flickered there.

Nobody would dare steal from me, he told her.

Then his hand was on the nape of her neck and he'd brought her face down to his, so he could take her mouth once more.

And Indy stopped worrying about *parking*.

He'd shoved her skirt up and out of his way, wrapping his big hands around her thighs to pull them even further apart so she was mashed down against the thick bulge of his cock, a glory against her clit. And his fingers had slid beneath her thong in the back as he'd skated past her ass to find her wet folds. He'd opened her, then penetrated her with one finger.

Then another, finding her wet and hot and crazy for him, writhing to get even closer to him—his cock, his fingers, whatever worked.

He'd let out a long spate of swear words again, but that time, it had sounded like a song. Then he'd shoved her tank top up, securing the fabric beneath the strap of the little backpack she'd forgotten she was wearing, so he could get his mouth on her breast.

God. His mouth. On her breast.

In Prague, remembering, Indy felt herself flush all over.

Back in Budapest, she'd arched back as best

she could between the steering wheel and his hard body, letting her head fall back into sheer bliss.

Indy had been lost somewhere between his mouth on her nipple as he sucked, hard, and the way she rocked her own clit against his cock. He was shockingly huge, and his fingers were blunt and too clever as they plunged inside her from behind.

In her head, it had gone on forever, but she doubted it had. Because she couldn't take it and came again, clenching hard on his fingers.

You are a witch, he'd muttered.

Indy had felt like a witch. Sex was always fun... but this was something else. It was like every single part of her had been made for every single part of him. As if nothing he could possibly do to her would feel anything but amazing. Because they'd been built for this.

She'd looked at him and been his. Their eyes had met over a gun, for God's sake, and there they were—and all Indy had wanted was *more*.

Reality couldn't intrude. It hadn't.

He'd reached between them. Indy had sat back as best she could, aware of the steering wheel digging into her in a way that should have been unpleasant, but wasn't. She'd liked the little spear of not-quite-pain, because that had meant it was real. It had really been happening.

This liquid heat, this glorious, endless explosion had truly been happening.

And his cock was a thing of glory.

He'd pulled it out, wincing because he was so hard. Indy's mouth had actually fallen open as she'd gazed down at where he rose between them. She'd felt her clit pulse and her core go molten.

You know what to do, he'd told her, and though his voice was quiet, there was that roughness to it, that command, that made her entire body break out in goose bumps.

But she'd felt that she did know what to do. That her entire life had been a dress rehearsal and that night in that SUV on an empty street in Budapest, of all places, had been the show, at last.

Indy had thought that very distinctly: *At last*.

She'd felt like crying. Like weeping with joy that she'd gotten to kneel up, even though her knees were still scraped—and that should probably have bothered her more. She'd felt emotional and beautiful and so connected to him it had hurt. It had *hurt*, when Indy was all about her fun and her orgasms, but even the hurt of it felt good.

And that was before she'd braced herself with one hand on the headrest behind him. Then reached between them so she could guide the massive head of his cock to her pussy at last.

At last.

Because it had felt like she'd already waited a lifetime and she hadn't even known his name.

But Indy had known it was true, even then. She'd been looking for him, for that wildfire connection between them and his dangerous saint's face, for a lifetime already without realizing he'd been her goal all along.

Something she couldn't have realized until she'd seen him, could she? Because only then had it been clear.

His hands had not been gentle. He'd shoved one into her hair and the other had gripped her ass, hard.

Indy had known many things then. That he was not a good man in the way she'd previously conceived of that phrase. That what she was doing was not a good idea, no matter how it felt. And that no one would ever understand how this had not only happened—but why she had *made* it happen.

But she had never been the good sister.

Because she also knew—as their gazes had clashed again, as she had notched the wide head of his cock at the mouth of her pussy—that this man was her fate.

That she had always been meant for this.

Right there. With him.

Now, he'd ordered her.

She hadn't understood until then that she'd been waiting for that, too. For him.

It had felt like running to the edge of a terrible cliff and then throwing herself off. And not caring at all, in the final moment, if she would fall or fly.

Indy had slammed herself down, impaling herself on him.

And she'd screamed out as she did it because he was so big that it hurt, so big that it was wildly, astonishingly uncomfortable to take all of him like that, and so *fast*.

But she'd known there was no other way to do it. It was like a kind of virginity because it was him. Them. It was *theirs*, the agony she was prepared to put herself through for one staggering beat of her heart. Then another.

And it had been entirely worth it when his mouth crooked up in one corner.

Foolish girl, he'd said in that quietly dark way of his that made everything in her sing. *I like that you want to suffer for me.*

Then he'd moved.

And any suffering she'd felt was gone that easily.

Because he'd fucked her like he'd known all the same things she did.

Like his cock, that big, battering ram of a cock, had been specifically designed to hit everywhere she'd needed it. He'd kept his hard hand on her ass, lifting her and slamming her in time with his thrusts, so that all she could do was melt into it. Become part of it.

His other hand, tangled in her hair, had kept her arched back so he could get his mouth on her throat, her lips. Down to her breasts and back again as he liked.

And he'd liked.

Indy had lost track of how many times she'd come. Again and again. Over and over. Because it turned out that what he liked, she liked, too.

And on he'd gone anyway, because he'd been making them one.

It was some kind of magic, fusing them together. Imprinting them on each other, because this was fate.

Maybe it might look like a simple fucking, but Indy had known better.

He was making them real. He was making sure the both of them knew that neither one of their lives would ever be the same.

Because how could anything have been the same after that?

When he came she could feel him inside her, scalding her, and she'd loved that, too.

And then, for a while, they'd had to stay like that. Slumped into each other in the front seat of his SUV because neither one of them was breathing too well.

He'd recovered first. He'd lifted her, muttering

another curse when she'd made a little sobbing sound at the loss of his cock. He'd set her in the passenger seat beside him, then winced as he'd folded his cock back into his jeans.

I am Stefan, he'd told her in that growl of his that had made her think of wolves again. She'd smoothed her red skirt down toward her thighs and shivered. *Stefan Romanescu.*

Indy, she'd replied. *Indy March.*

Indy? He'd sounded as if he was tasting her name the way he'd tasted her nipples. *What kind of name is this?*

Short for Indiana.

Indiana, he'd murmured, another long, deep taste.

Indy had nearly come again, just from that.

He'd looked around—out to the street and in his mirrors—in a way that told her more things about him. That he had some kind of military background. That he was just as deeply danger-ous as she'd thought he was, if not more, because he wasn't anything so simple as a *thug*.

But none of that had changed the fact that he was hers.

Nothing ever will, a voice in her had intoned, solemn and sure.

She'd curled her knees up beneath her and hadn't cared where her skirt fell. The thong she'd simply moved to the side made her pussy feel even more wet and swollen, because it kept grabbing at her. Reminding her.

Not that she'd needed reminding.

We didn't use a condom, she had pointed out.

You American girls are all on the pill. He hadn't even looked at her as he started the car, then pulled out, roaring away from the curb and into the dark Budapest streets in a manner that told her he knew them well. *And if you give me something, eh. Then we both have it. A memento, maybe.*

She'd laughed, then shrugged when he'd shot a dark look her way. *I don't have anything. Yours is the only cock that has ever been inside me without a condom.*

His gaze had caught at her, intense and too blue. *The only one that ever will be, Indiana.*

And she'd accepted that, because she'd felt it, too.

Fate.

Stefan had driven her straight to the airport.

I don't know what your travel plans are, but they must change, he'd told her, another command. It came easily to him, she'd understood. It was who he was, maybe. *You must leave here. Tonight. And do not return.*

But—

I need time, he'd said with an urgency that she'd felt inside her like her own heartbeat. *Two years. Then I will deal with this. With you. Do you understand?*

Two years? She'd blinked the unexpected emotion away, not sure what was happening to her. Not sure words existed to describe what had already happened, much less what had still been happening. *Stefan...*

He had taken her jaw in his hard hand. *Keep that pussy greedy for me, foolish girl. And enjoy as many inferior fucks as you can with my blessing. I want you limber.*

He had given her the key, told her a time, made her memorize the address.

And she hadn't heard from him since.

Indy blew out a breath at her café table in Prague. She drank down the last of her coffee.

She hadn't told anybody what had happened to her in Budapest. Because what could she say? Instead, she'd flown back to the States. She'd surprised her sister and moved in with her when her latest disappointing roommate had moved out.

She had cried when her skinned knees healed, because it had felt as if the loss of those scrapes took Stefan away from her. And she'd spent the last two years in New York because she'd lost the thirst for it. She'd been everywhere. She'd seen everything. And she'd found what she'd been looking for without knowing it—but she couldn't have him.

Yet.

Yet, she would whisper out loud in her bed at night, holding on tight to that key. *Yet*.

For a while, she hadn't wanted to bother with sex—for pretty much the first time since she'd discovered it in high school—because what was the point? When you'd had the very best, why backslide into less than that? The first time she'd let a cute boy in a Brooklyn bar take her home, it had made her feel as close to empty as she'd ever been.

But when she thought of sex as keeping herself fit enough to be worthy to fuck Stefan again, that changed everything.

Indy had impatiently waited out her two years. She had kept herself limber.

And now she was ready.

She left the café with only twenty minutes to go before the meeting time. The gorgeous old city gleamed bright in the summer sun, but all she could think about was the house up in the hills that she'd stared at on Google Maps a thousand times.

Indy took a cab out of Prague proper, crossing the river and scaling the hills into a neighborhood she'd read a lot about, these past two years. Upscale. Quiet. Wealthy.

Her heart was going wild in her chest and she pressed the heel of her palm hard against it, feeling something like giddy that this was finally happening. She knew that if she'd told anybody what she was doing, they not only would have told her something was wrong with her, they would have tried to talk her out of coming here today. They certainly would have tried to impose their grubby reality all over what she knew was her destiny.

Her older sister in particular, bless her.

The cab dropped her off in front of the correct address, a house that sprawled over a sizable piece of property right on the road. Indy pulled out her key and walked toward the door, unable to hear anything but the way her blood rushed through her. She thrust it into the lock on the front door, held her breath, and turned it.

The bolt clicked open.

Indy pushed her way inside, having absolutely no idea what to expect, but aware that she was no longer holding her breath. Because the key worked. *It worked.* She hadn't let herself think about what she would do if it hadn't. She slipped it back over her neck as she shut the door behind her, taking comfort in the familiar weight between her breasts.

Inside, the house seemed light and airy—or possibly that was just the foyer she stood in that soared upward to a set of skylights. She could hear music playing, something smoky and instrumental, and her impressions of the house seemed to shudder into her from afar. Clean. Nearly stark, were it not for the odd pieces of intriguing art set here and there. Or the surprisingly ornate banister of the grand stair directly in front of her.

She followed the music through a sitting room on the same floor that opened into another, nearly blinding her with all its great windows that looked down over Prague and the Vltava River that cut through it.

But the music wasn't coming from those rooms or the bright gallery beyond, so she kept going. She wound her way down a hall until she came to a study at the end of it, drenched in the same sunlight.

And froze, because he was there.

Stefan sat in an armchair next to a bookcase, far more beautiful—and brutal—than she'd recalled. His poetic blue eyes came to hers. Held.

And she was sure she heard some kind of thunderclap in the distance.

It still felt like fate.

Better still, that gaze of his on hers felt like a command.

Indy only realized then—as she started moving toward him, unable to tear her gaze from his—that she hadn't been afraid that he *wouldn't* be here. That hadn't really worried her. But she had been afraid that he *would* be here—but that she wouldn't feel this again.

That she wouldn't feel all this heat and glory, greed and longing.

This sense of coming home in a strange place.

And through it all, fate making them one.

The way she knew they had always been meant to be.

As if she'd been built for him alone.

Indy kept moving until she stood before him. She shrugged off the small backpack she wore and tossed it aside. Then she sank down on her knees, there before his outstretched legs, and smiled up at him as if he'd given her the world.

Maybe she thought he had.

Already.

"Finally," she whispered, gazing up at him.

"Finally," Stefan agreed, with a voice like gravel and a hard, bright light in his gaze that made her feel like she might be shimmering. Inside and out. "We can begin."

CHAPTER THREE

STEFAN ROMANESCU WAS not a man of faith.

In anything.

But he had seen a vision in a shitty back alley two years ago. And even though he would have said he believed in visions even less than in the dour Orthodox god of his childhood, long since happily renounced, he had immediately known one thing above all others.

A man should never turn down a vision, no matter how inconvenient it was.

Though the word *inconvenient* was a mild way indeed to describe how he'd spent the past twenty-four months.

None of his former associates—because a man like him didn't have friends—had understood. But then, how could they? All they'd seen was Stefan systematically dismantling a network he'd worked hard to put in place, removing himself completely, piece by piece.

For no good reason, he was sure they would have said if he'd encouraged such conversations. Because his network made money and for a long while, that was the only thing he'd cared about. It was the only thing that mattered to most of his associates, as it had to him, too. Before.

Only people who had always lived safe and secure—and rich—ever imagined that money wasn't power.

But he'd met her in Budapest and everything had changed.

He couldn't have explained it himself. He'd seen Indy March, bright with a fresh beauty though it had been the middle of the night. And no one who was wandering around that particular neighborhood at such an hour could possibly have been *fresh* in any sense of the word. Still, she was such a tiny little thing, with glossy dark hair and a heart-shaped face. Picking her way through the rubble and ruin of the world he lived in as if she hadn't noticed the state of it.

She'd looked at him the same way.

His heart, that useless organ, had stopped. Then kicked back in, hard.

She had looked like an angel, and what fallen man could resist?

He couldn't. He hadn't.

And now here she was on her knees again, only this time Stefan had no gun aimed at her head. No collection of associates he barely tolerated himself. This time, she appeared before him of her own volition. Not because she'd wandered down the wrong alley in the wrong part of the wrong city.

Not to mention, she'd had two years to think better of the whole thing.

These were all important distinctions.

His cock might have been rock hard, the way it always had been every time he'd thought of her since he'd dropped her at the airport in Budapest, but he was in no rush now. Not now.

Because she was here. And Stefan could see from the expression on her face that her hunger was as fierce as his.

"Welcome to Prague, foolish girl," he murmured, settling back in his chair and regarding her almost lazily. "Why don't you tell me, at last, how you ended up in that alley?"

Her chest moved, telling him she was breathing too hard. He liked it. And though he saw a kind of dismay on her face, or possibly impatience, she didn't argue with him. She settled back on her heels, giving him the opportunity to miss that flowy little red skirt she'd worn before that had fueled any number of fantasies since. She shoved the silken mass of her hair back from her face and smiled at him.

As if this was a proper dinner date in whatever squeaky-clean world she came from.

Though he knew what her world was like. All its fresh, bright, happy details. A man might trust a vision all he liked—but a wise man verified it.

Only wise men survived the kind of life Stefan had built for himself, then destroyed.

"I was at a club," she told him, and her voice was as lovely as he remembered it. Sweet and sultry all at once, with that American Dream accent of hers. "It was just down the street in some crumbling-down warehouse I couldn't find again if my life depended on it. I wanted a breath of fresh air and a little walk and then there I was. In the middle of your… Situation."

That was significantly less celestial. He studied her, the laziness giving way to a frown. "You wanted to *walk*. At that hour. You didn't notice what kind of neighborhood you were in?"

Indy shrugged, and his eye was drawn to how delicate she was. She was such a little thing. He remembered, vividly, picking her up. Holding her against him, his imagination wild with all the ways a man of his size could indulge himself with a tiny little creature like her—but he'd urged himself to be careful.

He might not have been a good man, but he didn't break his toys.

Then she'd proved herself more than his equal. She'd showed him a libido to match his and better still, the ability to take his cock even if she hurt herself doing it.

Men changed their lives for far less.

That night had been warm, as he recalled. She'd worn a strappy little tank top, a tiny little backpack like the one she'd tossed aside here, and that filmy red skirt that had haunted him ever since. And loads of necklaces and bracelets that marked her as one of the carefree backpacker set who polluted most of Europe—and the world—with their vast privilege wrapped up as wanderlust. Today she wore skinny gray jeans that seemed pasted to her and a flowy sort of T-shirt that did as much to expose her midriff as cover it. She still wore a ton of bracelets, but the only necklace she wore today was the key to his villa.

Back in the alley, his first thought had been *angel*. His second thought had been bohemian— in the sense of a certain beach culture style popular with both Californians and those who aspired to look like Californians. Not in the sense of the Bohemian region where they currently sat that had nothing at all to do with Californian anything.

When she'd spoken, he had not been surprised to hear that she was an American, though he hadn't known how to feel about that. And then he hadn't cared, because it made his path clear.

He had practically been able to see the white picket fences of her people stamped all over her.

"Those kinds of clubs are always in terrible neighborhoods," she was saying, almost dismissively. As if he was being…silly. Something Stefan had never been in his life. "I never got into trouble before."

Stefan leaned forward. He rested his elbows on his knees and got his face close to hers.

She was even more perfect than he'd recalled. Flawless, really. That pretty face of hers, eyes like chocolate and that sweet and dirty mouth. She looked soft and breakable, but he knew better, didn't he? His Indiana was wild, and a little crazy, and her pussy was voracious.

God, she was perfect.

Even if, right at this very moment, he was pissed at what could have happened to her if he hadn't been the *situation* she'd stumbled into.

"Do you know how much trouble you were in?" he asked quietly. "Do you really know?"

Her melted chocolate gaze glittered. "I think the gun to my head was a clue."

Stefan reached over and slid his palm over her jaw, her cheek. Not sure if he was holding her there…or assuring himself that she was real.

That he had not simply lost it in that alley two years ago, as many had claimed since. That there had been a reason and it was her.

That she was *here*.

"The man who held a gun to your head no longer exists," he told her, making no attempt to keep the darkness from his voice. "But he was a very bad man, Indiana. You should have been terrified of him. Why weren't you?"

She smiled and pressed her cheek deeper into his palm. "I don't know."

"I gave you that key and an address. You could have come here any time you liked, but you didn't. You could have forgotten all about one strange night in Hungary, but you didn't. You waited two years. You came to Prague. You showed up to-night at precisely the right time and now look at you, down on your knees with your skin already flushed with arousal." He shook his head, his gaze all over her. "Why?"

"I trusted you." When his scowl deepened, her smile widened. "And it didn't occur to me to come here any sooner. I guess I could have come straight to Prague after Budapest, but I went to New York instead. And by the time it occurred to me, much later, that I had the key and could come over here and see if it fit in anytime, I was too busy... Recovering."

He searched her face intently, something in him going still. "You were hurt?"

She shook her head. "No. But it was..."

Stefan nodded. Because he knew. "A beautiful catastrophe."

Indy's eyes glowed. "Yes. And then I thought I

might as well wait. You had been so certain about the time period. Why was it two years? Why not two months? Or five years?"

He could have told her. That he had always had an exit strategy, because longevity was not a feature of the life he'd chosen after he'd left the army. He'd been planning his escape almost from the day he'd started. Meeting her had simply expedited those plans.

Instead of sharing any of that, he lifted a shoulder. "There were things I had to do."

It was her turn to study him for a moment. "Like… A divorce?"

Stefan had not been expecting that. He laughed. "A divorce? What makes you think such a thing?"

Indy let out a small sigh, once again nestling her cheek a bit deeper into his palm. "It seemed like the kind of thing you might have had to get out of your way. I've never slept with a married man, to my knowledge, but then we didn't do much talking."

"I have never been married." The very idea was ludicrous. "Have you?"

"Never."

"And no unpleasant diseases," he said, finding his thumb moving over her cheekbone. "Or I would have known soon enough."

"Right back at you. And yes, I'm on the pill."

"I suspected these things. I am happy I was right."

"You strike me as the kind of man who's usually right." Her eyes were big, but she smiled. "Or usually thinks he's right, anyway."

He was a lot more than that, but Stefan saw no reason to share that with her. Not until this all felt like less of a dream.

"You are even more beautiful than I remember," he found himself saying, almost as if it wasn't up to him. As if the words simply came out of their own accord. "How is that possible?"

Indy let out another sigh, her cheek in his hand and her gaze bright with heat. "Do we really have to do all this talking?"

She leaned forward, sliding her hands up along the inside line of his thighs. And still Stefan couldn't quite believe that she was here. Right here with him. That he hadn't made her up as he'd thought he must have over these last dark months. Even though he could remember her taste. And that fierce grip of her tight little pussy on his cock.

He still couldn't believe that she could possibly be real.

But he took her hands before they reached his cock and held them away from him, smiling a little as he gazed down at her.

"I like it that you are still so greedy, my foolish girl," he said. "But there are things we must discuss."

"Can't they wait?" she asked, her gaze between his legs in a hungry way that almost made him think, *what the hell*.

The way he had in Budapest.

Almost.

"You flew all the way to Prague for this, Indiana. You can wait a little longer."

Her eyes were a little bit wide as she looked up at him, and he could see the hunger there. The same greed that burned in him.

"I would have flown even farther," she told him. "But why make the anticipation even worse? It's been two years in the making for one night. What if it's not worth it?"

He regarded her for a moment, taking that in. She thought this was one night. That felt a lot like a blow.

But the flip side of that surprising notion was that she'd waited two years and flown all the way to Prague for that one night.

"It will be worth it," he assured her. "But you should know something about me, Indiana. I am… Bossy."

"A lot of men are bossy," she said softly. She smiled. "Not all of them have your cock. So… I'm okay with it."

"Excellent."

And then, Stefan thought, it was time to reacquaint themselves.

He settled back in his chair and inclined his head, not surprised that she understood his command immediately. Watching the change in her made him even harder. She flushed, swallowed hard, and then reached for him again with hands that trembled slightly.

Because she continued to be perfect in every way.

Indy angled herself closer to him and this time, when she ran her hands up the inside of his thighs, he let her. He looked down the length of his torso as she knelt there between his outstretched legs. Her glossy dark hair flowed down her back and her heart-shaped face looked fierce as she concentrated on unbuttoning his jeans. Then that ferocity turned into something far hotter as she reached into his jeans and pulled out his cock.

She made a soft little humming noise, wrapped both her hands around the base of him, and leaned in.

Then she licked him, swirling her tongue around the broad head. She took her time learning his length before she tried her best to suck him into her mouth.

Stefan thought he could die happy, watching this tiny, impatient woman—his woman, whether she knew it or not—try to suck him off.

She returned her attention to the head of his cock and began to move her hands up and down his shaft, not exactly gently. That mixed with the hot suction of her mouth, and the way she used her clever tongue, and that fire in him began to build.

Indy took her time, teasing him. Swirling her tongue around and letting her hands play him like he was nothing but her instrument. Something he should have hated, but he didn't.

Not with her.

The fire grew higher, more intense. So did she.

Until the marvel of it took him over.

Because this was already better than all his expectations, and his expectations had been extreme.

He let his head fall back against the chair while he gripped her hair with one hand, holding her head to his cock and feeling her as she worked.

And when he came, it was with a roar.

Stefan wasn't at all surprised to find she drank him down, then sat back on her heels and smiled up at him as if he'd given her a gift.

This woman was going to kill him.

He was going to let her kill him.

"Take off your clothes," he told her, doing nothing to soften his voice.

She shivered a little, still smiling, and stayed where she was as she stripped her shirt off, then tossed it aside, without a word. Her small, perfect breasts weren't contained by any bra, so he could see her hard nipples immediately, and he liked that. Then she knelt up higher on her knees, unbuttoning her jeans and shoving them over her hips, with another one of those thongs that he vividly recalled from Budapest. Tonight it was hot pink, a detail he suspected would live within him always.

He hoped it would.

When she sat back, she rolled back so she could stretch her legs out in front of her and pull her jeans the rest of the way off.

So smooth, so easy.

"You take your clothes off well," he said. "Almost as if you have done it before. For money, perhaps?"

He knew she had. But would she admit it? It wouldn't ruin anything for him if she lied on this, their first night. Stefan knew too well the risks of oversharing, or even the faintest attempt at transparency. But if she lied, it would give him an insight into her. And her relationship with shame.

Indy's smile was wicked. And completely shameless. "You should see me on a pole."

"Is that what you do when you're not roaming about bad neighborhoods in Europe? Strip?"

She shook her head. And she knelt so easily before him once more, he was already hard again. "You know how all the girls like to say that they're stripping to get through college, right? I actually did. It was fun."

"Then why did you stop?"

She considered him for a moment while she knelt there, perfect and naked and within reach. After all this time, he could simply extend a hand and touch her as he wished.

Part of him still couldn't believe it. Not even now, after she'd sucked him good with that wicked mouth of hers.

"I think that stripping is the kind of thing that could quickly become pretty much the opposite of fun, if it went on for too long and became about, for example, paying rent. And here's something about me that you should probably know, Stefan." Her gaze was steady on his. Her voice was quiet. "I don't want to do it if it's not fun. Whatever it is. Because what's the point of that?"

"Life is not always fun, foolish girl. I would say it is very rarely any fun at all. How have you never learned this?"

She was so young, he thought. A product of the country she came from and the splendid life he knew she'd lived there, white picket fences and shiny dreams and all the rest of that New World crap. While he had been born into the ruins of the very, very Old World, had been raised dreamless and dark, and knew better.

But when she smiled, she seemed neither young

nor naïve. "Whether life itself is fun or not isn't the point, Stefan. How I choose to live is fun or I don't choose to do it. Do you understand?"

"I understand that you are a privileged American girl, no? So maybe it is easier for these things to be fun for you while for others, living is not so delightful. It is merely the better option."

"Maybe," she said, and though he studied her expression he could see no indication that she took any offense at his words. He couldn't tell if he liked that or not. "Or maybe I don't think that we all need to be *quite so* serious all the time. Really. We don't. No one does."

"And if I tell you that I'm a very, very serious man?"

Another flashing smile and something like wisdom in her gaze. "I like how serious tastes. And I'm guessing you like how fun tastes, or you wouldn't be here either. Would you?"

He laughed at that and then he stood, leaving his jeans unbuttoned. And enjoying the look of her there, still kneeling at his feet.

His beautiful, foolish girl.

Stefan reached down and picked her up, but he didn't set her on her feet. He lifted her even farther, liking the way she laughed a little and melted against him. Making it the easiest thing in the world to lift her so high that she was kneeling on his shoulders.

Indy laughed. "You aren't really…"

"I would hold on," he advised her. Sternly.

Then he gripped her ass, made sure he was holding her securely, and brought her pussy directly to his lips.

He licked his way in, finding her wet and sweet and hot and in the next moment, coming against his mouth.

Just as he remembered.

He teased her clit, sucking on it and raking it gently with his teeth. He saw how many more times he could make her come as she gripped his hair so hard it hurt and arched her body there where she knelt on his wide shoulders. She tossed her head back, writhing against him and showing him that she fully trusted he would not drop her.

Her trust made his cock so hard it nearly hurt.

And only when he was satisfied with the way she screamed and rocked against his face did he lower her down his body, handling her with an ease that made him ache, to finally slam his way inside her.

This time, her whole body formed a perfect bow. She wrapped her legs around his hips, her mouth wide open as if the scream was trapped inside her, and he could no longer tell if she was coming or about to come again.

He didn't wait for her to accommodate him, because she was molten hot and so sweet it almost burned. Instead, he moved her, using her to fuck himself, loving the feel of her in his hands. That tight fist of her pussy, wetter and hotter with each stroke.

The longer it went, the more she moved into it, letting her back arch once more. Letting her head fall. Closing her eyes and once again trusting him to hold her where he wanted her, to move her as he liked.

Taking all of him and making low, greedy noises as if she loved every inch.

And when he felt her pussy clamp down on him once more, she sobbed wildly, another orgasm taking her over. Stefan found his own release, emptying himself into her with a few hard, deep, glorious thrusts.

Then he held her there as she collapsed against him, her mouth wide open in the crook of his neck as she fought for air.

He was still inside her and carried her that way, enjoying the little noises she made when he took the stairs up to the second floor. He carried her to the loftlike master suite and into the bathroom, where he set her down outside the massive shower stall. He reached in and turned on the water, smiling with deep satisfaction when she made her way in a moment or so later, but had to hold on to the tiled wall as if her legs weren't quite steady.

He stripped, then followed her into the hot spray, already steaming up the room.

"Oh," she breathed, gazing at him in what looked like awe. His cock certainly thought so, and stood proudly. "I've been wondering what you look like naked."

She reached over and traced the tattoo that took up the better part of his chest, then wrapped around his back. It was a phoenix etched in bright colors and utilizing all his scars, its tail ending in the small of his back. And Stefan had always loved his tattoo, the story of how he always rose from any ashes, but never so much as now. Because Indy moved closer and began to trace it with her fingers. Her soft little hands. That hot, dirty mouth of hers.

"What are these?" she asked softly, finding his various scars concealed in the lines and swirls.

"Knives and guns." He grunted as she found a different ridge. "The odd boot."

Her dark eyes rose to meet his, then dropped. But she kissed his scars a little bit longer.

After the shower he dried himself, then took her towel from her and amused himself with drying her, too. She combed her tangle of hair with her fingers, then braided it, letting the damp mass of it fall over one shoulder.

"I left all my clothes downstairs," she told him when he pulled his jeans back on.

"You don't need clothes." He studied her. "Are you hungry?"

She considered, and then her face lit up. "Ravenous, as a matter of fact."

He had her walk before him down the stairs so he could watch her move. So he could contemplate the sweet line of her spine and the flare of her hips as he imagined taking her from behind.

Would his hunger for her ever end?

Once on the ground floor, he settled his hand on the nape of her neck and steered her into the kitchen at the back of the house that looked over the terraced grounds, green by day. Tonight the pool gleamed turquoise and beyond, down in the valley, the city of Prague lay like ribbons of light.

"Tell me about this place," she said, jumping up lightly to sit on the counter as he moved around the kitchen, assembling a simple meal of savory pancakes, a Romanian staple his grandmother had always made him when he'd visited her. "This villa. The art on the walls, the air of old-school elegance mixed in with all these modern lines... None of this seems to go hand-in-hand with an alleyway in Budapest."

"I think you would call this *layers*, no?"

"Are we naming all these layers?"

He glanced over at her, but she didn't look avid in any way. Just... Interested.

In him.

Not what he could do for her. Not what she could get. Just him and whatever story he might tell.

It felt like a new kind of magic. He remembered he'd called her a witch, and it fit.

Stefan cleared his throat. "My father was a hard man. When I tell you this as a Romanian, you must understand that I do not mean hard in any American sense. I mean the real thing. A real kind of hardness that went deep inside him. He should not have married, but then, even monsters get lonely. After my mother died he stopped pretending to be a father, not that he had ever taken to the role. He was a jailer. I mean *hard*, you understand." He moved his shoulders to do something about the tension in them, not sure why he was telling her this story. There was a reason he wasn't much for sharing. But he didn't stop. He couldn't. "It was a relief to escape him when I joined the army. But then, the army takes all men and makes them hard. I think this is true everywhere. Afterward, I found other ways to fight. And learned to live by my own laws."

"Meaning outside everyone else's laws."

He nodded. "But my grandmother left Romania a long time ago and settled in Old Town. Far away from her troublesome son-in-law and her memories of the daughter she lost. I visited her here in Prague as a boy. And I bought this house early in my…career, let us call it. Maybe as a monument to her. I always knew that someday I would retire here."

"You don't look old enough to retire."

"The kind of business I was in…" Stefan shrugged. "If you are lucky enough to retire, you do it young. Or not at all."

For a while she didn't say anything, and he finished preparing the meal. He brought a stack of the savory pancakes over on a plate that he set down on the counter next to her, and then stood there himself, watching her as she ate. Eating himself, until it felt as if that, too, was a kind of sensual act.

Simply being with her was a sensual act.

He was going to have to find a way to get used to it.

And for more than *one night*—but he did not intend to argue that with her. Not when there were far more interesting ways to make the same point.

"You still have not told me how you ended up in Budapest." He shook his head. "Did you travel the world, finding dark alleys to wander down alone?"

She paused in the act of licking her fingers and smiled at him. "As a matter fact, I did."

"You were a backpacker."

"Yes, though I always traveled a bit more lightly than proper backpackers. If I needed something I would buy it or borrow it. And then when I didn't need it anymore, I'd gift it to someone else. I didn't tote around a mobile office or anything. I just had my phone."

"And who funded all this aimless wandering?"

"If I didn't have money, I worked." She took another bite of her meal and chewed happily, then smiled when she swallowed. "Budapest was a stop along the way, though I didn't really have a destination in mind. I've never been one for itineraries. I was thinking that I was going to head back toward Australia, to keep the summer going, but then you happened."

He liked that. "As if I am some storm?"

"I didn't see the point of traveling anymore when all I wanted to do was come here." That almost sounded like a confession, but she looked so casual that Stefan thought he must have misunderstood. "So I went back to New York instead, where I've been living with my sister ever since."

"Is your sister like you?"

"Bristol? Oh no. No, not at all." Indy laughed. Almost too hard, in his mind. "She's a very serious person, like you. She finds me... Delightfully trying."

"But what is it you *do*? You must do something. Everyone does."

She lifted her chin, and though her voice stayed light when she answered him, her gaze was not. "I thought I told you. I do whatever makes me money and if I don't feel like doing it anymore, I don't."

"Indiana." He sounded severe, but he didn't modify his tone. "That is playtime. Not real life."

She sighed. "Everybody says that. A lot, actually. But none of them are particularly happy, are they? So why would I listen to them?"

"Does this mean you did not work in New York?"

"I worked in a lot of different jobs in New York." Indy shrugged. "I like temporary positions. Right when they get boring, you move on to the next."

He studied her, sitting so carelessly on his counter, eating food he'd made her with his own hands. Naked and unselfconscious. Perfect in every way.

The ways he wanted her should have horrified him, but they didn't. They never had.

Still, he wanted to know her. Not what he could dig up on her, but *her*.

"Surely you must know that the kind of life you lead is only possible because you're young and beautiful." He tugged on the end of her braid. "It cannot last, this wandering here and there with no thought to your future. That is the thing about the future. It finds you, always."

"All the more reason to enjoy it then," she replied with maddening calm. "While I can."

"You must have some kind of dream. Some ambition."

"Must I? Ambition is for people who don't like what they have. But I do." She frowned at him. "And if I have a dream, I go after it."

He didn't believe her. But he didn't press. She wanted one night, so that was what he would give her. Because there were a lot of things a man could do in the course of one night that might just teach his foolish girl how to want a few things she couldn't possibly be sure she could get.

And to learn how to long for them, like everyone else.

"Lie down on the counter," he told her then, all command and heat. "Face down."

The heat in her eyes kindled, but she still took her time licking her fingers. Then stretching sinuously, like a cat, so he had no choice but to watch the way it made her breasts bounce. She rolled herself over, sliding herself across the countertop until she was stretched out before him.

"Enjoy the stone on those greedy little nipples," he invited her.

Stefan gripped her hips, pulling her back toward him so her legs hung down over the edge of the counter and he could line her up with his cock again.

He slid inside, sheathing himself fully. She made a cute little grunting sound, wiggling this way and that because he filled her so completely and she needed to make a little space. He had the notion then that no matter how many times he took her, she would always be this tight, always gripping him just like this, always precisely this perfect.

This time he went slow, because he wanted to enjoy looking down at her the way he'd imagined so many times before. Feeling her cute little butt against him as he plunged deep, then drew back. The line of her spine, the swell of her hips, the soft nape of her neck.

She stretched her arms up so she could grip the other end of the counter, giving herself a little bit of leverage as he worked.

Slow. Deep.

Relentless.

He watched as her skin reddened, everywhere, and listened as her breathing changed. She came differently in this position, one wave into the next, an easy kind of roll. But Stefan wanted more than waves, so he reached beneath her to find that eager little clit and played with her until her intensity skyrocketed.

On and on he went, drawing out her responses, learning the difference between those light little climaxes and the wilder, deeper ones that made her whole body seem to shatter around him.

The ones that made her sob. Real tears.

And only when he thought he could read her well enough did he build her up to one more bone rattling, screaming finish.

Then follow her.

But he still wasn't done.

Because she thought this was only the one night.

And Stefan knew full well that one night wasn't going to be enough.

CHAPTER FOUR

INDY WOKE UP with a start instead of her usual sweet ease. There was sunshine all over her face and she had no idea where she was, but that wasn't particularly unusual in and of itself. Normally she stretched, smiled, and happily looked around to see where she'd ended up the night before.

But then she didn't normally wake from dark, erotic dreams, unsure what was real and what she'd imagined. She blinked in the bright light, the contrast to the cascade of images in her head making her feel almost lightheaded.

Then the night came back to her in a rush, far more erotic than any dreams she might have had. Her body reacted as if it were happening all over again. She was dizzy and molten, hollowed out with longing, and a little bit drunk on all that sensation within her.

She sat up slowly, gingerly, and looked around the room, half expecting to find Stefan watching her from some or other vantage point.

But she was alone.

And when she took a breath or two, she decided she was glad of it.

Because clearly, she needed to take stock of... this.

Of what had happened to her here.

What she'd wanted, so desperately, last night and now...

Thinking about all the things she'd done last night—all night—made her flush, everywhere. Her nipples pebbled into twin aches and between her legs, the rush of sheer longing made her squirm against the soft sheets. She pressed her hands to her cheeks and found them hot, and that, too, made her shudder.

Inside and out.

Indy hardly knew who she was, sitting upright in a shaft of Czech sun, her hair falling all around her in abandon, adding to the shocking sensuality of the morning. Since when had she ever been *embarrassed*? Or even this affected, the morning after and alone? She'd meant what she'd told him last night. She only did things that were fun. She followed that fun wherever it led. The more people who told her she couldn't dance her way through life, footloose and fancy free and whatever else they liked to call it, the harder she kept on dancing.

And sex had always been the sweetest and best

dance of all. Fun from start to finish, every time and everywhere.

But Stefan had switched things up last night. She knew exactly when he'd done it. When he'd taken that electricity between them and jacked it up to high. It was when he'd had her spread out across the kitchen counter like a dessert, and suddenly, without warning, it was as if he'd thrown a switch.

That suddenly, everything had been far more... intense.

Until she'd felt scraped raw and needy in a way that had nothing to do with laughter. And it was still with her this morning, as if he'd peeled off a layer or two of her skin and left her naked in a new way.

A lot like that night in Budapest, but this time, there had been no dark alley or scary gun in sight.

It had just been...him. Stefan.

He had carried on like that throughout the night. Until she'd found herself sobbing, in a frantic, mad frenzy to find her release—so she could start all over again, ripping herself wide open and giving him things she hadn't known she had it in her to give.

Indy was not used to intensity.

That night in Budapest, sure. The situation had been intense.

She'd come here for the connection, but on some level, Indy had figured nothing could *stay* so intense. One night of intensity was one thing. She didn't want to repeat it.

You avoid intensity, a voice inside her pronounced and she couldn't say she cared for that, either. *Like the plague.*

Intensity left a residue, she found. She felt stained with it.

She rubbed at her face, waiting for that flush to fade from her cheeks, and wished the unsettled feelings churning around inside her would go away with that heat. Then she sat there in the sunlight and took her time re-braiding her hair.

As if curbing its wildness would settle her, too.

But it didn't help as much as she wanted it to. And eventually she could see no other choice but to get up and face…whatever there was to face on the other side of a night like that. At least after Budapest, she hadn't had to face Stefan. She'd imagined facing him, but that was different.

Everything about this was different.

Indy suddenly found she related to all those stories other women had told her over the years. The ones she'd laughed at, but there was no laughter in her now. Instead she had a strange flutter in her belly. She had *feelings.* And an emotional hangover that made her bare feet against the distressed wood floor feel both sensual and unsteady.

The truth of the matter was that she had no idea how to feel anything less than perfectly confident when it came to sexual politics or bright mornings after dark nights. Much less how to navigate the unexpected wallop of all this *emotion* churning around inside.

She remembered crying over her healed-up skinned knees, curled up in a ball in the closet that passed for her bedroom in the Brooklyn apartment she shared with Bristol. Actual tears for her own healed flesh.

Why did she feel like that again today?

Indy looked around the stark yet somehow welcoming bedroom, dimly recalling that she'd left her clothes on the floor she'd first knelt on. Downstairs. She opened the first drawer she found, something inside her lurching a bit at the discovery that Stefan was…neat. She pulled out a T-shirt and tugged it on, because she didn't want to be naked.

Or maybe she'd wanted the softness of the fabric against her sensitized skin, so soft it told her he cared about the things that touched him. And the faint hint of whatever laundry detergent he used that teased her with a part of why she wanted to bury her face in his neck and inhale that scent. Forever.

"You need to get a grip," she advised herself

then. And avoided looking at her reflection in the mirror as she left the bedroom.

Another new thing she couldn't say she liked.

Then she slowly walked down the stairs, her bare feet silent in the quiet house that loomed around her. It was too bright everywhere, and slowly, it dawned on her that it wasn't actually *morning*. The sun was overhead. Had she really slept that hard? Maybe it was the jet lag she should have had yesterday, catching up to her at last.

Because it certainly couldn't be a deep reaction to what had happened between them. Indy didn't have reactions. She moved on.

She always, always moved on, like a flickering flame never quite committed to any one fire. She burned on and on without burning out.

Indy padded through the house, appreciating it all the more now that she wasn't in such a rush of anticipation, wondering if he'd actually be here. Today she wasn't bristling and wild with two years of pent-up need. Now she could take her time with the surprising art gracing the walls and the quiet, understated elegance of the rooms she peered into. This wasn't a designer's take on a rich man's house. This was a home of modern lines and a crisp aesthetic, run through with an old-world undercurrent.

Not unlike the man who lived here.

But she didn't want to think too much along those lines. It made her feel even more unsettled than she already did.

You need to find him to say goodbye, she told herself sternly. Because their night was over and it had been as overwhelming as the first, if different. Maybe she'd need three years to recover this time.

Maybe more like five.

She found herself rubbing absently at the gap between her breasts, as if that could do something about the ache inside.

Indy headed for the kitchen, but it was empty, and she could admit—if only to herself—that she took it as a reprieve. She helped herself to a glass of water, drinking it down hungrily. When she was done, she rinsed it out and set it on the drying rack, then drifted over to the big glass doors that looked out over the slope of the hill. There were gardens rolling down the slope of the yard on the far side of the gleaming pool, green trees almost concealing the other houses tucked away on this hill, and in the distance, the silvery ribbon of the Vltava carving its path through Prague.

That was where she found him. He was sitting out on the terrace off the kitchen with Turkish coffee and a laptop before him on the table, though he was looking at a newspaper, turning the pages with a kind of efficient crispness that indicated he was a habitual reader.

The June sun adored him. It cascaded all over him, lighting him up and making him seem made of some kind of melted steel. Gleaming and lethal in a pair of loose, casual trousers and a T-shirt much like the one she was wearing. And something shifted in her as she looked at him. Because she'd really never imagined Stefan, her dark and dangerous man, who'd been there in that alley and had haunted her dreams ever since…sitting at a table in the sunlight, looking edgily domestic and burnished with heat and light.

While *reading*.

Indy didn't understand why something so unremarkable should sit on her the way it did, like a set of heavy weights. She only knew she could hardly breathe through it.

Stefan glanced up at her, a glimmer of blue that seared through her, but he said nothing. He only picked up the small pot at his elbow and set it in front of the other place at the table. That was when she noticed that there was a plate waiting for her with the traditional Czech breakfast she recalled from her last visit here. Slices of thick bread with a choice of butter, honey, and jams. And a selection of cold meats and cheeses.

He returned his attention to the paper, leaving Indy to sit down and pour out the thick coffee Stefan had prepared. She sipped at it to find it smooth and silky and still hot, with a hint of sweetness and other spices that gave it a richer, deeper taste. Even that struck her as sensual today.

The same feeling she'd had upstairs returned to her with a vengeance, slapping at her and then sinking in deep, though she did her best to fight it off. She concentrated on the coffee with its texture against her tongue, glad it was sweet and savory and strong. Just what she needed.

Maybe it would clear her head. And wash away whatever cobwebs these were, cluttering up her chest.

It felt a lot like baggage, this intensity hangover, and Indy didn't do baggage. She always had much, much better things to do. She found herself scowling down at the plate of food before her as she thought about that. And this electric reunion between them that was not how she'd anticipated it would be at all. It was all supposed to be that rush of wonder and dark joy she had experienced in Budapest. That *certainty* that had changed her so profoundly, down on her knees in that alley. The sudden clarity like a punch, telling her she was exactly where she was meant to be and with the man she was meant to be with, above and beyond everything else.

Not this…*unrest*.

"Is something the matter?" he asked, his voice mild.

She lifted her scowl to him, but he was still

reading. *Reading*, of all things. "What could possibly be the matter?"

"If you do not wish to eat, do not eat," he said in that practical yet jaded way of his that made her think of the house rising behind her that represented him all too well. Functional with that old-world spin. "You surely don't have to look at it as if it is plotting your death."

"You don't know," she replied. "Maybe the honey is looking at me funny."

He put the paper down then, shifting all that intense blue to her. Was that what she'd wanted? Indy felt a different sort of sensation shiver all the way through her. It took her a moment to recognize it.

Uncertainty.

She rarely felt such a thing. And it hadn't occurred to her, until just now, what a gift it was to always feel she knew her place. Her sister liked to tell her—sometimes laughing, sometimes not—that she was filled with unearned confidence. Indy had never understood that as a criticism. Why should confidence need any earning? Bristol had always believed that a person gained things like confidence—and self-worth, and bragging rights while she was at it—by accomplishing things.

But that meant there was a measure and others might assess it differently.

Indy had always felt real confidence was innate. It was about being open to anything. To being fully prepared to say *yes* to whatever came. She had done that in spades, always.

The only other time she'd felt *uncertain*, this man had held a gun to her head.

"Do you still have a gun?" she asked.

But she regretted it, instantly, because that was exactly the kind of question that she prided herself on not asking. It wasn't that she didn't *care*, she'd explained to her sister once. It was that there was no point digging in deep to things she couldn't hold on to. Better by far to accept what was given and make do.

And okay, she acknowledged internally. *There might also be some power wrapped up in* seeming *not to care about the things people usually care too much about.*

The power thing was especially clear now. As she'd just given hers away.

She watched as Stefan took in that question. His expression changed as he sat with it, growing unreadable as he gazed back at her. Not quite like armor, she thought. More like the suggestion that he could, at any moment, produce an entire armory.

"Not that particular gun," he replied, and something jolted in her because he didn't pretend he didn't know which gun she meant.

Or maybe it was all the implications about his relationship with guns wrapped up in that succinct statement.

"And are you…the sort of person who spends a lot of time pointing guns at people's heads?" Again, she didn't know what on earth she was doing. Or what she hoped to gain. This was why she never asked questions like this. She preferred to let people tell her their stories as they liked, the bonus being she never felt so *messy* while they did. But now that she'd started actually asking him questions she wanted the answers to, how could she stop? "It was a while ago now, but if memory serves, you were holding it pretty confidently."

"I was in the army for some time. I hold all guns confidently."

"Are you really not going to answer me? We met up in Prague after what certainly couldn't be called a *meet cute* Budapest. Two whole years ago."

"Thank you." His dry tone and all that gleaming blue made her…edgy. "I had forgotten all of this."

Indy plowed on because she'd never skidded over this particular cliff before and she didn't have the slightest clue how to stop herself. "There has been no communication in all of that time, yet here we are. Surely that means, at the very least, we owe each other a little bit of honesty. Don't you think?"

"I live for honesty." And it occurred to her that that little undercurrent in his voice, the one that matched the gleam in his eyes, was amusement. "Why don't you tell me why you're so nervous?"

Nervous. Indy wasn't *nervous.* She was never *nervous.*

And yet, as wrong words went, that one seemed to hit her in all the places she felt raw.

"I'm just wondering if I've flown across an ocean to shack up with the Big Bad Wolf," she said tartly. "Maybe this wasn't my smartest move."

"I thought we were being honest." Stefan shook his head, though his hard blue gaze never left hers. "We met in a dark alley with my gun in your face. That didn't stop you from fucking me blind not ten minutes later. And it didn't stop you coming here for more, years afterward, knowing nothing about me except that alley. Are you afraid of me, Indiana? Or are you afraid of yourself—and the fact that you don't care what I am?"

She felt caught by that, in a hard, tight grip. As if the honesty she'd demanded was choking her—but Indy forced out a laugh anyway. And maybe she gripped her coffee cup tighter as she settled back in her chair, wishing she'd come down naked.

Because that would have been a distraction. And a distraction was obviously better than... whatever this was.

Indy opted not to acknowledge the uneasy sort of knots that drew tight inside her at this unwelcome awareness of how she operated. Almost as if she wasn't the carefree, fun-loving creature she'd always been so sure she was.

"This is getting pretty heavy for a morning after," she said as her laughter faded. "And besides, aren't conversations like this better during sex? To spice it all up a little."

She expected the usual reaction when she said even the most nonsuggestive things, as long as sex was implied. Explicitly stated, she expected his eyes to drop where his T-shirt rode up on her thighs. She expected his hands on her, touching her like he couldn't bear not to for a single moment more...

But Stefan remained as he had been all along, lounging in his chair and regarding her far more closely than was comfortable. Not as if he wanted to jump her bones. More like he wanted to forensically examine them, then jump them.

Indy didn't like it.

"Do you have discussions when you're not having sex?" he asked, with entirely too much *mild amusement* for her taste.

"I'm having one right now."

"Are you?" There was a hint of a smile on his hard, sensual mouth, but only a hint. "Because it seems to me that *discussions* are not something you wish to do. Most people reveal themselves in sex, Indiana. But you? You hide."

That felt a lot like a terrifying mirror shoved straight in her face. And after she'd gone to the trouble of avoiding that actual, nonmetaphoric mirror upstairs.

She made herself laugh again, though she didn't love the sound of it in the summer air. Had she always felt so forced? "I have sex when I'm having sex. I don't put any extra, weird weight on it. I don't understand why people do."

"Do you not?"

The way he said that felt a lot like an accusation. Or maybe a dare.

Worse, it butted up hard against all those raw and hollow places inside her.

"I keep forgetting we're strangers," Indy said, and laughed again. Longer this time, because the *summer air* could bite her. She drew her legs up onto the chair, pulling the T-shirt down over her knees, then resting her chin on the little shelf she'd made. "Let me give you the story of Indy March. First and foremost, I'm not like other girls."

Stefan considered her. "I have lived in many places, you understand. Not only different countries with different languages, but in many conditions. Rich, poor, and many shades between. And I have never met a person who introduced themselves to me by telling me how special they were who was, in any way, special."

But this was where Indy sparkled. She didn't take offense. She didn't glare at him. She only laughed. Because where everyone else went intense about their identities, she went effortless.

It felt as if she'd been treading water since she woke up this morning, and suddenly she'd found the bottom. And could finally stand.

"I don't attach to things the way most people do," she told him with a shrug. A smile. "That isn't to say that I don't have feelings, because of course I do. But some people make feelings their whole life. To me, feelings are just experiences. I have them, I put them aside, and then I move on. Sex is supposed to be fun. Not an opportunity to dredge up the dark and let it take you over. Because where's the fun in that?"

"You're talking about run-of-the-mill, boring sex," Stefan said dismissively. "Anyone can have this kind of sex. With any person they happen to meet. With their own hands, even. It is not so thrilling, this kind of sex, but it gets the job done."

"I wouldn't call the sex we've had boring or ordinary." She wrinkled up her nose at him. "But it's been fun."

"Fun." It was his turn to laugh, and Indy found she *really* didn't love it when he did it.

Not like that. Not *at* her. "Is this what you tell yourself?"

"Fun is what matters to me," she told him. "Or I wouldn't have come here, would I?"

"Indiana."

He still didn't lean forward. She didn't understand it. This was a perfect opportunity for him to reach out and put his hands on her, so they could both feel the kick of that wildfire connection and get lost in that for a while. But he didn't do it.

And yet, somehow, she still felt caught tight in that gaze of his. It was too blue and far too knowing. She had the shocking notion that he could see straight through her.

For once in her life, a man's dick wasn't getting in the way of his gaze. Indy would have sworn that wasn't possible.

Her heart began to gallop. And his gaze only seemed to pin her to her chair.

"The first time we've fucked you had just had a near-death experience. The sex was many things that night, but not fun." Stefan's mouth did something, some near-curve, that made her feel lightheaded again. "It changed you. I know, because it changed me. And now here we are, two years later, and nothing that happened last night was *fun*. It was intense. Provoking. It also only scratched the surface. Because this thing between you and me?" He did that thing with his chin, indicating the two of them. "This is not fun. It's too big. Too dark. And you are terrified of it."

She tried to make herself laugh, because she always made herself laugh, but she couldn't quite get there. "You have me confused with someone else. I don't get terrified."

"You like to fuck your way across this planet," he continued, in that same too quiet, too confronting way. "You like your little candy-coated orgasms, like sugar. But you and me? It's blood and fire, my foolish girl. This is life or death. Do you think I didn't notice that the more intense it got, the less experienced you seemed?"

"That's me." Indy's voice was rough. She told herself it was Czech allergies, nothing more. "A born-again virgin, just for you."

He was really smiling now, no question, and it burned through her. "What are you afraid of? Don't you ever ask yourself what the point of it all is if you're always too scared to truly strip naked?"

Indy's heart was pounding at an alarming rate inside her chest and all the rest of her was in a knot. She wanted too many things, most of them at odds with each other. *What if you picked one?* something in her asked, but she ignored it. And switched tactics.

Anything to disrupt the steady way he looked at her.

"I know I can't be understanding you correctly," she said, and the light tone she used was a struggle. But she did it. "Do you really mean to tell me that this is how a man like you rolls around? Ranting about intensity to every girl he touches?"

"Not every girl I touch." His smile made his lean, almost-cruel face a kind of portrait, painted in the light all around and her own rapid pulse. It made her think of poetry again. "This is how I know the difference. If I wanted a quick fuck, Indy, I could get that anywhere."

She was pretty sure it was the first time he'd called her by her nickname, and there was no reason she should dislike it. But she did.

And she hated that she'd even noticed. "Wait, wait. Are you telling me that despite your snide commentary on the number of countries you've lived in and the number of times people have claimed to be special only to prove that they were not... I am, in fact, not like the other girls?"

He leaned forward then, but for emphasis. Or so she assumed, because he didn't reach across the table to her.

"This is what fascinates me," he said in that same mild tone that was completely belied by the fire in his eyes. The fire that matched hers, and that was what was going to kill her. She knew it was. "Why would you fly all this way, two years later when anything could have happened in the meantime, only to pretend you did such a thing for *fun*?"

There was the knotting inside and the way each little snarl pulled painfully tight. There was the clatter of her heartbeat, the din of her pulse. And now Indy found her throat was dry, which would tell him all the rest if he heard it, wouldn't it?

"What else would it be?" she asked, in a vain attempt to sound lazy and unbothered.

But Stefan only smiled.

That damned smile of his that made her melt where she sat.

"You had better eat before you go," he told her, sitting back again and resuming that *lounge* of his, as if a man as lethally built could ever look truly languid. "Regardless of whether or not you hate the meal that had you scowling so ferociously, you expended a lot of energy last night. For all that fun we had."

She stared at the meal in question as if she'd never seen it before. Then lifted her gaze to his again. "Where am I going?"

"We agreed on one more night." He shrugged, looking entirely unbothered. "The night is over. I assumed you would be in a hurry to get away. After all, Indiana, the world is stocked full of the kind of fun you claim to love so much, is it not? Why would you waste your time here?"

Indy knew that this was a part of the game he

was playing and clearly, she'd walked right into his hands. Because even though she'd been planning to leave when she woke up earlier, had been very nearly eager to get away and settle herself down, she'd gotten sidetracked in all this...light and heat.

It felt like a gut punch.

She wanted, more than anything, to pull out a measure of that effortlessness that usually came so easily to her. An airy laugh. A languid hand. She could stand up, stretch, and grin mysteriously down at him as if she already had six more lovers lined up for the next twenty-four hours. Because both of them knew she could make that happen. She could pile her hair on top of her head, because it was rare that she did that in front of a man without him itching to get his fingers in it.

Indy had never considered these things games of her own, but she could see now—with uncomfortable clarity—that they were. That she'd been playing all kinds of games for a long time. The difference today was not only that Stefan could see through her.

The difference was that she could, too.

And it didn't matter anyway, because she couldn't seem to move.

"One night," she managed to say, fighting to sound anything but thrown. "Yes. That's what we agreed."

"Are you not satisfied?"

That darkly mocking note in his voice should have been all she needed to hear. It should have sent her running for the door—or in her case, sauntering with purpose while doing her best to look as unbothered by this as possible.

But sure, a voice inside chimed in, as mocking as Stefan. *You're not a game-player at all.*

"It's not a question of satisfaction," she replied. And even managed a smile. "This is what I'm trying to tell you. I'm always satisfied."

He didn't actually call her a liar then. He didn't have to.

"Terrified," he said softly, instead.

"Maybe," she heard herself say, filled with a wild, dizzy sensation that was certainly not *terror*, "I'd like to renegotiate the one night we agreed on."

"Because you want to see?" His voice was so rich. A dark ember, already lodged deep inside her, yearning to catch fire. "What can be?"

"Not at all." Because she didn't. Did she? She couldn't. "To prove to you what it is."

He took a long time to smile at her then, though his poet's gaze gleamed bright. Like everything else where he was concerned, it pierced her. She was sure he could see straight through her as if she were glass.

Indy had never thought that she was trying to

fool anyone, but she knew without question that she wasn't fooling him.

"Very well," Stefan said. He inclined his head slightly. "Convince me then. Show me how much *fun* you're having, Indiana. You have one night."

CHAPTER FIVE

STEFAN EXPECTED HER to crawl directly onto his lap to work her magic the way she knew best, but she didn't.

Instead, Indy seemed to relax, though he didn't believe it for second. Still, she sat differently, still curled up in the chair opposite him. His T-shirt seemed to grab at her, or *almost* let go to show more skin… And he suspected there wasn't a lot his Indy didn't know about the way her body moved, how it looked from all angles, and what those things meant.

She shook her hair out of its braid so that it fell all around her in a silken, heavy mass of dark waves. The smile she aimed at him rivaled the summer sun above them. And then she dug into her breakfast at last, looking for all the world as if she was totally unaware of the pretty, sexy picture she made.

Stefan knew better.

He would wager that Indy March knew exactly

the effect she had on him. On anyone and everyone, but right now, just him. She sat there naked
with only his T-shirt on, her hair wild from the
last time he'd had his hands in it, eating with such
relish it became a sensual act when she licked her
fingers. Looking totally unselfconscious, though
he knew better.

It wasn't that she was calculated. He wouldn't
accuse her of that. She was far too generous with
her body, her responses, her need. It was more that
she was *aware*.

The thing was, he liked it. His cock liked it
more.

She had slept in late, which wasn't surprising
after her travel the day before—not to mention the
night they'd had. He had gotten up with the sun,
as was his custom no matter what kind of night
had gone before. It had long been a way he had
exercised control over a life that had sometimes
seemed to be forever careening where it wished.

One of the only things life with his father had
taught him.

He had gone for a long, looping run through this
quiet neighborhood, the kind of place he couldn't
have imagined well enough to dream about back
when he thought his father was the whole of the
dark, unkind world. Stefan had pushed himself,
trying to clear his head of all that need and passion…if only to prove he could.

As always, he had failed.

Indy had still been asleep when he'd returned, curled up in a soft ball in the center of the bed he'd put to use in a hundred different creative ways, all night long. Her face had been hidden by a thick curtain of her hair, so he had brushed it back, sighing a little at the curve of her cheek. The way she looked so serious as she slept, a far cry from the laughing, flickering creature she was by day.

Mi-ai intrat în suflet, he'd said, because he knew she couldn't hear him. And even if she could, he would not translate the Romanian phrase for her.

Because she did not need to know that she had entered his soul. Become a part of him.

No matter what happened.

His chest had ached enough that he'd found himself tensing, and he'd left her there as he'd showered and dressed, then had gone about his day as if it were any other. As if he hadn't been aware that she was finally here, in this house, where he'd pictured her a thousand times.

Stefan had never trafficked much in imagination. His father's backhand had taught him the folly of expectation early, a lesson he had taken to heart. But when it came to Indy, he found himself indulging in the kind of *what-ifs* that he knew better than to entertain.

The man he'd been two years and one day ago would not have recognized him now.

He chose to take that as a good thing.

A very good thing, as men who lived as he had often found themselves dead.

Whatever else happened, he told himself now, he would always be grateful that an unexpected vision in the form of this foolish, beautiful girl had appeared before him in that alley. Then led him out.

Because it had been in the dismantling of his various operations that he'd truly seen how much the cancer of it all had spread. It was possible that had he not pulled out when he had, he would have found himself incapable of it later.

That would mean, among other things, that this house would have stood empty. That he would never have discovered what it was like to wake up in a place he loved, a place where no one would show up at his door uninvited, bringing their ugliness and violence with them. That he would never have known what it was to sit high above Prague on a summer afternoon, across from a beautiful woman with the wind in her hair.

That he would never have known *this*.

It would have been a loss worth grieving, though he never would have known what he'd missed. Somehow, that made it worse.

He sat back in his chair. He enjoyed the sun on

his face. He waited to see what his Indy would do next.

After she finished with her coffee and breakfast show, she sat back and stretched. Stefan noticed with great appreciation how her hard nipples showed against the soft fabric of his shirt. As if she knew it, Indy pulled the T-shirt off, shooting him one of her liquid, sparkling glances as she got up. Then she sauntered over to the edge of his pool, pausing for a moment at the edge.

Appreciation wasn't a strong enough word to describe his reaction to seeing her there above the deep blue water, naked and lush and perfect, a better monument to Prague than all the statues on the Charles Bridge down below.

Indy tossed back her hair, then dove in deep. He stayed where he was, watching as she swam beneath the water, sleek and sure.

She surfaced, slicking her hair back, and then smiled at him as she floated there, another vision. This one drenched in light.

"Don't you want to join me?"

He only smiled. "I prefer to watch."

And he got why she'd said she wasn't like other girls. She didn't pout as many would. She didn't try to cajole him. She shrugged as if it didn't matter to her if he did or didn't join her, then turned and went back to her swimming as if that was what she'd wanted all along.

Stefan understood why she had a trail of lovers behind her, a battalion or two at least, each and every one of them determined to pin her down.

But he wasn't concerned about that. Because he knew what all of them didn't. He knew the truth of her. He'd seen it.

And even if he hadn't, she'd come back to him.

Proving, whether she cared to admit it or not, that the intensity between them had wrecked her the same way it had him.

Stefan almost felt bad for her. Because he had changed his entire life to make it here. To find himself sitting on this terrace today. He had the feeling that she'd spent the same two years frozen, waiting, which meant she had yet to change the way he had.

He couldn't wait to taste it.

And he meant it when he told her he would rather watch her move through the water, slippery and sure. That was what he did, settling back in his chair and enjoying the sun, the sky. Prague below and the scent of flowers in the air. It had been a long road and yet if this was the reward, Stefan thought he would walk it again a thousand times.

Indy took her time, floating for a long while in the clear blue water of the pool. Sending the message that she'd forgotten he was there, which he assumed was the point. When she was done she swam to the side and lifted herself up, displaying that easy grace of hers that he found spellbinding. Still. Then she made her way toward him, fully and unapologetically naked. And she smiled as she walked toward him.

"You don't look like you're having fun," she said.

"Do I not?"

She didn't answer him with words. She shifted to kneel down before him, dripping wet and gloriously naked, her hair in a sodden tangle as she reached forward and helped herself to his cock.

Stefan was only too happy to let her have it.

And as she set to work licking all around the thick head, then wrapping her hands tight around his shaft—one on top of the other—he wondered, idly enough, if she actually knew how manipulative she was. Or if she truly believed that this was all in aid of the kind of *fun* she thought she liked. Most men would be putty in her hands at the spontaneous skinny-dipping. Much less after she got finished turning him inside out with that wicked mouth of hers.

But then, Stefan doubted very much that she'd ever met a man like him before. That was why she was here, wasn't it? He was perfectly capable of coming down her throat with a groan and still being just as much of a problem for her when he tucked himself away again.

"You keep staring at me," she said mildly when they were back in the kitchen some time later that afternoon. She had gone upstairs to shower off the pool and to dress in another flowy, shapeless sort of dress that made him think of fairytales. It allowed her to pad around the villa in bare feet, her hair around her like a cloud, looking ethereal and making him long to eat her up in one bite. "As if you're waiting for me to turn into a frog right before you."

"Not at all," Stefan replied. "I would prefer you stay in your current form. Frogs are not so appealing."

He had poured them both a small glass of *țuică* and had tossed his back as he set about frying eggs to put on the bowls of his grandmother's *tochitură* for a late lunch, a thick pork stew that reminded him of her few visits when she would command the kitchen, ignore his father, and cook. Indy was sipping at hers, not his favorite way to consume his favorite plum brandy, imported from Romania with his own two hands. But he noticed she avoided the counter where he'd laid her out the night before and tucked that away as a little bit of ammunition. Maybe she *should* make sure to keep her wits about her.

"I'm thinking about the way you handle men," he said as she took another sip. "It makes me wonder where you learned this. Was your father a man you felt you needed to handle?"

She laughed, as he'd expected she would. "This sounds like another one of these very deep conversations you always want to have at the strangest times."

He watched as she tossed back the rest of her *țuică* and hid his smile. "If it is too painful for you, I understand."

"My father is the most decent man in the world," she told him, her dark eyes flashing. "There's nothing painful about it. He's solid. He loves my mom and his daughters and that's that. He works hard, fishes whenever he can, and still dances cheek to cheek with all the women in his life. That being the three of us. He didn't require handling. He doesn't."

"Who then?"

He took the bowls over to the table that sat in the small nook off the kitchen, sunny like the rest of the house, this one with windows that let in the green and the gardens. And he was not surprised that she trailed after him.

"Is this because I sleep around a lot?" she asked, sounding ever-so-faintly bored. "I have to have daddy issues?"

"You're not *required* to have daddy issues, no."

"Good. Because I don't. And to be honest with you, I don't really have any other issues. It's amazing how easy life is when you make the conscious decision to...make it easy."

He waved her to a seat and took his. "It is not that you have a lot of sex. It's the rest of this thing you do. All day I have been debating whether it's a deliberate manipulation or, instead, an innate understanding of how to smooth over a moment with sex." Stefan studied her response to that, but indicated the food he'd made. "Eat."

She did not eat. She stared back at him, looking thrown, which he found he enjoyed. "I don't think I do either of those things."

"Do you not? And yet if I were to take a poll of people who know you, what would they say?"

"I live in the moment, Stefan. I don't spend a lot of time calculating possibilities or manipulating people. Or worrying what other people think about me. That's all gross. I just do what feels right."

"Innate it is, then. Fascinating."

"I'm sorry if this is disappointing for you." Indy sounded sweet then, yet the glittering light in her gaze was anything but. He liked her fierceness. He wanted to bathe in it. "I realize that men really, really want me to have some kind of deep inner wound only they can heal. With their penises. And I hate to break it to you but I really just like a lot of fun and a lot of sex. The end."

Stefan could have told her that while that might

have been true in her past, it wasn't now. Because if it was, she never would have showed up in Prague. She never would have come back to him.

Because what happened between them in Budapest was the most intense thing that had ever happened to Stefan. And his whole life had been intense. None of it, before her, in a way he would call *good*. If what Indy said was true, her life had been a monument to avoiding intensity—meaning, she could have continued doing that. She could have very easily stayed in New York.

But she hadn't.

And if she didn't understand that yet, all he could do was sit back and enjoy the show while she came around to the truth. He intended to do just that.

"Tell me how you lost your virginity," he said, picking up his utensils. "Let me guess. It was *fun*."

"Yes, it was fun," she said, her soft eyes gleaming. "He was an older boy, scandalously. I was a freshman in high school and he was a senior. Do you have freshmen and seniors here? Or… In Romania, I guess?"

"We have American television, Indiana," he said dryly. "So it is all the same."

"We dated a long, long time," she said with a laugh. "Meaning, most of the fall semester. He wanted to do it and I finally told him it was fine as long as it felt good. And it did."

"In the backseat of a car, I can only hope. What could be more American?"

"It *was* the backseat of a car!" She sounded delighted. "A Chevy, no less. It didn't really hurt—he made it fun as promised, and that, I'm afraid, is how I began my downward spiral into the fallen woman you see before you today."

He waited as she tucked in happily to her meal, but the silence dragged on.

"Do you want to know how I lost my virginity?" he asked.

"Not really." She glanced up at him, her dark eyes laughing. "It doesn't have the same resonance, does it? When and how girl gives away her V card is a *clue*, isn't it?"

"Or a story."

"Don't be naïve, Stefan," she said, waving her hand in the air so the spoon she held gleamed in the light. He tried to remember if anyone else had ever called him that. But of course they hadn't. But his pretty little bulldozer charged straight on. "For men, who cares? The only reason it would be relevant would be if you were still a virgin. Otherwise, it's assumed that men shed their innocence the way a caterpillar sheds its skin, then carry right on."

"I am not a virgin," he said, not sure if he was amused or…something else. "In case you wondered."

"I didn't. Now you think you know things about

me, don't you? When what you know is that I gave it away when I was fourteen. But that's not the shocking part." Indy paused, waiting for him to ask. When he didn't, she rolled her eyes. "The shocking part is that I don't regret it, and it wasn't a horrific experience. Maybe I was always destined to be a whore."

"The sounds like a lot of baggage, does it not?"

"It's not my baggage," she said, with another one of those light, airy laughs. "I slept with Jamie Portnoy in the backseat of his father's Chevy because I wanted to. And even then, there were people who wanted to shame me for that decision. Because it turned out Jamie was a bragger. So I broke up with him and then I told even more people than he had. Why should *I* be embarrassed?"

And he thought he understood, then. She wasn't pretending. It was all unconscious. She hadn't needed to handle her father, maybe, but an older boy who had bragged about her and the people he'd told. She'd taken what could have been shame and called it fun, and he believed she felt that. It wasn't a put-on.

It wasn't quite real joy, either.

But this was about fun, he reminded himself. Or her attempt to convince him that *fun* was what they were having here. What he really wanted from her could wait.

After they ate, she played music from her mobile and danced around the kitchen. She made him laugh and once she did, she climbed into his lap, reached between them, and worked his cock deep inside her. And then sang along to the song that was playing as she rocked against him, until they both came in the same swift rush.

That was how it went. Light, airy.

She took a nap in the early evening, flushed and warm in that bed upstairs while he tended to business concerns that couldn't wait. Later, after she woke, he drove them down into Prague so they could walk through Old Town and sit in one of the restaurants opened up to the summer night. In public, where there was no possibility that she could revert to nakedness or sex when she wanted to change the subject.

That it also tortured him was worth it, because he could see—as the color climbed her cheeks and her eyes got brighter—that being forced to simply sit there and *talk to him* was driving her crazy.

"Have you been to Prague before?" he asked sedately when she looked as if she might be considering starting a scene to divert his attention.

"I came through twice during my two years of travel," she said, squirming in her chair. Stefan knew full well that she was wet and ready. And more, that the prospect of this long dinner stretching before them was sending her over the edge.

Good. He hoped it did. He doubted Indy would be any quieter than that famous movie scene.

"Only twice? Some people would stay here forever if they could."

"I would always think I'd found the perfect place," she said, her smile taking on a slight edge. "Every place I go, I'm sure it's the one. But then I go somewhere else. I meet someone else. And I fall in love all over again."

He opted not to take the bait. "So nowhere is home, then?"

She squirmed again, taking a long pull from her water glass. "I guess when I think of home I still default to Ohio, but it's not really *my* home. It's my parents' home. My sister and I vowed we would get out as soon as we could, and we did. And I haven't lived there in a million years. I complain when I have to go back, the way I do every Christmas. But still. You say home, and that's still what I think."

"What makes it home?"

Indy sighed, and he thought he could see the very moment she remembered that she didn't like to share anything but her body. "Do you have a home?"

"No," he said. "I grew up in various Romanian cities. Bucharest, mostly. But none of the places I lived were *home*. I don't fall in love with places."

"That makes me sad." She was tracing patterns on the side of her water glass. Around them, tourists talked loudly, languages blending together on the warm night air. "That's the whole point of travel, as far as I am concerned."

"But I did not travel as you did." His smile was harder, then. "Flitting about the globe, finding myself in questionable pop-up clubs in dark, dangerous cities. This was not available to me."

"Budapest isn't all that dangerous."

"There is no place in the world that is not dangerous if you are a pretty, careless girl," he retorted. "As you discovered."

But she only rolled her eyes at him. "The world is the world. I refuse to live in fear. If you assume goodness, most of the time, goodness is what you're going to get."

"That or guns to your head when you walk down the wrong alley."

Indy shrugged. "That's my case in point. A gun really was to my head and yet here I am, wined and dined in beautiful Prague for my trouble."

"I think you know better."

"What about you?" she asked, her dark gaze on his with more heat than he thought she meant to show him. "If the world is so dangerous, surely you should be walking around with an armed guard."

"Not in the Czech Republic. It is not necessary." Stefan didn't quite smile. "There are some places it would not be wise for me to go, and so I will not go to them. But I am the reason pretty young things should not venture into alleys in the first place. I am not afraid of the world so much as it is afraid of me. And rightly."

She studied him. "I can't decide if you want me to be afraid of you or if you just like boasting about how mad, bad, and dangerous you are."

"I think you should be afraid of me, Indiana," he said quietly. "And I do not boast."

"You've never seemed particularly dangerous to me. Sorry. I feel like I would have seen it by now."

"But that is where you are wrong," Stefan told her. "It is you who are in the most danger."

For a moment, her gaze clung to his.

But then she waved her hand, picked up her menu, and let that roll away too, as if what he'd said was sheer nonsense. Maybe she wanted it to be.

He knew better.

After they ate and left the restaurant, she took his hand. She linked her fingers with his in a gesture that he told himself felt as foolish as the rest, but he didn't disengage. Then she led him out into the cobbled streets of Old Town Prague, tugging him along through the crowds until they became a part of the same great energy of the ancient city on a clear summer night, like so many before them. Like everyone around them.

"Should we pretend to be tourists?" she asked, smiling up at him outside Prague Castle.

"I have never been a tourist."

He looked down at her, still holding his hand like they were anyone. As if he were a regular person like all the other men he saw around him tonight. Soft, unwary. Was it that simple? Change his life, shed his old skin, and become what he had never let himself imagine he could?

With her fingers threaded in his, he almost believed it.

He wanted to believe it, and maybe that was worse.

"Then there's no time like the present," Indy declared. "We can be tourists right here."

Stefan let her tote him along with her, walking the length of the Charles Bridge and then back again. He posed for the inevitable photographs. He even smiled winningly as they took them, which made her nearly cry with laughter.

"What? Even I know you must smile in these things."

"Yes, Stefan," she murmured, standing on her tiptoes to adjust the angle of her mobile. "You're a regular old selfie-taking fool like everyone else. It's obvious."

And she was still laughing, later, when instead of following him back to where he'd parked his car so they could drive back to his villa, she tugged him into a dark alley. Then let her smile go wicked as she melted against him.

"Is this the real truth?" he asked her gruffly as he leaned back against the nearest wall and let her sprawl against his chest. "You cannot keep out of alleyways?"

"Let's call it symmetry," she whispered back.

And she wanted it fun and light. Flirty and fun.

But he didn't.

Stefan kept it slow. He lifted her up and wrapped her around his body, then pinned her back against the wall so he could hold her there and take his sweet time.

He drew it out, teasing and tempting her, so that by the time he moved between her thighs she'd been shuddering on the edge instead of tipping over into her sugarcoated orgasms.

That was why he eased inside her, slow and sure. Filling her but never quite giving her what she needed to make it over that cliff.

And he fucked her like that, slowing down every time she tensed against him, until she was beating at his shoulders with her fists. Glaring at him, her eyes damp with her sensual misery.

"This is supposed to be fun," she hissed at him.

He smiled and slowed down even more. "Maybe this is fun for me, Indiana."

By the time he finally let her come, she had to bite her own fist to keep from alerting half of Prague to their illicit behavior.

When she tried to put a little distance between

them as they walked back to the car at last, he didn't allow it. He pulled her tight, wrapping his arm around her shoulders, and kept her close. Making sure she could feel the heat in him just as he could feel it in her.

As if it marked them both.

When they got back to the villa he did the same thing all over again, but this time stretched out in that wide bed upstairs until she was nothing but a sobbing, writhing, begging mess.

And in the morning when she wouldn't meet his gaze he fed her, fucked her again, and when she made a move to leave once more, only smiled at her.

"Surely not," he said. But lazily, as if he didn't care one way or the other, which made her eyes darken, there where she was sitting cross-legged on the bed. "You had your fun. Surely it's time I had mine."

"You already had your fun," she flared at him, pausing in the act of braiding her hair again to glare at him. "Ruining mine in the process."

"You seem ruined," he agreed. "But not in the way you mean, I think."

"Whatever. I told you, this is supposed to be—"

"Fun, yes." He lifted a brow. "I never thought I'd see my foolish girl, unafraid to walk into dark alleys and take her chances with questionable men... Afraid."

"Is that… Are you *daring* me?"

Stefan shrugged. "If you are too afraid to play with a little intensity, Indiana, I cannot help you with this. I have learned to live with other disappointments."

He saw a series of emotions move over her heart-shaped face. Temper. Dismay. And then, more interesting, that amusement she usually wore so easily. He had never seen her put it into place in quite that way before. Like she was settling into a mask.

She laughed, because she always laughed. Because he thought she'd decided that made her seem exactly as fun—and as bulletproof—as she thought she needed to be.

"You're reading this all wrong," she told him lightly. Always so lightly. "I'm not afraid, I promise. I'm just not an intense person. It's not how I'm made."

He thought of the way she'd sobbed beneath him last night, her gaze slick with hunger and need, every part of her so tuned into him it was like its own, sweet agony. He thought of the way she had kissed her way over his scars, finding them in his tattoo and taking her time. Making sure she found every last one of them.

And he knew that she was used to controlling things this way. Her carelessness. Flitting from place to place, lover to lover, to the endless soundtrack of her own laughter.

But Stefan knew she was a liar.

All he did was study her until she flushed. And she did, bright and red.

"Bullshit," he said.

And he made sure that when he smiled this time, it was a weapon.

CHAPTER SIX

HE WASN'T EVEN touching her and yet Indy felt splayed wide open like they were back in that alley.

She'd thought she'd made such a good choice after playing tourist. After wandering around in the summer night, making them part of the crowds doing the same—and therefore not strung out on their connection and all that electric, breathtaking need—she'd thought she could pull him into a dark alley to reframe the admittedly intense beginning of their relationship.

The joke had been on her. Because he'd wrecked her.

Indy felt turned inside out. She didn't like it.

"It's not bullshit," she said, frowning at him.

It was another beautiful, breezy summer's day in the Czech Republic. Everything outside the endless sweep of windows was green and lush and beautiful. She could see the bridges spanning the Vltava and the spires of Prague Castle from the center of Stefan's bed, where he'd ruined her fun. Repeatedly and deliberately, all night long.

Last night she'd been so sure that she had this situation under control. She'd been convinced that she could simply *be herself*—because she didn't accept what he'd said, that she was manipulative or unconsciously trying to handle anything—and he would somehow start behaving in a way that made sense to her.

Yeah, she thought now, finishing up her braid while holding that gaze of his. *That didn't work.*

Today she was a little bit wiser, maybe. And dressed, thank you. Because she certainly had no intention of prancing around naked in front of him when he was far too good at using her own body against her. One more thing she'd never experienced before, she could admit. Normally she was the one who used her body. And she'd never met anyone who was better at it than she was…until now.

But that didn't make her afraid. And it didn't make him right.

"It is bullshit," he said again, his voice implacable.

And God, the way he looked at her. That hard and steady gaze that left her in absolutely no doubt that he could see straight through her. That he saw everything. Maybe even things she didn't know about herself, a notion that made her feel far too trembly deep inside.

That and his marvelous accent, that made her think of the taste of that plum brandy on her tongue.

"I understand you like to play this carefree, languid character," he continued in the same way, all steel and certainty. "But even your orgasms tell the truth, Indiana. You like the easy way out. You don't like the commitment of anything more. You don't even want sex if it demands too much of you. You tell yourself you're made that way, when as we have proven, what you're made for is me. This." His blue eyes gleamed, brighter than the sky that stretched on forever outside the windows. "Us."

Indy told herself she was tired of the earthquakes he kept setting off inside her. The fault lines she hadn't known were there, tangled and fragile and *shaking* while her heart beat too hard. In parts of her that her heart shouldn't have been.

"You don't actually know me at all, Stefan."

She knew that sounded more defensive than she wanted to sound in his presence. Why not bare her throat to his teeth and see if he really was the wolf she thought he was? She knew he would read too much into it. She knew he would take that tone as *proof.*

But she couldn't seem to help herself. There was something beating in her along with her wild pulse, feeling far too much like panic.

She smiled. Politely. "The fact of the matter is, we had a lot of sex. And I don't know how to break this to you, Stefan, but that doesn't make you special."

"If you say so." His blue eyes gleamed, but not with the fury she'd wanted. It was something far more like amusement. Only hotter. She could feel it connect to all the shaky places inside her.

She waved her hand in the air, a dismissive gesture she hoped he would find insulting. But he didn't look insulted. He looked hard, everywhere, as he stood near the windows, his expression something like indulgent. And mouthwateringly hot. And gloriously wicked while he was at it. He wore only the pair of athletic shorts he had tossed on this morning when he'd left the bed, heading out for a run while she was left limp and soft and wheezing for breath. And she had so dearly hoped that he would somehow be diminished by rolling around in the kind of clothes that any random guy would wear. By doing mundane things like *running*, meaning that body of his wasn't simply his by chance...

But not Stefan. There wasn't a single part of him that wasn't commanding or powerful. He wasn't a *guy*. He was a man, all man, and he was so far completely impervious to her fervent wishes that he might magically, suddenly, have less of a hold on her.

"I'm not trying to be mean," she began.

"Are you not? That must be a bit of your kind of fun, yes?"

She ignored that. "We met under bizarre circumstances. There's no denying that. And we both like sex, clearly. A little rough and spicy, maybe. We spent two years apart after only being together for a few hours. And now, what? It's been two nights?"

"I applaud your ability to count."

"Basically, Stefan, we've shared a weekend stretched over years. We're still strangers no matter how many times you've made me scream in the course of that weekend. That's just the truth. And so when I tell you who I am and what I'm like, I think you can trust that I'm the expert in the room on that topic."

"Indiana. Please." Everything was the blue of his gaze, then. Too hot to bear. "Do I strike you as the kind of man who leaves things to chance?"

That panicky thing inside her seemed to pick up speed, or maybe it was simply that she couldn't catch her breath. *Maybe you need to stop trying.*

"I don't know what that means," she threw at him, panic and all those other dark and nameless things pulsing too hard inside her. While, even then, her pussy melted, as if the way she wanted him was hardwired into her. "You left a thousand things to chance. Whether or not I would show up.

Whether I might just take the key you'd given me, come to this address, and rob you blind at some point over the past two years. I could pick a thousand ways this could have gone that did not involve me showing up here, desperate for another taste of you." She sniffed as if she were above all this, hoping the sound would steady her. And if that was impossible, the way it sure seemed to be, at least let her pretend. "Sounds like a gambler to me."

Stefan laughed. "I gave you a key, yes. There is also a security system. If you had attempted to access this house with your key alone at any other time you would have found that further security measures are required to get inside. They were waived because I was here. So no, there was no gambling involved."

"You didn't know if I'd even show up," she argued.

"Maybe not." But he didn't look unsure in any way. It made her question why she was nothing but. "I built a certain life for myself—you know this. And after I cleaned up the mess I made in Budapest that night, I had a choice. Continue with the madness I began in that alley or go on as if it had never happened. Continue my life as it was. Maybe show up here on the time and date I'd given you, maybe not. That was something I could worry about two years later, if I chose that route. But before I made a decision, I studied."

Something in her hitched at that, though she frowned at him. Ignoring the way her heart fluttered.

"What do you mean, you studied?" She heard the panic in her voice and made herself laugh. "Between you and me and the college I attended, I was never much for studying."

"You, Indiana. I studied you."

Indy felt as if she was coming apart. She found her hands in fists as she stared mutely back at him while all the implications of what he'd just said pounded through her.

And made her pussy ache all the more.

"Don't be silly," she managed to say softly. She wished she weren't sitting on the bed, wearing nothing but cutoff jeans and a tank top. She wished she was swaddled in protective gear and far, far away—*where you would only wish you were here,* a voice inside chided her. "This is shallow water, Stefan. No need to study a puddle. It is what it is."

His gaze seemed to sharpen on her at that but he stayed where he was, lounging there with his back to the windows, the very picture of a certain insolent ease. If a person ignored the heft and majesty of his body, that was. Which Indy didn't think she would ever be able to do.

"What fascinates me is not that you would say such a thing, which of course is false," he said after a moment. "But that you appear so invested in me believing it."

Her heart was starting to *hurt* her. "You don't have to believe it. But I wouldn't want to disappoint you any further. Because that's where this is going. You know that, right? You can imagine me to be anything you want, Stefan. I can't stop you. But that doesn't make it real."

Stefan considered her for a moment, and she wanted to *do* something. Anything. But she felt pinned into place by that gaze of his. "You are so dedicated to performing this party girl persona. Even when it doesn't suit you."

"It's not a performance. It's my life."

"You're very easy to track, Indy." It was official. She hated when he called her that. Though she refused to ask herself why. "You put it all out there, all over social media. This party, that party. Hints of new lovers everywhere you go. Suggestive photos in dark clubs. Naked flesh on sunny, topless beaches, all of it calculated to show off your beauty and your inability to stay in any one place for long."

She forced herself to uncurl her fists when her fingers began to cramp. "I am who I am. I post what I feel like posting. You could always not look at it if you don't like it."

"And yet, if all of this were true, surely you would have developed a drug habit to go along with it as so many do. How else to fuel all those late nights and erotic dances? It is common enough. Yet instead, though you spent more time committed to your strip club than your college, you graduated a year late with suspiciously average grades. And with a hefty savings account and investment portfolio. These things do not match."

"How are average grades suspicious? They're just average." But her mouth was dry. "I'm not embarrassed by that."

"Your bank account demonstrates that you are not average. You were able to not only save, but invest to a profit. It suggests you deliberately downplayed your abilities in the classroom. I cannot be the only person who has noticed this, surely."

But no one else had ever looked at her this closely. Indy had made sure no one could. And she felt as if he were clawing her open. As if he were digging his hands deep into her chest and pulling her wide. She had to look down at her own front to make sure that wasn't really happening.

It wasn't. Of course it wasn't. Indy sighed as much in relief that she was still in one piece as anything else. "I'm good at being naked, Stefan. But as I said, not so good at studying."

"Then why didn't you fail out?" He sounded so calm. So reasonable. It was maddening. "Why did you continue your studies at all if it meant so little to you?"

"Now you sound like my father." She managed a frosty sort of smile. "Which is not hot, by the way."

He didn't laugh at that, but the look on his face felt about the same. "You are the one who said you did not have daddy issues. Or was that another lie?"

She made herself laugh to try to break the tension. Before it broke her. "I'm not a liar, for God's sake. I was a middling student. I was a much better dancer. I had some regulars who gave me great tips and suggested I bank what I could. It's not a mystery, Stefan. It's not a clue to my wounded inner child. And as I already told you, I stopped doing it because it stopped being fun. Or I thought it would stop being fun eventually, whatever."

"What is this 'whatever'?" he asked, sounding irritatingly *patient*. "I have known many strippers over the years. Very few of them *invest*. This is what you did while paying for the school where you were pretending to be terrible student."

"I don't know what part of me not liking school you're not getting."

His blue gaze was bright then. Knowing in a way she not only didn't like, but felt rush through her like a cold chill.

"Is it that you don't like school?" he asked. "Or is it that your sister is the scholar and that means that you cannot be?"

It would have been better if he'd hauled off and

hit her. It would have shocked her a lot less than…
that. Indy moved then. She crawled over to the
side of the bed, wishing her head weren't spinning. Wishing her belly weren't knotted up tight.

Wishing this had stayed as simple as it had been
that night in Budapest.

Live. Love. Leave.

"My sister?" She could barely get the words out.
"Why are you talking about… How do you even
know about my sister?"

"I know everything about you," Stefan said,
mildly enough, which only made it worse. Because
it was so matter-of-fact and everything inside her
was a mess. Knots and shivering and what was he
doing to her? "I made this my business. Because
when I choose a path, Indiana, I expect to commit
to it totally. Or I do not do it."

Foreboding settled in her, making her bones
ache.

Indy stood up abruptly, holding her palms up
as if trying to ward him off—though he made no
move toward her. He looked as if he was relaxing,
in fact. Standing by his windows while the summer breeze blew in. Enjoying the lovely day, not
eviscerating her.

Not turning her inside out with every word.

"This has all gotten way too intense for me,"
she told him, fighting with everything she had to

keep her voice from shaking. "And I told you, I'm not about that."

"I am unsurprised to hear this." Stefan shrugged in that way of his that was not, in any way, a gesture of uncertainty. Somehow, when he shrugged it was aggressive. A decisive critique—of her. "Maybe you should ask yourself why dark alleys do not scare you. Why men with guns do not stop you. But intensity makes you run."

Her lips felt blue. She couldn't feel her own face. But she still tried to fight. "Maybe you should ask yourself why you think it's okay to dig around in someone's life without permission. Then use it as bait."

"I have never pretended to be a good man, Indiana." His voice was harsh. But something about the way he was looking at her was kind, and it made her want to give in to the sobs she could feel inside, threatening her ribs. "I never promised you anything at all, except a time and place. This is not a redemption story. I do not require your forgiveness. Did you believe that you might meet me as you did and I would be anything at all but this?"

"I've never given any thought," she managed to say.

His blue eyes lit up with an unholy glee. "Liar. But it is not me you lie to, I think. It is yourself."

Indy had never been so grateful that she packed light as she was then, with all that emotion surging around inside her, making her feel misshapen with it. Because all she had to do was pick up her little pack from the floor and shrug into it, then gaze at him almost sadly.

"I get that there's this big movement for everyone to act as if what they really want from life is to be known," she said. "To be wide open and vulnerable so that any passing stranger can take a glance and see exactly who they are. If you want to talk bullshit, that's what *that* is. You think you know me because you looked through some social media posts and hacked my information? You don't. *You don't.* I don't perform, but I also don't think that the sum total of a person is a collection of photographs. Carefully curated photographs at that."

Stefan didn't look particularly impressed with that speech. "I'm not following. First you were a puddle. Now you cannot be discerned through the pictures that you post. Surely both cannot be true."

"I have no interest in being psychoanalyzed," she bit out. "If I wanted a therapist, I'd get one. And knowing me, I'd probably sleep with him. That's how I roll."

"I know how you roll, Indiana. I know you use sex to hide from your life, not to embrace it." His smile lanced through her. "I told you—I know everything."

"Then you already know what I'm going to do, don't you?" She was finding it hard to stand still when she wanted to run. But she made herself do it. "That's handy. It means I have no need to tell you myself."

"You will storm out." Stefan sounded almost bored—unless she looked at the way his eyes blazed at her. "Though I expect you will do it slowly. An easy, carefree little walk so I'm not tempted to jump to the wrong conclusions. So that no one could suggest that you are having an emotional response. And off you will go. I expect to a bar, where you will surround yourself at once with men who do not challenge you. Who will fawn all over you, buy you drinks, tell you that you're pretty. And if you let them, give you those empty sugar-high orgasms you like so much. But not for long, because there's always another cock to ride, is there not?"

Her whole body jolted with every word he said. Indy could hardly see past the strange heat clouding her gaze. She had given up on her breath. She either seemed to be panting, or holding what air she could inside her, and either way, she felt… Unhinged.

"Do you think that you're the first person in my life to try to run me down so that I'll do what they want me to do?" she managed to ask.

"I'm not trying to influence you one way or the other," he said with a laugh. Still lounging there as if he not only didn't have a care in the world, but as if none of this was getting to him. She was falling apart, but none of this was touching him at all.

"You can't really believe I don't know what I want, can you?" she demanded, though she knew she should have already made her exit.

Again, his shattering blue gaze moved through her like a storm, making her wish that he would shout, flip a table, punch a wall—do *something* to indicate that this was as ruinous for him as it was for her. That it mattered to him that he was ripping her apart.

That I matter to him, a voice inside said, and she didn't want that. She didn't want to feel these things. She didn't want to *feel.*

"I imagine you want any number of things," Stefan said with all that quiet intensity that had ruined her from the start. "But I know what you need. And so do you, I think, which is why it scares you so much. When you are ready, you will come back. And we will do this dance as many times as it takes, Indiana. Because in the end, there is nothing you want so much as the things you are afraid to need. Deep down, you know this."

"Goodbye, Stefan," she managed to bite out.

And then she turned, his words heavy inside her as she did exactly as he predicted. She made sure she kept her stride little more than an amble as she left the bedroom and headed for the stairs.

She moved through the light and airy house, the

sunshine pouring in from all sides feeling like an affront. She wanted it dark and moody to match what she felt inside, but Prague wasn't cooperating.

But she didn't need it to rain to do what she needed to do.

She threw open the front door and walked away from Stefan Romanescu and all his simmering *intensity*, telling herself she had no intention of ever going back.

No matter what.

Because she, by God, was going to have some *fun*.

CHAPTER SEVEN

THOUGH *FUN* WAS NOT her first thought as Indy stood there outside the house, breathing in the summer morning while she tried to take stock of what had just happened.

What she'd just done.

A part of her wanted nothing more than to turn around and race back inside. She'd waited two long years for this and she was bailing already? Surely it made sense to just go back to him and see if she could salvage this somehow—

Salvage what? asked a caustic voice inside her. *You know what you're good at and it's not this.*

She blew out a breath, and started down the road, thinking a nice long walk would suit her perfectly, thank you. It would settle her down and let her think.

Prague glimmered there in the distance as she made her way down the hill, dance music in her ears to remind her that she liked her mood light and her parties never-ending. And it was the beautiful fairytale city it always was, but she hardly saw it. Because she was too busy going over every single thing Stefan had said to her.

Indy had always been a mediocre student. That wasn't a question. Why had he made it a question? And why now, years after she'd finally graduated, when it didn't matter what kind of student she'd been in the first place?

Her sister had been the student in the family. And it wasn't that Indy had set herself up in opposition to Bristol. It was that there was no point competing with her sister for a crown Indy didn't even want. She'd always thought that Bristol had become serious about her studies to put herself in an unimpeachable place where studying was all she did. Because Indy had been much better at flitting around their small-town schools, doing the popular thing.

There was no point doing things you weren't good at, was there?

No one's good *at paying bills, Indy,* Bristol had cried in exasperation at one point during their time as roommates. *I'm not* good *at being responsible, I just don't have an option not to be. Why don't you understand that?*

Maybe you don't have a choice, Indy had replied, hugging Bristol even though her sister tried to shrug out of it, even batting at her a little because Bristol didn't feel like *not* being frustrated.

But you maybe also love it a little bit at the same time, don't you?

Bristol had given up. But Indy had taken it as confirmation. She gravitated toward the things she was good at in life and that was why her life was a delight. Bristol might claim to enjoy what she did, but she had sure seemed endlessly stressed out about all of it while she did it, didn't she? Her grades in high school. Her GPA and course load in college. Her masters and then her doctorate—it was all *stress stress stress*.

One thing Indy had avoided, as much as possible, was stress.

She couldn't understand why anyone would want the kind of intensity Stefan had showed her. That just seemed like a whole lot of stress in all the places where life was supposed to be the most fun and she wanted no part of it.

"I'm fine the way I am," she muttered out loud as she left his street behind.

It took her a while to walk down into the city and when she did, she found herself wandering through the city streets until she found a shop that sold newspapers and magazines in English.

And stopped dead, because there was her sister on the cover of several. Front and center.

Go Bristol, she thought.

She found a place to sit down by the river and read them all through. Then she got her sister on the phone, the way she did as often as she could while Bristol was off adventuring in tabloid splendor. If only for a few moments.

"Did you know that you're on the front page of every single tabloid there is?" she asked when Bristol answered.

"What do you mean by every tabloid?" Bristol sounded annoyed, but Indy was looking at a whole series of pictures of her face. Soft and open and splashed across the papers—and Bristol was an academic, not an actress. Something in Indy turned over at that. "I'm not comfortable with *one* tabloid."

"Then I have some bad news for you," Indy said merrily. "They're comfortable with you. And you do know you have a little something called the internet at your disposal, Bristol."

She laughed, picturing the annoyed expression her sister was certain to be making, off in her Spanish island paradise with one of the richest and most famous men alive. *Nice for some*, she thought, though she knew she didn't actually envy Bristol. It was that look on her face in all these pictures, though. It made Indy wish she were different, inside and out.

But she wasn't. "You can access this exciting new invention with the newfangled handheld computer you're using to talk to me, in a totally different country, *right now*."

"I access the internet all the time, asshole," Bristol replied in her typically snooty way. All big sister bossiness and the suggestion, right there beneath her words, that Indy was wasting her life. It was oddly comforting today. "And yet, oddly enough, it's not the tabloid newspapers I look for when I do."

"Well, good news, then," Indy said brightly. "You look amazing. What else matters?"

Bristol let out her trademark longsuffering sigh, but Indy could hear that her out-of-character adventure was already changing her. Because Bristol was doing the exact opposite of the things she normally did. She was celebrating finishing up her doctorate and not knowing exactly what to do with the rest of her life by doing something completely outside her normal range. That was how she'd ended up on the arm of Lachlan Drummond, one of the most eligible billionaires in the world.

She even sounded happy.

And as Indy sat there glaring at the river after the call ended, that felt like yet another jolting sort of indictment inside her.

Stefan's breakdown of what she was going to do once she walked away from him seemed to simmer inside her, taunting her, because she knew he was right. Wasn't that what she always did when she found herself on her own? Maybe after a long night. Maybe after an adventure where she'd lost track of her companions. She could walk into any bar, anywhere. She often didn't even have to walk into a bar. A few suggestive glances and she was sure that she could have a man eating out of her palm no matter where she was. But to what end?

She could hear Stefan's voice in her head. *Those empty sugar-high orgasms you like so much*, he'd said, and she was very much afraid he'd ruined them for her. Because who wanted hollow junk-food sex when there was…him?

Meanwhile, despite her *Bristol-ness*, her sister had sounded happy.

Happy.

And for all that Indy had spent her life pursuing fun at all costs, had she remembered to make sure that she was happy while she was doing it?

Do you even know what happy is? asked another voice inside, this one sounding a whole lot like her father.

She called home, smiling when she heard her father's grumpy voice on the other end.

"Do you know what time it is here?" he asked, instead of saying hello. "Don't tell me you forgot to look at the time change. I think we both know you do it deliberately."

"Hi, Dad," she said, affection for him racing through her and warming her. "You sound deeply stressed out. Isn't it a Saturday?"

She heard his laugh and could picture him easily, back in that house where she'd grown up. It was a little after six o'clock in the morning, Ohio time, but she knew perfectly well he hadn't been asleep. Margie liked an extra few hours to catch up on her beauty sleep every weekend, but not Bill. He worked all week, as he liked to say, and therefore liked to be up and at it on the weekends to squeeze out every drip of leisure time available.

"It's a fine Saturday," her father said. "I have big plans. The hardware store, a little project in your mother's vegetable garden, and I'm going to fire up the grill for dinner. Did you call to hear my itinerary? You're not normally the itinerary sort, are you, Bean?"

Bean. She couldn't remember why he'd started calling her that, only that he always had. And that something inside her would break forever if he ever stopped.

"I want to ask you a life question, Dad," she said, and though her voice was pleasant enough, her heart still hurt. Walking down from Stefan's hillside villa hadn't helped at all.

"You're the one gadding about in Europe. Mysteriously. Seems you have it figured out."

She hadn't told him—or anyone—where, precisely, in Europe she was. Because everything concerning Stefan had seemed too private. Too personal.

And because if she told them what she was doing, she would have to tell them why. Which could only lead to explaining things better left unexplained. Or, worse, coming back after a night or two and having to explain that instead.

Better not to risk any of that. "What is *gadding* anyway?" she asked. "No one ever says, *oh, I think I'm up for a* gad. *Come join me in some* gadding."

"Is this one of your internet games?" She heard sounds she recognized. Her father puttering around in the kitchen. The cabinets and the fridge opening and closing as he made himself the English muffin he liked to eat every morning, getting out the honey and butter to use when the toaster made it the exact shade of tan he preferred. "You know I don't like being recorded."

"That was only the one time. I told you I wouldn't do it again. And besides, you were amazing. You still have fans on my page."

"Then my life is complete," Bill said dryly. "Every man needs fans on a webpage."

"Are you happy, Dad?" Indy asked before she lost her nerve. "I mean truly happy?"

There was a small pause, and Indy screwed her eyes shut. But when she did, all she could see was her dad at the kitchen window half a world away, staring out at the backyard and the woods, his brow furrowed in thought.

"Are you in trouble, Bean?" her father asked, his gruff, joking tone changed to something quieter that made the knots in her seem to swell to twice their size. "Because you know that all you have to do is say the word and your mother and I will be on the next plane. No matter where you are. Or what you're doing."

And something flooded her then, bright and sweet, because she knew he meant that. Her parents, who had always seemed so deeply content to be exactly where they were—who didn't take the kind of trips their daughters did, or even their friends did, and never seemed all that interested in far off places—would think nothing of racing to her side if she needed them.

Shouldn't she be happy with that? Why did she need more? Why did anyone need more? There were a whole lot of people who didn't even have what she did.

"I'm fine," she hurried to assure him. "I was just thinking about what happiness really is. And you and mom always seem so content, I figured you must know."

"You always said contentment was a fate worse than death," her father reminded her, though he laughed when he said it. "When you were thirteen, you and your sister made solemn vows to leave this town and never come back, because neither one of you had any intention of *settling*. You were very sure of yourselves."

"I'm always sure of myself, Dad." That was true enough, but saying it out loud gave her pause. Why was she so sure? That she was bad at school. That she was shallow. That she only wanted what she knew she could get, and even then, only for a little while. She found herself rubbing at her chest again, though she already knew it wouldn't keep her heart from aching. "But that's why I'm calling. I'm asking what you're sure of, for a change."

She expected him to shrug that off. Make a little joke, maybe. Keep things light and easy.

"I think that a happy life is earned," her father said instead, sounding…thoughtful. "Because life itself isn't one thing or another. It's not happy or sad. It just is. Like anything, it's what you make of it. Your mom and I have had some hard times and we've had easy times. But the hard times are better, and the easy times sweeter, because of the work we put in."

"That's something people like to say," Indy whispered. "Putting the work in. But they don't ever say what it means."

"It means you don't let your life just happen to you, Indy," her father said, not unkindly. "You have to live it, good and bad, boring and exciting, one day after the next. It's not meant to be fun all the time. That isn't to say you can't enjoy it, but a life that's only one thing isn't much of a life."

And though she changed the subject then, even talking to her mother for a while when her father passed the phone on because Margie was actually up before nine for a change, it was that part that resonated with her.

A life that was only one thing wasn't much of a life.

She couldn't let it go. She tested herself, finding her way into a bar, and, sure enough, letting a few men flirt with her while she sat in it. But she did not take them up on any of their invitations.

Or their candy-coated anything.

Because her life had been only one thing for a long, long time.

And she hated that Stefan had seized on the reason for that being Bristol, because she loved her sister. Adored her. Supported her, cheered her on, and wanted nothing but the best for her. That didn't change the fact that way back when they were kids, Indy had decided that she was going to go a different way.

Maybe *because* it was different.

Was it that easy? If you made a decision when you were young were you doomed to repeat it ever after?

But no, she thought as she found herself in Old Town Square again. She watched the statues of the apostles appear in the famous Astronomical Clock, doing their thing while the crowd cheered and took pictures. The statue of death waved. And Indy felt a kinship to the funny old thing. Because the clock put on its show at the top of each hour, and it was wonderful. But the rest of the time, no matter how beautiful and old, it was just a clock.

Maybe, for the first time in her life, she didn't want to be the same old thing she'd always been.

And she could admit, then, that Stefan was right about this part, too. Intensity terrified her. The things that Stefan said to her, and all the implications, terrified her even more.

But maybe she'd come all the way to Prague to be terrified. Maybe it was good for her. The fact was, if she paid attention to her orgasms alone, the man knew what he was talking about. Everything with him was dialed up to one hundred or more. Everything with him was *more*. Longer. Deeper.

Better.

What did it say about her that all she'd wanted was to finally come to Prague, to meet him here, and yet she'd run off the minute it got to be too much for her? Was she really that person? Deep down, she knew she'd woken up scared silly that first morning and had been running ever since. Because he'd touched things in her she hadn't known were there.

Over the past two years she'd convinced herself that she'd imagined the intensity. That it had been the circumstances, not the man.

But the truth was, Stefan still felt like fate.

Like destiny.

She might like to tell anyone who asked that she was shallow and silly, but deep down, she didn't think of herself that way. And Stefan was the only person she wasn't related to who didn't take her at face value. Who looked at her and saw depths. Who saw more than her body or her face or what she might look like beside him.

And she knew she should have been horrified that he'd treated her like a research project, but she wasn't. Who else had she ever met who wanted to know *more* about her when they'd already had sex with her? Who refused to accept what they saw?

Even though she'd run off from his house and even though she hadn't been faking her outrage while she'd been there, Indy knew the real truth was she liked it. All of it.

She *liked* how intense he was, little as she knew how to handle it. He'd been that intense the first night she'd met him. Despite what she'd told herself since, she hadn't imagined that part. And she liked what he seemed to be suggesting, that he'd been as shaken by her as she'd been by him. Maybe she just needed time to acclimate to that. To him.

To fate.

Maybe she'd needed to know that she could leave so that she could return.

Because that was what she did, climbing out of a taxi at his front door once again, and this time noticing the security pad on the wall. She let herself in with the key that still hung around her neck, finding the house as bright and sunny as she'd left it. She wandered through the beautiful rooms, amazed that a man she'd met in such a dark and gritty place had made himself a sanctuary like this one. Amazed that he felt the same way, impossibly bright when he should have been something else entirely.

She saw him standing out on the terrace, looking out over the pool toward the city in the distance with his mobile to his ear. He'd changed his clothes, putting on jeans and what looked like a well-loved red T-shirt that made the muscles in his wide back enough to weep over.

He was talking in what she assumed was Romanian when she opened the glass doors and stepped outside. He turned around, his blue gaze coming to her and staying there.

Bright and hard.

He finished his call and shoved his mobile into his pocket, then did nothing at all but regard her where she stood.

"Yes," Indy said, as if she was making proclamations. "I'm back. I went to a bar, just as predicted. Are you happy?"

"Ecstatic."

"I did not have sex with the numerous men I could have had sex with." She studied him for a moment, that face carved of stone that had haunted her for years now. "I think you should take that as a statement of my intentions."

The light in his blue eyes changed. Like a lightning storm. "I will make a note."

"I don't know how to do intensity, Stefan." That sounded a little more uncertain, but Indy didn't let that stop her. "I don't know how to do any of this. This is not the kind of thing I do."

"But you do, foolish girl. You have from the start."

She blew out a breath and then crossed her arms, as if that could help her. "That's very opaque, thank you. Anyway. Here I am. You get your night of wild intensity."

His smile made everything in her seem to stand at attention. "No. I am afraid that is no longer on offer."

"It's not?" And she was… Crushed. There was no other word for it.

But he was still holding her gaze. "A night will not do it. I'm tired of these one-night games. You will give me a month, Indiana. And then we will see where we are."

"A month?" She thought her teeth actually chattered. "I don't know if I can."

"You can," Stefan told her, and *he* was sure. He was commanding and certain in all things. She liked that, too. Maybe too much. "Because it is a month or nothing. Which will you choose?"

And when he put it like that, it was simple.

CHAPTER EIGHT

JUNE FADED, TURNING into a sweet, golden July that seemed to stretch on into forever.

Maybe he only wished it could.

Stefan had never spent much time contemplating the seasons. They marched on, one after the next, and what mattered was surviving what they wrought. Summer had simply been warmer than the bitter winters, but life had carried on the same. The less said about his childhood the better. Ditto the army. And since then, he'd been far too busy catapulting toward his dark future to spend any kind of deliberate time in the light.

But this summer he was in Prague. The only place on the planet that he had ever viewed not just as an escape, but as safe. It was where his grandmother had showed him that there was more to life than his father's heavy fist.

And now, fittingly, Prague was where he and his Indy were finally coming to terms.

I'll give you a month, she'd said that first afternoon. When she'd left him but come back, looking jittery and wide-eyed and still somehow stubborn.

Still stubborn, even as she'd surrendered.

Even as she gave him what he wanted, she did it her way.

He'd thought again of a splash of red in a dark alley. And how quickly, how irrevocably, this woman had happened along and changed everything. It was a good thing he had always been a practical man, or he might have been tempted to tear down a wall or two. With his bare hands, just to feel them fall.

Anything to feel as if he could control the things he felt for this woman. As if he could control himself the way he always had before her.

But he had a month. And Stefan intended to use it.

Let me guess, she'd said that first afternoon, when all he'd done was gaze at her, victory and something that felt too much like relief pounding through him. *You require nudity at all times. Blow-jobs morning, noon, and night. Is that the kind of intensity you have in mind?*

It is never a bad place to start, he'd said, already amused. *As I think you know.*

She had already told him that not indulging in her usual behavior, out there where she could have lovers eating from her hand with a single glance, was a statement of her intent. But Stefan didn't think he was the only one who thought that really, when she crossed the terrace to kneel down at his feet, then held his gaze while she took him into her mouth again, that it was a new set of vows.

And for the first few days, it was enough to simply have her near. To know that there would be no renegotiation come the dawn. That she had promised him a month and that meant she wouldn't sneak out when he was on his run or while he was dealing with the inevitable phone call.

Not that she struck him as the type to *sneak* anywhere. But then, before her, he hadn't been the type to worry about what a woman might be doing. Or about anything at all save getting richer and staying in one piece.

"I thought you walked away from your business," she said when he finished one of those calls, standing out in the dusk and testing himself. Not looking back into the house to see what she was doing. Not checking to make sure she was where he'd left her.

He supposed that was trust. Or a gesture in its direction. And in him, trust was a muscle that had atrophied long ago—but for her, for them, he would work on it.

Stefan had been cooking Indy a traditional Romanian dinner when the call had come in. He walked back in now, something in him shifting—

not quite uncomfortably—at the sight of her standing there at his stove. The kitchen was warm and
bright, filled with the scents of his childhood, and
Indy there in the middle of everything. She was
barefoot, wearing those cutoff shorts that he had
become a little bit obsessed with. Her hair was tied
in a big knot on the top of her head, letting him
look at her elegant neck and her shoulder blades
beneath the airy tank she wore. Her bracelets sang
small, happy songs every time she moved.

He felt his heart beat harder in his chest, the
way that it did now.

And he knew that two years ago he would have
called what surged in him then a kind of horrify-
ing neediness. He would have found it unpardon-
able. A weakness. He would have tried to excise
it with his own fingers, if he could.

But that had been before. Before she'd walked
into his world and knocked it straight off its axis.

"I walked away from my major business, yes,"
he replied. "The part that would be frowned upon
by any number of law enforcement agencies."

"Then why are you still taking business calls?"

Once again he was struck by the fact she simply sounded interested. Not trying to score any
points. Not building toward some kind of agenda.
Just interested in him as a person.

And only when he acknowledged how rare
that was could Stefan also admit that he liked

it. That he wasn't sure how he'd lived without it all this time.

"I always intended to retire from the more dangerous part of my business eventually," he told her, and opted not to share how difficult that had turned out to be. It was clear to him that if he'd stayed in any longer than he had, exiting would not have been possible—and he didn't like that at all. He'd always imagined himself in control of the things he did. "I only expedited the process. I am sure I told you this."

She looked over her shoulder at him, laughter in her gaze. "I guess I didn't realize you had a legitimate arm of whatever had you gun slinging in an alley in Budapest."

Stefan went over to the stove and took the wooden spoon from her hand, nudging her away from his pot. "My money is perfectly legitimate. And as you know, money invested wisely makes more money."

"That's what you do? Invest?"

"Isn't that what you do?"

"I travel all over the globe, wherever my mood takes me," she said airily. "My investments fuel that lifestyle, sure, but so do the jobs I take when I want some cash. But what about you? What do you like to do?" She lifted up a hand when he started to answer that. "Don't say me. You had a whole

life before you met me, Stefan. And in the years
since. What is it you actually *like*?"

Another question no one had ever asked him.
A question he'd hardly dared ask himself some
years, because how could it matter what he liked?
He had needed to focus on surviving, like it or not.

"Art," he said, without letting himself brood
about it.

And he cautioned himself against putting too
much weight on the fact that he'd never told anyone
that before. His grandmother was the only person
in his life who might have been interested in such
things—but she had been a stoic, stern woman. It
had never been her way to chatter idly.

Still, he found himself looking sideways to see
what Indy's reaction might be. Would she laugh?
His heart kicked at him. Would she laugh *at* him?

He had never put himself in this position before. Where another person's opinion could hold
so much weight.

The truth was, he did not care for the feeling.

But all she did was nod, looking off across the
room. When he followed her gaze, he saw that
she was looking at a bold piece he'd bought years
ago in Cluj, known for an avant-garde art scene to
rival Bucharest's claims of being Romania's artistic capital. He'd had it installed here in this house,
his cathedral to what could be.

What could be—and now was.

"All the art you have in this house is beautiful," she said, moving that dreamy look of hers to him. "Interesting and confronting and lovely. Is that why the rooms are so airy here? So that the art is what's seen?"

"I spent most of my life in dark, desperate places," Stefan told her, and his voice was rougher than he would have allowed it to be for anyone else. But this was Indy. And he could hardly demand her vulnerability if he wasn't prepared to share his own, could he? "My mother did her best to make the places we lived feel more like a home, but my father always ruined it. Any extra money we had went to his debts or his drink. After she died, there was no point bothering."

"I'm surprised you remembered art existed at all," Indy said softly.

"Art is not something a person forgets." He scowled down at his pot, this sentimental meal from one of the few good moments of his childhood, as if only just noticing that there was no part of what he was doing here tonight that wasn't emotional. But he couldn't seem to stop himself. "The perfection of a finely drawn line. A pop of color that changes everything. I saw pieces I liked over the years and had them sent here, telling myself that one day I would come here, live here, and have them all around me all the time. But that day never seemed to come any closer. Then I looked up from an ordinary evening of the typical darkness in my life, and there you were. All your fine lines and a splash of red in the night. I knew you were art, too."

He snuck a look at her and found her gazing back at him, her lovely eyes filled up with tears.

Stefan could tell that she was trying out this intensity thing, as he'd asked her to do, because she didn't dance away. She didn't start singing, or change the subject, or move closer so she could put her mouth on him and distract them both. He almost wished she would. Instead, Indy let him see her respond. React.

All those emotions he knew she would have said she didn't possess. Right there in her eyes like the finest chocolate.

"My grandmother left me her flat down Old Town when she passed," he told her, because he couldn't seem to stop. Maybe he didn't want to stop. "It was filled with art. Maybe she was why I never forgot the power in it. I bought this house before she was gone, but it wasn't until then that I began to make it mine. Even if I only made it here once a year, if that, I knew it waited here. I knew that I could come, walk these rooms, and let the art I'd chosen make me believe I was a different man. A better man. I told myself it didn't matter how far off *one day* was. For a long time, knowing this was here was enough."

Indy drifted close and bumped him with her shoulder, a kind of unconscious gesture that about laid him flat. Because it was the antithesis of any of the ways they touched. It wasn't sex. It wasn't the prelude to sex. It didn't have anything to do with sex at all.

But it was intimate.

And even though Stefan was the one who'd confidently thought he'd already done all the changing necessary, he felt something in him crack wide open.

"It seems like you do have a home after all, then," she'd said quietly, her eyes shining. "That's not a small thing, is it?"

And he didn't know how to tell her than nothing that happened between them, or because there was a *them* at all, had ever been small.

But later that night, after he'd tied her up so she didn't have access to her usual bag of tricks, then made her sob and scream until he was satisfied that she didn't have a single thought in her head without his name on it, Stefan lay in the dark with the soft weight of her in his arms and wondered what he would do if a month was not enough.

Because he did not think that any place would soothe him now, not when he knew how much better it was when she was here. Lighting up already bright rooms with that smile of hers, making the world stop again and again while she did it.

He knew it did no good to worry about the future. There was only now.

July continued on.

Some days he bossed her around, because he could. Because it made both of them hot.

"I think, foolish girl, that I will have you naked today," he would say.

Sometimes she grinned wickedly and looked thrilled at the notion. Other days she had different reactions, not all of them positive. One morning she scowled at him, blinking the sleep out of her eyes while she did it.

"Why do you call me that? Maybe I should call you *foolish man*. Would you like that?"

"You can call me whatever you like," he told her. "But you will always be my very own foolish girl, who wandered into the dark and brought me out into the light."

And he watched, sprawled there beside her in the bed they shared, while she melted at that.

"Well." Her voice was grumpy, but her eyes were bright and shining. "I guess it's okay then."

"Naked," he reminded her.

Because naked days were all about power and surrender and all the marvelous things a man with his imagination—and the wicked delight she could never repress for long—could build between them.

"I thought you'd be like that all the time," she panted one night, after the kind of naked day that left her so limp and boneless that he'd had to carry her upstairs, bathe her with his own hands, then put her to bed.

He did not mind these tasks, to be clear.

"Like what?" he asked.

"You know. The way you are on naked days. All the rules. All the kneeling. I assumed you'd demand to be called Master Stefan or something and go crazy with nightly spankings and all the rest of that stuff."

He was amused. He was stretched out, propping himself up on one arm, toying with a strand of her hair while he looked down to that heart-shaped face of hers that only grew more beautiful. When surely that should have been impossible. "Is that what you want?"

"Sometimes," Indy replied, grinning up at him. "And sometimes not."

"You do not like a steady diet of anything, Indiana," Stefan said in a low voice, because he knew. And sometimes she was not in the mood to hear all the things he knew. He tugged on the lock of her hair, gently enough. "You thrive on variety. But then, so do I."

"You're the one with a big house full of art. You must like some steadiness in your diet."

He smoothed his hand over her face, her soft cheeks, where heat from her bath still lingered.

"I like you, foolish girl," he said, though he

knew he should not have. "Have I not made that clear?"

She smiled at him, though he thought he saw shadows in her gaze. "I'm not really a dietary staple. I'm more of an occasional dessert."

"I like dessert, too," he offered.

But she laughed and ran a hand over his chest, then down over his ridged abdomen. "*Do* you?"

The days passed. Stefan watched her, closely. He expected her to show signs of claustrophobia. To act as if it was sheer torture to stay in one place, with one man, for so long. He wasn't sure she'd ever tried before. He anticipated that she would make it clear she was *doing him a favor*.

And yet, as one week became another, and another, if Indy was restless she failed to show it.

"I asked my father about happiness," she told him one afternoon. "I wanted to know if he was as happy as it seems he is."

They sat in the shade outside, beneath a trellis draped in blooming roses. He was working on his laptop while she curled up beside him, reading a book in between her dips in the pool. Not naked, sadly. It seemed the tiny little bright yellow bikini she wore was, apparently, one of the surprising number of items she'd managed to roll up and stick in that tiny pack of hers.

"I never needed to ask my father such a question," he had replied, not looking up from his screen. "I already knew the answer. It was his fist, preferably connecting with my face."

"I guess I can understand that," she said with a quiet ferocity. "Because I'd very much like to plant my fist in his face. And imagining it makes *me* happy."

He looked up then, entertained and touched in equal measure that his carefree, relentlessly non-judgmental Indy had it in her to sound so bloodthirsty. Much less on his behalf.

"He died as he lived, never fear," Stefan assured her. "As we all must."

Indy had her book open in her lap and she turned it over then, frowning at him. "In a way, that's what my father said. But how can you tell if you're living life the way you should be?"

"There is no *should*. There are only the choices you make in each moment, strung together to make a day. A week. And sooner or later, a life that is the sum of its parts."

There was the sound of the breeze rustling through the trees. Lawn mowers growled in the distance while up above them, birds sang and bees hummed. But Indy didn't return to her reading.

"The thing is," she said after a moment, haltingly, "I never saw myself in competition with Bristol. It was so important to her that she be the smart one. And if she was the smart one, then I got to be the pretty one." She blew out a breath. "For a long time, that was all I really wanted."

"I've seen your sister," he said, though Indy knew that already. She called her sister daily and had told him, with glee, that she was responsible for her sister becoming girlfriend to Lachlan Drummond, the billionaire who couldn't seem to keep his face out of the tabloids. The same tabloids that featured Indy's sister, now—and that she liked to brandish at him. "Whether she is smarter or not, I couldn't say. But she is also pretty. Surely you both know this."

"She's gorgeous, obviously. Hello. She's my sister." She smiled while she said that, but it faded. She toyed with the spine of her book. "It seems silly now. But for some reason, back when we were kids, it seemed absolutely crucial that we choose. We had to make sure that there was always a critical and obvious distance between us. Bristol disappeared into her books. And I…"

For a moment it seemed as if she didn't intend to go on.

"And you?" Stefan asked.

To his surprise, she flushed slightly. "I did what I always do. I flitted around from group to group. I was everybody's best friend, but they were never mine. I kissed all kinds of boys, even before my fateful relationship with Jamie Portnoy." She shook her head. "If anyone had asked, I would've sworn on a stack of Bibles that I was a born extrovert."

He had a sense of where this was going now, but he only waited, sitting back to better watch her lovely face as she spoke. And to enjoy the way she used her hands as emphasis, drawing pictures in the air.

Stefan wanted to tell her that already, she had bloomed here. That the frenetic edge to her was gone, because she didn't have to plan her quick escape. Because living as they were, only the two of them in this house, it was impossible to maintain any kind of performance. He had seen her in all kinds of moods. The ones she would cheerfully admit as well as the ones she pretended she didn't have. He'd held her when she sobbed at a movie, then pretended she hadn't. He held her when she sobbed out her pleasure, then gave it back to him tenfold.

They woke every morning tangled around each other, as if in sleep they instinctively wanted nothing but to get closer.

Indy had not retreated from any of this. She had not run.

"But for weeks now," she was saying, frowning at the roses, "I've been here. With you and all these books. I think I forgot how much I like to read. And how, if things had been different, I might have liked to disappear into books, too."

"I'm glad," he said, and meant it. "You should."

She shifted, turning her body so she could hold his gaze. "But I was really good stripping, Stefan."

He laughed. "This I believe."

"It was fun. And I mean really fun. Maybe partly because I was actually paying for college, *and* saving, *and* doing something illicit at the same time. You may not know this about me—" and her eyes sparkled as she gazed at him "—but I really do kind of love it when people try to shame me for the things I enjoy."

"Shame does not sit well on you, Indiana." He wanted to reach for her, but checked himself. Because once again, this was not a sexual moment. He felt something more like sacred, and he was determined that he would honor it. "I am glad of that, too."

And she didn't have to tell him that they were only his, these moments that were all the more intense because they were not about sex. He could feel it in his bones.

"I stopped going to classes in college because I liked them too much." Her voice was solemn, then, as if she was making a painful confession. Her eyes lost some of that sparkle. Stefan still waited. "I was getting an A in one class, so I made sure to skip out on the final because it was half my grade. And I had already made my choice, hadn't I?" She searched his face for a moment. "How did you know that? Because you knew that, didn't you?"

"I suspected."

"No one else has ever thought there was anything more to me than a good fuck," Indy said, her voice hardly above a whisper. "Not even me."

He picked her up then. He hauled her into his lap and held her there, smoothing one hand over her damp hair and then holding her face tipped up to his so there could be no evasion. No hiding.

"There is much more to you than that," he told her, his voice nearly a growl. He reached between her legs, beneath the damp scrap of her bathing suit, and found her molten hot. Swollen with need, as always. "Your pussy is one of the great wonders of this world, Indiana. But it is only an addiction because it's yours."

He stroked her, playing with her slippery folds and circling her clit until she moaned.

She bucked against him, her breath feathering out. "I've spent my whole life hiding, but you saw right through me. I still don't understand how."

"You understand."

Stefan held her clit between his thumb and forefinger, pinching it in time with her pants. When she moaned again, he twisted his wrist and plunged two fingers deep inside her clinging heat.

"You called me into the light," he growled. "But I found you in the dark. We fit together, two halves of a whole. There was no possibility that you could ever be anything but exactly who you are, not if this was to work. Beautiful, yes. Uninhibited and remarkably sexy, always. I will never get enough of you but even if this—" and he sped up the rhythm of his thrusting fingers, loving the way she clung to him, her fingers digging into him, her eyes half closed "—went away, even if I could never fuck you again, it would change nothing."

"Bullshit," she whispered.

He pulled his hand away, then laughed when she glared at him.

"Who do you want to be, Indy? It's no longer a choice you made as a child. It doesn't matter how you spent your years. We are here now. What do you want to be here?"

She was breathing heavily, her gaze something almost like hostile as she stared back at him—but Stefan knew that had more to do with the fact he hadn't let her come.

"I will tell you what I know in only these short weeks," he said. "You have spent no time at all maintaining your online life. I never see you huddled in a corner, scrolling through your phone, certain you've missed something. You seem genuinely happy. Maybe the trouble is that you don't believe it."

He saw her sit with that. And saw, too, that she didn't like the weight of it.

"The trouble," she said solemnly, "is that you are not inside me."

"You know how to fix that," he growled at her.

And when she went to straddle him, he turned her around. She pulled her bikini to one side as she wriggled against him, arching her back as he pulled out his cock so he could slam himself inside her.

For a moment the sheer wonder of it swept over him. Her too, he knew. They both paused, reveling in that impossible fit.

She might think it was this house. His art collection, or this new, pretty life he'd made for himself. But Stefan knew the truth.

His home was her.

But that wasn't something he intended to tell her. Not yet. He wrapped one arm around her middle, holding her as he began to pound into her. He turned her head so he could take her mouth, because there weren't enough ways to taste her.

There never would be. Not in a lifetime.

Maybe more.

And then he showed her what he could not put into words, and fucked them both home.

CHAPTER NINE

"I'M TRYING TO DECIDE what my great passion in life is," Indy announced one morning into her mobile, and wasn't surprised when Bristol, off in some or other city on her world tour with Lachlan Drummond, laughed.

"I thought that was obvious," Bristol said. "Isn't it?"

Indy had been on her way toward the kitchen when she'd been sidetracked by her current favorite room in Stefan's house. She'd left her book in here yesterday and when she'd come in to retrieve it, had sat down and called Bristol. Her favorite room in the house changed by the day. This one was arranged around a white-bricked fireplace, with only a few throw rugs and a deep red painting to break up the color scheme.

It appealed to her sense of drama.

"Thank you, asshole, but I like sex for fun, not for profit." She let out a theatrical sort of sigh because she knew it would make her sister roll her eyes. "Believe me, if I felt otherwise, I've had ample opportunity to take up sex work."

That was all too true. She'd been offered all kinds of fascinating positions. Some people wanted her to be a dominatrix. Others thought she should lean into the erotic dancing. Or try the yacht-girl thing at Cannes and see if she could make that into an enterprise. One of the women she'd met in the South of France had told her frankly that these days, the internet made it so easy to conduct a personal escort service without having to cut anyone else in, that any woman who *didn't* make money that way was a fool.

Indy had found all of these offers and suggestions fascinating. Surely it said something kind of fabulous about her that so many people thought she could make money from an act she would have done anyway—and for free?

Anyway, she had always chosen to take it as a compliment. No matter how it was meant.

"I would ordinarily express dismay at that sentiment," Bristol said, sounding... Not happy. Not sad either, but almost... Rueful. "But you know. Pot meet kettle and there I am in the middle."

"Signing a contract to be somebody's girlfriend isn't sex work," Indy said loyally. "Not really."

"I think you'll find it is."

"Not at all." Indy waved a hand at Stefan's

white fireplace, as if her sister could see her. "It's nothing more than a prenuptial agreement for a relationship that isn't a marriage. Totally socially acceptable."

"I'll let Mom know then. She'll be so proud."

"Sometimes," Indy said, in a confiding way, "I'm pretty much positive that Mom and Dad might just be bigger freaks than we think. We had to come from somewhere. And maybe there's a reason they've always been perfectly happy to stay home and settle in to that Ohio life. Why bother going out when you have everything you could possibly desire right there with you already?"

"Ew. What? No."

"I'm telling you—I think they have a rollicking—"

"Anyway," Bristol said loudly, cutting her off. "Why are you interested in finding a passion? I thought you always had all the passion a girl could need or want. I thought you liked it that way."

"Men are a passion of mine, it's true," Indy said lightly, because it was expected.

But a bolt of something far more complicated than need went through her as she said it, because when was the last time she'd thought about men in a general sense? She only thought about one man now. And for the past two years, really. *Only and always*, something in her whispered.

Even as she thought that, she was aware that

it wasn't how she operated. She would have said she didn't have that kind of possessiveness in her, but she held on to it anyway. As if it was something precious.

Only and always didn't scare her.

Which, really, was the scariest thing yet.

"Your passion was always academics," she said to her sister, trying to shake that off…whatever it was. But her hand found its way to her heart and stayed there. "I don't really think that a meaningful life is built on an unquenchable thirst for socializing. We can both agree that I've tried."

"You tell me, Indy," Bristol said. "You've had a million temp jobs in the last year alone."

That shouldn't have stung. She told herself that the fact it did meant only that she was tired. And who wouldn't be tired? The kind of demands Stefan liked to make could take whole nights to work out.

Especially because he liked to take it slow.

She shivered. "Yes, yes," she said into her phone. "I can never settle down. I'm not serious. Lack of responsibility, careless and undependable, blah blah blah."

"I didn't mean that as a dig." Bristol's voice was even, and again, faintly rueful. "In a way, I'm envious. You've had the opportunity to try on a hundred different lives without having to commit to any of them. Did none of them appeal to you at all?"

"I guess I didn't think of them as trying on lives," Indy said, considering. "Maybe I should have. They were just jobs that I could leave whenever I wanted. It never occurred to me that someday, I might want... I don't know. A career. Or at least a purpose."

There was a long silence. Indy found herself sitting up straighter, her heart pounding. Because she'd just admitted something, hadn't she? Whether she meant to or not.

Something she hadn't admitted to herself before.

"And what exactly has prompted all of this fascinating speculation?" Bristol asked after a moment, sounding far more intrigued.

Bristol was stubbornly refusing to ask what exactly Indy was doing, and where, despite Indy breezily saying things like *I'm summering on the Continent, Bristol. As you do.*

That meant, as a matter of sisterly principle, Indy could not tell her.

"We all come to these crossroads, Bristol," she murmured. "One way or another."

And though she'd meant to sound mysterious, the words landed in her as if they'd been carved in stone.

"I can't tell you what to do," Bristol said, and again, there was that note in her voice. Maybe it wasn't *rueful*, necessarily. Maybe it was a kind of *aware* that echoed a little too sharply inside Indy just at the moment. "I wouldn't dream of trying. But I can tell you that I've always admired your fearlessness."

Of all the things her older sister might have said, she hadn't been expecting that. Indy had a sudden flashback to a particular day of playing games of make-believe with Bristol in their backyard, running around and around the old oak tree that had stood there for hundreds of years. They'd decided it was their castle.

I'm going to be the princess, Indy had announced, though really, she was looking for Bristol's permission. As the oldest and the bossiest, it fell to Bristol to make the decisions. *I'm always the princess.*

Bristol had looked back at her with all the bone deep weariness a ten-year-old could muster when faced with a younger sister.

That's actually because you decided *to be the princess, Indy*, she'd said loftily. *You could decide to be a wizard instead. Or a warrior. You know it's up to you, right?*

Indy could remember that moment so clearly, which was funny, given she hadn't thought of those games they'd played in a million years. Eight-year-old Indy had stared back at her older sister, a part of her desperate to leap out into the unknown. To take on a role she'd never played before and *decide* to be whatever she wanted.

But she hadn't.

Was it really Bristol deciding to get serious about her studies that had sent Indy down this path? Or had she been the one who'd chosen it all along?

Because she'd chosen the part of princess that day, out there playing make-believe. It had been familiar. It had required nothing of her. She could have played that role in her sleep.

In a way, she'd been playing it ever since.

"My fearlessness?" she echoed now. Then laughed. "I guess I fooled you, then. I don't think I'm fearless at all."

"Maybe that's not the right word," Bristol conceded. "Maybe it's that no matter if you're afraid or not, I've never known you to let that keep you from doing something. Even when we were kids. You always jumped in, no matter how deep the water was. No matter if everyone and their mother told you not to do something, you wanted to see yourself. And you did. I admire that, Indy. I always have."

"I love you, too," Indy whispered.

And then they'd mutually hung up on each other as quickly as possible, so there would be no sniffling.

But her sister's words stayed with her when she

got up from her white chair in the white room with its powerful splash of red. They haunted her as she wandered through the house, looking for Stefan the way she did more times every day than she would have imagined possible. Given that she'd never been one to *look for* a man before.

He isn't just a man, a voice inside her chided her. *And you know it.*

She knew that he'd come back from his run this morning because he'd woken her up then. He'd flipped her over on her belly and had her digging her fists into the mattress and moaning out her pleasure before she'd even opened her eyes.

Indy had never been the kind of woman to claim she didn't like morning sex. She'd never understood the complaint, because what wasn't to love? A hard cock moving deep inside her before she was awake, so she fell out of sleep and into an orgasm without having to do anything at all. It was like a gift.

But she'd never loved it more than she did with Stefan, who made it something far hotter and deeper than any mere *gift*.

Sometimes he used the gym he'd installed on the lowest level of the house after his run, but he wasn't there when she looked. She trooped back up to the kitchen, eying the ibrik that sat by the stove—the correct name for the pot he used to make Turkish coffee, as he'd informed her when she'd called it *that thingie*—and even though he'd showed her how to make it herself, she didn't. Because she liked it better when he made it for her.

She looked around outside, down by the pool and in the gardens. His laptop sat closed on the table in the shade of the rose trellis, but Stefan himself was nowhere to be found.

Maybe you'll just have to sit here with your thoughts, she told herself wryly. *Instead of hoping he'll distract you.*

Indy sat there at the table, because that felt a lot like a challenge. She frowned out at the view, telling herself that she was *fearless.* Bristol had said so. And surely, if she thought about that enough and didn't try to avoid it in the heat of another orgasm, her heart would open up wide and give her a passion.

A purpose.

A life she wanted, not the one she'd chosen when she was a kid who didn't know any better.

And that was where Stefan found her sometime later. With his usual disconcerting telepathy, he set a cup of Turkish coffee before her, as if he'd been standing about invisibly in the kitchen and had watched her decide not to make her own.

"You look distressed," he observed, his accent washing over the way it always did, like a caress. "What could possibly have happened since I left you, limp and moaning out my name?"

"Many things, Stefan. Many important and exciting things, none of which I'm going to tell you if you're going to keep bragging about your sexual prowess. It's so unattractive."

His blue eyes gleamed. "Is it?"

She laughed as he sat down beside her.

"I like that," he said.

"What?" she asked, though she was already distracted by his proximity. Indy had never been into the drugs that, he was right, had been a huge part of a great many of the scenes she'd frequented over the years. Strip clubs and all kinds of other parties, in all different countries.

But Stefan was far more potent than any party.

It was amazing what all this time with him was doing to her. Day after day of this. Of them. It made everything seem to take a different shape. Though the way she wanted him only seemed to increase, it was different now. Because she knew that she would have him.

Sooner or later, she would have him again.

It made the waiting hotter.

It made the wanting deeper.

"When you laughed now, you mean it," Stefan said quietly. "I like it."

And he didn't wait for her to react to that, the way he sometimes did. He didn't study her, tracking every stray emotion as she had it. This time it was a matter-of-fact statement. Then he picked up his laptop and cracked it open.

Leaving Indy there beside him with the sweet and rich taste of his coffee on her tongue, and a new ache in her heart.

It took her some time to compose herself. To gaze at the roses, let their scent fill her, and remind herself that she'd fooled at least one other person into believing she was fearless.

"How did you know that you'd be good at…what you used to do?" she asked.

The look Stefan shot at her was amused. "I did not know. I did it and did not die. Again and again. This is how I decided it was good." The corner of his mouth kicked up, and she knew by now that it was his real smile. She could see the way it made his eyes gleam. "Also I made money. This was also good."

"Some people have a calling, you know." Indy sighed. "Is something wrong with us that we don't?"

"If you want there to be." He reached over and tapped her on the nose. "Yes, some people have a calling. But everybody has a life. You are not required to choose your path once, long ago, and never deviate from it again. Maybe those who live that way are lucky. But then again, maybe not. Maybe it is better to try many things, so that when you choose, you know you chose well."

"Says the gangster who's made himself an art dealer."

His smile sharpened. "All art dealers are gangsters, Indiana. Ask any artist."

That night, everything seemed hotter. Brighter.

She knew by now that the kind of intensity she'd been so afraid of was both better and worse than she'd feared. Better, because it didn't wreck her and it made everything sing, in and out of bed. But it did ask more of her than she'd ever given before. It was the intimacy of this month together. It was staying put and more than that, letting herself enjoy what that was like. To relax into the time. To do it without daydreaming where she'd go next.

It was the conversations they had, rambling and endless, picking up and carrying on from one hour to the next. From one night into the next afternoon, making her think things like *forever*.

It was Stefan himself. This wild thing they'd built between them.

And it was worse, too, because it had an expiration date.

But Indy didn't like to think about that.

It was a long night. Stefan woke her again and again, taking her in every way he could, almost as if he was marking her. Imprinting himself on her and inside her, making her body his so that there would be nothing left of her that wasn't his.

A thought that made her come all around him, screaming out his name.

The next morning he was there when she woke, looking down at her with a stark expression on that beautiful face of his.

She blinked, then moved closer, searching his gaze as she fit her palms to his jaw. His beard had come in and scraped at her skin, but she loved it. She loved the heat. She loved—

Careful, she warned herself. *Be very careful.*

"What's the matter?" she asked him.

"Today is a naked day, foolish girl," he said, darkly. And she remembered, vaguely, that she'd once complained about that endearment. When now it was like a song inside her, sweet and long. "And it will be intense."

"Isn't it always?"

But she had hardly recognized the smile he gave her then. It didn't make it to his eyes.

"This will be different," Stefan told her. "Because this will be the last."

CHAPTER TEN

"Stefan…" Indy began.

But he didn't want to hear it.

Because their month was up tomorrow and the only thing she seemed to want to talk about was how to find her passion.

Meaning, clearly, it wasn't him.

He was going to have to find a way to be okay with that.

Tomorrow.

"Quiet," he said now, his voice low. "Today will be a day of silent reflection."

Indy laughed, and not in the genuine way he loved. "I don't think that it will."

"If you are not quiet," he continued in the same tone, feeling the anticipation in him surge, "I will find a way to encourage you. You do like it when I spank you, don't you?"

"You can do whatever you want," she said. "But first—"

"No," he said, cutting her off. "No *first*. On your knees, foolish girl. There's much to do today."

Indy looked a little surly, but she obeyed him. Because she knew by now that when it came to naked days and power exchanges, he meant what he said.

And she loved that he did. She told him so, but even if she hadn't, the way she melted in his hands would have done the trick.

"You might want to do something about the insolence in that gaze of yours," he murmured as she sucked him in deep. "Or you can be sure I will."

She lowered her lashes immediately, but he knew full well that he would have the opportunity to express himself as the day wore on.

Because Indy loved to play sex games, but she was only submissive when she thought it was hot. It wasn't a lifestyle.

Too bad, he thought, because if it were, he would simply order her to stay with him and that would be the end of it.

But that wasn't who he was, either.

He came with a roar, his hands deep in her hair. And he watched, feeling himself heat up all over again as she swallowed him down, then smiled as if she was the one in control.

Sometimes he couldn't tell either.

And this was the last day, so he knew this was going to go, didn't he? The only mystery was how she would leave. He didn't think she would creep away in the night. He thought she would put on one of her performances. A lot of laughter, probably some sweetness, and then she would dance away into what was left of the summer, leaving him here with whatever was left of him.

He would have to find a way to accept that.

Because this was the tyranny of wanting things he couldn't simply take. This was the problem with the intensity he demanded from her. For the first time in his life, he had something to lose. He would have to live without her, knowing what it was like to have her.

He hated it.

And he took it out on her delectable body.

They both liked toys, so he fitted her with one of her favorites, then made her walk down the stairs with it in. He made her keep it in, so that even the act of standing with him in the kitchen while he calmly made coffee made her blush and shift from foot to foot, moaning a little.

"Do not come without my permission," he said as he poured the Turkish coffee into two cups and then carried them outside. Where he had her sit in the sun, letting the light dance all over her skin while she squirmed in her seat and looked at him like he was the best kind of monster. "Or you will regret it."

"I already regret it," Indy retorted, her voice

rough and greedy, just the way he liked it. "It's torture."

"It is not. But it could be. Is that what you would like?"

"I would like to talk—"

"A spanking it is, then."

Stefan pushed back his chair and patted his lap, lifting one brow.

Indy stared back at him, naked but for the way her hair tumbled down over her shoulders. And oh, he loved to watch the expressions that moved over her lovely face. At first she looked mutinous. He saw the distinct flash of her temper. And then, almost despite herself, the heated awareness that became a flush. Her nipples hardened. Her lips fell open.

She muttered something beneath her breath but she got up, crossed to him, and draped her naked body over his lap. Deliberately making it awkward when he knew how graceful she was, as yet another level of protest.

"I'm not really into this, you know," she told him as he widened his legs to keep her where he wanted her. But could feel the way she melted into him, no matter what she said. "Not when you seem mad. Which, by the way, you do."

"Yes, I can see how not into it you are," Stefan murmured, his hands playing between her thighs. He gripped the base of the toy and fucked her with it until goosebumps broke out all over her back and the sweet curve of her ass.

He was not mad. But he did not wish to tell her what he was.

Maybe he didn't know where to begin.

"Stefan..." she started. Again.

"I told you to be quiet," he reminded her. "But there are some lessons you do not want to learn, Indiana. Maybe today, you will."

He removed the toy. And then he paddled her. He didn't go easy on her, either. He spanked her until her ass was red and she was sobbing with a mixture of outrage and pleasure. And the more she sobbed, the slicker and hotter she got between her legs.

When she melted against him again he pulled her up to bend her over the table before him, fumbling with his trousers before he thrust himself inside her.

Inside her, where he belonged.

Stefan pounded into her, making sure he smacked up against her reddened ass with every thrust.

Then she was coming, sobbing out his name. Then he was too, and it was all heat and intensity and how could she walk away from all this?

Because she was Indy. That was what she did.

He pulled out of her, but she stayed where she was, looking thoroughly debauched, tossed across the table.

"Will you make it?" he asked her dryly.

She didn't open her eyes. He bent over her, wiping away the moisture beneath each eye, and found himself tenser than he ought to have been—at least until she smiled. Sleepily, but smugly, as if she'd gotten exactly what she wanted.

"That's almost as good as your Turkish coffee," she murmured.

Stefan didn't keep her in the sun too long, but he did keep her naked.

He took her back inside and commandeered one of his sitting rooms. He let her recover from their first round, but when she was awake again and sitting up—if gingerly—he started all over again.

And this round, he really took his time.

Indy finally screamed out her release and shattered. He followed, but recovered far more quickly. He brought her a tall glass of water and some crackers, setting them down near the couch where he'd left her, seemingly dead to the world.

Then he watched her as she slowly came back to life.

First she opened her eyes. Then she slowly pulled herself up to sitting position. She gazed back at him for a time, almost without comprehension. Then she looked a bit more like herself, and reached out for the water. She drank deep, ate a few crackers, and frowned at him.

"I get that you like intensity, Stefan. But this seems over the top." She considered him for another long moment. "Even for you."

"Then let us make it more intense," he suggested. He was already sitting across from her, so he settled into his seat. Then waved a hand. "Make yourself come."

"Now? Really?" She sputtered a little. "When we just...?"

"Now," he ordered her quietly. "It may take some time. And I do not want you to close your eyes, Indiana. You will look at me. The whole time."

He could see what she thought of that. Not much at all. Her cheeks were almost as red as her butt as she shifted around on the sofa. She shoved her hair back from her face, then stared at him as if she didn't have the slightest idea how to find her own pleasure.

That was no problem. Stefan was happy to tell her.

"I want you kneeling," he said. "Right there on that sofa. Thighs apart, breasts thrust toward me, and your hands between your legs. Go on, Indiana. I won't ask again."

She shivered, and he knew her too well now. He knew she wanted to fight him. He knew she was even now weighing whether the punishment might well be more delicious than the obedience.

And he saw the precise moment she decided not to test his will.

Not then, anyway.

Indy knelt up on the couch, arranging herself just as he'd ordered. He heard her breath leave her in a little sigh as she ran her hands down her thighs, then tracked her way up again. Then, holding his gaze again, she trailed her fingers up the length of her torso until she found her own nipples.

He expected her to say something. Something racy, no doubt, but all she did was hold his gaze.

Just as he'd demanded.

Then she played with herself, her hair tumbled all around her and her eyes big, wide, and hot on his.

And Stefan was hard. He was always hard when she was around, but that wasn't the worst of it.

The worst was his heart. This last month had made it grow in ways he would have thought impossible had he not lived through it.

Now it beat, didn't it. For her.

Only and ever for her.

And she was still the most perfect thing he had ever beheld. There wasn't a single part of her he hadn't tasted, touched, studied, and made his own. She was his in every possible way. He'd seen to that.

But she was the only one who didn't seem to know it.

Slowly, still obediently holding his gaze, she let her hands move down her body again, settling them between her thighs.

And then, slowly, she began to rock. She thrust her hips into her own palms, again and again. Stefan thought it was the hottest thing he'd ever seen. He saw as she stopped worrying about him and tuned into her own need.

Because she began to pant, her hands moving faster and her hips thrusting, while her wide brown eyes became glassy.

But still she worked, until her skin began to glow from her exertion, and it took everything in him to stay where he was. To stay seated, watching her put on a show.

A show just for him.

Stefan knew that in the days to come, this is what he would hold on to. Indy, so wild and so abandoned, doing as he asked because he'd asked it. Because she wanted to do it. His beautiful Indiana, finding her own heat. He loved the flush on her cheeks and, as she got closer and closer, the way that same flush rolled down her neck until even her breasts looked rosy.

He loved the unmarred perfection of her flesh, when, if asked, he would have said that not only did he generally prefer a woman with tattoos but that Indy seemed the type to have a vast selection of them.

But she didn't. As if she knew, somehow, that no matter how depraved or debauched she might become of an evening, she would always look untouched.

It was mouthwatering.

He loved the way her hair moved with her, and his fingers itched to bury themselves in all that dark silk.

His beautiful girl. His perfect match.

And when she came, she tilted her head back, letting her scream come out like a song.

He let her sob. He fought to catch his own breath. And when she lifted her hands, still shaking everywhere, he crooked his finger at her.

She was still gasping for breath as she moved, coming over to stand before him, shuddering again when he pulled her into his lap.

Stefan was painfully hard, but he did nothing about it. He only held her there, licking her fingers clean as she nestled into him.

And then trying to control the thunderstorm where his heart should be as she drifted off into sleep.

He knew, intellectually, that the day was no longer or shorter than any other. It was a day; that was all. Yet still he would have sworn that this one was the fastest that had ever been.

He cooked as night fell, because it was the only thing he could do. He fed her, then fucked her, but as the night wore on he took her upstairs, spread her out on his bed, and held her to him.

She fell asleep almost instantly. But he refused to give in to any slumber. Not tonight.

He knew that he could have woken her at any point, and that they were so attuned to each other by this time that no matter how tired she was, her body would answer his. With that same joy that marked each and every time they'd come together.

His cock was hard and ready, and more than willing.

But still, Stefan only held her close. And stayed awake, because he wanted to remember every breath. Every small little noise she made as she burrowed deeper into him.

He thought of all things he'd lost, one after the next. His mother and grandmother. The father he should have had, who he'd seen glimpses of now and then, which it only made the reality of his father he actually had worse.

He thought of the things he'd given away, and more, the many things that had been taken from him.

All of it, all the things he'd considered *his whole life* before her seemed to fade away. He would live without her, because he would have no choice.

But he didn't fucking want to.

Stefan knew that living without her, waiting for

her, was the only possible way to win her in the end. Because he knew her now.

And because he knew her, it wasn't surprising in the least that she'd decided she needed to pursue whatever passion she wanted. Or that she would use that passion, whatever it was, as a way to put space between them. The truth was, he'd expected her to fight more against the intimacy he'd asked for here.

Instead, in true Indy style, she'd given him everything.

Was that worse or better, in the end? He couldn't tell. Maybe he would be better suited to handle her departure now if he didn't know how perfectly they fit together.

"I will remember this," he promised her sleeping form. "I will remember everything."

She had not merely become a part of him, as the overwrought Romanian phrase would have it. She was far more than that.

Because if he knew anything, it was this. A man was not meant to hold on too tight to a vision. The vision itself was the gift.

He had made this house of his beautiful. Inviting. A place where a woman like Indy could be comfortable, and stay a while. But she had made it home.

Stefan had already changed the way his world revolved for her. What was waiting a little longer?

Because he knew that chasing this woman of his, filled as she was with wanderlust and that stubborn streak, would only chase her away.

So he held her close as the dawn crept ever closer, settled in, and talked himself into setting her free.

Because that was the only way she would ever come back.

For good.

CHAPTER ELEVEN

INDY SHOULDN'T HAVE BEEN surprised to wake up the next morning to find Stefan gone from their bed.

He had taken intensity to whole new levels yesterday. She sat up carefully, and could feel her body, tight here and a twinge there, in case she'd forgotten. She hadn't.

Good thing it made her feel a little too hot all over again.

She made her way into the shower and stood there a long while, letting the hot water revive her. When she got out and toweled off, she realized that everything inside of her was clear. At last.

Their month was over. He had chosen to end things with that endless, sensual-intensity marathon that made her feel shivery and molten just thinking about it.

She could picture his face, looking somehow more cruel as the day wore on. Even as those hard hands of his took such care with her, though they were the same hands that had spanked her. They'd moved over her body, coaxing her to just one more peak.

Then one more after that.

The man was a sorcerer.

But the thing about his kind of magic was that, here on this most momentous morning after, Indy finally felt swept clean.

All the muddling around, all the *wondering*, was all gone. Everything clicked into place.

She felt it hum through her, like awareness. Like attraction.

Like certainty.

Like fate, a voice inside her whispered.

She let her hair do what it liked, shoving it behind her ears as she walked back into the bedroom and slipped on her flowy dress. The one she'd been wearing when she'd tried for symmetry in that alleyway, only to have Stefan teach her a lesson about intensity.

A lesson he kept teaching her.

But because she'd learned that lesson, maybe too well, she knew what he'd been doing yesterday. It had been different from what had come before. She'd understood that while it was happening, but it made even more sense now.

Stefan had been saying goodbye.

She padded her way down the grand stairs, running her fingers along the smooth length of the banister as she moved, as if she needed the sensory input. When, maybe for the first time in her whole life, she felt full up.

Indy never liked to think of herself as having a wound that needed healing, or an empty hole inside her, as she'd been accused of more than once. But she couldn't help noticing how different she felt here on the other side of a month of intense intimacy with Stefan.

Her whole life there'd been a kind of edginess in her that skittered over her skin and made her bones feel itchy in her limbs. The urge to keep going. The need to always leave where she was and find something new. But no more.

She'd always been preoccupied with seeing and being seen, but not because she had anything to prove. Indy had discovered early on that when she was feeling lonely—or feeling anything, really— the best cure was to go out somewhere and pretend she was happy.

Until she was.

And when that wasn't on offer, there was always social media, which could amount to the same thing.

At the bottom of the stairs, she slipped her mobile out of the dress's deep pocket, and pulled up her favorite personal account. She took a quick scroll through, on the off chance she'd forgotten what was there. Because she hadn't posted anything since she'd come to Prague.

But the evidence was there before her. It was curated joy.

It wasn't that it was fake. She'd taken all those pictures and had posted them, too. But she understood, in a way she wouldn't have month ago, that while she might not have been trying to prove anything to anyone—the account existed so that any time she felt any emotion she didn't like, she could scroll a little bit and feel like herself again. *Fun*, first and foremost. She collected pictures of the fun she had so in less fun moments she could look at it, remember it, and get back into that space.

And then somewhere along the line, she'd decided fun *was* happiness, and had built her life around it accordingly.

But happiness wasn't a screen of pretty pictures.

Happiness was what happened when there were no screens around to record it.

Indy shoved her phone back into her pocket and wandered toward the kitchen, her feet bare against the smooth floor. It was another bit of input, all of it like whispers next to a shout when she walked into the kitchen and found Stefan there at the counter where he'd once spread her out like a dessert, then feasted.

He didn't seem to move or acknowledge her

presence. He was looking down at his laptop, but she knew. Indy knew full well that he knew she was there.

That it was possible he'd heard the moment she sat up in bed upstairs.

She wouldn't put it past him.

"Am I allowed to speak today?" she asked, coming to stand on the opposite side of the counter, as if they were facing off with each other.

Stefan closed his laptop with a decisive click. His blue gaze pierced through her, lighting her up and leaving scorch marks.

She liked it that way.

Even if his expression was about as closed off as she'd ever seen it.

"You can do as you please," he told her, his voice perfectly even. "You kept your promise. The month is over. The world is yours, Indiana."

"I do love when the world is mine." She smiled. "But surely I can get a little coffee first."

To her delight, or maybe that wasn't the right word for the way her heart leapt in her chest, she saw a muscle move in his lean jaw.

Very much as if Stefan Romanescu was not as in control of himself as he usually was.

As if maybe, just maybe, he was finding this as overwhelming as she did.

She really hoped he did.

He stalked over to the stove, and set about making her the Turkish coffee she was pretty sure she was addicted to now. There were spices, fine coffee, a bit of sugar, and then the boiling. Three times, and all the while, she stood on her side of the counter and took the opportunity to study him.

Because maybe he was the real addiction.

She'd spent two years imagining and reimagining the little bit of time they'd spent together in Budapest. Now she'd had a month and two days. She knew him far better. The sex seemed to get more fantastic every time he touched her. She hadn't been anything like bored.

And it still wasn't enough.

There wasn't a single part of his powerful body she hadn't explored. Her mouth watered just thinking about it. Today he wore jeans and T-shirt, and as usual, elevated both to the kind of art he liked to hang on his walls. A study of a powerful man, she might call it, though the only kind of painting she wanted to do involved her fingers on his skin.

He turned back when the coffee was done, sliding the thick brew into place before her. And his eyes were still poet's eyes, brooding and emotional and all the things he acted as if he wasn't. His mouth was still sensual, and she knew how it felt at her breast, and all the other places he liked to put it.

He was a dream come true, but he was real.

This was *real*.

And she reminded herself that she got to decide what she made of this. Of them. Of her life and what was in it.

She picked up the delicate little cup and sipped at it, sighing a little bit at the first taste of the coffee she never could seem to get enough of.

"Stefan," she began.

But a flash of blue cut her off again.

"Stop," he ordered her. "I know already how this will go."

Indy put her cup down on the counter between them. "Do you?"

"I changed my whole life after that night in the alley," he told her, not sounding quite so even any longer. "This is not figurative speech. I am not exaggerating. I was one thing, then I saw you and I became another. There are some parts of some countries that will remain forever closed to me because of this. I accept it."

"Will people come after you?" she asked, momentarily diverted from the fact this was the end of the month they agreed upon, and he was acting... the way he was acting. "Are you safe?"

Something glittered there in all that blue. "I would never have risked meeting you here if I was not." She saw that muscle in his jaw again. "I would never have risked *you*. That part of my life is over. It is not merely a closed door, you understand. I set it on fire. It is better that way."

"Stefan, I really want—"

"You will listen to me, Indiana."

His voice was a command, but she could see he wasn't as in control of himself as he usually was. And the longer she looked at him, the more she began to suspect that this—that hectic glitter in his gaze and that muscle flexing in his jaw—was Stefan's version of messy.

Of wild.

Once again, she felt her heart swell to three times its size. All the parts of her that had been knotted tight loosened in a rush.

But she was still holding her breath.

"I have never worried about emotion," he told her, his eyes too bright and his voice too dark. "It is not a factor. I like sex. I like women. I like them when they come to me and I do not miss them when they go. Then there was you." He shook his head, as if he was trying to clear it. As if he was the one muddled now. "Nothing about that night made sense. Why were you there? Why weren't you afraid? How was it possible that I could meet a creature such as you over the barrel of a gun?"

"I asked myself a great many of the same questions."

"There is only one thing that makes sense," he continued, his voice gruff. "I fell in love with you the moment I saw you, Indiana. It was that fast, and that mad. This isn't intense between us because I'm an intense person. I never was before. Not with any other woman. It's only you."

Indy understood, then, that this was him stripped naked. That she could see so much in his gaze, he was telling her these things—this was how Stefan Romanescu ripped himself wide open.

"I love you," he said in the same way, as if he was delivering terrible news. "And I will tell you, I did not want to."

She smiled, though her heart was thumping at her. "How flattering."

"I wanted nothing to do with any of this," he growled at her. "What place is there in a life such as mine for a creature as soft as you are? You are too little, too breakable. You clearly have no sense of your own peril. You are American, of all things. And yet I knew that you were it for me. Instantly."

She blew out a breath, shuddery and long. "Why are you telling me this as if you're saying goodbye?"

And the way he smiled then changed him. He made her want to cry.

Maybe she did.

"I fell in love with *you*, Indy," he told her, almost hoarsely. "And I don't want to change you. I don't want to tie you down. I threw out my entire world so that I might try to deserve an angel in an alleyway. How could I pluck off your wings?"

An angel in alleyway. It sounded like a poem,

and even though Indy still felt as if she might cry, there was something laced through it. Something so beautiful it hurt.

"It doesn't take much to deserve me," she told him, though her voice was thick. "I think you've already cracked the code."

But Stefan shook his head again, looking down at where he had his hands braced on the counter. "You have spoken a great deal about how you want to find your passion. I want this for you. And I know who you are, Indy. I know you are not a girl who stays put."

"Stefan—"

He ignored her, lifting that blue gaze to hers. "But I will. I want you to understand that I'm not afraid of anything you might find out there, or anything you might do. I have never been a patient man, but for you, I will wait." He managed to indicate the house with one of those shrugs of his. "I will be here. And I know you'll come back. Maybe more than once. And maybe one day, you will stay."

Indy stared at him, stricken. That look on his face was doing odd things inside of her. He looked so stoic. So resigned. And yet here he was, making this sacrifice, when she knew there was not one inch of this man who was at all good with either waiting, letting go, or sacrificing himself in any way.

She knew it.

She knew *him*.

Maybe what she knew most of all was the two of them, together.

"This is what you think will happen?" she asked softly. "You think the passion I want to find involves going back out there and continuing to do what I've always done?"

That muscle in his jaw twitched, but his gaze remained steady. "If that is what you want, I won't be the one to stop you."

Indy wanted to throw something at him. She wanted to throw herself at him. Hug him a little and maybe shake him while she was at it.

But she didn't do any of those things.

"Well," she said. And maybe made a little meal out of the word. "Look at that. You don't know everything."

Whatever response he'd expected, that clearly wasn't it.

Stefan blinked. His head tilted slightly to one side. And she watched those impossible blue eyes change once more.

Taking on a shade she recognized.

Danger, not sacrifice.

Which was to say, *him*.

"I woke up this morning and everything made sense." It was her turn to look at him steadily. To hide nothing. "Yesterday was so intense it's like it was a key in a lock. You wouldn't let me speak and so I couldn't make excuses. Not even in my own head."

"You don't need to draw this out. You can simply leave. I told you this already."

"And in the middle of all that intensity, the whole world boiled down to this," Indy said, ignoring him. "I didn't think that I was searching for anything, but then I found you. I think you know I've had a lot of steamy nights. I don't normally pay them any attention. They fade away as soon as the sun comes up, and I go on to the next. It was different with you."

"Maybe it was the gun," he suggested, with a glimmer of that dry humor she loved.

She smiled at him, and even she knew that it was a real smile. Because it was for him.

"It was you, Stefan. I thought of nothing else for two years, and then I came here to find that you're everything I had imagined and so much more." Her heart was thundering at her. She felt almost shaky standing still. But she looked at him and none of that mattered. "You were right—there was part of this that terrified me. I walked away, but really, I think I only did it to see if I could. To see if you'd let me. And you did."

"I'm doing the same thing now," Stefan gritted out. "But I should tell you, I was never much of a martyr. The longer you stand here, not leaving, the less I can remember why I'm not convincing you to stay."

"You can't convince me to stay," Indy said softly. "No one could ever convince me to stay. Because a long time ago, I decided that I needed to be a rolling stone. That I could never stay in one place too long. That it would take something from me if I did. Do you know what I think that was?"

Another hint of dryness. "Not daddy issues, I understand."

"Because I thought I had to be different from how I started. Just like I decided I couldn't do well in school because my sister did. I had to distinguish myself." She pulled in a breath. "I took something that might have cut a different girl off at the knees, a dumb older boy taking private things and making them public, and I owned it. And do you know what, Stefan? It felt good. Powerful."

"As it should."

"I tasted that at fourteen and all I wanted was more. So I had whatever sex I felt like having. I was a stripper because why not? I liked taking off my clothes, and more than that, I liked people's reactions when they found out that's what I did." Indy had never talked about these things like this. She had never laid out her life, not like this. But it didn't feel like *her* life any longer, did it? She focused on him. "And ever since then, I've done exactly as I pleased. I've gone wherever I wanted, taken lovers and friends as I liked and left them, too, without a qualm. You're the only man I've ever come back to. Twice."

"This is how I know you will come back again." His voice was a low, rough sound. "As I have told you, I will wait for you."

"But yesterday taught me something," Indy said, as if he hadn't spoken. "It taught me everything. I already know what my passion is, Stefan. I finally figured it out."

She watched him gather himself, as if he expected a blow. And she could tell that he was a man used to taking blows, and returning them in kind. Those hands might curl into fists but she knew, deep inside, that he would never strike back when it was her.

"It's you," Indy said softly. "My passion is you. And with you, Stefan, I can do anything."

He let out a sound she didn't recognize, because it was low, almost animal.

And she didn't wait. She vaulted onto the counter, and then crawled across it until she was kneeling there in front of him, her face to his. Then she took the jaw that had given him away in her hands, and held him there.

Fully aware that he allowed it.

But this would be their life, she understood then. He would always allow her to leave, and so she would stay. And she would have this power over him, because he let her—and because she would never abuse it.

"You need to be sure," he said, his voice a mere scrape of sound. But his gaze was loud. "Very, very sure. Because if you choose me, this, now… I will not have it in me to be quite so forgiving as I might have sounded."

"I don't want forgiving," Indy told him fiercely. "I want you, Stefan. I'm not afraid of your darkness. I know all about the light and I think deep down, beneath everything, it turns out I've been a jealous, possessive, dark kind of woman all along. Can you handle that?"

His smile was a long time coming, but when he finally surrendered to it, it took over his face. "I can handle it. Can you?"

"You and me," she said. "No one else. I dare you."

He was picking her up, holding her in his arms and then lifting her up above, as if he needed to look at her in the sunlight. She gazed down at him, aware only when her cheeks began to ache that she was smiling so hard, so wide, she might as well have been the sun herself.

"I will never understand where you came from that night," he said, his voice as intent as his gaze.

"All that traveling. All those adventures. All of them were leading me to you." Indy wrapped her legs around his waist when he let her slide down his body, smiling even brighter when they were face to face. "I love you, Stefan. I thought love at first sight was a myth, but then there you were."

"I love you," he replied.

And she kissed him, or maybe he kissed her, and everything was a tangle of heat and need and better still—best of all—love.

When he pulled away again, neither one of them was breathing steadily.

Indy hoped they never would.

"Now," he murmured, his bright blue eyes turning wicked. "About that dare."

Then he showed her how he met a challenge, right there on the counter again. How he would always meet a challenge, especially if it was her.

How they would always find their way back to each other, to that perfect fit that was only theirs.

Their hot, sweet, life-altering love, that was worth changing a world or two.

So they did.

CHAPTER TWELVE

Ten years later, Indy shivered in the cold on the front porch of a sweet little old farmhouse she and Stefan had spent the last six months renovating.

Right there on the outskirts of the same little Ohio town where she'd grown up. The town she'd been so certain she would never return to, ever.

She reached down and slid her hand over her gigantic belly, feeling even bigger beneath all the layers she was wearing, smiling. Because life, it turned out, did what it wanted.

Especially when a person finally wised up and stopped living it all in one way.

Her parents had thought that when Indy called home at the end of the summer to announce she'd met a man and *oops*, had accidentally married him on a beach in Bali, it was more evidence of her well-documented *flightiness*.

Then they'd met Stefan that Christmas. It had been a banner holiday in the March family. Bristol had come home with Lachlan Drummond, and it had been a strange few days of too many men in a house that had never had that problem.

Lachlan and Stefan had bonded. Bristol and Indy had realized, too late, that this was a potential cause for concern.

"We are brothers now," Stefan had said, a wicked light in his eyes, there in her childhood bedroom.

Where he'd proceeded to wash away all the ghosts of Jamie Portnoys past.

But quietly, so as to be respectful.

Indy's parents had been instantly impressed with their new son-in-law. Bill had a few beers with him. Margie had taken Indy aside and told her, with great confidence, that a man like that would settle her down. Eventually.

That wasn't quite how things had worked.

She and Stefan had followed their passions, whatever they might be. They didn't need to work, or wander off into think tanks like Bristol and Lachlan, so they indulged their whims instead. And over time, their whims tended to shift back and forth—something worthwhile for every selfish bit of hedonism. Art appreciation and buying trips all over the world. A year of volunteering in the rain forest. A summer scuba diving off the Great Barrier Reef. A season in Antarctica on a research expedition.

There was no need to waste her time on silly

love affairs with men not worth remembering. Not when she had everything she could ever want, and more, in Stefan.

Indy had never wanted to settle. She and Stefan had attended Bristol and Lachlan's wedding a few years after theirs, and while she'd loved watching her sister so happy, she was even happier that she and Stefan had married in private.

Because that kind of happiness, to her, was real.

And it made settling fun. Even the most domestic, hum-drum activity in the world was fun if she did it with Stefan.

"Are you ready?" she asked when she heard him come out of the house behind her. "Christmas morning waits for no one, Stefan. You should know this by now."

She turned to look at him, this beautiful man of hers. He still looked as dangerous as ever. He still had the bluest eyes she'd ever seen.

"For you?" Stefan grinned. He did that a lot more now. "I am always ready."

"You know we Marches take our holidays seriously." She smiled when he moved his hands over her belly, too. This baby they'd made, a little boy she was already madly in love with, would be joining them at any time. "Just wait until he comes. He's going to be worse than all my sister's kids combined."

Stefan's hand settled at the nape of her neck,

possessive and perfect. The snow had come in last night, but he'd been up early to clear off the steps and the walk to their car. And now he helped her navigate her huge, unwieldy body down the wintry steps.

"My son will be properly reserved and contained," Stefan told her. "I will teach him myself."

"You're not reserved at all, foolish man," she said softy.

His gaze seared through her. "Not anymore."

He helped her into the car and she sat there as he rounded the hood, looking at this place they intended to call home, at least for part of the year. So that Indy could be near her mother and the child could be near his grandparents. And they would always be close enough to Columbus that they could fly away at a moment's notice.

Because she liked to spend a good chunk of her summers in Prague, where they'd become them.

That was what she'd learned. Life was what she made it. It was never all one thing. She and Stefan got more solid by the day, happier and better, and none of that prevented them from playing the kind of games they liked best.

Give and take, year after year.

Carrying their home with them wherever they went, because the two of them, together, were what they needed. That was the passion that made life worth living.

Together they were rooted deep and tangled up in each other.

And yet, when the mood struck—and it always struck—they could fly.

Out of that alley in Budapest into a bright future, laced through with the most delicious darkness, and all for them.

"I love you, foolish girl," Stefan said when he climbed into the car. He turned the engine over, but didn't move. He was too busy studying her face.

"I know you do," she replied. She frowned. "I love you, too. But I think we need to head to the hospital instead of my parents' house."

"The hospital—?" But he cut himself off. "Now?"

"I'm pretty sure my water broke."

They stared at each other. Then both of them grinned, so big and wide it was brighter than the snow outside.

And they might have stayed there forever, but the little contractions she'd been ignoring changed into something she couldn't have ignored if she'd tried.

"Okay?" Stefan asked, searching her face, when it passed.

"Intense," she panted at him..

Then she strapped in, because Stefan drove like a man on the run when he liked. She opted not to ask him how or when he'd learned to do that.

Two short hours later, Indy beamed up at him from a hospital bed as he held their son. Stefan looked at her in wonder.

And together, plus the brand new love of their life, they started their greatest adventure yet.

* * * * *

TEMPTING THE ENEMY

JC HARROWAY

MILLS & BOON

TEMPTING THE ENEMY

JC HARROWAY

I dedicate my final DARE to everyone who loved this line—the authors for their fab stories, the Mills & Boon team for their expertise, and the readers for their support. It's been an amazingly fun ride for this romance author, one I'll always cherish.

Love, JC

MILLS & BOON

CHAPTER ONE

Ava

IF YOU WERE going to gatecrash an office party, the lavish shindig thrown by BLD Global Ventures would be the one to choose. It's a shame I'm not here for fun. Driven by desperation, I'm hunting Sterling Lombard, head of the New York division of BLD, which is housed in his building, Bold Tower—a gleaming, state-of the art skyscraper in Manhattan's financial district. Hopefully, the elusive billionaire, who's been dodging my attempts to secure a face-to-face meeting, will make an appearance as host of his own staff's function.

As work parties go, this one is a blast—delicious canapés, an open bar, a band and dancing. It's what I'd expect from Lombard, one of America's wealthiest men and one of three partners who head up BLD, or Bold, as it's often termed.

Just like his partners, Hudson Black and Monroe Dove, the renowned businessman Lombard has the Midas touch. His handsome face regularly peers out from the covers of the *Financial Times* or *Bloomsburg Businessweek*—sandy blond hair, piercing green eyes and a smile to rival any male pin-up on the planet. His success is as eye-watering as his good looks and confidence.

But even the little people deserve an audience.

I smooth one palm down the skirt of my little black dress and glug a mouthful of champagne as I scan the cavernous, multi-level room for my enigmatic quarry.

Part of me is impressed that my grandparents' small logistics company, the company I inherited from them after their recent deaths, attracted the attention of a hard hitter like Lombard. But what were they thinking, signing over so much equity to BLD, which now owns the controlling stake? Times must have been hard, even harder than they are currently under my leadership…

Ava tries hard but logistics isn't her forte.

I stand taller. It doesn't have to spin my wheels. I owe my grandparents everything.

I wander over to the windows, concealing my frustration with a serene smile. It's pasted on my face as if I'm totally okay with flying solo at a glamorous party where I know no one and don't belong. But needs must when it comes to safe-guarding my business.

It's all I have left.

Ignoring the lower Manhattan views of the Brooklyn Bridge lit up over the East River, I scour the forty-seventh-floor office once more. Familiar panic rushes through me like the fizz and pop of champagne bubbles. The same panic that keeps me up at night—I can't let Pops and Nonna's company fail.

I shake off the pessimism threatening to drag me under and eye the mezzanine level, which seems to be where all the top BLD executives are congregating. All I need is five minutes of Lombard's time in which to convince him he wants to sell me back his shares. If only he were here...

After ten more fruitless minutes of cruising the entire room, I surrender to a final defeated sigh and drain the glass of champagne I've managed to make last over an hour. In the three months since Nonna died, when I discovered BLD's investment in Hamilton's from the lawyers, Lombard has evaded my attempts to secure an appointment. Trespassing his staff party was an audacious long shot I hoped might win me full ownership of Hamilton Logistics.

Not that you had anywhere else to be on a Friday evening...

Dejected, I leave the party and clip across the marble foyer towards the bank of elevators. What do I do now? I won't just give up. My mission is deeply personal. Hamilton's is my last tie to my family—my grandparents and, through them, my parents.

All four of them are now gone.

I was fourteen when my parents died and my grandparents took me in. Ever since, I've focused on helping out—working for them after school, interning as warehouse manager through college and eventually running their business after graduating, when Pops's health took a downturn. Making Hamilton's a success is what keeps me too busy to actually feel my life's losses. Bone-deep exhaustion staves off any unhelpful comparisons: wondering what my life might've been like but for a drunk driver in a souped-up sports car losing control on the Brooklyn Queens Expressway one fateful night.

Failure drags at me until all I can think about is donning my snuggliest pyjamas and comfort eating my way through a huge bowl of pasta. I glance up at the digital reading for the elevator, craving my cluttered apartment—a Williamsburg brownstone in Brooklyn, filled with memories. I can't bear to throw out any of my parents' personal belongings—their books, their old vinyl collection and their favourite kitchen paraphernalia.

The electronic ping of the elevator's arrival snaps me from ruminating how I've spent most of my adult life rudderless.

The brushed steel doors slide open and I step forward towards the car. I start, my eyes clashing with those of the only other occupant—the man himself, Sterling Lombard.

For a split second, I'm frozen with shock on the threshold, one stiletto-clad foot in and one out. The sparkle in his green-grey eyes makes me double-take. He's way more attractive in person, taller than I imagined, his body lean and toned and his tailoring immaculate.

And he oozes power and success.

'Going down?' His deep voice somehow renders the innocent question sinful and seductive. He smiles and I'm jerked into action by the dazzling sight, the grooves in his cheeks and the sexy stubble on his strong jaw, the way he seems to fill the elevator with his commanding persona alone.

'Yes, thank you.' I step fully inside and clutch my purse tighter in an attempt to slow the gallop of my pulse. I can't believe my luck. After an hour and a half of boredom at his party, my chance of a one-on-one with the boss has landed conveniently in my lap.

I stare straight ahead as the doors close, urgency gripping my throat like a vice. I have probably less than a minute to persuade him to hear me out. But I've got this. Work is pretty much all I do. I know all there is to know about Hamilton Logistics.

Say something. Now!

I turn and offer him a friendly smile. What is it about elevators and sharing an enclosed space with a total stranger that pushes us so far out of our comfort zone? In his case, it's a good kind of discomfort, full of intrigue and possibility.

'Leaving the party early?' he says before I can engage my brain to speak.

I'm fascinated by his sexy, anglicised New York accent. I recall reading somewhere that he studied at university in London and spent years living there before returning to the States. I imagine his dirty talk, how that voice would sound strangled with desire…

What the hell? Focus.

'Yes, I am leaving, although it's a fabulous bash.' I struggle to ignore his extreme masculinity and highly engaging charisma. I've seen him a hundred times in the business news, but in person he's just so much more imposing, attractive and mesmerising. 'Are you done too?' I'm supposed to be propositioning, not seducing him. But there's something about him that I wasn't expecting.

He nods. His body fills his suit to perfection— wide shoulders, narrow hips and strong thighs. My eyes want to devour him. But that's not why I'm here. I run through my opening spiel, trying to remember my mission before we arrive at his floor and I miss my opportunity.

I wanted to talk to you actually… I'd hoped to

meet you tonight... Do you have a second to discuss some business...?

This was easier in my head.

'I'll let you in on a little secret.' He leans close conspiratorially, and I'm doused in the delicious manly scent of him. 'I'd rather be working than attending an office party.' Before I have time to clear the lust fog in my brain, he thrusts his hand in my direction. 'Sterling Lombard.'

'The man with his name on the door. Ava Hamilton-Wade,' I say, giving him my full name, although I usually shorten it to my mother's surname alone for professional clout. Sparks fire my erogenous zones as I shake his big, warm hand. Gorgeous and friendly. I wasn't expecting him to be so down-to-earth, personable, and...hot.

'I know what you mean about parties.' I glance at my watch and roll my eyes. 'Before nine and I'm all dressed up but headed home. I work sixty hours a week,' I add in explanation. 'Sleep is my downtime.'

Pathetic...

'Ah, I see we have something in common,' he says, as we share a knowing grin. Unexpected flirty banter wasn't on tonight's agenda, but I can't seem to help myself.

I shiver with desire, looking away. I should just launch into my pitch, right here in the elevator. It's the opportunity I came here for.

But…

It's almost a shame to ruin this moment with business. From looks and instant chemistry alone, this guy is exactly my type. And I'm enjoying the distraction from constantly worrying about the prosperity of Hamilton's. To say it's ailing would be a terrifying understatement I try not to think about.

He shifts beside me. 'Of course,' he says, 'what good is success if you can't celebrate it every once in a while? That's what the party upstairs is all about.'

'I agree.' My pulse leaps, arousal pooling in my belly.

He's flirting with me, and my body is fully on board. It's as if I've awoken from a long hibernation, my libido unfurling into the warmth of the sun. *That's* the reason my reaction to him is so violent—I've practically been a nun for the past ten months. But my grandparents were sick, one shortly after the other. Part of me is convinced that Nonna died of a broken heart without Pops by her side.

The sudden, stomach-sinking slowing of the car tells me we're about to stop on his floor. I shake off the sadness of losing Pops seven months ago and Nonna four months later, pressure building in my temples. If I don't act quickly, Sterling will disappear and I may never again have this chance.

I swallow past my dry throat and flash him my alluring smile. 'Perhaps we should head back upstairs and enjoy a drink together, snatch that chance to celebrate?' My rusty seduction skills seem to surprise us both. But a friendly drink could be exactly the way to butter him up and secure the appointment I came for.

Yeah...that's why you're breathing hard and imagining his body under the clothes.

His stare takes a lazy tour of my face, ending on my mouth. My lips tingle as if he's touched them with more than just his gorgeous green eyes. I realise I want that. He looks as if he'd be an excellent kisser and probably a sensational lover.

Lombard presses his lips together in a curious half-smile. 'I have a better idea.' The lift stops and the doors slide open. He presses the button to hold them apart. 'There's some twenty-five-year-old bourbon in my office. Can I tempt you?'

Probably into the fiery pits of hell...

'I could be persuaded.' I melt under his focused eye contact and that intense, seductive look on his face. But a private chat works even better for my purposes.

What the hell am I doing? Surely I intend to use my good fortune for my cause, not just to entice this man out of his ten-thousand-dollar suit?

Why not both...? Maybe we can laugh about this in the morning before we move on to business?

He holds out his arm, indicating the direction. 'After you.'

I exit the elevator and follow him to the only lit office space on this floor. He holds open the door for me and I smile, murmuring my thanks. I'm a sucker for some good old-fashioned gentlemanly manners.

This guy's positive attributes are growing.

His massive corner office boasts a sleek wooden desk and twinkling views of lower Manhattan's financial district and the bay beyond. There's a luxurious seating area with plush leather sofas, a colourful contemporary rug and convenient bar in one corner. A single lamp on the otherwise uncluttered desk lights a solitary laptop, leaving the rest of the office dimly lit and intimate.

For a second, I'm distracted by thoughts of my own cluttered workspace, the organised chaos of invoices and logbooks and potted plants on my desk. Sterling is a serious neat freak. An intriguing, nice-to-look-at neat freak.

'Tell me, Ava,' he says, shrugging out of his suit jacket and hanging it on a hook near the door, 'do you work for Bold? I don't recall seeing you before and I'd have definitely remembered.'

He loosens his tie and rolls up his shirt cuffs, his gaze swooping over me with clear interest. His compliment sends electricity dancing over my skin.

Now would be a good time to tell him exactly why I'm here. Instead I tilt my head, flashing my good side and subtly rolling back my shoulders so my breasts look their best in my slinky black dress.

'No, I came with a business colleague from one of your companies.' *Just a little white lie.* 'We've never met before, although of course I know you by reputation.'

And now we've met I suspect sparks would fly were we to take this flirtation to the next level.

And why shouldn't I indulge? I've spent years working my ass off for Hamilton's, and I was happy to do it. Not only is the business my grandparents founded my legacy, I also owed it to them to join their company, which literally grew out of their love. After all, rearing a moody teenager whose world had fallen apart would have been no easy task.

One night with the famous Sterling Lombard could be my reward for the long hours and the lack of work-life balance I've tolerated for too long.

'I see.' He nods and heads to the bar. 'So what do you do?'

I watch as he reaches for and then uncaps the bottle. The fine cotton of his shirt moulds to his muscular chest and arms. His narrow waist tapers to the most delicious butt. He must spend a lot of time doing squats in the gym.

'I run my own business, but I don't want to talk shop right now.'

'Fair enough.' He returns with two glasses. 'Take a seat.'

I slide onto his leather couch and accept the glass, which is half-full of amber liquid and ice cubes. I take a sip as he joins me on the sofa. The bourbon is delicious—smoky and smooth with hints of caramel.

'So this is how you spend your Friday evenings? Working late while the rest of Manhattan parties?' I wince at the hypocrisy of my question. I'm practically a hermit. I usually spend my downtime relaxing in the kitchen, cooking from my mother's dog-eared handwritten recipes and freezing healthy meals for the working week ahead.

'Yes, I'm afraid you've saved me from myself tonight. And perhaps I've saved you, too.' He smiles and touches his glass to mine with a clink of expensive crystal. A delicious spasm jolts through me. 'To you, Ava. And to chance meetings that make Friday evenings a million times more interesting.'

I take a sip, my stare held captive by his, then lick the bourbon from my lips. What am I doing? I'm supposed to be convincing him to sell me back his shares in *my* business, not thinking about how long it's been since I had sex and how I've never physically reacted so strongly to a man I've just met.

But Sterling Lombard isn't just any man. I always thought the rumours about him couldn't possibly be true—wealthy, intelligent, with a reputation for dating glamorous ladies—but, now I've met him in the flesh, his sexual magnetism speaks for itself. Directly to my aching nipples, which are peaking through the thin fabric of my dress.

'That's what I love about New York,' I say. 'In a city of eight million people, you just never know who you'll meet and where it will lead.' The alcohol moves through my blood, warming and relaxing as it travels.

'Where do you want it to lead?' he asks directly. His voice turns gravelly. 'Because you should know that I'm definitely going to want your number before you leave.'

His confident, forthright manner is a major turn-on. His eyes seem to see right through me. It's not unpleasant, kicking up my heart rate and flooding me with thrilling heat.

I should present my case for Hamilton's, but now that I've experienced our fierce chemistry, my heart is no longer in it. I'll have another chance. I could give him my number—he's exactly the type of man I'd date if we met under different circumstances.

I eye him over the rim of my glass, my pulse flying. Why does he make me feel so reckless? Is it his power and success, a serious aphrodisiac?

Is it because I didn't expect to share anything in common with him? Or is it just pure, unadulterated and uncontrollable lust that's made me desperate to kiss him since we left the elevator?

'I don't want to interrupt your work.' I glance at the desk and his lonely laptop.

He holds my stare, his thick-lashed eyes intense. 'It can wait. Can you?'

My breath is trapped in my lungs. This wasn't the evening I had planned, but why not? Who knows—perhaps it will smooth the eventual business negotiations?

I shudder out a sigh and clank my glass down on the low coffee table. 'No. I can't.'

I lean in close. He leans too.

My hands find his strong biceps as he slides one hand to my thigh. I'm not sure who kisses who first, but it doesn't matter. Our lips collide, a sublime yielding, give and take. Power and life pulse to the tips of my fingers and toes. It's been way too long since I've felt this degree of attraction, and I fall into it headfirst.

I slide my fingers around his neck, urging him closer. He presses one hand between my shoulder blades, crushing my chest to his so I'm encircled in his strong arms. My lips part to welcome the surge of his tongue, and my nipples tingle against his rock-hard muscles.

I was right about the excellent kissing.

He pulls away and I actually moan in protest.

'Well, that was a surprise…' He cups my cheek and glides his thumb over my skin, his aroused stare searching mine and a hint of amusement twitching his beautiful mouth.

I can't help my own smile. My business plan is completely sidelined by this fierce and unforeseen want. Of all the things I'd hoped to achieve tonight with Sterling Lombard, pleasure wasn't one of them, but when opportunity knocks…

'I'm full of those,' I say, tugging his mouth back to mine.

CHAPTER TWO

Sterling

HER STARTLING BLUE eyes brim with desire as we break for air. How long has it been since I felt chemistry this intense? Too damned long. I grip her exquisite, heart-shaped face and direct her lush mouth under mine once more, kissing her the way I wanted to the moment our eyes met.

The minute she stepped into the elevator, her silky black dress hugging her pert breasts and rounded hips, the hemline flirting enticingly just above her knees, my lousy Friday improved. Being with a woman intriguing and beautiful enough to make me forget the call I received earlier deserves my undivided focus.

'If I'd known you were at the party,' I say in between kisses, 'I'd have stuck around longer.' I'd shown my face early on out of duty, greeting a few high-profile clients, but parties aren't really my thing. Not the kind going on upstairs anyway, which will likely result in a fair bit of embarrassment between colleagues on Monday morning, not to mention a few hangovers tomorrow. A party for two with a beautiful woman over a glass of excellent bourbon is more my style.

It reminds me of where I am and how I arrived here, surrounded by markers of the success Marcus Brent—my *stepfather*, though I'm loath to call him that—told me I'd never achieve. My lavish office in a Manhattan building I own, where I head up the New York division of a global private equity company, would suggest otherwise. A testament to my years of hard work, long hours and the determination to prove a naysayer wrong.

Why am I thinking about *him*?

'I'm glad I left when I did.' Ava groans into my mouth.

I curl my fingers into the fabric over her hips, satisfaction streaking along my nerve endings. I don't normally seduce women in the elevator, but since my divorce four years ago I've grown accustomed to beautiful dates like Ava. And there's something special about her—a stunning figure, luscious dark, glossy hair I want to twist in my hand and a full mouth practically made for kissing.

Without breaking the kiss Ava slides off the killer stilettos I'd first admired upon seeing her and straddles my lap. She hoists her dress up her thighs. I catch a glimpse of black lace and my cock surges against my fly. I want this woman, badly.

Lucky for me, I always get what I want.

'You have no idea how much I needed you tonight,' I say, dragging her closer so her breasts crush against my chest.

She laughs, her eyes sparking with arousal and playfulness. 'Bad day at the office?' She strokes my hair, which has a tendency to flop over my right eye, away from my face. It's a trait I inherited from my deceased father.

The gesture speaks volumes about the kind of woman she is—I'm definitely going to want to see her again.

'Something like that.' I press one hand between her shoulder blades, chasing her lips with mine and chasing away the lingering annoyance I've battled since this afternoon's phone call from my mother.

Through the same calculating streak he likely learned from Marcus, my stepbrother, Josh, persuaded her to exert her influence where he's failed. I have something Josh wants: Brent's Express.

Marcus sold his neglected company to me six months ago, just before he died, cutting out his son in a bid for cash. I refuse to show Josh more sentimentality and family loyalty than his own father. Josh might have convinced my mother that with him at the helm of Brent's, Marcus's name can live on, but I'm fully in control now. Of my own success, and the fate of Marcus's company.

I must make some sound of dissent. Ava pulls back and stares down at me. 'Are you okay?'

She rocks her hips, massaging my erection between her legs, a reminder of all the fucking awesome things I've engineered in my life since I left home and escaped my stepfather's hateful influence.

'I'm fantastic. You?' I slide my hands up her back into the long, silky mass of her softly tumbling hair, fisting the glossy strands. How can I be thinking about my stepfather when the most fascinating and attractive woman I've met in years is looking at me like she wants to eat me alive?

She nods, her glazed eyes hooded with pleasure as she leans over me and kisses me as if I'm the last man on earth.

Get your shit together, Lombard. There'll be plenty of time for your revenge.

Ava's hands leave my shoulders and she tugs my tie loose, sliding it from under my collar and tossing it beside us on the sofa. Her breath comes in sexy little pants, her stunning blue eyes dancing with mine. She reaches for the top buttons of my shirt, her teeth tugging her bottom lip with a hint of uncertainty. 'Do you have a condom?'

I nod, cupping the cheeks of her ass and guiding her hips forward where I'm hard between her legs. I grind us together until we both groan. 'I do.' I press a kiss to her pouty lips, swollen and lip-gloss-free, thanks to our make-out session. 'But there's no rush.'

Having her in my bed all night can be my reward for a distracting day.

Clearly determined to torture me, she begins a sexy lap striptease, sliding first one strap of her dress and then the other from her shoulders. The fabric sits above her generous breasts in a taunt that makes my blood pound harder.

'There's a zip at the back.' She leans forward so I'm engulfed in her divine-smelling hair. I reach around to slowly undo the zip. Every second of the metallic scraping shunts my testosterone higher. She shoves the dress to her waist, staring at me with uninhibited invitation. Her breasts are perfect, just big enough, her nipples pink and inviting. I cup them both and slide my thumbs over the tight peaks, watching with fascination as desire darkens her eyes to almost turquoise blue.

'You like that?' Who is this alluring creature? I already know that one night isn't going to be enough. My divorce has curtailed my desire for a anything long-term, but some things are worth indulging in more than once.

Ava nods, her plump bottom lip caught under her teeth as she releases a soft moan I could listen to all day.

'I want to see you.' She unbuttons my shirt and bares my chest, her pupils flaring in appreciation that make the hours spent in the gym worthwhile. She presses her mouth to the base of my throat. I close my eyes and relax my head back on the sofa, enjoying every kiss and lick she lavishes over my throat.

'Where did you come from?' I ask, need hot in my veins. I feel her answering smile against my skin.

'I was born and raised in Brooklyn.' Her soft chuckle, the hint of her sense of humour, makes me smile.

Beautiful, sexy, and funny.

I store this nugget of information away for later, too turned on for conversation but burning up to know everything there is to know about this woman. Have I ever clicked so quickly with someone? She's distractingly beautiful—the glossy black hair and blue eyes a striking combination.

Just then she palms my dick and my mind blanks of everything but the way she's making me forget my past and the burr under my skin that today's outlandish demand from Josh created. I want more of Ava, and, as my shitty stepfather would soon see if he were still alive to witness my plans for his business, I'm a man of my word.

'Hold tight,' I say, gripping her hips and rising to my feet in one smooth move.

She squeals, laughing and wrapping her arms around my shoulders and her legs around my waist. 'Where are we going?'

She smells fantastic, spicy and feminine. Her scent is already embedded in the fabric of my shirt, so I know I'll be able to smell her on my sheets after tonight.

'Somewhere more comfortable...' I push open the door to the bedroom adjoining my office and the automatic lights illuminate the space in a sub-dued glow.

'Oh, wow. You even sleep at your office.' She looks around the king-sized room and ensuite bathroom beyond.

'Sometimes.' I grin, mildly embarrassed that I've become something of a workaholic since I moved back to New York three years ago and took Bold global. My ex, Monroe, stayed in London and our third partner, Hudson, moved to Tokyo.

In two strides we're at the bed. Ava shivers as I lay her down against the cool linen, then she props herself up on her elbows and watches me undress.

'This is very convenient,' she says, her eyes moving over my body. 'You don't even need to leave the office to date.'

I laugh. 'It's pretty handy for the frequent nights I work late and can't be bothered to go home. Or for that once-in-a-lifetime occasion when an exquisite woman seduces me in the elevator.' I kick off my shoes and remove my socks.

'Yes, I guess I did do that…' She releases a breathy sigh, perhaps of longing, as I quickly shed my clothes.

'I'm not complaining. Just in case you have the impression that I'm horribly lazy, you should know that I do normally leave the office to date. I know how to show a lady a pretty good time, something you'll discover when you give me your number in the morning.'

She smiles, her eyes narrowed playfully. 'You can show me a good time now.' Her painted toes curl into the comforter under her as I prowl closer. I want to kiss her from her head to those elegant toes, but I'm wound too tight with desire to go slow the first time, despite stating earlier we had all night.

'Oh, I intend to.' When I shove my boxers down my thighs and kick them aside, her mouth hangs open. I could scale skyscrapers from the admiring expression on her face.

'You have too many clothes on.' I tug her black dress over her hips and groan when she's left in only black lacy panties. 'Fuck, you're gorgeous. Leaving that party when I did might just be the best decision of my life.'

She chuckles, the sexy sound soon dying in her throat, because I can't stop my hands from roaming her soft skin, up her slender thighs, over the curve of her hips, across her stomach and back to the breasts she's shoving into my hands as she writhes on the bed.

I put one knee next to her hip and lift one breast to my mouth, triumph spicing my blood when she cries out my name and curls her fingers into the sheets. I lave her nipple, dragging out a series of breathy moans from her, and then I suck down until she's twisting my hair in her hands and all but begging me with her eyes.

'I haven't done this in a while,' she says, panting.

'Don't worry—can't you feel how good we're going to be together?'

She nods, her pupils dilating to swallow most of her brilliant blue irises.

'I want to taste all of you.' I treat the other breast to the same attention while Ava grips my cock and strokes her fist from root to tip, honing in on the sensitive spot under the crown. It's distractingly good, but I want to know all of her gorgeous body intimately. She's better than twenty-five-year-old bourbon—decadent and rich and memorable.

I rear back, planning to pin her hands beside her head so I can really go to town on every inch of her exposed skin, but before I have a chance she sits up.

'Me too.' She grips my cock and takes me into her eager mouth.

'Ava,' I bark in warning, loving the sight of those plump lips, which are red from our kissing, wrapped around me. I fight the urge to close my eyes as intense pleasure grips my entire body. I enjoy her sucking for a few minutes, fisting her hair and holding her head to keep her eyes on mine while she works me with her tongue. I look down and she looks up, her eyes blazing with lust. I'm lost in her stare and the desperate moans she makes and the increasingly vigorous sucking.

'Stop.' I jerk my hips back before this is over too soon. 'My turn.' I scrape the lace panties down her pale thighs and press a kiss to her mound. I push her thighs wider, taking a good look at the sweetness between her legs.

'You're beautiful.' I kiss her inner thighs, teasing her and chuckling when she shudders. I trace one finger over the strip of dark curls until I locate her slick clit. She gasps, shoving up onto her elbows so she can watch. I part her lips and push two fingers inside her, twisting my wrist as I plunge them home through her wetness.

'Yes, don't stop,' she pleads.

'I'm not going anywhere, sweetheart.' I lave her clit with the tip of my tongue, sucking in the erotic scent of her on a low growl I can't hold in.

'Oh…my…' Her neck arches back. She grips

my head in one hand and holds me in place. Her eyes lock with mine and connection, urgent and undeniable, zaps between us. I was right to trust my instincts with this woman. She's just the well-timed balm I need.

Her hips jerk, rocking in small thrusts against my mouth. Ava's not one to lie back and take it, and my heart beats against my ribs at how perfect she is. I plunge my fingers in and out and suck down on her clit, watching in fascination as pleasure streaks across her exquisite face. Her hair is a wild tumble around her flushed cheeks, the ends curling over her shoulders, down to her breasts. Her cries grow more desperate, her voice breaking as ecstasy grips her in its brutal hold. She falls into her climax with a long wail, and satisfaction roars through me.

I snatch a condom from the drawer beside the bed and quickly cover myself, then spread her thighs again and guide myself inside her soaking pussy.

'Yes,' she cries. 'I wanted you the minute I saw you.'

'Me too,' I confess as I glide through her wet core.

She grips my forearms, which are braced beside her head. Her breasts bounce with the force of my thrusts. She lets go and reaches overhead to prop her arms against the headboard, providing counter friction to my pounding hips that has me seeing stars.

'That's it,' I say, reaching down between us to stroke her clit once more. 'Come for me again, beautiful Ava.'

She whimpers, her eyes wild on mine. My orgasm tears through me, pleasure blasting through my brain like a flash of white light as I spill into her. The feeling is amplified when her cries and the way she squeezes me tell me she's indeed there with me.

I collapse on top of her, already planning an entire night of seduction. We can shower together, chat and get to know each other, swap numbers and perhaps even catch breakfast at the deli around the block.

I roll my weight off her and remove the condom, wrapping it in a tissue and tossing it in the bin. We look at each other, both chuckling. Her flush tells me she's a little self-conscious as the endorphin high trickles away.

'You *are* full of surprises,' I say, kissing her shoulder, which is dotted with golden freckles.

Her soft acknowledgement makes me smile—an amazing feat after Josh's infuriating cheek today. Soon Marcus won't even be a memory. Not for me, or the employees he overlooked in his final years in charge of Brent's.

I sling my arm over Ava's waist, my eyes growing heavy. Just five minutes of shut-eye and I'll be good to go again.

When I wake an hour later, the biggest surprise of all awaits me: no Ava, no goodbye, no phone number.

CHAPTER THREE

Ava

THE FORTY MINUTES it takes me to compose one email to the manager of our freight team should be a prediction of the day to come. I take an unsatisfying slurp of my cold coffee, frustrated that I've allowed myself to be distracted by a single night of great sex.

I'm normally more productive on a Monday, refreshed and ready to attack anything awaiting me at Hamilton's. Except this weekend, while I tried to catch up on work, shopped for groceries, took a yoga class and lost myself in the kitchen and the ritual of making fresh pasta, I couldn't forget the explosive one-night stand.

I stare at my computer screen, the spreadsheet blurring as my mind wanders back to Friday night and Sterling Lombard. Delicious shivers break out all over my body. A body that remembers every touch, every kiss, every moan even when I want to switch off my mind and focus.

There is no forgetting a night like that.

But it should never have happened.

'Stupid, Ava, really stupid…' I jab at the delete key to erase the mistake I've just made. I should have told Sterling what I really wanted from the minute he introduced himself.

I just wasn't expecting our chemistry to flare up like a bonfire. I'd wanted him more than an appointment in that instant in the elevator. Crazy, because this business represents everything to me—all I have left of my family. All I have in the world…

Has that always sounded so pathetic?

I glance around my comforting but eclectic office—no sleek, modern sanctum here. Instead memories and ghosts lurk in every cluttered corner. The set of bookshelves are the ones my mother took to college. Nonna and Pops rescued the coffee machine from my parents' restaurant before it had to be sold. I have pictures of Mum and Dad sitting on the battered sofa under the window the day they came to this very office to tell my grandparents they were engaged.

I sigh and drop my head into my hands. Why did I sleep with Sterling, of all men? It's only made things more awkward. Unprofessional. Now I'll have to contact him and say *Hey, remember me, the woman from the one-night stand on Friday? Well, guess what? We co-own a business I'd really like back.*

Exactly the kind of call I want to make on a

Monday morning when nothing seems to be going right...

Itching with self-accusation, I rise from behind my desk and pace to the window. My office sits in a warehouse complex on a lot of land my grandfather bought before my mom was born, near the Brooklyn Navy Yard. From the far right of my window I can just see a strip of the East River and half of the Manhattan Bridge beyond the redbrick industrial buildings. It's a view I've stared at many times while trying to figure out my life.

And I find myself here again.

At fourteen, I stood here to grieve my parents, my face hot and swollen from all the tears I'd shed. I couldn't contemplate school, but I couldn't stand to be left alone for fear of my intrusive thoughts, which were determined to torture me with the horrific way my parents died. I spent hours in this very room, staring at that sliver of blue water through unseeing eyes, oblivious to my grandfather chatting to clients on the phone and numb to his painstaking two-finger typing on the computer. Yet I always felt his watchfulness. Sensed his and Nonna's concern for the teenage girl they had no idea how to reach. I lost track of the number of times I curled up on the sofa under a blanket with my eyes closed, pretending to sleep so my grandparents wouldn't worry as they tried to get on with their own lives and run their company. The only thing I knew with any certainty back then was that nothing could ever fill the void left behind by the accident.

And I'd been right: nothing ever has.

Nonna and Pops changed too after losing Mum, their only child. I owe them so much for taking me in in their twilight years. They raised me while they grieved for their daughter. They even gave me a career, a secure job—first as office gofer after school, then part-time warehouse manager during college, then, once I'd completed my MBA, more and more managerial responsibility. And now, when their beloved business, their life's work, is in my hands—when I've saved every penny I have from the modest inheritance left to me by my parents in order to take full control and steer Hamilton's back into the black—I'm here again, in this very same spot.

So why did you blow your chance with Lombard?

Because I wanted to feel like a woman. To embrace the unexpected and fierce connection and switch off my brain's incessant worrying for a few minutes of relief. For a brief, indulgent moment, I wanted to banish my loneliness and feel like a success.

A frustrated sigh gusts out of me. My parents' death taught me that security and certainty were luxuries I could no longer take for granted. If I put in the hours, return Hamilton's to its glory days, surely I'll find exactly the peace of mind and sense of belonging I crave. And the first step is claiming back the equity sold to Sterling Lombard.

So what are you waiting for?

If I call his office and leave my name, he'll probably take my call. He wanted my number, yet I sneaked out like a coward instead of facing him and confessing the real reason I attended his party.

But I can explain all of that.

I'm just about to turn away from the view when a flashy grey Porsche convertible pulls into the parking lot below. My stomach flips with familiar grief—the driver who hit my parents was driving something similar, speeding while intoxicated. The car looks so out of place amid the row of bicycles propped in the rack and the modest Hondas and Fords belonging to my staff that I assume the driver must be lost, but a sixth sense prevents me from returning to my desk.

I focus on the sole occupant as he kills the engine, seeing only the back of his sandy blond head and broad shoulders.

I freeze. Dread floods my body with chills.

Sterling Lombard climbs from the low-slung vehicle.

Breath hisses out of me as he buttons his suit jacket with one hand and glances up at my fourth-floor window. I dive back from sight, panicking as the events of Friday night come crashing down around me.

What is he doing here? How did he track me down? A man of his relentless resourcefulness would have no problem locating the woman who seduced him in the elevator and then fled from his bed while he slept without so much as a 'goodbye and thanks for the orgasms'.

I wince, struck with fresh guilt. I'd wanted to stay, but the minute his breathing turned shallow and regular, telling me he'd fallen asleep, remorse had pressed down on me until I feared I'd never move again. I debated shaking him awake to confess, but it made me feel like I'd somehow used him sexually, when I'd simply been carried away by his hotness and my body's reaction.

Looks like now I'll have my chance to explain.

With my heart in my throat, I race to my desk, uselessly shoving piles of papers around in an attempt to tidy up but achieving nothing. I open the door and call to my assistant, Judy, with instructions to delay him. Then, ridiculously, I duck into my tiny private bathroom and check my flushed face in the mirror.

Hair caught up in a utilitarian ponytail, check.

Cheeks pink in a way that makes me look guilty, check.

Eyes bright with both excitement and dismay, check.

'Shit, shit, shit,' I say to my reflection as I smear on some fresh lip gloss and ignore the way heat sizzles through my veins at the idea of seeing him again. Even in the cold light of day he's so gorgeous—confident and sophisticated. Sexy and charming. Hung and talented...

Forget about him naked and plead your case for Hamilton's.

Right.

Back at my desk I wonder if I have time to scoop all the clutter into a bin liner and then calmly and professionally instruct Judy to escort him in. Before I can move a muscle there's a hurried knock at the door.

Judy's flustered face is puce with embarrassment. 'There's a Mr Lombard to—'

'She knows who I am,' says Sterling, stepping around Judy and instantly shrinking my office to half its size with his impressive physique and commanding aura.

'Question is, who is *she*?' His eyes shine like shards of sea glass as he pins me with an accusatory stare.

That fizzle of awareness snakes across the room. He may be all buttoned up now, his angular face clean-shaven and his hair tamed, but all I can see is the man who kissed me like there was no tomorrow and made me cry out his name.

Twice.

I swallow, speechless, my eyes taking a once-over of his magnificent body. This suit is charcoal, tailored to within an inch of its life, and hugs his powerful frame in a way that tells me it's bespoke. His white shirt is so crisp it wouldn't dare wrinkle and the mauve tie makes the green of his eyes pop even more than they did when he was buried inside me husking out a feral growl.

I want to hide. Instead I sit behind my desk and calmly cross my legs, as if being interrupted by irate investors I've screwed is an everyday occurrence with which I'm perfectly comfortable.

'Thank you, Judy,' I say, my voice tight with nerves as my assistant flees. I drag my longing glance from the door and reluctantly meet Sterling's stare. 'Well, this is a surprise.'

The fact that he's come to my office means he's connected the dots and knows exactly who I am and how we share ownership of Hamilton's.

'Is it?' His tone is short. That deeply seductive voice a distant memory.

But my body remembers. *Come for me, beautiful Ava.* Have I ever felt so physically worshipped? So in tune with another person? So entranced?

No wonder I can't forget the sex.

'You didn't leave me your number.' His nostrils flare. 'I assume that meant you wanted no further contact with me.'

I burn inside with shame that I had a great time

in his bed but left without warning. My reasons now seem hazy and cowardly. I can't fathom what I was thinking. I only know I'd gone into Manhattan Friday night for one thing and it wasn't meeting a man who pressed all my sexual buttons and then some.

'And yet you tracked me down in your luxury European sports car.'

His lip curls.

Why am I judging and antagonising him when he clearly has an axe to grind? I should just apologise and explain. But where do I start?

'And what do *you* drive?' he asks. 'A scooter? One of those bikes outside? Rollerblades?' He eyes my outfit, a self-congratulatory smile stretching his mouth when his inspection reaches my feet.

I have a penchant for heels, the higher the better, but there's a pair of sneakers in my closet for the walk home.

'I don't drive at all.' I regret the unguarded response instantly. I don't want him to know any more about me than he's already discovered from the internet.

To prevent him asking why, I plough on, demanding the most pressing answer. 'How did you find me?' There's accusation in my tone now, but I always fight fire with fire. It's in my passionate Italian blood. He came here prepared for a showdown, when all I did was ghost him.

He shrugs. 'I had your number within an hour of waking up alone. You really should address your online discoverability—there are a lot of creeps out there. I can recommend a security company in which I own stock, if you're interested.'

'Thanks for the heads up.' I bristle, horrified to acknowledge any vulnerability to this ruthless version of him, when only sixty hours ago I entrusted him with my body and my pleasure. When I wanted him with a ferocity that eclipsed my goal for seeking him out.

'I'm glad you're here, actually.' I clear my dry throat. 'I wanted to talk to you and you've saved me a trip into Manhattan. Won't you have a seat?'

I can salvage this. Sure, it's a bit more awkward than I would have liked, but my gatecrashing stunt on Friday had the desired result—I have his attention captive. He's in my office. Time to ignore how I still want to remove that suit with my teeth and present my business proposal.

'I'll stand,' he says, his stare somehow mocking as if he already knows what I want. Turning his back on me, he wanders around, eyeing the old industry award certificates on the walls and the framed pictures of Pops breaking ground for the building we're currently standing in. This office abuts our fifty thousand square foot climate-controlled warehouse facility next door.

'Okay.' I wet my lips and drag my eyes away from his rear. I can appeal to his sense of integrity and fairness. 'Well, as you've discovered, I'm the owner and operator of Hamilton Logistics—'

'Part-owner.' His voice is eerily calm as he looks at me with suspicion over his shoulder.

'Yes…part-owner.' Surely he's a reasonable man. All I did was leave after the sex was over. A woman must have done that to him before. 'I only discovered your interest in Hamilton's recently from the company lawyer. You see, I inherited the business from my grandparents, who founded it in the sixties.'

He turns from peering out of my window and nods, urging me to continue while his expression remains unreadable. Considering the length of time I've had to perfect my pitch, this is going decidedly badly. If only I hadn't slept with him, hadn't blurred the line…

You still want him, that's why you're tripping over your words.

I clear my throat nervously. 'Pops—that's him on the wall—' I point to the photo of a smiling, fair-haired man wearing a hard hat, from whom I inherited my blue eyes '—he started specialising in valuable and difficult-to-ship items, so he found a niche in the market at that time. It grew from there and now we service the entire East Coast…' My voice peters out at his continued silence, which is more foreboding than the annoyance he displayed when he first arrived.

'You knew who I was in the elevator, didn't you?' he utters in a quiet voice. 'Before I introduced myself...'

I bite my lip, guilt hot like sunburn. I should have come clean about my reasons for being there Friday. When I look up from my fidgety fingers, which are ineffectually straightening papers on my desk, his stare is full of ice as if I've committed the crime of the decade.

'Yes,' I admit. 'I was desperate. I've been trying to arrange an appointment with you for months.'

'So you lied your way into Bold's office party, which was for loyal employees and select partners only.' The English lilt to his accent is more pronounced when he's angry. More haughty. He's like an American Mr Darcy... I try not to find it sexy but fail miserably.

'No... Kind of.' It was a last ditch attempt to speak to him, and then once we'd slept together, I felt overwhelmed. 'I wanted to get your attention, that's all. To meet you and request a face-to-face conference during office hours.'

If only he'd agreed, none of this would have happened. His implacable stance is beginning to grind my gears. As if I'm guilty of committing some sort of industrial espionage or single-handedly eating the supply of Bold caviar from the buffet.

'I know you're a busy man, but the little people deserve to be heard, too. Without companies like mine, you'd have nothing in which to invest.'

His stare turns flinty. Somehow I'm making this worse, not clearing up the misunderstanding. 'And without me, Hamilton Logistics would have sunk into bankruptcy years ago.'

'Oh, well, aren't you noble?' I wince, hating that he knows my company as well as he seemed to know my body, playing me to near exhaustion with his wicked mouth and sexual finesse. 'Look, I don't dispute that my grandparents must have needed help—at the time they came to you I was away at grad school. Although, I don't understand why someone like you would bail out a small troubled company.' I silence the reminder on my phone telling me I need to be in the warehouse in five minutes. 'But to get back to my point—'

'So you slept with me to get an appointment? I have to say, that's pretty cold—not the impression I had of the sensual woman I met on Friday.' His eyes glitter, a glacial smile on his lips as if he expected the appalling behaviour he's accusing me of.

'I did no such thing. We seduced each other.' Heat rushes up my neck at the memories of the way I behaved. One look at his hotness is the only excuse I can muster. 'I've been fobbed off with your associates for months. I wanted to go straight to the top. I planned to approach you at the party—'

He paces closer, an air of danger pulsing around him. I should heed it. He's dangerous to my good sense, to my instincts, to my self-preservation— even now I want him still. 'So you stalked me and seduced me? This keeps getting better and better...'

'No. Yes... I mean, I didn't stalk you. I was leaving because I thought you wouldn't show up.' I grip my hands together in turmoil.

How can he affect me so much? It was just sex.

Amazing, unforgettable sex. *Admit it, he's the hottest man you've ever met. For a moment in his arms, with his kiss on your lips, you didn't feel so...alone.*

He tilts his head, his stare moving over my face leaving me even more flustered. I recall that look. He used it on Friday night when I was naked and panting and watching him go down on me.

Only now, with his bad attitude, it's tainted. He's like a different person today, not the charming, considerate lover of Friday.

'So,' he shrugs, 'make it right. I'm here. This is the shot you say you've been waiting for.' He crosses his arms over his chest and grips his biceps.

I should be relieved—this is my chance to appeal to him professionally. Instead, warning buzzes over my skin like static electricity. It feels like he's toying with me. Like I'm a mouse and he's sharpening his lethal claws.

'Okay.' I hold his challenging eye contact. Hamilton's is important enough for me to swallow a slice of humble pie. 'I want you to sell me your Hamilton's equity.'

He has the temerity to laugh.

Shards of contempt pierce me in that moment. I at least expected integrity, manners and professionalism from him.

Yet you weren't professional on Friday...

That was ill-judged lust.

'Fine.' He paces closer. 'I'll take the bait and ask—why would I do that?' His stare narrows but to my consternation it's still there, the connection we shared in the elevator. Like fingers of temptation licking at my skin. No matter how much we both wish our one-night stand had never happened, it seems we can't avoid the thing that brought us together.

'Well, as you know, the company has been struggling for a while.' I lift my chin, hating to admit any weakness. 'I'm sure you have many other investments that outperform us. What's one little third-party logistics company to *you*—the great Sterling Lombard?'

'If that's the case, if Hamilton's is floundering, surely you need more of my investment and expertise, not less. You're not even in a position to buy back the stock.'

My stomach pinches. I didn't want to go into this much detail. I hoped he'd be relieved to offload a company that must be a pretty low priority for a big hitter like Bold.

I suck in a breath, veering perilously close to a bottomless emotional chasm. Hamilton's is more than a company to me. It's inexorably linked to my sense of belonging. The only way I can connect to my parents so I don't feel the sheer panic of being utterly abandoned.

I close my eyes for a second, sucking in a bolstering breath. As I often do, I hear my parents' voices.

Food is more than nutrition—it's a part of our rich history. Always remember your roots, Ava. Without them we can't grow.

The words force a lump to the back of my throat. They often used our time together cooking—the ritual of making fresh pasta or kneading bread—to impart parental wisdom, or just connect. We spent hours talking in the kitchen. I usually play music while I cook now to counter the overwhelming silence.

I swallow, seeking my composure as I answer his question on my finances. 'I have some savings my parents left me. With a small loan it will be enough for what the shares are worth.'

His eyes are trained on mine as he faces me across my embarrassingly cluttered desk. 'How do you know what the shares are worth?'

I stand too. He already has the height advantage and the surprise factor to his credit. This is *my* office, warts and all.

'Well… I'm a company director. I—'

'I'm not talking about dollar value,' he interrupts. 'I'm talking about the value to *me*, personally. Why do you want to own all of the sinking ship anyway? Wouldn't it be better for us to drown together in the hopes that I'll cast you another financial lifeline?' His smile borders on cruel even as his stare swoops over me.

I huff in outrage, any lingering feelings for the time we shared destroyed by his obstinacy. 'Why would my company mean anything to *you*?' I say, appalled. 'I want the *sinking ship*, as you put it, because it's everything to me. It's my inheritance. My heritage.'

All I have left of my loved ones…

He shrugs, completely unfazed by my pleading tone and my private admission. 'I would've thought you'd be relieved to unburden yourself of such a crippling liability. This company was struggling when your grandparents came to me three years ago, and it's in even worse shape now. Which is why I'm here to tell you that your cunning little plan to get close to me has worked in your favour. Congratulations.'

'What do you mean?' Ice slithers through my veins at the look of hostility in his eyes. I recall them sparking with arousal and I wonder where that warm, considerate man has gone. The one with the winning charm, good manners and sexual magnetism.

A cruel smile that makes me shiver twists his gorgeous mouth. 'I mean, Ava, that I intend to amalgamate Hamilton's into a bigger company, which I'll then sell to the highest bidder. And there's not a damned thing—including seducing me again—that you can do about it.'

CHAPTER FOUR

Sterling

SURROUNDED BY THE nostalgic clutter of her office and the memories plastered over the walls, she seems so down to earth. More approachable. Vulnerable. And still shockingly beautiful. She's wearing another pair of skyscraper heels, a navy blue pants suit and an emerald silk blouse that makes her eyes brighter. I recall those eyes shot through with arousal and my cock flickers in my pants.

Dream on, buddy.

This is the same temptress who all but propositioned me in my own damned elevator in order to get close to me and seduce me out of my shares in her company.

No, now it's *my* company. A company Marcus had wanted but failed to procure. When Ava's grandparents came to me for investment three years ago, shortly after I returned to New York, I jumped at the chance to best the man who'd made half my life miserable.

Looking at Ava now, her face pale, her astounding blue eyes wide, and disbelief visible in the way she's holding her luscious body, I have to lock down my violent attraction to her.

Her surprise drains away to be replaced by the flush of anger. 'You can't sell Hamilton's. It's my job...my life.'

She's not vulnerable; she's conniving, deceptive, ruthless. I know better than anyone that appearances can be deceiving. Wasn't Marcus a pillar of the community in strangers' eyes? He attended all the right functions—charity galas, fundraisers and business events. He'd married his friend's widow after becoming a widower himself and taken on a young stepson. I was the only one, it seemed, who consistently saw the real man. My mother must have hoped for a doting stepfather. To this day she's blessedly unaware of what a despicable bully her second husband was to her only son.

I've tried to protect her, so she doesn't know the full extent of Marcus's psychological manipulations. I only hope she fared better against his cruel streak. A boy should never hear his mother cry behind a closed door. I couldn't stop Mom's emotional abuse at the hands of Marcus any more than I could stop my own.

But I can execute my plans for both Hamilton's and Brent's.

Despite Josh dragging Mom into his whining justifications for claiming Brent's—something that should be between us, man to man—I've no desire to enlighten my mother. She's lost two husbands. I won't cause her more pain.

The same impotence I felt as a boy beats at me now as I stand before Ava. 'On the contrary, I can do what I like with our company.' I grind my teeth to hide how much I still want her. My body clamours to get close, get inside her again until I feel restored and she learns I'm not a man to be hoodwinked and used.

I'll never be weak again. Weaknesses can be exploited. Marcus taught that life lesson to a ten-year-old boy still grieving the death of his father. Then I was powerless to the tyrant who subtly criticised everything I did and said. The man who constantly compared me to my stepbrother and was quick to highlight my failures. Quick—through jealousy I hadn't understood at the time—to slander my kind, hard-working policeman father, despite their friendship.

You'll never amount to much, just like him.

Your father isn't here because he was too busy protecting other people to care about you.

If only you could make your mother proud the way I'm proud of Josh...

The recollection of Marcus's vile words spoils my satisfaction at Ava's shocked reaction to my statement.

'If you no longer want the company, why not sell it back to me? Surely that makes the most sense.' She blinks her pretty blue eyes.

I won't succumb to her charms a second time. Discovering her true identity replicated the powerlessness I felt under Marcus's control.

'I'm not interested in making sense. Only money and *all* of the decisions. That's why I negotiated the equity stake with your grandparents.' I have a plan for Hamilton's, one that involves Brent's Express, which is based in Chicago. It's a plan I intend to stick to, and it doesn't involve weakness or sentiment.

I feel Ava's animosity buffet me from across the room.

Good—I'm an expert at withstanding indifference and dislike. What I won't tolerate is failure or its reminders.

Ava's stare turns murderous. 'You took advantage of my grandparents.' Fight stiffens her body. 'They were elderly and desperate, otherwise they'd never have come to a shark like you.'

That she questions my integrity after what she did boils my blood. I want to kiss her just to silence her unfounded accusations.

And because you can't get her off your mind.

That's just sex. This is business.

'I did no such thing.' My brittle smile seems to enrage her further. 'I invested heavily in their business for the controlling share, and they were eager to sell. They said they needed the money to help their granddaughter with her college debts.'

She looks away and pricks of remorse make me wince—she clearly didn't know.

Her phone emits a second alert. She silences it quickly, her shock morphing into an impatient frown that tugs her mouth flat. 'I have a meeting with my warehouse foreman—we'll need to re-schedule this…discussion.'

'I don't think so.' My denial jerks her eyes back to mine.

I won't be brushed off again. Waking up to find her side of my bed cold and no sexy little note was dismissal enough from the woman who blasted through my dull Friday night like a comet. These days, people underestimate me at their peril.

Marcus did. Josh, too, is quickly waking up to the realisation that I won't be manipulated. As stepbrothers, there's little love lost between us. He failed to show me any sort of brotherly kindness growing up. I'd looked forward to having an older sibling, but, at seven years my senior, Josh wasn't the role model I hoped for. Instead he despised me at worst and ignored me at best.

'This isn't a social call,' I continue, taking a seat

and watching with satisfaction as panic steals the colour from Ava's cheeks. 'You've already run out on me once so I'll wait right here for you.' I've had to cancel a business trip to visit the other Bold directors in Tokyo this week, so I have nothing better to do. 'But be assured, Ava, I can do whatever I like with this company. I hold the deciding share.'

When I invested in Hamilton's, its only value to me was the one-upmanship I achieved over Marcus. But, now I know how Ava Hamilton manipulated and used me, I'll take even greater pleasure in doing what Marcus couldn't: amalgamating Hamilton's and Brent's. I'll add my golden touch, rebrand and sell them as a Lombard success story.

Selling Brent's at triple the price I paid for it will show Marcus, once and for all, how he underestimated me…even if it's only his son who remains to witness my revenge.

'What are you planning to do to Hamilton's?' Her appalled question is tremulous.

I shrug, brushing a speck of lint from the leg of my pants, as I harden myself against the confused desperation on her face. 'Why should I tell you my intentions? I don't trust a single glorious hair on your deceitful head.'

I trail my stare over the rest of her, recalling every inch of her sexy, voluptuous body.

Ava fists one hand on her hip and I'm momentarily reminded of my ex, Monroe. A woman I still admire and care about enough to stay business partners with, despite our personal history and failed marriage. Ava has the same graceful elegance, the same forthright spirit and the same confidence and smarts.

But I've been there, done that. Relationships are another way to be vulnerable to attack. To feel powerless. To harbour regrets.

After her mother died, Monroe pushed me away. I tried not to internalise her grief, but that part of me beaten down by Marcus felt defeat, nonetheless. No matter how hard I tried, I just seemed to make things worse. I let her down. I couldn't be what she needed. Some long-forgotten part of my brain was awakened by Marcus's condemnations—after all, he'd predicted from the start that our marriage wouldn't last. I wasn't totally to blame for the divorce, but didn't that sting the worst, to know he was proved correct?

'Trust me or not,' Ava says, her voice tight, 'we're currently business partners—fifty-fifty.'

I snort. 'More like fifty-five, forty-five in my favour. As there's no time like the present, I'd like a tour of my assets, please.' I stand, move to the door and swing it open so she knows it's non-negotiable. 'I've already seen the…um…offices—' I glance around the cramped space with a nice view of the parking lot '—why don't I accompany you to the warehouse?'

From the venomous look she shoots me—white-hot sparks turning her irises arctic—I'm surprised I'm still standing. But those sparks ignite my blood the way they did when our lips connected, the same potent chemistry at work.

They say love and hate are two sides of the same coin...

I sling my hands in my pockets and wait for her to realise that, unlike Friday night when she held the upper hand and I was ignorant, now she's completely at *my* mercy.

'Fine,' she huffs, scooping up her phone and purse. She struts past me to the outer office, leaving a trail of delicious scent in her wake. I momentarily close my eyes, my mind and body awash with memories of her in my bed. Her passionate cries, her nails digging into my shoulders, her pleading stare, begging for release.

'Judy—I'll be in the warehouse. Mr Lombard would like a tour.' She shoots me an exaggerated smile of saccharine sweetness that makes me want to tug her into my arms and remind how much she'd wanted, no, *needed* me, the other night.

She flicks her glossy hair over her shoulder and leaves the room, expecting me to follow. I do just that, sniggering under my breath. She reminds me of the ancient bulldog my grandparents owned—all snarly bluster on the surface but fond of a good tummy rub underneath. I've seen her other side.

The sexy seductress who came apart in my arms. The passionate woman who sucked me until I almost lost my mind.

Oh, she might have set out to entrap or manipulate me, but her reactions in bed, her breathy kisses and wild moans—they were as real as it gets. Physically she was as overcome as me.

Except she had an ulterior motive.

We reach the ground floor and exit the building, a hostile mix of distrust and pheromones swirling around us like smoke. I want to switch off that part of my brain that finds her incredibly alluring. I don't want to notice the sexy sway of her hips as she walks, or the slope of her neck when the wind gusts, lifting her hair. Her scent carried on the brisk breeze is particular torture.

Remember what she did. How it made you feel like that helpless kid again.

My determination strengthens with every clip of her heels across the concrete. I'll never be manipulated again, no matter how tempting the inducement. And they don't come more tempting than this woman.

Perhaps I imagined that glimpse of vulnerability in her expression earlier. It was likely just surprise at me showing up unannounced and catching her out on her subterfuge.

Fighting the impotence of wanting her still, I drag my eyes away from her gorgeous ass.

'Why did you sneak out while I was asleep?' Now, why did I ask that? I don't care that she left without so much as a goodbye. She knew who I was before I laid a single finger on her. She used me while I was oblivious, while I was already picturing where I'd take her for our second date.

So why didn't she stay to press her advantage?

'I didn't sneak. I just left.' Her thick, dark lashes bat as she blinks rapidly, watching me with curiosity and a small smile playing about her full lips. 'Don't tell me your ego was bruised when you woke up alone…?'

'My ego is just fine.' I step close as we reach the warehouse side door and she keys in a code with gratifyingly twitchy fingers. I swing the door open and then block the doorway, turning so we're face to face, only inches apart.

'Perhaps I just hadn't had my fill of you.' I dip my stare to the vee of her blouse, where a flash of cleavage and a glimpse of lace tighten my groin. Damn, but I want her just as fiercely as the first time, conniving temptress or not.

Her pulse leaping in her neck and the hint of arousal in her eyes as she looks up at me are way too satisfying. Resenting each other hasn't diminished our desire one bit. There's no reason the flames in the bedroom would dim just because we're now on opposing sides. Only, now that she's revealed her true colours, I'm confident our chemistry is something I can not only control but also use to give me the upper hand.

'Let's just stick to business, shall we?' She moves past me and snags a couple of hard hats from the selection hanging on the wall. She thrusts one my way, her smile mocking.

'Something amusing you, Ms Hamilton?' I take the hat and adjust the strap before perching it on my head.

She dons her hat without ceremony, telling me she's not just used to running things from her disorganised office, but she's comfortable on the shop floor, as it were, too. I wonder if she can also drive a truck or operate a forklift...

Now, that I'd love to see...

'No, I just wish the *Financial Times* could see you now, that's all.' With a twitch of her lips, she heads through another door and into the warehouse's main facility.

The noise of the climate control system and the various industrial vehicles moving around the cavernous space prevents further conversation. When we enter the office in the corner the noise level drops dramatically.

'Hi, Sam.' Ava addresses a man in his late fifties with greying hair. 'This is Mr Lombard. Would you please give him a tour of the facility while I take a look at the invoicing system?'

The foreman nervously takes me in but jumps

to his boss's bidding, grabbing his own hard hat and leading me back out through the door we just entered.

I'm only half listening as Sam describes the square footage, the state-of-the-art loading docks my investment paid for, and the inventory management system and electronic data interface that makes things run like clockwork. My mind is occupied with more pleasing thoughts—like how Hamilton's will complement Brent's. Throw in the New Jersey–based SeaFreight, the shipping company I own, and with some management restructuring and a shiny new business name I can create a very profitable national logistics company. And erase Marcus Brent from my life once and for all.

Despite how he treated me and Mom, despite what he said about my father out of envy, I'm ten times the businessman he was.

As we walk back to the office, I ask Sam what kind of a boss Ava makes. I'd like to believe my curiosity is intelligence-gathering, but I suspect I'm just intrigued—this is traditionally a male-dominated industry. She's clearly a very hands-on boss. It's all a complete turn-on I'm battling to ignore. I tell myself that it's good to know your enemy, and preferably keep them as close as possible.

Yeah, you just want her back in your bed...

'She's amazing,' Sam says with genuine affection.

I fight prickles of jealousy to level an encouraging smile on the older man. I want to keep him talking.

'I've known her since she was a little girl.' He chuckles. 'She'd come in here with her grandfather in a kid's-sized hard hat—all wide eyes and chatter.'

Much like the talkative Sam.

I stay quiet, deeming it the best strategy to learn more about my new adversary from a personal standpoint. I've already compiled a résumé from the information I gleaned during my internet searches. She has an MBA from New York University and she's worked her way up through the ranks at Hamilton's.

'Of course, that all changed when her parents died. But she's worked here at Hamilton's ever since—after school, during college and then later full time.'

The news about her parents takes me aback for a few seconds—I noticed a glimmer of sadness in her eyes. But I can't allow any weakness around this woman—she'll take full advantage, just as she's already proved.

Perhaps realising he's said too much, Sam shuts up. But with what I know, it's enough. By the time we make it back to Ava, I'm burning up with curiosity and reluctant compassion I have no idea where to place. She used me, made me feel a powerlessness I haven't experienced in years. I don't want to feel any positive emotion, beyond the lust I can't seem to control, for a woman who played me so well and so relentlessly.

She joins us outside Sam's office. 'Have you seen enough?' Wariness wars with defiance in her eyes.

'On the contrary,' I say, lifting my chin in thanks to Sam, who beats a hasty retreat from the atmosphere surrounding Ava and me. 'I propose a business lunch. I have some suggestions and many questions I want answered.'

She shakes her head at my audacity.

Better get used to that, darlin'. When you make a deal with the devil, you can't complain if your fingers get burned.

'I don't eat lunch. And I too have questions. Like, where have you and your plans been for the past four months since I've taken over sole management? Why would I take guidance from you, a man who knows nothing about logistics? And why not sell to the prospective buyer right in front of you?'

'That's a lot of questions—let's address them over lunch.' Before she can reiterate that she doesn't eat lunch I add, 'You can watch me eat.'

'I never realised you were an asshole when we met.' She stares me down. 'The media fail to mention that side of your character.'

I smile, inching closer so she has to tilt her head back to keep her challenging eye contact.

'And yet you wanted this asshole between your thighs. In fact, you want me still.' It's time for her to realise I hold all the power, professionally and perhaps personally, too. I know I get to her. I made her tremble in my arms. I can exact revenge over her body while I plot the demise of both her company and Brent's.

'You're insane if you think that's happening again. Not now I know what you're really like…'

Her challenge brings forth my easy grin. I allow my stare to linger on her lush mouth. Her breaths are shallow. Her lips part. Her pupils go wide with arousal.

'We'll see about that,' I say, not above using our mutual attraction against her. I can punish her with sex for her crimes. Slake this desire for her until I've worked it out of my system, while we work together to offload her company. I can appease both my desire and my vengefulness.

Oh, yes, there'll be a reckoning. The only question is, her bed or mine?

CHAPTER FIVE

Sterling

OUTSIDE THE WAREHOUSE, I indicate she should follow me across the lot towards the Porsche. As I open the door for her, sparks of hostility and sexual heat surround us.

'Of course you drive this...' she mutters as she slips into the passenger seat.

I grin as I close the door of my customised gunmetal-grey Porsche 911 Cabriolet. I round the back of the car and slide in beside her, my body on high alert at her closeness. Now I've had the idea to settle the score, I want her again as soon as possible. I'd bet my share of Bold that I could render her helpless as I did on Friday. She may hate my favourite car, but she can't stop casting me longing looks.

'Where's good around here for lunch?' I ask, my finger poised over the GPS display.

She looks at me with scepticism, as if she can't

equate the man who makes her moan with the version who wants to sell her family's business.

'Heaps of places.' She shrugs. 'What do you want to eat?'

'Surprise me.' I drop my hand and she types in somewhere called Gianni's a few blocks away on Havenmeyer Street.

I cast her a look as I pull into traffic. 'So what do you have against my Porsche? What has she ever done to you?'

Ever since my first car, a 1984 Chevrolet El Camino, I've been hooked. I was sixteen when the trust from my father's family purchased the vehicle. For me, it signified more than a set of wheels. For the first time I had some independence. I could get away from Marcus and the control he wielded over my life, over the house and at times even over my mother. I could leave and just drive. Clear my head and feel light-hearted. It didn't matter where. Fortunately I had school friends who lived upstate whose parents often tolerated me for the weekend or holidays.

Ava rolls her eyes. 'It's not *this* car in particular. I'm not particularly fond of sports cars, period. And I prefer to use the subway in the city.' She shoots me a withering look, but I notice she can't seem to stop looking my way any more than I can ignore and forget her. My day, my week, my plans for the merger would be a lot easier if I could clear her from my consciousness.

'I see. In that case, I can't wait to show you the rest of my collection and convert you.' It's juvenile. Petty and adversarial. But I can't seem to move past my need for retribution. Starting with our chemistry. I'm going to enjoy every minute of her sensual punishment.

A very satisfactory way to make her pay for her subterfuge…

Ignoring my jibe, she clenches her hands in her lap and confronts me. 'You had suggestions? About Hamilton's.'

I should keep this business-focused instead of planning ways I can drive her wild.

Whether Hamilton's implements any changes or not, the writing is on the wall. Acquiring Brent's Express six months ago, having already owned equity in Hamilton's, gave me the idea to improve and then offload my stepfather's business. Now that Josh has enlisted Mom to emotionally blackmail back what he thinks should be his, the reminder that it's time to part with them couldn't be more timely. Soon Ava's company will be incorporated into something bigger and better—Lombard Logistics. Yes, that has a nice ring to it. Let the business world, Josh and Marcus—from the grave—see that Sterling Lombard can turn a profit where Marcus Brent failed.

I wave a dismissive hand. 'Just ideas for streamlining some of your operations. I have people, strategic advisors, who do that sort of thing very well—I'll send them in.'

Ava's eyes narrow. 'I'd be a fool to dismiss any form of cost-cutting measures. But *I'll* be the one to oversee any changes you plan on making. It's my name on the letterhead. I don't need you ploughing in after showing no interest in Hamilton's for years and changing everything my family has built.'

I concede with a tight grin, 'It's your name on the letterhead, *for now*. But you don't seem to be grasping the fact that from here on, I'm calling the shots.' I moisten my lips and watch with gratification as her stare follows the movement.

My comments, and perhaps the fact that she's still attracted to me, seem to once more ignite her ire, turning the bright blue of her astonishing eyes frosty. She glances out of the window, trying to bluff nonchalance.

'You are so arrogant.'

'Perhaps, but I'm good where it counts. Ask my ex-wife.' We stop at some lights and I take in her outraged reaction.

Her eyes roll at my brag. 'If you're so perfect, what made you a shitty husband?'

I bark out a humourless laugh. This woman is so good at pushing my buttons. 'Well, that's a whole other story… And this is a business lunch.'

The reminder that I'm a divorcee triggers guilty

memories of how I let Monroe down when she needed me most—when she was consumed with grief after her mother's death. I tried to keep Marcus out of my head during our marriage, but as pressures increased, so did his voice of doom. Monroe played her part too, holding back from me emotionally at a time when we should have pulled together.

I grit my teeth. I loved Monroe—and part of me always will. Except seeing her—like during my upcoming trip to London—will resurface my deep regrets that I wasn't a good enough husband to weather any storm. It sickens me that on that score, Marcus was right about me and my marriage.

I couldn't control the series of events that led to my divorce, but I can control everything else in my life.

Especially my business plans.

Ava's pupils dilate as her stare moves over my face. 'Okay, but there's more to business than making a profit,' she says, drawing me back to the hot topic.

I snort at her idealism. 'Maybe for you. But, as you pointed out, Hamilton's is small fry. For me the equity has become a means to an end.'

She gasps in outrage. 'Hamilton's is a part of local history. We employ two, sometimes three generations of the same Brooklyn families. We've been part of the landscape for sixty years.'

God, she's gorgeous when she's fired up. How I want to render her incoherent with arousal. To hear her beg for me and what I do to her. To know she may hate what I'm about when it comes to Hamilton's, but she craves my touch all the same.

I swallow, trying to keep my tone bored when all I want to do is drag that sultry mouth of hers to mine and kiss her senseless. 'Very noble, but completely irrelevant.'

Her lips press into a firm line. 'How can you be so…pig-headed? And cold? And…ruthless?'

Ignoring her insults, I take a left turn and slide into a parking space close to the restaurant. I kill the engine and lean close.

'I wasn't cold when you lost your mind in my bed. When you begged me to give you what you wanted.' I hear the revealing catch in her breath and watch her eyes widen, thick lashes batting as she tries to assimilate my nearness.

I want her begging for me once more, until she's fully at *my* mercy. Then we'll see how much *she* enjoys being manipulated.

'That was just sex.' Excitement darkens her eyes to almost navy.

I enjoy the effect I'm having on her pulse, which is fluttering in her neck. 'Well, any time you want to burn again, you know where to find me.'

'I'd rather freeze.' Her mouth says the words but I can feel the wall of heat generating between us across the centre console. If I'd pulled into a secluded alleyway instead of parking in a street, I know we'd be on each other in seconds—it's written in her eyes.

'Instinct tells me I'll have my revenge over your body sooner than you think,' I say. 'But if you prefer denial for now, so be it.' I watch her lips thin, remembering the taste of her and her wild, passionate responses.

'And what if I have my revenge over *your* body? You still want me, too.'

Her telling statement fills me with urgency, because she's not moving away or leaving. 'You're right, I do. I have every intention of slaking this compulsion until it's extinguished. Just let me know when you're ready to stop fighting it, and we can both get it out of our systems.'

Sheer hatred pours from her eyes, bathing me in renewed resolve. My physical weakness for her is manageable and the only weakness I'll allow.

We'll have our retribution, Ava and I. And only one of us can rise to victory. I put my money where I always put it: on me.

When, out of nowhere, she lunges for me, I'm momentarily blindsided. She grasps my neck and drags my mouth down to hers with an impatient mewl. I part my lips on a grunt, meeting her kiss with my own sensual assault, my tongue surging against hers, my hands cupping her face and my defiant stare locked with hers.

Testosterone roars through my blood, deafening me to all else. The disappointment I felt when I opened my eyes, searching for the woman who'd breezed into my life like a breath of fresh air. The familiar feeling of failure I felt when I discovered her identity and how she clearly had an ulterior motive for being at the Bold office party. And the vicious, helpless craving I still felt when her office door opened and I wanted her, despite it all.

But our desperate, angry kiss is short-lived. Ava pulls away first. She shoves at my chest so I release her, pressing her body into the door to get as far away as possible.

'Surely you have enough money,' she spits, returning to our argument, completely ignoring the fact she's just kissed me as if her life depends upon it. 'Why are you so intent on selling Hamilton's for a huge profit when you have an invested buyer right in front of you?'

Part of me of admires the hell out of her tenacity. She'd certainly get along like a house on fire with Monroe.

'Don't be naïve. Money is more than money—it's power. You can't ever have enough.' I straighten my tie and try to wrangle my heart rate and my arousal pressing at the fly of my pants back under control. 'It suits my purposes to offload Hamilton's. I own a similar company. Together they'll become an international contender.'

This time, my cruel smile and her answering outrage brings me no pleasure, presumably because my wanting her physically has eclipsed every other desire I possess. 'Besides, I'm not interested in being second best—didn't you discover that from the business news articles?'

Her ravaged mouth gapes. 'No. I assumed you had a scrap of integrity, that, by helping companies to grow, you cared about the little people like my grandparents. But now I see I was mistaken. You seem to care only about cars and cash.'

'And revenge. Don't forget revenge. Right now that's currently my most pressing priority.' I process her scathing character assessment, torn between wanting her and wanting to live up to her poor opinions of me.

'Well, I won't be any part of *that*.'

'Ah, but you will. As that kiss proves, you crave me, even as you spit fire and brimstone in my direction.'

Her breath comes in choppy pants. 'So? That doesn't mean I'll sleep with you again.' She swipes her hand across her beautiful mouth as if she can erase the memory of my kiss.

I smile, control returning like a comfort blanket. Everything is working out in my favour. I'll have Hamilton's, I'll annihilate Brent's and I'll exact my sensual retribution over Ava, if the way she's looking at me is confirmation.

In her case, revenge is best sampled between the sheets.

I lean close and lower my voice. 'We'll burn this explosive attraction out one way or another. Revenge sex isn't a bad way to do it.'

She shakes her head in disbelief. 'No. You're out to destroy everything my grandparents worked their entire lives for. I don't trust you one bit.'

My lip curls as renewed certainty fizzes in my veins. 'Who said anything about trust? Trust is for weaklings. Trust blinds people and I don't trust *anyone*, least of all a woman intent on manipulating me for her own ends.'

She huffs, but her tongue swipes her lips in a nervous gesture. 'Do your worst with my company if you must, but I won't watch from your bedroom.'

My coup de grace falls into the tense silence inside the vehicle. 'Oh, you'll be much closer than that. I know things about you, too. You know logistics. Your staff told me you learned the business from the cradle. You have the qualifications I need to advise me on the merger of what will become Lombard Logistics.'

Her blue eyes widen with dawning alarm. 'What do you mean?'

I drop my voice to an intimate whisper. 'If, as

you say, you're keen to avoid sleeping with me again, you'll have plenty of opportunity to display restraint—you're going to be working for me.'

CHAPTER SIX

Ava

THE BUCATINI DISH is sublime in its simplicity. I know the recipe is handed down from Gianni's nonna. The pasta, coated with the richness of a red pepper and sundried tomato sauce, and topped off with crunchy seasoned breadcrumbs, reminds me of happier times as a little girl.

Yet I can't enjoy a single forkful.

I'm still too turned on by the man across the table from me and too outraged by both my own body's betrayal and his outlandish statement in the car.

Work for him…? No way.

I pick up my fork and stab the tines into the pasta, while I watch him eat as if he hasn't a care in the world. How dare he be so composed after both the incendiary kiss we shared and after dropping such a ridiculous bombshell? The only reason I'm still here is that, now I understand his despicable intentions more clearly, I'm extra-desperate to procure those Hamilton's shares back from the man and take him down a peg or two in the process.

Nothing to do with how his suggestion of revenge sex has left you crazy horny and plotting ways to make him pay...?

Oh, he'll pay all right. *I'll* be the one making him beg...

I take a bite of pasta on autopilot, trying to detangle arousal from outrage.

That my grandparents sold a stake in their company to him in order to help me out financially leaves me unsettled, almost tearful. If I'd known, would I have studied for so many years? I assumed they could afford the luxury, or that they'd dipped into the money left to me by the sale of my parents' restaurant. Knowing they cared so much about my future and the future of Hamilton's only strengthens my resolve that it both succeed and carry the family name.

Then the delicious flavours caress my tongue again and I forget where I am and who I'm with, because I could be in my *nonna*'s kitchen or my parents' restaurant, surrounded by love and security and belonging.

A small involuntary moan leaves my lips as I chase the drop of rich sauce at the corner of my mouth with my tongue.

'I thought you didn't eat lunch,' Sterling says, reminding me that he's sitting opposite me at *my* table in *my* favourite Italian restaurant. I often eat my meal in the bustling kitchen with the chef and owner, Gianni. He was a friend of my parents, and I've known him my whole life.

Sterling's jaw is tight, as if he's gritting his teeth, and the way his eyes dip to my mouth every few seconds tells me he's distracted, too.

Time to wrestle back some control. Let the games begin.

I hide my smile and enjoy the power coursing through my system—the first time I've felt like myself since he walked into my office this morning. He's right—there's no avoiding our chemistry. That doesn't mean I can't play dirty.

'I don't usually eat lunch.' I swirl my fork through the pasta and raise it to my mouth. 'But this is the best Italian restaurant in the five boroughs. I know the chef. This recipe is a hundred years old.'

I take the mouthful inside slowly and deliberately. Keeping my stare locked to his, I chew, swallow and then run the tip of my tongue unapologetically over my bottom lip in a seductive swipe.

'Mmm… I haven't tasted anything so good since…hmm—' I tap my chin, pretending to think '—Friday night.' I shudder at the widening of his eyes.

Bingo.

I take a sip of Sicilian red wine, a small smile lifting my cheeks at the expression of lust on his face and the way he takes a pained swallow.

'How's your risotto?' I ask, adrenaline pumping through my veins at the ease with which I can I get to him physically. If only I could influence him professionally as easily. Isn't that what he accused me of?

Perhaps his ludicrous suggestion that I work for him has merits. I can stay close while I fight my corner for Hamilton's, and I can make him pay for his ruthlessness, render him as helpless as he's made me feel. In some ways, seducing him in that elevator has achieved exactly what I wanted—he's here, isn't he?

But I haven't gained everything I want, because Hamilton's still isn't mine. What if he won't sell me the stock back?

Panic dries my throat.

'The risotto is excellent.' He runs a finger inside his collar, clearly trying to claw back control of his body.

At least I'm not struggling with our chemistry alone. Only I'm here to quiz him, not fall into his seductive trap. If he thinks he's getting the upper hand, he's mistaken.

I'll have my revenge over your body.

Why did his assurance have such a profound

effect on my libido when my brain screamed at me to laugh in his face? Instead I returned the challenge, the promise, and then kissed him.

Good move, Ava.

'So you like Italian food?' His grim expression contradicts his benign question. Perhaps he can't believe he's having lunch with a woman he sees as an enemy. Perhaps he's still trying to conceal his arousal—he returned my kiss with that edge of dominance I expected. For a minute I thought we'd go all the way, right there in his convertible.

My guard rises at the personal slant to the small talk, but I offer some explanation. 'My grandmother was born in a village outside Genoa in northern Italy. My parents owned an Italian restaurant, so I grew up on simple dishes like this one.' I look down at my bowl, my brain awash with stark and painful memories. My first job in the restaurant was folding napkins and filling water bottles after school. With those skills perfected I progressed to table-laying and then fresh pasta-making with my mother. We'd hang the pasta to dry on wooden racks overhead. Some of my happiest moments, our most memorable conversations, happened under a canopy of spaghetti and linguini.

He nods, his green eyes searching mine. 'Sam, your warehouse foreman, told me about your parents. I'm sorry to hear that they died.'

'How indiscreet of him,' I mutter. I look away from his handsome face, reluctant to acknowledge the sincerity in his expression. It's easier to fight my attraction if I dismiss his principles.

Except the agony of his reminder is like a slap, momentarily seizing my breath as it has done intermittently for the past fourteen years. Contrary to popular belief, that pain never lessens. I've just grown used to dealing with it, shoving it down and keeping busy.

'He wasn't to know that we're enemies.' His tone is conciliatory, as if I'm delicate. 'To be honest, I had the impression that Sam is proud of you—he said he's known you since you were a chatty little girl in a hard hat.'

I can't help my twitch of a smile, remembering how I loved my red hat, which was emblazoned with the words 'The Real Boss.' Except Sterling knowing anything about me feels as if I'm conceding points, and he's already at an advantage.

Yes, I'm keeping score.

'My parents died a long time ago,' I say. I was another person. A person I knew. I had a promising and fulfilling life. Now I feel as if I'm treading water in an endless void, waiting for my real life to click back into place.

But how can it? The life to which I belonged, with my family, the restaurant, is gone for ever. Probably the reason I give my heart and soul to

Hamilton's. Would there be any Ava left without my company?

'How old were you?' He's still, watching me with rapt interest. My automatic answer dies on my lips, replaced by the taste of bitterness. I don't owe him a thing, least of all my confidences.

'Why should I tell you? We're not friends, we just spent the night together, and now you want to destroy my business.' I made myself vulnerable to him and this is how he repays me—with accusations, distrust and selfishness. 'At this stage I feel you could use any information against me.'

The corners of his mouth tug down. 'We spent *part* of the night together—you ran away once you'd got what you came for, remember? And I don't want to destroy anything. You'll be a very rich woman when I have my way.'

Frustration blasts from me in a sigh. Life isn't just about profit and self-interest. Sometimes it's about obligation, honouring departed family members, and belonging to something bigger than yourself.

I'm done being polite. 'I told you I *did* go to the party in the hopes of meeting you, but what happened after the elevator…that was all spontaneous and stupid. Believe me, if I could take it back, I would.'

Liar. Why would you take back the best sex of your life?

He looks mildly thrown by my admission, as if he's unwilling to cut me any slack. 'My father died when I was eight years old.' He shrugs one broad shoulder, his white shirt tugging across his defined chest. 'Now we're even. You know something about me, and I know something about you.'

The tightening of his mouth affirms the vulnerability he feels in the wake of his confession. It softens my resolve and I can't have that, so I look down at my now cold lunch. I don't want anything in common with this man beyond the incredible time we shared in the bedroom, although a part of me realises my instincts are geared to keeping me safe from feeling. If I give in to emotion I remember the past—no good comes of that.

I swallow a sip of water to ease my tight throat. 'I was fourteen.' My pulse thumps in my head.

Don't think about twisted metal. Flames engulfing the wreck. The idea that the 'died on impact' story was concocted to spare you the horror of them burning alive.

To my relief, just then, Gianni ambles out from the kitchen at the rear of the restaurant and heads our way, his face split in a warm grin of welcome. *'Ciao, Ava.* I didn't know you were coming in today.'

I'm engulfed in the comfort of Gianni's big bear hug, to which I willingly succumb. He smells like warm bread and Italian coffee—so reminiscent of my father I want to bury my face in his shirt and sob like a little girl who's scraped her knee.

Of course, I rally. 'I didn't know I'd be coming in today or I'd have asked you to save me some of your famous cannoli.' My warm smile slides from my face. 'I'm here for an impromptu business lunch.'

Sterling is already on his feet, so I'm forced to introduce them and then explain to Sterling, 'Gianni owns this restaurant. He and my parents were friends, so I've known him my whole life. His cannoli are the reason I need to jog.'

Sterling praises Gianni for the delicious lunch, once more the polite and affable man I met at Bold Tower. I can't un-see the other side of him now, the vengeful, ruthless side, so I look away to regroup my defences.

Gianni eyes me with speculation. He thinks this is a date—he's always trying to fix me up with one of his single sons. I clasp my hands together to prevent a tell-tale squirm advertising my discomfort. The sense of my worlds colliding this way—business and pleasure—makes my hairs stand on end. I need to get away from Sterling and analyse everything I've learned today. Work out what it means for me and formulate a new plan to salvage Hamilton's from his grasp.

I could never forgive myself if I lost my grandparents' business. One they built together, loved and made sacrifices for. Sacrifices for me and my education...

The sudden urge to go home and bake ciabatta takes hold. The kneading and patience involved usually helps to clear my head.

After a few minutes of small talk, Gianni shakes hands with Sterling. He kisses both my cheeks in farewell. 'I'll let you eat. Any time you want recipes or the best ingredients, you come to me, okay?'

When he heads back to the kitchen, I want to chase after him. To hide in the kitchen, chatting about food while we prep for dinner. I once dreamt about following Mom and Dad into the restaurant business. Until the age of fourteen it was all I'd known.

But I'm doing okay on my own. I just need to get Hamilton's back on track so I can recapture the sense of belonging, somehow. Because *I'm* a Hamilton. Of course I belong.

'So, back to business,' I say with renewed resolve as I retake my seat opposite Sterling. 'What did you mean earlier in the car about me working for you? I assumed you were joking. I already work sixty hours a week and you're the last man on earth I'd want for a boss.'

Sterling shrugs, his stare laced with defiant heat. 'I know how hard you work. I know a lot about you, Ava.'

The gravel in his deep voice leaves me convinced he's talking about my helpless physical response to him, not the contents of my résumé.

Infuriating man. He's so composed when, being at Gianni's, remembering Mum and Dad, fighting for Hamilton's, I feel as if I'm disintegrating. I ignore his attempt to get under my skin over the sex. 'You seem to think I'll be helping you to dismantle my family's legacy. Why the hell would I do that?'

He glances away, as if with reluctance. 'Hamilton's as it stands today is over, Ava.' A flash of regret dulls his green eyes. 'The sooner you accept that, the better.'

A red mist clouds my peripheral vision. I've just confided in him about losing my parents as a kid. He already knows that I recently lost my grandparents, too. And I confessed earlier that Hamilton's is my life.

How ruthless can a person be to dismiss all of that because it doesn't fit with his selfish plans? Has he no compassion or tact or humanity at all?

He opens his hands, palms up, in a reasonable gesture. 'You can either work with me and influence the direction of the merger and the formation of Lombard Logistics, which, by the way, is my proposal and preference. It's in your interests too. Or you can step aside and simply collect your cheque when the sale goes through.' He raises his glass of wine as if offering a toast to the brilliance of his destructive and unyielding plan.

'You really have no heart, do you?' I knew he was cut-throat, but this is next-level coldness.

He touches the knot in his immaculately straight tie. 'When it comes to business and getting what I want, you're correct—I have no heart.' He leans close, resting his forearms on the table and piercing me with his cool stare. 'I learned from a young age that sentiment makes you vulnerable to attack. You helped me to remember those formative lessons the night you left without declaring your true intentions. So, thank you.'

The violent pang of curiosity and compassion his statement elicits is overwhelmed by the violence of my indignity. It's easier to indulge the animosity and undiluted resentment in my head than wonder what's shaped him to be so callous and self-serving.

His sinful mouth lifts in a small, victorious smile that leaves me more determined than ever to best this billionaire. 'What's it to be, Ava? Are you in or out? Are you tendering your resignation from Hamilton's, effective immediately? Or can I expect you at Bold tomorrow, bright and early, for a strategy meeting?'

My blood boils. Hateful, soulless man. He has me exactly where he wants me. The best I can hope for is that working alongside him will afford me an opportunity to reverse the power imbalance and fight my corner for Hamilton's.

I'm not above using seduction if I have to—he already thinks me capable of such underhanded tactics.

'I'm in,' I say before finishing my wine. Right now, I want my company more than I want this man out of my sight. As for my body, I can use that to punish him in return. If I'm going down in the flames we lit on Friday, he's coming with me.

CHAPTER SEVEN

Ava

I'M POWER-DRESSED FOR battle in a fitted powder-
blue dress, matching jacket and my favourite killer
heels. I arrive at Bold early the next morning. Out-
manoeuvring Sterling Lombard requires me to be
on my game, but, thanks to a restless night, where I
dreamed about green eyes slashed with both desire
and detachment, I'm far from well rested.

The body wants what the body wants. Unfor-
tunately for me that's the man in my professional
sights. But I can control our chemistry the way he
plans to: with revenge seduction.

Sterling's friendly and efficient assistant, Todd,
ushers me straight into his light-filled office. The
first thing my eyes land on is the magnificent
man himself. He's dressed in another fine suit.
His sandy hair is brushed back from his face with
the exception of that one stubborn lock that refuses

to be tamed, which hangs over his eye. My fingers tingle. I remember how that lock of hair felt between them, how his eyes darkened to the colour of the ocean in a storm when I held his face as a prelude to our kiss.

My gaze darts to the sofa—the place all my troubles began. Despite the mess in which I landed myself, my core clenches with the memories—delicious Bourbon, reckless kissing, a tour of his private bedroom.

Chills douse me. A seismic shift happened in this office. Meeting Sterling has thrown my professional existence into turmoil.

I've also never felt so...alive.

'Ava,' he says, his hand engulfing mine in a perfectly businesslike shake that shunts my heart rate skywards as if he's touched me intimately.

'I thought you might bail out on me this morning.' Humour twitches his decadent lips. 'I'm glad to see you're not that easily rattled.'

To the dismay of my lady parts, he drops my hand and smooths his grey tie over his flat abdomen. 'Please, take a seat.'

I follow him to the conference table in front of the window, and my legs tremble as if my body has muscle memory of the intense pleasure and unexpected connection that happened in this office. I shudder, both wishing away and welcoming my uncontrollable reaction to him—tingling nipples, pooling pelvic heat and a frenzied pulse.

I've been in his company less than a minute and already I'm a contradiction of desire and dislike.

'I'm here because Hamilton's is everything to me—nothing to do with assisting your nefarious plans, believe me.' I swallow, stating my business the way I wish I'd done in the elevator at our first meeting. Then none of this would have happened. Because I'm certain he's digging in his heels over Hamilton's in response to the way he thinks I manipulated him.

So appeal to his integrity and business acumen.

He chuckles and pours two glasses of water, and then takes the seat at right angles to mine. 'I admire the fact that you're so plain-talking and driven.' He leans back in his chair, perfectly comfortable in his domain.

Why shouldn't he be comfortable? He thinks he has things exactly how he wants them. I should've insisted we meet at *my* office, so that I could have the psychological upper hand.

I try my best to look equally calm and collected as I cross my legs.

His stare, which flicks to the movement for a gratifying split second, feels hot and heavy.

'If we'd met under other circumstances, I think we could have been good friends, Ava.' His voice handles the words *friends* the way he growled against my pussy when I came.

Nothing friendly about that. But oh, so addictively memorable.

'You don't know me,' I snap with frustrating petulance. He just knows which of my buttons to push...

'I know enough,' he quips. 'I know that you're passionate about Italian food. It lights you up, making those startling blue eyes of yours shine like diamonds.'

'Well, fortunately for me, I have enough friends without *you*. What I don't have is sole proprietorship of my company.'

'Ah, Ava, Ava... Stop making me respect you—it's messing with my evil plans.' The look he shoots me is pure sin.

I look away from the challenge and appreciation gleaming in his eyes as he moves his stare over my face. 'If you respected me, my wishes and my appeal to your integrity, I wouldn't be here listening to how you plan to destroy everything I love. I'd be in Brooklyn running my company without your interference. Let's get down to business, shall we? I need to be back in my office in ninety minutes.'

I slide my phone onto the table so he sees the timer ticking down the minutes I've allocated to this meeting. It may be his turf, but I'm in control.

Rather than open the laptop in front of him, he rests his elbow on the arm of his chair, strokes his clean-shaven chin with his capable fingers and watches me in silence from narrowed eyes.

'I hope being here doesn't make you uncomfortable.' He waves a hand in the direction of the sofa, and the bedroom door beyond.

Bastard.

'Not at all,' I lie, shivering as those currents of longing shift through my limbs. How dare he be so in tune with my body? How dare he be the kind of lover who's hard to forget? How dare he plant seeds of glorious retribution sex in my mind and then stand back and watch the fruits of his labour bloom in me?

'Okay. First item on the agenda,' he says, still pinning me with that sexy stare. 'Are you free tonight?'

I splutter, flushing hot and then cold. 'You *can't* be serious.'

He shrugs his wide shoulders. 'And yet I am.'

My breath gusts and my nipples tingle at his bossy tone.

'It's just a business dinner, Ava. Surely you've had one of those before.' His eyebrows lift. 'Unless you're worried you might kiss me again? Go too far this time?'

Come for me again, beautiful Ava.

Oh, help me, yes...

Stop. He's destroying my livelihood and all I can think about is sex.

'No—dinner is off the table.' I lift my chin, meeting the challenge of his stare with my own. 'Whatever business we have we can discuss now.'

I push my hair over one shoulder and glance pointedly at the display of diminishing minutes on my phone. With any other businessman I wouldn't hesitate to conduct meetings after hours. But yesterday, him walking into my office changed everything.

'Why so nervous? Afraid to be alone with me?'

'Just because I have no choice other than to watch you like a hawk and keep an eye on my company, doesn't mean we're dating. We're not even fucking.'

'Not right now, no. Although the desk is sturdy if you want to change that.' His expression drips sarcasm and seduction—an impressive combination to pull off.

'Maybe I do,' I say, taunting him back. I want to kiss him and bite his full lower lip until he hisses.

He smiles but there's ice lurking in his stare.

'Item two,' I say, my tone clipped as I cling to my frazzled composure. 'I need the details of the other companies in your proposed merger.'

'I'm glad you brought that up.' He issues another satisfied smile. 'You'll need to accompany me on an overnight business trip to Chicago. The logistics facility I own there, Brent's Express, is similar to Hamilton's. I'd like you to compile a report for the merger—areas where the companies overlap with or complement each other and how I can trim away any fat once I take them national.' He slides a document folder my way. 'Brent's Express company prospectus—basic facts, statistics, sales projections et cetera. I prefer not to lay off too many staff, so if you can suggest other efficiencies once you've visited the site, we can avoid the pain of redundancies.'

My head spins at the abrupt shift he takes from adversary to colleague. That he's thinking about how his plans impact the current employees of both Hamilton's and this Chicago-based firm casts my assertions into doubt. Maybe he's not the total asshole I want to believe he is. Maybe he cares about the merger beyond the money he'll make.

That doesn't change the fact that I want Hamilton's back.

Reluctant to allow him any concession, I flip open the file in silence. Aside from a glossy prospectus, it contains a travel itinerary and hotel reservation.

'This itinerary is for tomorrow...' I'm aware my mouth is hanging open.

He nods. 'Todd checked with your assistant, Judy. Your schedule is clear. If it's not convenient for personal reasons, we can postpone, but the sooner we get things underway the better, I think. I'm sure that prolonging this…this professional association unnecessarily benefits neither of us.'

His statement shouldn't sting. It's only what I've told myself—I can't wait for him to be a part of my past—but I'm insulted just the same. 'No. You're right. How very efficient of you.' That he can seemingly overcome the sexual undercurrents and focus on work leaves me irritable and ready to slap myself in the hopes I'll snap out of the sensual spell being near him casts.

'So, agenda item three—how I see Hamilton's featuring in the new company.' He opens his laptop. 'Let's discuss it.'

We spend the rest of the hour going through the strengths and weaknesses of my company and what changes are required to bring Hamilton's in line with the other companies he owns—Brent's Express and a shipping company called SeaFreight.

Begrudgingly I see his vision. The amalgamation and subsequent cost-cutting will make the new company an attractive proposition to potential buyers. But that's not what I want. A large, slick, corporate operation isn't the business my grandparents founded. Hamilton's strengths lie in our ability to deal with the one-off and unusual solutions. The company began with the shipping of a delicate grand piano that belonged to Nonna from Italy.

'All Hamilton's really needs is some updated software which will allow us to link into national carriers and expand our services to other states.' I offer a solution, outline the benefits to both of us for turning Hamilton's profitable once more without cutting and pasting it into his grand plan. If he won't sell me his stock, perhaps I can persuade him it's a lucrative option to keep the company we co-own in his portfolio.

'Perhaps you'd be right, if that was my only consideration.' His gaze flits and I make a note to ascertain the other factors.

'I'm not naïve,' I press on, taking advantage of his concession and the fact I'm back in his office, this time with my clothes on. 'I can see how your amalgamation plans will have manifold cost-cutting benefits, greater leverage with national freight companies and even cut out the middle man to a degree.'

He nods, his eyes showing a glimmer of appreciation that I'd normally find flattering. After all, he's a world-class businessman.

'Bold invests in a number of freight-carrying and freight-forwarding companies. I can broker a beneficial deal for the new owner of Lombard Logistics that makes this an even more attractive purchase. If you're trying to talk me out of it, you're doing the opposite. You're smart, Ava. You can see how this benefits us both in the long run.'

How am I making this worse? 'Except for me it's personal.'

'Who says it's not personal to me?' His stare narrows.

He hinted at this yesterday but didn't elaborate. 'How?' There's clearly more than good business motivating him.

'Turning struggling companies profitable once more is why I love my job. Isn't that enough of a reason?'

Still evasive...

'If I only cared about profit alone...' I mutter. Eight months ago, with both of my grandparents still alive, I might have been on board with his plan. I'd have probably tried to persuade Nonna and Pops to sell Hamilton's. It's been limping along for a while. The glory years under my grandparents are long gone. When Pops developed Parkinson's two years ago and had to drastically cut back on his hours, I did what I could to compensate, but some previously loyal customers couldn't stomach the change of leader and deserted us.

I sigh, defeated. If only there were a few more hours in the day, I could work harder to rescue Hamilton's without Sterling's help. There's nothing to stop me implementing the same changes he's proposing alone, for the benefit of Hamilton's only. But without the controlling stake, he can sell it regardless, so what's the point in sinking my personal savings, my time and my energy into Hamilton's, only for it to feature in his…corporate yard sale?

'Listen, I'm in no doubt of your professional credentials,' I say. 'The whole world knows you're good at what you do—making money. But this is more than a job to me. Most of our staff have been with us for decades. It's an extended family of sorts.'

Or maybe that's simply how you feel because without Hamilton's you'd be truly alone… Because you have nothing else in your life. Too scared to chase a relationship because it makes you aware of what you've lost. Clinging to the past, because you're somehow emotionally stuck at the age you were when your parents died.

The vile voice in my head also warns me not to get my hopes up. 'But my loyal staff aren't enough to dissuade you from your course of action, are they?' My voice is flat. I already know the answer from his guarded expression.

'No, I'm afraid not.' His stare carries definite regret. What kind of personal reasons are stopping him from abandoning his plans?

'You still want to punish me for Friday, don't you?' I was foolish to think I could influence him with sound business sense. Thinking I had a shot to convince him with my insider knowledge, passion and sentiment. I should have known better— for a man like him, feelings and emotions don't enter the boardroom.

He glances at my phone and sighs. 'It's less about you and more about me, Ava, but I can see why you think I'm an asshole.'

If only I *could* relegate him to the asshole category. Dismiss him and take the moral high ground. But our physical connection—the generous, impassioned, playful side of him I saw the night we met—and the rare glimpses of intriguing complexity he reveals when his barriers lower hold me back.

He's like sugar: bad but so addictive.

'I think you consider I've wronged you and you want me to pay.' How could I have been so stupid and trusting? 'You probably invited me here just to toy with me.' Another notch on his belt.

I should tell him to stick his merger and his equity and walk away. Only, while there's a spark between us there's still a chance I might be wrong about him. That he might change his mind and see that some businesses are about people, not profits.

That's especially true of Hamilton's.

'Rest assured,' he says, his hard eyes glittering, 'I have very sound reasons for selling these companies.' Chills break out over my bare arms at the look he shoots me—both hostility and heat that reminds me of every touch we shared. 'And if I wanted to punish you for Friday, you'd be naked and coming by now.'

As if his words have lit a touch paper, my despicable body goes up in flames.

He closes his laptop and stands, signalling that the discussion is over.

I rise too, feeling dismissed and horny and furious that the two emotions can exist in me at the same time.

But one feeling overrides all others. I want my punishment and I want to punish him in return. For casting doubt over the future of Hamilton's. For showing me just enough of his good qualities to make me question the bad. For making me crave him while I bemoan that we ever met.

He escorts me to the door and holds out my jacket. How easily he can switch on the charm and control our chemistry, when it's eating me alive and spitting out the bones. How effortlessly he can look at me as if he's remembering how perfectly we complemented each other in bed, even while he maintains his hard line over Hamilton's.

I turn my back on him, sliding first one arm and then the other into the sleeves, my heart galloping that we're this close but not locked together with the passion I know we can ignite.

The heat from his body scalds my back. His spicy cologne floods my senses. His breath brushes the hair at the back of my head.

I freeze, my physical needs stilling every part of me but the thundering of my heart. Liquid heat gathers between my legs. If he wanted me now I wouldn't stop him, heaven help me.

When I can take no more of the escalating tension, I spin around and he's right there. We're face to face, chest to chest. I look up into those green eyes of his and feel his minty breath mingle with mine.

'Ava,' he says, holding out his hand as if in conclusion to any other meeting. He's so calm, whereas I'm a wreck: conflicted and inflamed.

I shake his hand, my palm sparking against his. My toes curl in my shoes.

One heartbeat.

Two...

With a curse under his breath, he scoops one strong arm around my waist. In two quick paces I'm crowded up against the door. My fingers spear his hair as his mouth claims mine. He groans, transmitting his desperation through the glide of his lips and the thrust of his tongue.

Triumph sings through my every nerve. Despite the passing of another day, he's no more in control of this than I am.

The kiss, which has been brewing since our

last one in his Porsche yesterday, consumes me. My mind clears of worry, frustration and doubt. There's only room in my head for Sterling and this reckless, defiant desire that won't be silenced.

I moan into his mouth, hiking my dress up my legs so his thigh slots home against my core, providing the friction I need. His hand replaces his thigh, and his fingers slide past my underwear and slip easily inside me. I'm so wet for him.

He tears his mouth from mine. 'Fuck…' He presses his forehead to mine, panting as if he too is trying to come to terms with the contradictory feelings of desire and animosity.

'This doesn't mean I like you,' I gulp, yanking his hips close by tugging the belt loops of his trousers.

'You like me good enough. You're soaking.' He braces one hand on the door above my head and looks down, fire in his eyes as he works his other hand between my thighs. His thumb circles my clit and my legs buckle.

'Do you like that?' he asks with a self-assured grin.

'No.' I spread my thighs, giving him better access while I cling to his corded arms to stop myself becoming a puddle on the floor.

'Liar.'

Our stares lock, challenge blazing between us in hot arcs like those from a welder's torch.

'Just because our bodies crave pleasure,' I palm his erection to make my point, 'doesn't mean we have to like the person delivering it.'

'Lift your dress higher,' he orders without denial.

I obey, both his willing pawn and his fierce opponent.

He drops to his knees and shoves my panties aside. I look down. My legs tremble at the look of furious lust slashed across his face.

'This is for leaving me hard and alone in my bed the other night,' he says, his voice low but tinged with malice.

He keeps his fingers inside me and covers my clit with his mouth. I gasp at the first decimating touch. I bite the back of my hand to stifle my cries, aware of voices in the reception area beyond the door.

He pulls back, triumph glittering in his eyes when I whimper out my dismay.

'Keep up those pleading noises and you'll get what you want.' He flicks at my clit with the tip of his tongue.

'Bastard. I hate you.' I spear my fingers into his hair and twist with just enough pressure to dictate the angle of his head. Not once do Sterling's eyes leave mine as he sucks me. His fingers plunging in and out are a poor substitute for his glorious cock, but effective all the same. He's enjoying my torture. High on the pleasure I couldn't hold inside if the building started to crumble around us. Momentary awareness of the timer on my phone and the alarm about to signal the conclusion of our meeting floods me with urgency. I'm desperate for him to finish my punishment, but I'll repay him in kind.

A disembodied voice I recognise as Todd's breaks the silence.

'Mr Lombard—your ten am is here, sir.'

The wave of delirium suspending me falters. My eyes plead with Sterling.

So close… So, so close…

He doubles his efforts. A low groan rumbles up from his chest as he senses my imminent explosion.

The last thing I see before my climax snatches me and deposits me on the ceiling is his victorious smile.

When it's over, when reality creeps back into the room, he rights my underwear, tugs down my dress and strides to his desk.

'Just a minute, Todd. Ms Hamilton and I are almost done.' He speaks to his assistant as if nothing has happened, as if I'm not leaning up against the door breathing hard and seeing stars. As if he isn't nursing a massive hard-on.

He casts me a look—part satisfaction, part regret, because he's the one who'll have to continue his next appointment unfulfilled.

Yet I feel like I'll never find all of my scattered pieces. I'm so discombobulated, my orgasm so powerful, I'm reeling. How can someone I should hate get to me so thoroughly? Know my desires so well? It makes no sense.

I need to leave, to walk out of here with my wobbly legs and my confusion and my questions. I swallow and run a hand through my hair, finding my balance without assistance from the door.

He's already putting himself back together, his tie straight and his arousal diminishing. It seems he was right: the only way to get through this period of professional discord, to see who'll come out on top, is to embrace that we're temporarily in each other's blood.

But I can't leave him thinking he has the upper hand. I need to remind him that I'll fight for Hamilton's until the end.

'One last question?' I say in an impressively normal voice, as if that incredibly hot few minutes hadn't happened. 'Ahead of our visit to Chicago tomorrow?' I wave the folder on Brent's Express at him.

'Okay.' His expression is once more closed and cagey, and part of me aches for the return of his passion.

'Why not offload this merger onto someone who works for you? Bring in a firm of consultants to slash through the redundancies, streamline, rebrand

and then sell.' I need to understand why this deal is so personal to him. He says he wants my report, but he seems to be doing all the work.

'You should know by now that I'm a man who enjoys a front-row seat when it comes to getting my own back.'

My heart gallops. Is he talking about the deal or what he's just done to me?

'I'll take great pleasure in watching Brent's benefit from Bold's Midas touch.' He slips on his suit jacket and adjusts the collar. 'I know you would deny me that pleasure, Ava. But there's no way out of this situation where we both get what we want, at least not professionally.' He arches one brow, a wry smile tugging at his mouth as he takes in what is no doubt my post-orgasmic dishevelment.

'Ah, yes,' I say, my tone caustic, 'a steamy fling will soften the blow of me losing my beloved company.'

He deflects my sarcasm with a shrug. But he's shown me a tiny chink in his armour and, just like him, I intend to use any weakness I can identify. 'You still haven't told me why.'

His mouth tightens, his beautiful eyes darkening to stormy. 'Because in the past, the man I bought Brent's Express from, the same man who once tried to wrangle Hamilton's from your grandparents at a bargain price, thought I'd amount to nothing.'

So it *is* revenge motivating his plans for Hamilton's. Just revenge over someone else, not me.

His malicious grin gives me goosebumps. 'I'd say he misjudged me, wouldn't you?'

CHAPTER EIGHT

Ava

A JOLT OF turbulence rocks Bold's private jet, snatching me reluctantly away from potent memories of yesterday. Memories of the annihilating orgasm in Sterling's office and my body's bitter betrayal. I glance Sterling's way, an involuntary scowl tugging down my mouth in answer to the knowing grin on his handsome, self-satisfied face.

I spent the rest of the day working like a demon, hoping for some reprieve from the constant mental lure of his uncompromising masculinity and the weakness of my thoughts. But the remission was brief. I arrived at JFK this morning for the ninety-minute flight to Chicago, to find a fresh and energised-looking Sterling waiting inside the luxurious company jet. His roguish grin of welcome and a huskily murmured, 'Nice to see you again,' made my core pulse with renewed need.

But today is about business. I won't waste my opportunity to evaluate Brent's Express, finding every flaw I can in order to disrupt Sterling's plans for Hamilton's.

Looking away from the man who dominates my thoughts, both wakeful and dreamt, I glance to the rear of the plane. The aircraft is outfitted with white leather sofas and thick grey carpet underfoot. It also boasts a media room and master bedroom—I'm fantasising about using that bedroom to wrestle back some power. For every time he dismantles me, I can ensure I torture him in return. I may not be able to control his business plans, but I can certainly avenge every orgasm he metes out.

Aside from using my desires against me, he's using Hamilton's to further his revenge over some man I've never heard of. It would be so much easier to walk away from him. To throw up my hands and concede to him over my business and regain my peace of mind, but there's still hope in me that I can change his plans.

It's not over till it's over. If I thought it would help, I'd show him exactly what the company means to me. But that would involve opening up and being vulnerable with him again, and that didn't work out so well for me last time…

I must make some sort of noise, perhaps a sigh at how I'm going to extricate myself from this pig-headed man's lure, because he looks over sharply.

'Are you thinking about me?' His stare is intense in that way that tells me he, too, is thinking about the conclusion to yesterday's meeting.

'There's nothing to think about. You're just an acquaintance I'll forget the minute I have Hamilton's back.'

'You tell yourself that if it helps you to keep your attraction for me in check.' He grins at my attempt to fool myself. 'But I think you'll struggle—we have plenty in common.'

'Such as mutual dislike?' I snap, clinging to the edge of remembered ecstasy. He'll get no concessions from me.

He smiles a conniving smile. 'And explosive chemistry.'

'Professional distrust,' I volley.

He's just as quick. 'An insatiable inability to keep our hands off each other.'

I look away for composure, trying to dismiss the urge to undo my seatbelt and his fly and render him speechless. 'If you must know, I was thinking about this company you own—Brent's Express...' I lie, changing the subject and dousing the flames between us.

'Ah, yes...' He accepts the shift in conversation. 'The man you're meeting is named Vic Matheson. He's been the manager there for years. The previous owner ran the business remotely from New York, so Vic will show you around the facility. You have the authority to observe anything you want. Full access to any information. You can also interview any member of staff. Understand?'

I nod, confusion tugging my mouth into a frown. 'Won't you be there?' I assumed his Bold business included accompanying me to Brent's.

Regret and something else—hesitation or vulnerability—cause his eyes to flick away from mine. 'No—I have other work to do.' He looks out of the small window beside him as the pilot announces the start of our descent into Midway Airport.

'Okay...' I conceal my puzzling disappointment. Since when do I need his presence every minute of the day?

Since he became a full-blown addiction, that's when.

'You're giving me an awful lot of power for an arch enemy...' I wonder what it is about this company that prods at his defences. In contrast to the supremely assured, confident and guarded Sterling, his flashes of humanity are messing with my head. 'I thought you didn't trust anyone,' I say. A pretty cynical standpoint I'd also like to get to the bottom of.

My temples throb with tension—I'm in way too deep. He's selling my company out from under my nose. He's even got me helping him to do it. Yet

I'm intrigued and want to know more about what has shaped him and what makes him tick.

He smiles. 'I trust your opinion in the logistics field, that's all.'

His admission leaves me restless, even though I don't trust him in return. I may crave him but he remains enemy number one.

Sterling continues, 'Brent's has been left to stagnate in recent years. The former owner—'

'A man you detest,' I interject.

His smile is brittle. 'He pitted himself as a savvy businessman, but he cared only for profits.' His caginess has returned, his eyes turning hard. 'I'm certain you'll find plenty of room for improvement, although Vic has done his best as manager.'

My hairs stand to attention. What isn't he telling me? His interest in a company *left to stagnate* makes no sense. From those *Secrets of My Success* articles, in which he regularly features, I know him to be an astute and driven investor.

'How long have you owned Brent's?' I ask. I don't want Hamilton's dragged down by association with a neglected business. My grandparents were well-respected in New York and I've done everything in my power to maintain Hamilton's good standing.

'Six months.' A muscle ticks in his jaw. He doesn't want to talk about this acquisition, which

doesn't sound like one of Bold's usual winners—
poised on the cusp of global success. But what
if his golden touch fails? What if all he achieves
with his revenge over Brent's past owner is to
ruin Hamilton's too? I won't watch everything
my grandparents loved, everything I've worked
my entire adult life for, disintegrate.

This is my livelihood.

'I don't understand. You're shrewd and have an
uncanny knack for spotting a company on the way
up. It doesn't sound like the usual high-return investment you're renowned for.'

He watches me, something admiring shifting
through his expression. 'With the rebrand, with
my name above the door, I'll clear all of the rot
allowed by my predecessor.' Those devastating
lips of his flatten into a telling line. I feel his animosity for this man and it makes our spat feel
like a misunderstanding, which is exactly how
it began.

'Why buy the company at all if it's in such bad
shape?' Why would a composed businessman of
his calibre allow feelings to influence this deal?

His smile turns cold. I'm reminded of the day
he stormed into my office with accusation and
revenge on his mind. It's the same ruthless determination he applied to pleasuring me against the
door yesterday.

'It was more of a personal conquest than a

professional investment. I've told you that the original owner underestimated me. I saw an opportunity to snatch up his company when he was desperate to sell and I took it. I knew the day would come when I could improve on the way he'd left it, tenfold.'

'So you bought his company for no other reason than to exact your revenge and prove him wrong?' And now Hamilton's is caught up in the crossfire.

'You may not understand my motivations, but I assure you I have very good grounds—the man not only neglected his company and his staff but was also a bully. An emotional manipulator who used other people's weaknesses to serve his own interests and feel good about himself. He deserved everything he got.'

My brows pinch together as I stare at this vengeful stranger I'm struggling to equate with the passionate and considerate lover I've experienced—even as I acknowledge distress that my grandparents might have fallen foul of the calculating man he's describing.

'I see…' About as clearly as peering through molasses. But I'm more desperate than ever to extricate Hamilton's from his grasp. His motivation for this merger is deeply personal. It's hard to be rational and objective when that degree of emotion is involved. I know—it's how I feel about Hamilton's, as if I can't exist if my company is no more.

As the plane continues its decent, Sterling takes a business call, terminating the unsettling conversation that leaves me with more questions than answers, but also filled with new resolve. I can't let my family down.

Sudden crushing loneliness descends on me, squeezing the air from my lungs as if the cabin has become depressurised.

I lost so much when I lost my parents, including my sense of direction. I was angry and withdrawn for most of my teens. I spent my free time locked away in my room. I refused to talk about my feelings to the two people who loved me and had taken me in. I even started skipping school until my grades suffered and I woke up to the fact that I could repay them by working at Hamilton's. I owe my grandparents everything, especially the fight to save their company.

Inside the car that collects us from the airport, I follow Sterling's lead and sink into silent reflection. We're complex beings, caught somewhere between lovers and enemies. I want to resent him and punish him and dismiss him, but the longer I know him and witness his struggle with his own demons, the farther away that possibility seems to slip.

While I tour the facilities at Brent's, Sterling is constantly on my mind. And it seems I'm on his, if his texts are any indication:

I'm sorry I'm not there with you—I hope you've been made welcome.

And then later:

I appreciate your help with this, despite everything.

I suspect that's as close to an apology as I'll get from him over his wild accusations and over Hamilton's. Not that I've given up the battle. In comparison to Brent's, Hamilton's is positively prosperous. Staff morale here is low, the warehousing needs a total overhaul and Vic, who's knowledgeable and motivated, tells me that they've lost three major clients this month alone. Brent's software is outdated, and they're losing money at an alarming rate, according to the firm accountant I talk to over lunch. That's the reason, I discover, that Sterling has been personally bankrolling staff salaries and operations since he bought the company six months ago.

By the time I make it back to the hotel I'm exhausted and full of questions that not even a long hot shower can expel.

With my hair freshly blow-dried and my body encased in a hotel robe, I pour a glass of wine, plagued by doubts. Seeing what bad shape Brent's Express is in has made me fearful for the future of *my* company. What if I can't turn Hamilton's around alone? With poor management and no one to help make a success of it, I could just as easily lose the loyalty of my staff and lose clients.

The desolate loneliness of earlier returns as I toy with the stem of my wineglass. As if to taunt me, memories of happy times with my parents rush in. They always feature cooking, which was a huge part of our lives before the accident. The three of us together in the kitchen. Laughter. Favourite recipes that felt like home. Working together to make their dream, their restaurant, a success.

In the years following my parents' death, without their guiding influence, I was convinced that nothing would ever be the same again. I abandoned my childhood dreams of one day working in the restaurant full time and merely existed, putting one foot in front of the other, breathing in and breathing out, going through the motions of studying and college and work in order to steer my mind away from actually having to think about my happiness, and my personal goals.

What if Sterling doesn't have a change of heart over Hamilton's? You'd be free to pursue a different dream.

While that seems more attractive than the colossal battle to save Hamilton's, I can't think about that possibility right now. The ramifications of losing my company feel too enormous.

The walls of my hotel room start to close in.

An oppressive ache rumbles behind my sternum. I reach for my phone, my paramount thought of the man I can't seem to forget even as an adversary.

The visit went well. The staff were very accommodating. I hope you've had a productive day.

I send Sterling the decoy text, my fingers trembling with the force of how badly I want to see him. How can that be? How can I become lost in his sea-green eyes when I've no idea what he's thinking or planning, but I'm certain I wouldn't like it? How can I want to spend time with him, even though I'm equally consumed by ways to professionally outmanoeuvre him?

I swallow a sip of wine in disgust, hating that I want him physically as much as I did the first time we met, or perhaps more... As much as I wish my grandparents and I had never met him, I know this lost feeling will dissolve the minute he touches me. Despite myself and my body's betrayal, I'll forget I'm treading water. My mind will clear for a few blissful seconds of pleasure before reality comes crashing back down on me.

How can I be so conflicted? How can I be so disloyal to my family? Why can't I just walk away from him?

Because the fight for Hamilton's is all caught up in your physical relationship.

Yes, I'm letting him get close, but it's necessary for the fight. And I'll keep fighting. I'll make him pay for his secrecy and his agenda and for seducing me.

A knock at the door shunts my already excited pulse to a gallop. I use the peephole. Finding Sterling on the other side of the door, I press my forehead to the cool wood and exhale a long breath of preparation. I can try to resist him. Demand answers to my questions. But I already know my weakness for him will win. Temporarily.

I swing open the door, trying to conceal my excitement. He's dressed down in denims and a T-shirt, his dishevelled hair damp from a shower. My fingers twitch to grab him and haul him inside.

When we lock eyes, his stormy green stare is haunted.

Something lurches inside me. Compassion? Understanding? Need? All I know is that nothing is as it seems on the surface. For either of us.

'Invite me in?' He frames it as a question but there's enough command in his voice that I know he too is battling demons tonight. Is it the man he hates? I shouldn't care. Losing my parents has made me wary of my interactions with others, never getting too close. But Sterling and I are linked in this inescapable fight to the end, and, as he said, only one of us can win.

I open the door wider, inviting him in. Wave after wave of physical longing buffets my system—my lips buzz for his kiss, my nipples tingle for his touch and I ache between my legs.

But I want to dismantle *him* more.

'It's been a long day.' I raise my glass of wine in explanation. 'Want one?' I hope he can't hear the tremble in my voice betraying my need.

He prowls inside, all caged energy. The intense chemistry that is our norm swirls around us like tendrils of smoke.

'Please.' He nods, his face taut and his eyes unreadable.

I pour him a drink. Our fingers brush as he takes the offering. My tiny gasp ricochets around the silent room. My game plan dissipates in the face of my desire for him.

'You look…agitated. Bad day?' I ask. If I don't say something I'm going to tear at his clothes and selfishly demand he make me forget my own worries.

He takes a swallow of wine, his eyes fixed on mine over the rim of the glass. But it's not hostility or distrust I see there. It's turmoil. It shifts something inside me, something new and fragile.

'Are we becoming friends now, Ava?' His deceptively calm voice—deep and with a steely edge—makes my blood rush and my skin heat the way it did when he ran his hands over my naked body our first time.

I shrug, feeling desperate and uncertain all at once. 'I don't know what we are—' I confess the truth '—but something's bothering you.'

And things are bothering me, too. Like the fact that I'm more intent on getting naked with him than I am on having it out with him over Brent's, and what my inattention where my business is concerned means. Am I just distracted by the way Sterling makes me feel? Or am I mentally preparing myself, shutting down some of the threads of emotional entanglement with the business I inherited in light of my visit to Brent's. It's hard not to draw comparisons between the two companies and even harder to shake the weight of responsibility for Hamilton's when I could leave that to him.

'Sounds like we both need some down time.' His stare dips to my chest, lingering where the robe sits just above my breasts. His eyes have the same regret they wore in his office yesterday.

'Perhaps we should talk. You seem to have things on your mind. And I also have questions.'

When his eyes land back on mine, they're even more tortured and burning up with coppery flames. 'You could take my mind off anything...'

He steps closer, bathing me with the scent of his cologne.

His stark honesty, his vulnerability, renders me immobile. Perhaps he's feeling as adrift as me. My breath hitches. Power and certainty thrills through me, setting off a series of delightful shudders.

Work can wait. Pleasure is the perfect antidote to my unsettling doubts over Hamilton's. I need to forget that the only certainty in my life right now is how much I want him.

I step closer too, dip one shoulder so the robe slips down my arm, exposing half of my chest. 'Is that right? Even though I'm the enemy?'

His pupils flare. 'We could call a temporary truce…'

He lifts his free hand slowly and traces one fingertip along my collarbone and over my exposed shoulder. The contact spreads through my entire body like warm honey, chasing away the last lingering seeds of mistrust and resentment, and bringing that glorious abandon I craved when I texted him.

He knows how to make good on that seductive look on his face. How to make my body sing. The wild fluttering of my heart tells me I'm addicted to his distracting touch.

'I know this will likely surprise you as much as it does me,' I say, 'but on this subject we agree.' I take another sip of wine and he does the same, his stare locked with mine.

Excitement floods my nervous system. Professionally he's the master of his universe, and he's even the master of mine at the moment, unless he has a change of heart about the merger. But physically, we're equals. Both driven to forget past demons with our sensual game.

I take his glass and place both mine and his on the table. My heart beats like a drum as I step close and tug the hem of his shirt, pushing the fabric up and over his head until his ripped, bronzed torso is revealed to my greedy stare.

Damn, he's a work of art. Broad chest, strong arms, toned muscles. When he held me close on Friday, for a few seconds I felt surrounded. Protected. Safe.

With my eyes locked to his intense stare, I pop the button on his jeans and slide down the zip. He stands there as if he expects my worship, and he's right to assume. I want to run my hands and mouth over every beautifully masculine inch of him, not for revenge, but for the pleasure it will give me, the pleasure I'll see in his ardent green gaze. But he's not unaffected—his chest rises and falls on ragged breaths.

He's hard, his cock straining behind his boxers, demanding my attention. I shove down his jeans and underwear and encircle him, sliding my hand slowly and provocatively over his rigid length until he cracks and bites out a curse.

His hand fists my hair with an impatience that's echoed deep inside me. I want him wild and on edge. I want him greedy and demanding. I want him quaking with desire before I cease the torture.

He drags my mouth up to his, delivering a crushing kiss that steals my breath and makes my fingers clutch at his arm. I dig my nails into his warm, satiny skin and sway against his hard chest, trying to stop myself from collapsing into him with the force of my longing.

'How are you going to punish me?' he growls against my lips and I feel the same sensation buzzing between my legs in recollection.

I whimper at the look of fierce, unadulterated need on his face. He's close to the edge.

'I'm going to suck you.' I pull back, watching his face contort with rapture. His pupils flare wide and I drop to my knees. I want *him* to lose his mind until he's not sure if he detests me or craves me. Until he wants me out of his sight one minute and is frantically searching me out the next. Until he's as helpless to stopping this as I am.

We're both trapped in this spiral. The question is: are we heading up, or down?

For now it doesn't matter. All I want is to taste him.

'This is for making me want you, even when

my head knows better.' With his eyes on me, I glide my tongue from the base of him to the tip, capturing his every reaction—the harsh intake of his breath, the tightening of his grip on my hair and his sculpted mouth falling slack with desire.

Not satisfied with anything other than his full surrender, I draw the head of him between my lips, tonguing him as if he's a delicious lollipop.

'Fuck...' He drops his head back, his eyes scrunched closed for a second as he adjusts to the intensity of pleasure jerking his body.

His thigh is steel under my hand, his hips thrusting uncontrollably as he watches the progress of my mouth over the most sensitive part of him.

'Mmm...' I hum low in my throat, losing myself in his pleasure and my power, easing off on the suction, teasing him, taunting him, punishing him. This inebriating sense of control chases off my earlier qualms. My memories. My loneliness.

I keep my lips pressed to the spot I've identified makes him shudder so I can stimulate him while I talk. 'You brought me here to do a job, but you haven't been honest with me.'

He glares down, wildness in his expression. The thrill of his transformation pounds between my legs. Gone is the sophisticated, commanding businessman. I'm in charge now that the tables are turned.

'Beg for your punishment,' I whisper, ensuring my lips hit the right spot as they form the words.

He grits his teeth, defiance warring with passion and need in his stormy eyes.

'Suck me,' he barks, his hips jerking as if of their own accord.

It's good enough. The desperation in the ferocity of his stare restores my confidence. I've got this and any other challenge thrown my way.

I smile, wrap my lips around him and slide my mouth as far down his shaft as I can. He hits the back of my throat, his salty, musky taste flooding my mouth.

'Ava!' His groan urges me on as his other hand joins the first in cradling my head. His fingertips flex against my skin and tangle in my hair.

His expression becomes shot through with vulnerability as he watches my mouth glide over his length. It's heady to know I can undo him as easily as he undoes me. That I'm not alone in this helpless obsession. That we're equally matched in the art of war.

But I don't want a draw. I want to win.

I keep my mouth on him as I free the belt of my robe, peel it open and then slide one hand between my legs. I'm wet for him, aching and empty and equally desperate. I graze my clit with one fingertip, spasms racking my body in rapturous waves.

'Don't you dare come,' he says, gripping my

hair in his curled fingers and thrusting his hips in an erratic rhythm. 'I have plans for you. I want you naked and coming all night. You robbed me of that last time, when you fled my room.' He grits out the words through clenched teeth, too high on arousal to do more than take what I'm giving him.

I want to argue, but denial would be a lie.

I grip the base of his cock and angle him back so I can take him deeper, suck him harder, drive him wilder. With every grunt and groan he makes, my pulse flies higher. I'm not alone in this hurricane. He's trapped too, somewhere between distrust and delirium. Enmity and ecstasy. Restraint and release.

I moan as I find the rhythm I need on my clit. This is so hot—the helpless, crazed expression on his face alone is enough to make me come. He may not trust me with business matters, but his body is mine in this moment, and I don't want to stop until he free falls and releases himself to our combustible chemistry.

He looks down and hisses out his breath, his eyes bouncing between my mouth and my hand between my legs.

Fresh determination slashes across his face. 'Stop.'

Regret is clear in his eyes as he jerks his hips back out of my reach so he slips from my mouth.

I cry out in protest, so close myself that I feel robbed.

In a single move, he drags me to my feet, pushes the robe from my shoulders and hauls my naked body against his hard chest.

'You drive me insane…' he grits out. We connect, shoulders to thighs. Scalding hot skin and quivering muscles. Helpless need rising between us. 'I can't stop wanting you.' His tongue dives between my parted lips and he growls out a feral sound.

Triumph blazes through me on a fiery wave that zaps my nerves—together we're part of something temporarily bigger than us, something compelling and insistent that won't be denied.

Not enemies. Not lovers. Caught somewhere in between.

Sterling yanks a condom from his pocket, his other hand still wrapped around my waist. He kisses me while he heels off his shoes and kicks away his jeans and boxers. I'm walked backwards towards the bed while my body goes into the meltdown I've grown to anticipate—a prelude to his addictive brand of sex.

For now I'm done testing him. I'm slick between my thighs, longing to have him thrust inside me with that sexy grunt he can't hold inside. Craving his loss of control, knowing it will drive us both over the edge into oblivion.

'Hurry,' I say. My hands move frantically on his warm skin, which is taut over rigid slabs of muscle. His body is a work of art: toned and powerful, unashamedly masculine, crushing me under his weight until I feel we're somehow joined, co-existing in a way I've never felt with another soul.

Like you could belong...

No—there's no room in me for such a dangerous thought. Alone is safe.

When my thighs hit the edge of the bed, he snatches his mouth away from our kiss. 'Turn around.' His hands on my hips urge me into the position he wants.

I obey his domineering order all too eagerly, sliding onto all fours on the bed and watching him over my shoulder. I know what's coming. His sublime and thorough possession. Unrelenting fervour I want with a desperation that terrifies me, because I need to cling to some semblance of animosity between us to fight him professionally for my past, my sense of belonging. My life.

He stares between my legs as he covers himself with the condom and then his eyes traverse my backside until they lock with mine once more. Understanding flares between us—we're in this compulsion together.

'Please,' I beg, because I know it will feed the fire in him and urge him on. And then I'll get my relief.

He steps up close, his thick thighs brushing the backs of my legs and buttocks and setting off a series of seismic tingles that travel to my core. I laugh and cry in triumph as I get what I want: his touch. Oblivion. Freedom.

His hand slips between my legs from behind, locating my drenched clit. He rubs over the swollen nerves, working me into a frenzy so I arch my back and bite my lip to contain the shock of pleasure.

But it's no use. It's too big to hold inside.

With his hands gripping my hips, he notches his cock at my entrance and I spread my thighs to accommodate him, urging his domination with fragmented words of encouragement that feel ripped from that tightly wound part of me that normally carries all of the weight and makes all of the decisions.

'Yes… Now… More…' My fingers dig into the bedspread as he pushes inside me, stretching me. I brace my arms, pushing back against him to increase the friction and take him deeper.

He curses, his fingers digging into my hips as he thrusts again and again. 'I can't decide what feels better, your mouth or your pussy,' he says, his breathing ragged.

I know what he means. Every time we're intimate I think it can't get any better, but it does.

'Looks like I'll have to try harder to make a distinction.' I squeeze my pelvic floor muscles until he gasps and bends over me to rub at my clit in retribution.

'Bad woman. What shall I do with you?'

I pass him the control of my pleasure so I can let go and simply fly. 'Keep doing this,' I say, scrunching my eyes closed as intense delirium holds me captive and wipes my mind clean.

He groans against my back, his prickly facial hair scraping the skin between my shoulder blades as he bucks inside me and strums his fingers over my clit.

'Ava,' he groans, the tone of his voice telling me how close he is to unravelling with me.

'Yes, yes!' I cry, my fingers joining his between my legs as my climax tears through me. We come together in a cacophony of ecstatic cries that echo from the hotel-room walls.

As I come back to earth I marvel at the depth of my hunger. How can I have needed him so desperately, knowing his plans for my business? How can I have started off punishing him but quickly surrendered? Because it's too good, that's why.

And good things end, leaving you alone again.

Sterling withdraws and uses the bathroom while I breathe through the frigid panic taking up residence in my chest. It's just the effect of endorphins. Who knew sex could be so gratifying and addictive but also leave me so raw…?

When he emerges from the ensuite bathroom,

I catch sight of his expression and my stomach sinks. Rather than appearing satiated and restored, he still seems haunted. I expect him to dress and leave, but he shocks me anew.

'Mind if I stay a while?' he asks, scrubbing a hand through his still damp and messy hair.

I shrug, still high from my orgasm. The sight of him naked and proud and somehow vulnerable sparks renewed desire in my blood.

My heart lurches. Perhaps we might be friends, when this is over. I have precious few of those and someone as professionally well-connected as Sterling could be an ally.

Perhaps he could be more than a friend…

Only I'm broken, my parts barely held together like a cracked eggshell. Trust, reliance on someone, only leads to pain and abandonment. And I feel as if I've already written the manual on those heartbreaks.

'Not at all.' I draw aside the covers and tap the bed beside me in invitation to distract from my terrifying thoughts. I sit up and try to rectify my disastrous hair. He sees my attempts, catches my wrist and then strokes the dishevelled mess back from my face with a tenderness that leaves me jittery and confused.

'I'm starving,' I say to cover my reaction. 'You'll have to watch me eat something from Room Service, I'm afraid.'

His smile touches his eyes, layering heat and something less tangible there. 'I could eat something from Room Service. I came around to invite you to dinner, but seeing you in that robe robbed my appetite.' He drops his hand from my cheek and collects our wine, depositing the glasses on the nightstand. He plumps the pillows and joins me in my bed as if we're an old married couple about to watch the late-night news together.

We stare at each other. I laugh. He grins. It feels good to break the tension after an unsettling day and the intense sex we've just shared. And the more intense emotions...

'You're on my side,' I say to hide the fact that I want to kiss him again.

'No, you're on mine.' His voice is a playful rumble. 'But at least we're not at odds over that, too.'

He raises one eyebrow—a reminder of where we started and how much more complex things have become between us since what was supposed to be a one-night stand.

My stomach knots with inevitability. He's right. Regardless of how hot we are together, we can't both have our way businesswise. Is that logic and objectivity talking—his merger makes financial sense, and I believe he will find a buyer and make huge profits—or am I simply slipping under his sensual spell?

Damn—that's not good.

CHAPTER NINE

Sterling

I WIPE MY fingers on a napkin and place my tray on the nightstand, a sense of calm satisfaction radiating through me. Astonishing after dealing with a string of irate calls from Josh today.

'I was a teenager the last time I ate French fries in bed,' I admit with a grin, trying to forget the demands of my stepbrother. My feeling in any way light-hearted being here—in Chicago, a city that connects me to Marcus, dealing with the dissolution of *his* company—is a testament to the power Ava holds. Not, as I first assumed, over my business decisions where Hamilton's is concerned, but over weakness of a different kind: my weakness for her and for this connection I can't seem to ignore or get enough of—the reason I asked to stay a while.

Being forced to remember the past, and Marcus's

role in my life, makes me forget who I am and what I've achieved in the years since I was a boy under his control.

Ava swallows a bite of her burger and wipes at her mouth. 'I can't imagine a teenage you doing anything quite so…mutinous as eating junk food in bed.'

Mutinous…? I guess it was pretty rebellious in Marcus's household, by his standards, by which I'd been forced to abide.

Discomfort grates at my skin; rebellion is exactly the emotion I've battled today. Rebellion against the urge to capitulate and hand over Brent's to Josh. Let him wade through the consequences of his father's poor management, underinvestment and years of neglect. It's about time he woke up to the man his father really was, the man he could be when driven by jealousy and tyranny over another man's child. Even discussing Marcus's business draws me back to a time in my life I hate reliving. A time of powerlessness. Impotence. Rejection.

But exposing Marcus to Josh means exposing Marcus's true nature to Mom. I don't want to be responsible for her pain by blackening his name— it's my job to protect her, and she likely knew his worst side anyway.

Except the vengeful part of you does want her to know everything.

No, I won't stoop to his level. I'll never be like

Marcus. Instead I'll make something successful and positive out of Brent's. Move on. Help Mom to do the same.

'Why can't you imagine my wild side?' I ask.

Her stare washes over me, hot and desirous. 'You're just so…neat and poised and ruthless. You need only compare our offices to see who loves minimalism and who thrives on organised chaos. I guess I assumed you must have always been that way.'

We share a smile that feels good: a ceasefire of sorts that began when she sent me that seemingly inconsequential text earlier. It contained nothing that couldn't have waited until the morning. It made me think that she wanted to see me, which was convenient because I'd wanted to see her.

'You're right—I wasn't much of a rebel.' I grew up showing absolute compliance with Marcus's rules. For the few short years that he lived with us, Josh seemed to take delight in feeding Marcus ammunition. I'd hoped having an older brother meant I'd gain a protector and mentor and, in the beginning, Mom encouraged the three of us to take *boys outings* in order to bond. I'd hated them. Marcus acted inconvenienced and Josh resentful. My stepbrother took every opportunity to try to divide our blended family—telling tales, siding with Marcus and being two-faced in front of Mom so I appeared bratty.

I learned to toe the line. Otherwise Marcus made me pay in a million little ways that added up to the mother of all retributions—withholding my allowance, grounding me, and worst of all taking away my car keys and my means of escape.

If those measures failed to bring me begging for *his* forgiveness, he'd take it out on Mom, forcing me to live with the guilt of causing the arguments and mind games that happened behind closed doors but still managed to infect the entire house with a bad atmosphere. As far as I'm aware, he never laid a finger on her. He didn't need to; his emotional manipulations were ten times worse than any physical threat. They ate away at your brain, your self-esteem and optimism, until it was easier to cave and kowtow to his authority.

'My stepfather was a tyrant, ' I say. 'The only time I could relax was when he was away on business.' Mom and I smiled and laughed more during his trips to Chicago, his home city.

'The weekend in question, my mother and stepfather were away at a wedding.' I return to the subject of eating in bed and teenage rebellion to keep things light between us, because they're complicated enough. When I'm with her I feel conflicted. I'm enthralled by her dry sense of humour, her love of our city, how we have opposite ideas on almost every subject but still manage to find common ground. Spending time with her, I see her sharp mind. Her compassion and loyalty. Her gutsy determination. Not to mention the frenzy of insatiable need to embrace our physical side again and again and again.

'I had the house to myself.' I stare straight ahead, swallowing down the bitter taste in my throat. Marcus's home never felt like *my* home, even though Mom had pooled her resources with his after my father's death to purchase the townhouse.

'So there was no one to tell me I couldn't eat French fries in bed.' I try to offer my charming smile so she doesn't think I'm a slob, but bad memories tighten my chest.

Why did I even raise the subject?

Because you feel closer to her.

Maybe, but closeness isn't trust.

I clear my throat. 'I invited a few friends over to play video games and hang out—all perfectly harmless teenage stuff. Hardly rebellion at all, really.' I remember how uplifted I'd felt once free of his constant criticism.

Your grades aren't as good as Josh's were...

Your mother will be so disappointed in your insolent behaviour...

Your father must have been too soft on you...

And hardly worth it once Marcus found an empty soda can under the table on his return and accused me of having a wild party. In her quiet way Mom jumped to my defence, which led to a massive argument. He'd laid into her, right in front of me, accusing her of mollycoddling me and defying his attempts to offer some male stability and discipline. He had a bully's knack of making *you* feel guilty while making himself the victim.

That was the first time I left home. I crashed with a friend for a week until I realised I'd out-stayed my welcome and was forced to return to Marcus's home. An apology for something I hadn't done had been the price of my re-entry.

But I did it for Mom.

Hiding my most unattractive side from Ava, who I can't seem to keep my hands off, I paste on a grin and use the pad of my thumb to wipe a crumb from the corner of her mouth.

'Thanks,' she says, her eyes wide, hesitant and bewildered at the intimacy of my gesture. Her re-action slides sandpaper under my skin—the burning itch of shame.

'You're welcome.' Yes, I felt initially manipulated by her attempts to attract my attention, but we've played equal parts in seducing each other since. I respect her as a person and a business-woman. She's kept Hamilton's afloat during some trying times in a competitive marketplace. She has a good insight into the current challenges faced by the business and creative ideas for improvement. She's intelligent, lateral-thinking and dynamic—

exactly the kind of person I'd employ at Bold, if we'd met under different circumstances.

You only want her for sex.

I can't be sentimental—Hamilton's has to be part of my plan for Brent's because it was the one thing Marcus wanted but failed to acquire. The minute I escaped his influence, I vowed that I'd never again concede to him. That I'd make something of myself and always protect my mother. That at every opportunity, I'd prove I'm not defined by his poor opinions of me, despite hearing the echo of his words in my mind.

Brent's has been a thorn in my flesh ever since Marcus died suddenly from a heart attack. I couldn't exact my revenge while he was alive, and now that Josh is sniffing around, I want the company out of my sight, out of my mind and out of Mom's, for good.

Aware I've fallen silent, I scrub my hand over my face, shoving thoughts of Marcus aside. 'What about you—any acts of teenage rebellion? I see you have a tattoo.'

She turns over her hand and glances at the artistic sunflower on the inside of her wrist.

'That's more an act of remembrance.' Her soft smile is bittersweet. 'It was my parents favourite flower and the name of their restaurant. Girasole. Sunflower in Italian.'

She traces the design with her fingertip. 'I got

this shortly after they died, with my grandparents'
permission of course, because I was only fifteen.
I was too respectful of my Nonna and Pops for rebellion and too grateful that they'd taken me in.'

'Was your parents' restaurant like Gianni's?'

She nods. 'Perhaps even better.' Her eyes glaze
over with fond remembrance. 'Mom learned to
cook from Nonna, who learned from her mother.
Before they had me, my parents spent two years
in Italy, travelling the different regions, studying
cookery, learning handed-down recipes from the
locals. The restaurant was their passion.' Her face
lights up—animated and breathtaking—shifting
something in me.

I haven't seen this passion from her for logistics.

'You never considered following your parents
into the restaurant industry?' She came alive at
Gianni's after sampling the menu, and when he
invited her to call on him for advice she looked as
if she was about to hug him to death.

Her happiness isn't your concern.

I'm not seeking a relationship out of this. I'm
just working the hot sex out of my system. I've had
my shot at commitment. Failure doesn't sit well
with me, and I taste it every time I see or speak
to Monroe. No, casual works for me. It feeds my
need for success. No reminders and no snide voice
in my head.

Her skin pales. 'I was only a kid when they

died,' she says. 'Nonna and Pops were too old to run both the restaurant and Hamilton's and they couldn't afford to keep it, so it had to be sold.'

Curiosity unfurls in my stomach. 'Is it still there under different owners?'

She shakes her head. 'No. It's a dry-cleaning business. I haven't been back to that neighbourhood in years.' She looks down at her unfinished food and then places the tray aside. 'Too many memories.'

I nod. 'I understand that—I steer clear of my father's precinct.' I don't know why I'm telling her this apart from a desire to find more common ground.

'Your dad was a police officer?'

I nod, taking my own trip down memory lane, wondering how different my childhood could have been with my family intact and a father figure who loved me unconditionally, encouraged my every effort and praised my achievements unreservedly. A man who loved and protected my mother, so I didn't have to worry that she was happy and safe.

'How did your parents die?' How would it feel to be so alone? To lose both your parents at such a vulnerable age?

I feel wholly responsible for the anguish in Ava's stunning eyes. I want to tear out my tongue for asking such a dumb and deeply personal question. But there's been some subtle shift between us.

Perhaps being out of our usual environments has forced us to re-examine each other. I'm witnessing a passionate, intelligent woman who's lost so much in her life but soldiers on regardless.

I take her hand, hoping to undo some of the damage wrought by my need to pry and understand her.

'They were killed in a car accident coming home from work one night,' she says. 'A drunk driver fell asleep at the wheel of a racy little convertible like yours and ploughed into them, head-on. They both died instantly.' She recites the tale in a flat voice as if she's practised the painful words out loud a hundred times. Yet she can't hide their impact—her hand trembles in mine.

'Fuck,' I mutter under my breath, gripping her fingers tighter. 'I'm *so* sorry.'

She shakes her head; she doesn't want sympathy.

Frustration knots my muscles until I could snap in two. 'I feel like an insensitive idiot for making a big deal about my car.'

'You weren't to know,' she says.

For the first time since I walked into Hamilton's offices and stated my intentions to sell off her inheritance, her stare softens with something close to affection and acceptance. It's as if I'm made of glass and she can see straight through me—a feeling I want to shake off with more sex.

I've been blinded by my rage over Marcus's reach from the grave and I haven't paid enough attention the way I normally would with a woman this consuming.

Has there ever been a woman this consuming?

No. I can't afford for her to be *all*-consuming. I can't afford to become sidetracked from the merger, from finally ridding myself of any trace of the man who tormented my childhood. For the first time, I look past her beauty and her grit and her pain, take a closer look at Ava's motivations for turning up to the Bold office party. What if she feels like Hamilton's is all she has left of her loved ones? That would explain any amount of ruthlessness to claim the company back. I'd go to any lengths to protect what's mine—Mom, Monroe and Hudson, Bold.

I've been too caught up in how Josh's aggressive interest in his father's company made me feel weak again. Too off-balance by meeting Ava because the powerlessness I feel for her physically reminds me of the same emotions I felt under Marcus's rule and also towards the end of my marriage.

Well, fuck that—I refuse to give Marcus any more power.

I drag our still joined hands into my lap, stroking the backs of her knuckles with my thumb.

'Is that why you don't drive?' Dumb question.

I try to picture a teenage Ava, try to imagine

the devastation of having life as she knew it ripped away in a split second by such a senseless, selfish and unjust act. I remember the shock and confusion of losing my father, but at least I still had Mom's guiding force and comfort. For the two years when it was just us, we found some sort of new normality and peace.

And then Marcus muscled in. They were already friends and had both lost their spouse—Marcus's wife died from cancer. I don't blame my mother for remarrying. Raising a kid alone is no picnic.

Ava offers a small nod. 'I tried to learn to drive once, but I couldn't do it. I kept thinking about them, kept seeing imagined flashbacks of the impact.' She shakes her head as if clearing her mind of horrific images. 'I didn't feel safe behind the wheel.'

'I can understand.' I make a mental note to drive her in my Audi SUV from now on, which is fully electric and has the highest safety ratings possible. The assertion that there will be more opportunities to drive her anywhere shunts my pulse sky-high. Once she's compiled her report on Brent's and the merger with Hamilton's, there'll be no more reason to see her professionally.

She half smiles, half frowns. Something about her expression, her past and her obvious loneliness, prompts a confession of my own.

I trace her tattoo with the tip of my finger. 'I'm kind of a bit of a motor head. Learning to drive saved me as a teenager.'

Ava's frown morphs into curiosity so I plough on.

'As a cop, my dad saw a lot of human catastrophe. I guess that's why he set up a trust for me with the money he inherited from his parents. The initial payment was when I was sixteen—for the purchase of my first car.'

This time her smile is tinged with indulgence that warms me. 'So how did it save you?'

Why am I telling her this? I normally avoid talking about or even thinking about Marcus as if my life depends on it. But a part of me wants her to know I'm not just a revenge-driven, ruthless mercenary.

I'm not perfect, but I'm fair and honest and protect the ones I love.

I drag in a breath and exhale slowly. 'My stepfather died five months ago, but he and I didn't get on. He was…controlling. Learning to drive and having my own car gave me independence. I could get away from his influence any time I liked. Without that my teenage years could've been much worse.'

I shrug and look away, bitterness a rock in my chest. I want his association with my life over once and for all. Offloading Brent's in a better condition than he left it will remind me I'm nothing like him and nothing like he predicted I'd become.

We fall into heavy silence. I grow restless to crush her to my chest, kiss her and never let her go. In reality, I should get up. Dress. Leave. What we're doing isn't about talking and confiding and knowing each other on an intimate level.

Ava's next question is almost whispered. 'Did your mother know that you didn't get on?' Her fingers tighten around mine, sending a slug of addictive endorphins through my blood.

I shake my head. 'I hid the worst of it from her. He was good at hiding it too—clever, subtle, cunning. As I grew older, his constant put-downs and humiliations fell under the guise of the discipline he said was *good for me*. And he treated Mom the same.' I scrub a hand over my face. 'I don't blame her for wanting me to have a father figure. On the surface Marcus was a respectable man—a widower with a grown-up son and a business.' His first wife knew my father from school, so the couples became friends after the Brents moved back to New York—an emotional connection Marcus played on after my father died.

'He sounds like a terrible human being.' Her lips press into a furious line. 'I'm sorry you went through that. Being a teenager is difficult enough without constant criticism.'

I flash my confident smile. I *have* amounted to

something. With the exception of my failed marriage to Monroe, I've proved Marcus wrong on every other count. Just as I will with Brent's.

Good business is about integrity and understanding people—not just bulldozing and bullying your way through life.

'Don't be sorry,' I say with renewed determination to finally offload the last of Marcus's legacy and lay his ghost to rest. 'I escaped Marcus Brent's influence a long time ago.'

A groove forms between Ava's eyebrows. 'Brent?' Understanding begins to dawn in her eyes.

Damn—I'd previously left out that part of the story. Time to confess all of the truth. 'Yes. The facility you visited today was once my stepfather's company.'

Something close to disappointment shifts in her stare. 'You bought Brent's Express from your stepfather?'

I nod. 'For a song—he was desperate to sell quickly so he could retire. He even cut out his son, Josh. If you think I'm ruthless, you should've known Marcus.'

Her hand stiffens in mine, but I continue.

'I'm just glad he didn't manage to steal Hamilton's away from your grandparents and that when they wanted to sell some equity, they came to me.'

My gut tightens at the remembered calls from

Josh earlier. Someone at Brent's is feeding my
stepbrother information. I suspect it's Marcus's
assistant, who still runs the office. That's the only
explanation for Josh's series of urgent calls. After
the first one I ignored the rest. I know what he
wants: for me to bail out Brent's financially and
hand him over the company he thinks is his birth-
right. A company not even his own father saw fit
to leave him when he sold out to Bold.

Marcus was likely as shitty a father as he was a
stepfather, so I understand Josh's resentment. Not
that he ever sided with me over Marcus.

Ava's teeth sink into her bottom lip and she
seems to contemplate her next words. Tension
shifts through me, a cold sense of foreboding.

'So Hamilton's is more than just another logistics company—you wanted it because your stepfather wanted it?'

'Yes.'

'I see…' She frowns. 'I think I'm beginning to
understand now. Brent's is in pretty bad shape. It
shows signs of chronic under-investment and lack
of passion at the helm.' When she looks back at
me I see a hint of the same condemnation I saw
when I first told her about my plans for Hamilton's.

Her eyes grow wary. She slips her hand from
mine and pushes her hair back from her face. 'I
wish I'd been party to all of the information before
I visited today. But now I see how the merger is

primarily about proving something to your stepfather.'

I bristle. 'You knew all you needed to know to complete your report.' It's complex. She doesn't get me. Doesn't see how I'm trying to create something good out of these failing companies while making a positive change in my life, too. Brent's has already benefited from my investment and invaluable attention.

I hold my ground. 'I admit Brent's has been on the back burner for me for a few months while I've been busy with higher priority companies, but I assure you that it's received considerable investment since I purchased it from Marcus.

'The merger will remove any lingering trace of the previous owner and turn the company around. A simple solution for us all.'

Even while she hates what I plan for her company, she must acknowledge that my instincts are correct. The merger will succeed.

Her mouth hangs open in disbelief. 'It's far from simple. I can't suggest measures that will turn around years of neglect and infrastructure underinvestment in one visit.'

'*I* can. I have the resources, expertise and industry contacts. By the time I've finished creating Lombard Logistics it will make a highly attractive proposition for some shrewd buyer. You can retire a wealthy lady, do anything you want in life.'

Surely she can see the benefits, not only for the company she loves, but also for her personally.

She could start her own restaurant…

At her exasperated expression my blood starts to simmer. I asked for her input with Brent's, and I value her insight. She knows logistics, but I know business. Investing and turning a profit is my bread and butter.

Ava grows more agitated, rising from the bed and covering up with the hotel robe. 'I understand why you'd want to rid yourself of his business, but you can't just make a patchwork quilt with these companies and hope it holds together long enough for some poor schmuck to take the bait.'

Her censure takes me back in time—a stomach tightening reminder of helpless times when I couldn't defend myself. But now I can. 'I find your insinuation patronising. Give me some credit. Don't you think I've done my research? Even if you can't see it, there's massive potential here with the right person at the helm. Sadly for both you and Marcus, the right person is *me*.'

I snatch up my jeans and tug them on, tired of justifying my actions. 'I know what I'm doing, Ava. This is my livelihood and I'm damned good at it. Bold is consistently in the Fortune five hundred list, year after year.' Why am I explaining myself to her? If her opinion of me is so low, why the fuck am I wasting my time?

There's no hint of concession in her demeanour as she fists her hands on her hips. I'm sorry I opened up to her about Marcus.

'You're so driven by the past,' she says, 'and I understand why. But I'm concerned that you can't be objective. You may not care about Brent's, but *I* care about Hamilton's.'

Of course I'm not impartial where Brent's is concerned… But her judgement stings. It's too reminiscent of Marcus's chastisement to sit comfortably with me.

'Thanks for the vote of confidence. Fortunately, I don't need your permission or your blessing in order to do whatever I like with my companies.'

She huffs in frustration. 'I may not be able to stop you selling Hamilton's, but I'll be damned if I watch you turn my years of dedication and my grandparents' life work into part of your—' she splutters then spits out the final words '—revenge plan.'

I snort with disbelief that for a moment there I allowed her to get under my skin, then jerk into my T-shirt. The sex is mind-blowing, but I know better than to trust anyone, especially someone who's adept at subterfuge and manipulation. Someone who's no more interested in seeing the person I am than *he* was.

I make sure my voice is icily calm when I speak again.

'Thank you for explaining what you think of me. Your emotional attachment to Hamilton's is understandable, but this is business. I think if *you* could be objective, you'd see the benefits for all concerned—you, Bold, and the employees of Hamilton's and Brent's, who rather than face redundancy will still have a job in six months, thanks to me.'

I grab my shoes and head for the door, pausing only to dispense my parting shot. 'But if you're struggling to see any good in my motivations and you don't want to watch the end of Hamilton's and the beginning of something bigger, better and more prosperous, then I suggest you close your eyes.'

CHAPTER TEN

Ava

IT'S BEEN THREE days since we returned from Chicago. Three days since I last saw Sterling. Three days in which I've had time to think—about our last serious conversation, about the future of Hamilton's, and most alarmingly about the direction of my life.

Rather than provide clarity, everything he does and says confuses me.

When we arrived back at JFK, he'd had another of his cars delivered to the airport—this one a spacious Audi SUV that felt as secure as a tank. He'd even given me the vehicle's safety statistics before he pulled out of the airport and then dropped me home. I'd been too choked up and overwhelmed to do more than utter my thanks and then watch him drive away feeling as if my stomach was somewhere on the sidewalk.

Sterling's shocking confession about his step-father's cruelty haunts me. I can't stop thinking about a younger Sterling and how powerless he must have felt. For an intelligent, masterful and compassionate man like him, being under some-one's control and destructive influence must have felt like slow and painful torture.

Of course he wants to dispense with Brent's—a company associated with negative memories and a reminder that, despite what he's achieved, he was once a defenceless boy at the hands of a bully. He's trying to make a positive change by eradi-cating Marcus from his life. I can even begrudg-ingly admit that he's right: it is sound business to amalgamate all three companies, combining their strengths, customers and resources under one um-brella instead of competing in the same market-place.

I've been consumed with how his plans affect me, overlooking the fact that, when incorporated into a larger company, the success of Hamilton's will safeguard the jobs of my loyal staff for the future.

This is bigger than me.

But…

That's the sticking point. Aside from betraying my family, losing Hamilton's threatens my sense of belonging. Where will I work? What will I do?

I take a shaky sip of my cocktail and try not to

glance at my phone for the time. I shouldn't have arrived so early. I've asked Sterling to meet me at the Brooklyn Heights Hotel, not far from my apartment, to show him my grandmother's grand piano, the instrument that started the Hamilton's journey. It's my favourite place to come and remember happier times—sufficiently impersonal that I can forget when I want to, but close and public enough that I can pop in any time I feel lonely.

Sterling arrives just then, striding into the bar with his trademark confidence and purpose. Nerves make my breathing erratic as he scans the bar in search of me. It hurts between my ribs to see him so composed and handsome and vital when I feel as if I'm falling apart. Broken. Incomplete.

Except for when you're in his arms, when you're driving him wild.

No—I can only rely on myself for strength and create my own safety net. People I care about have a horrible habit of disappearing.

And our last conversation left me wondering if I knew him at all. Can't he see that selling everything his stepfather touched won't bring him the peace he craves? Can't he see how important Hamilton's is to me?

He spies me, his piercing eyes landing on mine. For a second his expression shifts from searching to relieved. The same emotion pulses in my veins, a part of me renewed, blossoming at the fact he showed up, when we left things so tense and resentful between us three days ago.

I stand, flutters attacking my stomach at the gorgeous sight he makes. He strides my way, determination in his green eyes as if he's a predator and I'm prey. My body softens, heat building the way it does when we're naked and connected on an intimate level.

'Thanks for meeting me,' I say, breathing in the spicy male scent of his cologne and trying not to succumb to the unexplainable sting behind my eyes as he presses his lips to my cheek.

'I'm glad you called. We left things unnecessarily hostile between us.' He takes a seat next to me in the booth facing the view and signals to a waiter, ordering his favourite bourbon.

My tongue feels clumsy in my mouth. 'I hoped meeting here would diffuse some of that. Did you see the report I emailed you on Brent's?' It's easier to talk business than to dissect why I'm so comforted by seeing him.

I watch for the vulnerability that mentioning his bully's name might cause. All I've come to expect from Sterling is ruthlessness and orgasms, but he's a complex and haunted man. His motivations for selling his stepfather's company are completely justified. I might even support his plan if it didn't involve Hamilton's.

Yet it gives you a chance not many people get—
to change direction and chase your dreams...

No, I'm not ready to give up yet. That's why I've brought him here, to this particular piano bar. To show him exactly what my legacy means to me.

'I did, thank you. You very professionally produced what I asked for and I...' He scrubs a hand through his dishevelled hair, making my fingers itch to do the same, to feel its silkiness as I draw his mouth to mine and become lost in his kiss. 'On reflection, I should have given you all of the information up front,' he says.

'It wouldn't have made any difference to my recommendations. I'm afraid I tried to be objective about the merger, but, as you saw from the report, I also presented a case for keeping Hamilton's out of the sale. Brent's Express and SeaFreight together make an attractive proposition. But Hamilton's is different. We're specialist. I hope to persuade you to keep it separate.'

'I see.' His mouth tightens and I drag in a bolstering breath. I don't want to fight. I just want to appeal to his humanity.

The server returns with Sterling's drink, gifting me a moment to catch my breath and regroup my defences.

'What you said in Chicago—' to give my restless hands an occupation, I twirl my glass on the table '—you had a point. I am emotionally invested in Hamilton's, but I wanted you to understand why. That's the reason I suggested *this* bar.'

His stare shifts over my features intently. 'Without conceding that it will change anything, I'd like to understand.'

I nod, respecting him more than if he'd offered false promises. 'I want to tell you a story about Hamilton's.'

Curiosity is intense in his eyes. 'Okay. I'm listening.'

'Do you see the piano?' I point to the far corner of the bar where a man dressed in a tux plays soft, mellow piano music on a Bösendorfer grand.

A smile plays on his lips. 'It's a stunning instrument—I have a grand piano at my apartment.'

'You play?'

He nods. 'Do you?'

I shrug, my stomach turning hollow at the memory of another part of my life that fell by the wayside after I lost my parents. 'A little—I'm not very good.'

I continue my tale, battling the lust and confusion that seems to be my constant state around him. 'That piano dates back to 1899. It belonged to my great-grandmother, who passed it on to her daughter, my grandmother, Nonna Hamilton.'

He raises his brows, impressed.

'Nonna emigrated to the US in the fifties, but she had to leave her beloved piano behind in Italy because she couldn't afford to ship it. She met my Pops shortly after arriving in New York. They were married four months later. As a wedding gift, he had her precious instrument shipped here. That was how Hamilton Logistics began.'

I pause, glancing at the piano while nostalgia hijacks my breaths. I tinkled with those keys as a toddler. My mother played a halting rendition of the happy birthday song to me every year while my dad, Nonna and Pops sang along. I've kept a lot of my family's personal items but had to part with the piano for practical reasons.

'I see.' His lips compress but there's only understanding and regret in his eyes.

'There's no room for such an impressive instrument at my apartment, so I loaned it to the hotel indefinitely. It should be played and cared for and enjoyed.'

'As a player myself, I'd have to agree with you.' Out of nowhere he leans close and cups my cheek in his warm palm. 'I'm sorry that you can't have the piano at home.'

My heart lurches as if it's trying to close the distance between us.

I shrug. 'Maybe one day. You wanted to understand what Hamilton's means to me.' My voice shrinks, small and hesitant, because a part of me, the part too scared to trust feelings, wasn't expecting his compassion and sensitivity after our fight in Chicago. Now it feels as if I've committed an underhand tactic—emotional blackmail. My sentiment and nostalgia shouldn't influence his decision.

'It's always been more than a business. It's about love and family and…'

My voice cracks and I look down, away from the empathy and threads of desire in his eyes.

'And belonging?' His fingers squeeze mine.

I want to sob that he's so perceptive. That he gets me.

'I do understand, Ava. Hamilton's is your life. Your family's heritage, just like the piano.' He sighs, as if momentarily defeated.

I nod, overwhelming sadness filling me up. 'Yes, it is.' I laugh, a humourless sound. 'That seems pathetic all of a sudden. At least you've been married. You tried to build your own family and create a legacy you can pass on.'

What am I without this final tie to my loved ones? Can I really do anything else? Can I let go of the past and find myself somewhere new to belong? Somewhere that's more…me?

'No more pathetic than trying to outmanoeuvre a dead man.' Sterling winces, his expression slashed with uncertainty. But he recovers quickly. 'And I've been around a few more years. Plus, my marriage turned into a failure, so I don't boast about it.'

We share a sad little smile.

'Thank you for sharing that story,' he says. 'You had a point, too…in Chicago, I do struggle to be objective when it comes to certain aspects of my past. I'm very protective of my mother. Dissolving Brent's will help us both move on, I hope.'

'I don't blame you for wanting that.' I say as something unexpected, tender and promising buds inside me. 'We all struggle with objectivity when our emotions and loved ones are involved. I can even see how you must have felt manipulated when you discovered my identity and our shared business interest. I never planned to use you. The minute I looked into your eyes in that elevator I became distracted and a more pressing urge to seduce the sexiest man I've ever met took hold. You do believe that, right?'

It's suddenly imperative that his impression of me improves, and I can't say why.

He reaches for my hand. 'I do.'

Two simple words. But they're enough.

'The feeling was very much reciprocated.' He raises my hand to his lips. The way he looks at me from under his long lashes all but melts my bones. I'm not certain where we are professionally, but right now I'm struggling to recall that it matters. 'Have you eaten dinner?' he asks.

I shake my head. I was strung too tight with

nerves, although I spent the afternoon cooking—my proven calming technique.

'Clearing the air has made me ravenous,' he says. 'Would you like to grab some? I've had a rough couple of days, and seeing you has lifted my spirits.'

My pulse pounds in my throat at his admission. Raw emotion loiters in the depths of his stare, and I want to decipher it. Perhaps when this is over we might stay friends.

Warning bells sound in my head. My feelings are at risk with him. I need trust like oxygen. I need the security that trust brings. I'm careful who I date—I'm careful about everything. Life has taught me to be that way. Whatever happens businesswise, one of us will lose. One of us will feel betrayed. And yet that obstacle isn't enough to deter me; I don't want tonight to end yet, either.

I take a bolstering breath that feels as if I'm finally putting myself out there, emotionally after years of hiding in my shell. Years of being the dutiful granddaughter, but not knowing who I am. Years of having no idea where I belong.

But I do know what makes me happy, and for now, that includes being in his company. 'I have a better idea, if you're up for a short walk.'

He quirks a brow. 'Back to yours?'

I laugh and nod. 'Yes. I was thinking I could experiment on you...'

'A sexual experiment?' His eyes light up. Sterling in this flirtatious mood is dazzlingly hot.

I roll my eyes. 'For some classic recipes I'm trying out.'

He jerks to his feet with amusing eagerness. 'Lead the way. I'm starving and happily submit myself as a subject. You have excellent taste in food and sexual partners.'

His wink sends shivers through me, but I'm grateful for the shift in atmosphere. As we leave the bar, he takes my hand and that's where it stays for the four-block walk to my brownstone apartment. It feels good there. It reminds me of his display of old-school, gentlemanlike manners the night we met.

We hang up our coats and head for the kitchen, the only room—the only part of my life, in fact—that's organised and clutter-free. I'm conscious of his every move, anticipation fluttering in my veins that he's in my home, the place where I can be myself.

'Whatever you're making already smells delicious.' He lounges against my kitchen bench, watching me over the glass of wine I've just poured him.

'Wash your hands,' I say with mock seriousness, to hide the fact that I'm jittery with trepidation. 'There are no observers in my kitchen. You'll have to earn your dinner.' I don my apron, take a sip of my own wine and try to ignore his intense observation. It's as if he, too, feels every second of the three days since we last touched. As if the hand-holding on the way here was an appetiser—delicious but merely whetting the appetite.

He grins and follows my orders with surprising enthusiasm.

When he joins me at the stove, I reach up on my tiptoes to loop a spare apron over his head. 'To protect your shirt,' I say, boiling up at my proximity to him. Sparks zap between us, lighting his eyes, which are full of heat and laughter and promise.

Oh yes, he's missed me too. The sexual undercurrents sizzle hotter than the flame of my beloved professional range.

I hand him the wooden spoon. 'You have a very important job.' I indicate the pan under which I've switched on the gas. 'Just keep stirring.'

He laughs, tying the apron strings around his trim waist. 'Sounds simple enough. I must warn you, though—I burn water.' The pan spits as he stirs the minced onion and beef marrow through the butter that forms the base of the risotto.

'You'll be fine. I'm an excellent teacher, if a little bossy.' I step close to inhale the delicious steam wafting from the pan, our arms brushing. 'This recipe—Risotto alla Milanese—is from northern Italy. Some people omit the marrow, but trust me when I say it adds so much flavour and richness. You're going to love it.'

'I can't wait. What's in the oven?' His stomach growls in that moment and we share a look and a laugh.

'Ossobuco—slow-roasted beef shin.' I cut a couple of slices of ciabatta and place them on a wooden platter with a dish of olives in oil, homemade sundried tomatoes and slivers of prosciutto. 'Something for the chefs,' I say, dipping some bread into the olive oil and raising it to his mouth.

He holds my wrist and wraps his lips around my offering, licking the oil from my fingers.

To cover the trembling of my body, I take an olive and pop it into my mouth. At this rate, dinner might become breakfast. With one eye on Sterling's pan, I return to chopping the herbs for the gremolata that will finish the dish.

'Tell me about your rough few days.' I need a distraction from wanting to rip off his clothes. I tip the risotto rice into his pan and motion for him to keep stirring.

He swallows his second mouthful of bread— he even eats sexily—and washes it down with red wine. 'I was supposed to meet with my business partners, Monroe and Hudson, in Tokyo this week, but I had a family thing. A cousin of mine, Dale, died of lymphoma. I took my mother upstate for the funeral.'

I pause what I'm doing, my heart lurching, and touch his arm. 'I'm sorry. Were you and Dale close?'

He shrugs, looking conflicted. 'I'd sometimes spend the summers with him at my uncle's place. Dale and I would show off to impress girls by diving from the dock at the lake nearby.' He flashes a small smile at the memory.

'Now, why can I imagine that so vividly...?' I laugh, sloshing a ladleful of beef broth into the risotto pan he's manning.

'I wanted to come back to New York after the service, but Mom wanted to stay the night.' He falls quiet and pensive.

Knowing he takes care of his mother does something to me. I look at him anew. He's kind and dedicated. Profound and honourable. 'I'm glad you and your mom have each other.' A familiar, almost envious ache burrows between my ribs.

Another shrug, this one concealed with a glug of wine. 'She's lonely after my stepfather died.' His eyes turn dark and turbulent and tension radiates from his body. 'She's not happy about me selling Brent's.'

I hold my breath, wary of jeopardising our renewed closeness. 'Perhaps that's because she doesn't know how you truly feel about him.'

He stills, the wooden spoon coming to a halt.

I rush on. 'It might help if she understood why

you're rebranding and selling the company. I'm sure she'd be supportive.'

He begins stirring more vigorously, and the poor risotto takes a beating. 'I don't know, but I'm tired of his influence. I'm trying to make something positive out of the past. She's never discussed it with me,' his voice drops, telling me he's opening up, 'but I know Marcus emotionally abused her too.'

My throat burns for him, the boy he was then and the man he is now. He's caring and protective. He'd have hated not being able to defend his mom. 'I'm sorry that happened to you both. But she'd likely be sad to know you're struggling with the past because you didn't want to disappoint her. Because you were sheltering her.' My heart aches. He loves this woman. He's spent his life shielding her from an unpalatable truth.

I ladle some more broth into the risotto, my voice tight with empathy. 'Stir, please.'

He sighs half-heartedly, a small smile breaking out at my command.

'I'm not struggling with the past—I'm trying to lay it to rest.'

'By proving you're a better businessman than he was?' I ask without judgement.

'Yes. What's wrong with that?'

'Nothing. I think that goes without saying. You're so much more than a world-class businessman. You have nothing to prove. For example, you're pretty good at stirring the risotto, a job I was only trusted with when I'd graduated through fresh pasta making and kneading bread dough.'

I smile wider, trying not to think of all the other things he's good at.

That we're standing in my kitchen—a place of happiness and contentment for me—about to share a meal he's helped me prepare, terrifies me. I never expected to find any common ground with this man outside of the bedroom. He still has the capacity to ruin my business, but seeing him in an apron doing something as ordinary as cooking, hearing how he loves and cares for his mother... I see him in a new light.

Do I already have feelings for him?

No—it's just compassion. If I'd experienced his degree of bullying growing up, who knows what I'd be prepared to do to avenge a loved one...?

'So, you and Monroe are amicable enough to still work together?'

Why am I asking about his ex-wife? We've prepared dinner in the kind of relative harmony that makes me homesick for my parents. They must have done this a thousand times—cooked a meal with love, side by side.

'Monroe and I are friends now. That doesn't mean we didn't have to work hard to keep Bold intact after the divorce. But if something is important enough to you, you do what needs to be done.'

I nod as danger buzzes through my head like a swarm of angry hornets. That's exactly how I feel about Hamilton's. Except now there's the possibility of something more, both professionally and personally, that meeting Sterling has brought into my life… It's confronting. Uncomfortable and liberating all at once.

I want to avoid another heavy discussion so I make small talk while we eat. Sometimes all the evidence you need to see that life is pretty good is a tummy full of wholesome food and good company. When he devours everything on his plate, his praise vocal and plentiful, I want to kiss him. There's no better feeling than someone enjoying something I've cooked. Well, perhaps one better feeling, which still involves kissing.

We eat dessert—creamy panna cotta—in the lounge, where we talk some more about our favourite parts of New York. I'm distracted, re-living our journey through the lens of those many kisses we've shared: wild, passionate kisses; angry, vengeful kisses and heady, diverting kisses that block out the world.

Tonight, being here with Sterling, I feel as if we're safe inside our own sanctuary. As if we're the only two people who exist. As if he's enjoyed being here as much as I've enjoyed having him.

'You have a lot of books,' he says, observing my jam-packed shelves.

'Yes. Many of them were my parents'. I'm reading my way through their library.'

'And the vinyl collection?'

'Also theirs.' I rise and place one of my favourites—'Big Band Swing'—on the turntable. I return and sit beside him on the sofa. Intimate music swirls around the room, drawing us closer like magnets. Red wine and delicious food and his proximity have me in a state of heart-thudding arousal, but also something more—the desire for the same connection we shared at the stove where we laughed and flirted and seemed to develop a greater mutual understanding.

Almost as if we click together.

Can I be close to him and still protect myself from the fear that he'll hurt me, not just my company? If I let him in, can I still continue to find where I belong in this busy, lonely, changing world?

I take a shuddering breath that feeds me with courage. I'm so tired of being afraid. 'Would you like to stay the night?' I don't want him to leave. I feel as if I'm finally getting to know him, and despite the fact that it scares me, I've invited him into the very heart of my life: my home, my memories, my past.

'I'd love to stay.' His smile is both seductive and

uncertain, a combination that's wildly attractive and makes my pulse fly.

I want to spend the night re-learning everything I thought I knew about him. I understand his motivations and reasons. His desperation to be finally free of his past resonates with me on a deep level that makes me feel a bond to him. I too wish for some peace from overthinking every decision and asking *is this what my family would have wanted?* I crave a pathway forward that bursts alive with hope and possibility after every tentative step I take.

Sterling slides his fingers into my hair and guides my mouth to his kiss. He takes his time exploring, as if it's our first kiss, as if he's in no hurry.

I try not to compare this kiss to our others, but in light of all we've shared today, it feels as if I'm letting him in emotionally. An alarming pounding of my heart mixed with exhilaration flips my stomach.

I pull away to straddle his lap and tilt his head back to kiss him once more. Greater awareness seems to blossom between us with every brush of our lips. Every gentle glide of fingertips against skin. Every shared breath.

A new confession fights for freedom as I pull back to gulp air. 'It's my birthday tomorrow and I don't want to wake up alone.'

Shock slashes Sterling's expression. 'Why didn't you say something earlier?'

I shrug in answer. My grandparents tried, but I refused to celebrate my milestone after my parents died. Without them it seemed pointless. 'I don't make a big fuss of it—I prefer to have a quiet day of remembrance, recalling the happiness of birthdays past when my family was all together.'

His stare simmers with emotion that's mirrored in me. His compassion surrounds me, as palpable as if I'm in his arms which draw me close. 'You won't wake up alone.' He brushes my lips with his. 'I'll be here.'

To shut out the vulnerable feeling his words unleash, I tackle his shirt buttons and kiss a path over his face and neck and chest.

His expression is taut with concentration as we unhurriedly divest each other of clothing. We might have done this a million times; it feels so familiar and perfectly choreographed.

But we're new to this connection and it steals my breath.

I bury my face against his neck to hide. I'm aware of him locating a condom from his discarded pants. He rolls it in place and then cups my breasts, lifting one to his mouth. I drop my head back and allow pleasure to snatch away my thoughts. Live in this moment—the perfect end to a perfect evening.

Even if he doesn't spend the night, this is already the best birthday I've had in years.

With our eyes locked, I lower myself onto him, my heart straining to be closer to his with every beat.

'Ava.' He groans as I start to rock my pelvis. I want to close my eyes to install a barrier, but I don't. What if he doesn't feel the same way I do: that this time is different? More intimate.

With a clenched jaw, he splays his hands on my hips and guides me, dictating the rhythm, perhaps to assuage his own mounting desire.

The first flutters of my climax force a gasp from me. I curl my fingers into his shoulders as if I'm clinging to the edge of a cliff, about to hurtle headfirst into the unknown, but I can't break our eye contact. It's silent communication: *I see you. I know you.*

Our stares stay glued, our wordless connection intensifying with every second.

A rush of feelings pours through my veins as I surrender to my orgasm. I could no more stop it than I can stop the spasms wracking my body as Sterling holds me tight and pumps out his release with a feral yell. When I open my eyes, I see the same confusion that I feel tightening my throat etched into his expression.

Lost for words, I collapse against his sweat-slicked chest, my heart a panic of stuttering beats.

What if he deserts you? Takes your trust and your feelings and disappears?

With each restorative breath I talk myself back from the ledge. I'm good. Just because it feels so right in his arms, doesn't mean I need him in order to find a place where I belong. I can figure out where that place is tomorrow. I can worry about Hamilton's and sleeping with the enemy tomorrow. I can examine these emotions waking up inside me tomorrow.

We head for the shower, renewed desire already coiling around us.

Tomorrow will come soon enough.

CHAPTER ELEVEN

Sterling

THE NOISES OF the city stream in through the open window of Ava's bedroom. The glow from the streetlights casts her beautiful body in relief. We haven't stopped touching each other since the delicious dinner we prepared together. Since we shared parts of ourselves previously locked away behind mistrust and resentment. Since I sensed her loneliness and realised that the complexity of what we're doing is beyond casual.

Risky.

My opening up about Marcus and Mom and Brent's felt both wrong and right. This woman's hold over me leads me to be vulnerable. Perhaps because she puts herself out there, too. Perhaps because she's strong enough, because of her own loss, to handle my ugly truths.

You could cut free those ugly parts...

That's why I'm casting off Brent's. Finally

walking away from the last tie to the powerlessness of my past. Yet there's a tiny part of me that wonders if Marcus's words and predictions were true. Yes, I have it all financially, but the idea of returning to my dark penthouse tonight with its sleek, minimalistic décor feels empty. Compared to spending the night with Ava at her cosy apartment—cooking, laughing, kissing and touching... No contest.

Perhaps it's just *her* that makes all the difference.

My fingers dig into her hips reflexively. A satisfied smile kicks up her beautiful mouth. The pleasure that fills every inch of my body ebbs, replaced with the familiar hot licks of shame and guilt I feel whenever I look at her. I understand what Hamilton's means to her, and if this vulnerable feeling didn't remind of me of how weak I was as a child under Marcus's control—how I failed at the relationship I tried to have with Monroe—I'd consider selling her back the equity. Or just handing over Hamilton's so she can create a legacy to be proud of. One that commemorates her loved ones.

Except I'll still need to find a solution for Brent's. Marcus controlled my young life. Controlled my mother and disparaged my father. His hold was so pervasive; he even played a part in ruining my marriage. I can't be that weak again. I can't go back, so the only way is forward.

Watching Ava in the kitchen earlier, I realised the tense, combative version of her I've witnessed to date is nowhere close to the real woman I've seen drooling over menus. When relaxed and focused on creating the mouthwatering dishes we ate tonight, she became the animated and passionate woman I see now. Full of fire. Alive with humour, her energy incandescent.

That's the woman I can't scrub from my mind for even a second. That's why she was the first person I wanted to see when I arrived back in New York after the funeral. That's why I couldn't walk away tonight.

She strokes that stubborn lock of hair back from my forehead, the silence between us comfortable.

You don't want this to end—that's why you didn't go home tonight.

But how long can it last? I'm going to ruin this easy connection we have. She'll hate what I still intend to do to Hamilton's, especially after she showed me her great-grandmother's piano.

Could I help her start up a restaurant? It's what I do, after all, fund start-ups. Surely with her heritage and her passion and her talents, any venture in which she partakes will be a roaring success.

But we won't be a part of each other's future. With the completion of her report, which sits on my desk, Ava's contract for Bold is now fulfilled. There's no reason to keep seeing her, apart from the urgency that rides me hard whenever we're apart. I've had plenty of time to experience that need in the three days since Chicago. Even now, lying in her bed, there's no end in sight.

Fuck—this can't be about feelings. I've been there, done that with Monroe. I failed. I let her down. I allowed Marcus into my head when I should have been focused on making my marriage strong. How easily my self-beliefs toppled, for all my success. Because I only flourish at business, and given Marcus is dead, no amount of prosperity will achieve my goal of besting him. Every time I've tried to put emotions on the line in my personal life, it's been a disaster. Confronting Mom over Marcus—I tried before I left home. She became emotional and cried, confessed her concerns about me growing up without a father figure. Rushing into my marriage with Monroe only to discover Marcus was right.

I can't risk another failure by taking a chance on Ava. But I can reassure her that I'm the one with issues. She may feel in professional limbo, but at least her personal life can be fulfilling in the future.

'You asked about Monroe.' I grit my teeth to stave off imaginings of Ava with another man. I roll onto my back and stare at the ceiling as pricks of guilt rain down on me at how badly I let Monroe down when she needed me most. 'We met at university in London.' Newly engaged, I'd taken Monroe home to New York to show off my new fiancée and the ring I'd saved up to purchase to my mother.

It won't last—one day she'll see through you Marcus had muttered under his breath for my ears only as the women fawned over bridal magazines and discussed venues. I'd been irrationally furious as I confronted him in low tones so as not to upset Mom and Monroe. I'd told him to butt out of my life and keep his opinions to himself. I'd already tolerated his audacious bragging—how he planned to purchase Hamilton's—over dinner.

'We were young,' I say. 'We had heaps in common, but I guess we rushed into marriage.' One of the hardest pills to swallow, aside from the fact that Monroe and I had fallen out of love seemingly as easily as we'd fallen into love, was that Marcus's prediction was accurate. It haunts me still.

Coming back to New York without my wife I'd felt like a dog slinking home with its tail between its legs. Even the expansion of Bold into North America had felt muted. I avoided seeing Marcus and his dreaded snide expression. I felt like a child again—I'd done something wrong but had no idea what or how to fix it.

I've worked my entire adult life to break free of the effects of his poisonous condemnations. The success of Bold attests to that.

But not your personal life.

'What happened?' Ava's voice is a cautious whisper. Her fingers gently stroke my chest.

I want her to understand me. I'm not ashamed of my divorce per se. I regret allowing Marcus's vitriol to distract me, and I hate that I let Monroe down.

'Six months into our marriage, Monroe lost her mother. It was a very tough time for her, and it seemed that she changed overnight. She was grieving, of course. But she pushed me away. As if she didn't need me anymore. I felt like a failure, like I could do nothing right.'

Ava is quiet and watchful, so I press on. 'I hated feeling helpless. It reminded me of how Marcus made me feel growing up. He'd even voiced my shortcomings as a husband before the wedding. That he was right, and there seemed to be nothing I could do to fix us, made me shut down emotionally.'

And I've never opened up fully since.

'Truth is, I allowed him to get into my head,' I say. 'Every time Monroe and I argued, I felt like his prediction was coming true. I had no control. I just kept letting her down. I don't forgive myself for that weakness.'

For being too hung up on proving something to Marcus to focus on the more important relationship right in front of my face.

Shock registers in Ava's expression. 'It doesn't make you weak, it makes you human. Life and relationships are hard enough when you have the support of loved ones. When you're constantly criticised and worn down over years, it's understandable that you'd occasionally believe the negativity. Did Monroe know? About your past?'

I shrug, desperate to change the subject now. I don't want Ava to think less of me. I don't want to show her all my vulnerabilities. 'She didn't know everything. I kept the worst stuff from her because I was young. I thought I'd left all of that behind by the time I reached my twenties, but these things have a habit of rearing their heads when we least expect, especially at times of stress.'

'Yes, I agree.' Her voice is full of empathy. 'I'm sorry about your marriage.'

I shrug again, because part of me still has no idea how we went so wrong. 'My biggest failing as a husband was that I didn't communicate well. I kept things to myself, assumed my ex didn't need to know what was in my head. Turned out she'd wanted to know, just as I needed to understand the way she was feeling. When we needed to pull together, we pushed each other away.'

I drag Ava into my arms and kiss her until the feelings of inadequacy fade. It's as if I can't get enough of her—she's a balm for my body and mind. The only time I feel invincible.

'What about you?' I ask. 'Any serious relation-ships?' Perhaps she's happy alone. The thought depresses me more than it should.

She shakes her head, her eyes wary. 'I don't have time for relationships.'

'You'd make time if it was important to you.' Just as she's made time for this thing between us, even though she hates my plans for Hamilton's.

But this isn't a relationship.

'Can't you tell? I have abandonment issues,' she says with an overly bright smile that tells me how close to the truth her statement is.

I smile back, but as I wrap my arms around her shoulders and hold her close, one thought circles my consciousness: I don't want to walk away when this is over.

So keep seeing her.

'Can I see you tomorrow night?' I ask before panic robs me of speech. 'I'd like to take you out for your birthday, if you don't have plans,' I add to cover the feeling that, emotionally, I'm cracking open a dusty chamber full of cobwebs.

'I'd love that,' she says on a sleepy sigh.

'I'm taking you dancing,' I say as we exit the ride-share vehicle in the East Village. She's excited, her eyes bright as she grips my hand and follows me down a set of wrought-iron steps to the base-ment club. I've booked a table near the stage with booth-style seating. The bar is dark and intimate, reminiscent of a speakeasy. There's live music and a small dance floor.

At our table, we order cocktails and bar snacks from our server. I tug Ava under my arm while we listen to the band play a soul classic, which showcases the vocalist's amazing talents.

I press a kiss to her temple. 'Seeing your parents' vinyl collection reminded me how my parents loved to go out dancing.'

She smiles. 'I meant to ask you last night, before I became…distracted. What was your father like?'

'He was just a regular guy. A protector. Kind and hardworking, and made everything great—the opposite of Marcus.'

'Did they know each other?'

I nod and explain the connection. 'For a few years before my father and Marcus's wife died, both couples became friends. I guess that's what Mom felt she had in common with him, and perhaps the reason Marcus was jealous of my dad.'

'How did your dad die?' she asks, squeezing my hand so I know she understands.

'An accident. He was making an arrest. There was a scuffle and he lost his footing. He fell and hit his head—a bleed on the brain.'

'I'm so sorry.' She raises my hand to her mouth and kisses my knuckles. 'You must take after him—

you have the same qualities. Protective, kind, hard-working. Do you look like him too?'

I shrug. 'I guess. We have the same hair.'

She ruffles her fingers through my hair and we laugh together before sharing a long, distracting kiss that chases away my melancholy.

'I bought you a small gift,' I say when we break for air. I pull a heavy envelope from my breast pocket and slide it onto the table.

'You didn't need to do that.' Despite her repri-mand, she takes the envelope with that beautiful smile I've come to crave.

'I know, but I wanted to. It's no big deal.' I press my mouth to hers, lingering over another kiss, which feels like a massive deal. Because I don't want to stop. I want to put this dreamy, elated ex-pression on her face every day. I want to wake up with her burrowed into my side the way I woke this morning. And even scarier, I want to protect her from her sadness and ensure that she never feels alone again.

Fuck…never is an impossible length of time. Permanence. Commitment.

I don't do that. Not since Monroe.

But Ava is different. You're different. Older and wiser and no longer a target of Marcus's bitter-ness and antagonism.

Could I risk a relationship again once I've put Marcus behind me? A fresh outlook, a clean slate?

That's what I hope my gift gives Ava—new perspective and a chance to reconnect with her parents over something I know she loves.

She slides her finger under the seal and removes the document from the envelope. I watch with rising excitement filling my chest as she reads the information, her gorgeous eyes flicking down the page.

I know exactly the moment she realises the nature of my gift—an all-inclusive, month-long cooking retreat in Tuscany—because her eyes widen and she gasps.

'Sterling, I can't accept this. It's too much.' The hand holding the itinerary trembles.

'It's a gift—of course you can accept it.' I can tell she's enchanted. She's probably just a little scared of the possibilities. After the meal she created last night, she can't continue to hide her talents at home.

A frown forms between her brows. 'How can I go to Italy when there's so much to do here?'

'Easy.' I kiss away the worry pursing her lips. 'You ask for my help. If you want, I'll put a manager into Hamilton's while I implement the merger and sale. All you'll need to do is sign the paperwork before you board the Bold jet.' I cup her face and stare into her eyes. 'Summer is the only time to visit Tuscany, and the return flight is open-ended, so you can travel around the rest of the country afterwards if you want—revisit your roots.'

She shifts, breaking my hold. 'It's not as simple as that.' The look she shoots me is full of disappointment. 'So you haven't changed your mind…? About Hamilton's?'

I frown, my stare pleading. 'Is that really what you still want? Think about it. Don't just cling to the past. Your parents and grandparents would want you to be happy. Cooking makes you happy.'

'Cling to the past…?' She stares for so long that prickles of sweat form under my collar. 'Don't you think that's a little patronising, given your entire motivation for selling my company is linked to *your* past?'

She's right. I am being hypocritical. I thought I could give her something she'd love even if it can't be Hamilton's, and I expected a little resistance. 'I know it can't compensate, but I genuinely hoped you'd enjoy the trip.'

'Another way to look at it is that I'll also be out of your hair so you can complete your plans unopposed.' A small frown pinches her brows.

I say nothing, because she's right. The gift helps appease my guilt. I'm selling her family business and effectively rendering her unemployed. 'All valid points, but I don't want to argue tonight—it's your birthday. Please just consider going to Italy.'

I swallow, my chest tight at the idea if she spends months in Europe. But I want her to find her wings. To rediscover her rightful path, not the one to which circumstances led her. Just as her home is full of memories, so too is her current workplace.

I want her to be happy.

You care too much.

Maybe, but I hate any form of injustice. The fact that Ava's young life was devastated by some selfish, careless drunk fills me with protective urges. I have the means and the inclination to grant her any dream she has. I could set her up in her own restaurant tomorrow, if she asked. I'd rather use my money to help Ava than to gift Josh Brent's.

She nibbles at her bottom lip, clearly deciding whether to drop it or persist.

'Will you dance with me?' I ask.

She sighs and offers a reluctant smile. 'Yes, but I retain my right to revisit this subject tomorrow.'

'I'll take that concession.' I hold her hand and guide her onto the dance floor. The band, who are home-grown talent, is excellent. The playlist is an eclectic mix of R&B, rock and roll, soul and even swing music. I tug her close for a slow dance, my heart banging against hers the way it did this morning when I woke her with a sleepy, happy birthday kiss at the first light of dawn. Her eyes shone with unshed tears I kissed away as I pushed inside her and we made slow, heartfelt love.

Her eyes sear mine as if she too is remembering how we began this day. 'Where did you learn to dance?' Her hand grips my shoulder, one finger lightly brushing my neck above the collar of my shirt.

I swing her around, showing off my skills and distracting myself from the way her touch tightens my body with a need that makes me forget our business conflicts. Forget that I'm only interested in casual. That I never want to be responsible for a relationship failure again.

'I learned for my wedding. Before that I didn't know dancing could be so much fun—an excuse to hold someone close.' I press my hand between her shoulder blades so her breasts graze my chest.

'You have a lot of respect for Monroe, don't you?'

Warning bells ring in my head. I want tonight to be all about Ava. But I want to be honest. 'Yes. She's an amazing person. I have a lot of respect for both my business partners.'

Ava gives a small nod, her expression guarded.

'I'm meeting them next week in London, actually.' Why are we discussing this? I want to dance her into exhaustion and then take her back to my place and make love to her all night. A grown-up birthday to remember, to replace the ones frozen in time.

At her shocked expression, I realise I should have mentioned this earlier. I'll be out of town for a week, and right now that length of time away from her feels like a lifelong prison sentence.

So how will you watch her leave for Italy...?

I dip my chin and press my lips to the top of her head, inhaling the scent of her shampoo. 'I'm attending the memorial for Monroe's late mother. She, Hudson and I have tagged on a business meeting, so I'll be gone for five days. I meant to tell you.'

She stiffens slightly in my arms. 'That's very supportive of you.'

I pull back and stare into her eyes, trying to read her mind. What do I want to see? That she'll miss me? That she's jealous of Monroe because she cares about me the way I can no longer deny I care about her?

But there are more questions than answers in her blue gaze.

'I guess you're right, or perhaps I'm just compensating for my failure to do that when we were married.'

Her stare is hesitant. Then she shrugs. 'Like you said—we're both stuck in the past.'

She's crossing a line. I don't know whether to feel glad that she cares about me, or annoyed that she sees me so clearly.

Can you see her situation with greater clarity than you can see your own?

'That's why I think you should take that trip to Italy. You're clinging to an old life, a life that isn't wholly yours. A life that will soon be gone.'

Fire flashes in her eyes suddenly. 'Yes, because I've already lost so much… Letting go of Hamilton's would be easier if it was *my* choice, rather than having it thrust upon me.'

Guilt leaves me tense from head to toe. 'I know how much you've lost, and I wish I could undo your pain.'

Instead, I'm the one turning her life upside down.

'Do you? Your gift, as generous as it is, feels like a consolation prize. One I'm supposed to simply accept in lieu of my company.'

Her accusation kicks me in the gut—I don't need the reminder of how much I'm taking from her. 'I don't want to hurt you. I just want you to consider following your dreams once all of this is over.'

'I'll embrace a new life,' she says, her eyes stormy with emotion, 'if you abandon your plan for revenge over a man who's no longer alive to witness it.'

The air is sucked from my lungs as if I've entered a vacuum. 'It's not only about revenge. It's about rejecting the last tie with the unhappy parts of my past.' Can't she see I'm trying to finally move on?

She stops dancing. 'Do you really believe that revenge-selling Brent's will bring you lasting peace?' Her stare is incredulous. 'You'll still have your memories. Your mom will want to remember Marcus with fondness. She doesn't know what you went through.'

'Yes, it will help.' My tone is sharp. More softly I add, 'Turning something negative into a success is how I've built an entire empire. If, with the help of Hamilton's, I can achieve that with Brent's I can lay the years of bullying to rest.'

The song changes to something more upbeat, but we've veered into sticky territory, the atmosphere heavy with discord. The last thing I wanted on her birthday.

As we head back to our seats, I'm struck by the unsettling knowledge that just because I'm allowing her close doesn't mean she understands me the way I think I understand her.

And I can't shake the feeling that I've been here before.

CHAPTER TWELVE

Ava

I DON'T NORMALLY go running this late, but it's the first chance I've had in a busy day and, aside from when I'm cooking, it's when I think best. It's dusk. From the Brooklyn Heights Promenade, the setting sun strikes Brooklyn Bridge ahead and turns the skyscrapers of lower Manhattan across the harbour into golden turrets of an urban fairy tale castle.

Except reality bites at my heels, pushing me harder as sweat stings my eyes. I'm trying to outrun my restlessness, my thoughts, but there's no escape from my new reality or from the way I feel about the man who's been instrumental in its creation.

Earlier today, with a heavy heart and a trembling pen, I signed the legal paperwork for Sterling's merger. Only the documents are still on my desk. I couldn't bear to deliver them, still clinging to the hope that he'll relent. Because his feelings for me have surpassed his desire for vengeance.

Fear of the great unknown stretches out before me, along with another, more insistent anxiety: that I'm falling for Sterling. Nothing else explains my conflicted state. I want Hamilton's, but I want him more.

But what does he want, beyond his revenge? And if he cared about me, would he plough on regardless and destroy my last link to my family?

Over breakfast at Gianni's this morning—strong coffee and warm brioche—I reflected on my options. I could ask the new owners of Lombard Logistics to keep me on—my relationships with both the staff and customers would be a great asset to their management team. I could look for a similar role in a new company—my years of management experience would certainly be attractive. Or I could take my share of the profits Sterling promises and do something terrifying and brave. Something I'm scared to even voice aloud, so momentous is the possibility.

You could open the restaurant of your dreams.

As I listened to Gianni talk about his new menu and his busy day ahead, my excitement for the trip to Italy bubbled to the surface. I allowed myself to envisage a life without Hamilton's. I imagined what advice my parents would give if they were here. I asked myself what would make me feel content and secure.

My stomach pinches as a wave of memories slams home. It's been years since I opened my heart to dreams. Losing my parents affected every aspect of my young life. Schoolwork seemed irrelevant. I stopped caring about cute boys and securing my first kiss. Even my friendships suffered—some ending and some, a rare few, becoming more important and therefore all the more fragile. But, aside from the grief and loneliness, the worst aspect was the personal toll: I felt as if I had literally disappeared. As if I too no longer existed.

What did that teenage girl I was care for dreams? I was too busy surviving. Living with my grandparents, seeing them work hard, shaped me. They guided me along the path to follow them into their business. I never once stopped to wonder what else I wanted. For myself.

Until this feud with Sterling forced me to take stock and revaluate my goals. To ask myself the question to which a part of me dreads the answer: am I happy with my life?

I *am* passionate about Italian food. I love to cook. If my parents were still alive I'd have probably joined them in the restaurant. But can I really turn a love for Italian cookery into something more when I've previously only allowed it hobby status? Something I do to remember my parents and my childhood and my roots?

Why not?

I could take Sterling's gift and start a brave new adventure. But doing that would force me to acknowledge my feelings for him and admit that he understands me, despite the way we met and the revenge-seeking circumstances under which we began this affair.

He's right—I have been clinging to the past. It's been my happy place. Before my parents died, I felt safe and loved and belonged to something bigger than me. After their deaths, the world seemed huge and dangerous and unfamiliar. I was lost as if I'd never fit in anywhere again.

I'll never be able to repay my grandparents for their care, nor will I ever forget my parents, but it's time to do something for myself. Time to be brave and forge a new path. To dream big and put everything on the line.

Just like Sterling, I too want a fresh start.

Perhaps we could start afresh together…

Because I want him in my brave new world. I want to try dating him. We have plenty in common and the idea that I won't see him again once the sale of the newly formed Lombard Logistics goes through fills my veins with ice. But my heart is fragile. Untested and patched together like a frayed pair of jeans.

What if the stitches don't hold?

I pound the esplanade, heading for the bridge. Shame for the pangs of jealousy that ripped through my chest last night, when Sterling talked about Monroe, chases me. His loyalty and integrity towards his ex-wife heartened me but also forced me to acknowledge my feelings.

Feelings that seem to grow with every step I take.

But the combination of his marriage failure and his need to prove something to himself after Marcus means he's probably a league away from reciprocating those feelings.

My visit from a man I've never met before—Josh Brent, Sterling's stepbrother—proved that Sterling isn't ready to abandon his revenge. The betrayal was a blow strong enough to make me question if the feelings I have are the beginnings of love.

What else would bring such dreamy highs and crushing lows?

I slow my pace, heading down the steps to the street level that will take me under the bridge and back to the waterfront, down past the vintage carousel I loved as a girl. That's when I see Sterling waiting at the kerb, his tall, athletic body casually leaning against the hood of his SUV. The last rays of the sunset glint from his sandy blond hair as he looks down at his phone.

My breath catches as if I haven't run in a decade. Those deep, convoluted emotions writhe in the pit of my stomach. How can I love a man who stripped me of my livelihood and my heritage? A man so hung up on the past that he too has a brittle heart that may never heal. Even if he does have feelings for me in return, he's been married before. He allowed the past, Marcus and his inability to move on to contribute to the demise of that marriage. Can I risk the fact that the same destructive forces might decimate our relationship?

Could I stand to fall all the way in love with him, only to lose him too?

I can't pin my hopes for a new belonging on such feeble foundations. I need acceptance. Certainty. Security. I can find all of that within myself if I have to, although I'd rather find it with Sterling. But my bravery can only stretch so far. Unless he's meeting me halfway, I can't forge a new and terrifying career path and a serious relationship at the same time.

He looks up as I approach, his smile like a knife between my ribs. I go to him on instinct because I can't stay away. I press my sweaty body against his and take his ready kiss, because I need it more than the oxygen feeding my lungs.

His arms come around my hips, slotting me between his thighs as he leans back against his car and kisses me back as if we're a couple of teens on our first date.

'I couldn't stay away, not even for eight hours.' His confession is planted against my lips. His kisses are wild and exhilarating.

'How did you know where to find me?' I ask when I've found the strength to pull back for air. I'm probably a red-faced mess, but his stare swoops the length of my Lycra-clad body in appreciation and he's hard against my stomach. I want to make him sweaty too, so acute is my desperation for him.

But I want more than sex. I want *him* and I need to know if it's a lost cause.

'Judy told me.' He brushes a wisp of hair back from my cheek. 'She tracks your phone when you run as a safety measure.'

I nod, grateful that in a city of eight million residents—which can still feel like a very lonely place—I have people who care.

He cups my cheek, bringing my mouth back to his, making me feel every minute tendril of *his* care. He wouldn't be here if he were the ruthless, heartless man I once believed him to be. He wouldn't be here if his heart were filled to bursting with revenge.

But is there enough room for love?

Recalling my visit from Josh, who'd tracked me down following my visit to Brent's, I taste

Sterling's betrayal once more, like acid in my throat.

Why didn't he tell me Josh wanted his father's company? I'm open and willing to be as vulnerable as I've ever been for him, to invite him into my terrifying future, and he's cagey and uncommunicative, just like he said he was with Monroe. He doesn't even trust me professionally, when I've given him everything.

My business. My expertise. My blessing, not that he knows this yet.

Josh's fight for his father's legacy helped seal my decision. I want to fight for that part of my parents I miss the most: our shared love of food. I want a restaurant like Girasole. I can honour both my parents and my grandparents by being happy and by being myself.

'Let's go somewhere to talk,' I say, ignoring the desire building in me like steam. I need to confront him and give him a chance to explain. I want to know if I'll need to stop craving him, to let him go…

He reaches behind him to open the passenger door and steps aside, guiding me into the vehicle.

The promenade is popular with joggers, dog walkers and tourists seeking that iconic New York souvenir snap. There are too many people around for the conversation ahead, so I direct him a few streets away to an empty parking lot near the waterfront under the bridge, which overlooks the carousel in the distance. At this time of night most of the businesses in this area are closed and the streets are quiet.

For a few seconds after Sterling kills the engine, we watch the colourful lights of the carousel in loaded silence. Under other circumstances I'd find this moment, this setting—a twinkling Manhattan across the water, the string of lights across the bridge, the distant music of the carousel—incredibly romantic.

Except doubts flood me with chills. I feel them creeping up on me with futile inevitability. I rub at my arms and Sterling reaches for his jacket and drapes it around my shoulders.

'Thanks.' I meet his beautiful stare, something lurching in my chest. I knew I loved him as I signed on the dotted line today, releasing my company into his care, to do whatever he will.

I want him to be happy. If selling Brent's and Hamilton's will help him move on from his painful past, then I'll no longer stand in his way, even if it means I'll lose Hamilton's.

'I had a visitor at Hamilton's today.' Trepidation shudders through my rapidly cooling body. I'm so conflicted I want to jump out of the car and keep running rather than face this moment. But I need to know if what Josh told me is true.

And I need to know how he feels about me.

He casts me a side glance, wariness in his eyes. 'Who?'

I swallow hard, foreboding cramping my stomach. 'Josh Brent. He came in to tell me that he wants to buy out Brent's Express, urged me to use any influence I have to beg you to reconsider. He said you won't sell to him.'

Sterling's nostrils flare with distaste. 'How manipulative of him.' He looks away, his face taut with repressed frustration. 'I can only apologise for my stepbrother's behaviour, something he's inherited from Marcus perhaps.'

He's shutting me out, sticking to his hard line and retreating behind his resentment.

'It's okay.' My voice wobbles. 'I understand his…desperation.'

Sterling huffs. 'Do you? Don't feel sorry for him. His desperation stems from being told no. He seems to think I owe him loyalty but there's never been any closeness or family connection between us.'

I ache anew for the years that Sterling felt stifled in his stepfamily. 'I don't feel sorry for him, but I can empathise with his point of view when it comes to his father's company.'

My tone is harshened by my own frustrations and disappointment. Doesn't Sterling owe *me* loyalty? After everything we've shared, both professionally and personally?

'If you want to waste your time on Josh, go ahead. I can't stop you.' He stares straight ahead, his bullish attitude highlighting just how out of sync we are emotionally.

Can't he see how much I'm conceding and how little he's giving me in return? 'No, but you can stop the public sale. You could sell Brent's to Josh instead.'

His head whips around, his glare astonished. 'Why the hell would I do that? I owe him nothing. I was a ten-year-old kid when he came into my life and he was seventeen. He had a mean streak a mile wide. He took pleasure in calling me names until I reacted, then he'd watch with a smirk while Marcus dealt out some reprimand for *my* behaviour.'

'I'm sorry about that—'

'I foolishly imagined I'd have a big brother I could emulate and rely on,' he interrupts. 'Josh had endless chances to stick up for me, but he never took a single one.'

I reach for his hand on instinct, nauseous that I've brought his pain to the surface. 'I hate that you went through that, but he was a kid too. You'd both lost a parent.' I understand the confusion and devastation of that. 'Perhaps he was struggling with the fact that his father had remarried and become part of a second family. That can't have been easy.' I don't want to defend Josh—I know nothing about him—but I want to find something in Sterling's heart other than vengeance. 'And bullies are often bullied. Perhaps Marcus was as much a bully to him as he was to you.'

'Perhaps. But in that case we should have had more in common than we ever did.' His hand flexes into a fist in his lap. 'If Marcus wanted his son to inherit Brent's, why didn't he leave it to him in his will instead of selling to me in some sort of final power trip?'

Anger spikes in me—a rapid thrumming of my blood. 'I don't know, but can't you see the parallels here?'

'What parallels?' Genuine confusion creases his brow. It cuts deep. He really has no idea what I'm going through or how let down I feel by his refusal to sell to Josh and leave Hamilton's alone.

'If the building which housed my parents' restaurant came up for sale, don't you think I'd want to purchase it?'

His eyes brighten, momentary delight shining there as he comprehends that I've undergone a monumental shift in rationale. 'I guess you would. I think that's a brilliant idea.' He squeezes my fingers. 'But this is different.'

'No, it's not. Belonging is everything to me, Sterling. The idea that I'll lose my family's business has forced me to see that I can belong somewhere other than Hamilton's. I'm waking up to the possibility of another life. But isn't it the same for

Josh? His parents are dead. Nothing can change that. But what if running Brent's or even Lombard Logistics is what he needs to do to stay connected to his past? What if you owned my parents' restaurant but refused to sell it to me out of petty revenge? Can you imagine how distraught I'd be?'

'That would never happen.' He clenches his jaw.

I ignore his assertions; they're hypothetical, empty words. 'Would you really deny Josh that for revenge over a man who isn't here? You're bigger than that. You always have been. You've proved yourself professionally over and over again. There's no one left to impress.' I'm impassioned, pleading with him to understand. 'You think your past made you weak, but you're wrong. It's the opposite, in fact. It made you strong. Determined. Compassionate. A kind, honourable protector, just like your dad. This vengeful man isn't you.'

I release his hand and cup his face between my palms. 'Denying Josh won't make you happy. I know, because I just saw it in your eyes.'

He looks away, a muscle ticking in his jaw. He doesn't believe me. He can't see a different way out. Not even for me.

I press on, desperate to see a glimmer of hope, because if he can open his heart, perhaps he could return my feelings. 'If you could buy me that dry-cleaning business right now, would you?'

'Yes,' he says with zero hesitation that makes me want to kiss him. 'But I care about *you*.'

His words sing through my nervous system as if I'm seven and happy and riding that carousel with my parents. I want to believe him. I'm just so scared that he's more caught up in besting Marcus through Josh.

'But you care about Brent's and your revenge more.' My whispered accusation reverberates through the quiet interior of the car.

'That's not true.' His eyes flick about wildly. 'Brent's is a business decision. You...that's personal.'

I sigh, all my fears converging at the back of my throat. 'And yet I can't detangle the two where you're concerned. The personal has become more important to me than the business that's the last tie to my loved ones.' I blink away the sting behind my eyes. 'Answer me one question honestly—if I hadn't slept with you that first night, would you have sold me back Hamilton's?'

I feel every second that he calculates his answer pulse through my head. 'No, probably not.' He frowns, his admission flat.

A part of me crumbles then. The feeling is so familiar. I wish I was in my office, staring out of the window at that strip of the East River. Perhaps then I'd find the strength to do what I must.

'I signed over Hamilton's today,' I say, dredging

up my last shreds of courage. 'I trust you professionally. But also, I realised that I'm lost in the past and not living my own life. I want more—I want a fulfilling job and personal happiness. I want to chase my own dreams and I want to find a man to do that alongside.' If I can move on and face a brave new future, why can't he? 'Do what you will with my company. It's *you* I want.'

He looks desolate. Not pleased, as I assumed, that his merger can finally go ahead, or that I'm laying everything on the line for the possibility of us.

But there's no going back. Embracing hope means embracing how I feel. 'I'm willing to change my entire life,' I say. 'To stop fighting for Hamilton's in order to show you how much I care about you. I'm falling for you, and all I need to know is that you are willing to be open to a relationship with me without allowing the past to interfere.'

When he looks down for a split second, I have my answer. It's a blade clean through those stitches in my heart.

'I don't know what to say.' His eyes blaze. 'You say you're handing over Hamilton's, but you seem to be issuing an ultimatum—us or the merger. I can't have both.'

I fall apart then, like a cliff crumbling into the sea. 'That you think that tells me exactly what I need to know.' If he had feelings for me, he'd reorder his priorities. He'd support me the way he supports Monroe. He'd turn his life upside down to make us work, the way I've turned mine over and over. Not for him, but for *me*. Because I want him more than anything else.

With sudden desperation to escape the coldness in his eyes and the foolishness I feel for trusting my fragile heart to a man who can't love me back, I reach for the door handle.

'Good luck with the sale, Sterling. I hope you get everything you want from it.' I leave the car, ducking to issue my final remark. 'I hope your revenge makes you happy and that the emotional price isn't too high.'

I run as fast as I can towards my future, my feet twice as heavy knowing that he won't be a part of it.

CHAPTER THIRTEEN

Sterling

EVERY INCH OF me is tense, as if I'm made of steel. The brittle kind. One false move and I'll crack into jagged shards. The concern in Monroe's hazel eyes across the table from me amplifies the panic cleaving through my soul.

'Don't look at me like that,' I say, blocking out her perceptive stare by glancing around the elegant dining room of London's Dorchester Hotel where we've met for brunch on my last day in London.

This trip has been a disaster. I've been too distracted by how I handled things the last time I saw Ava to focus on Bold business. The interest in the newly branded Lombard Logistics has been overwhelming—several motivated buyers emerged way quicker than I anticipated. But I'm trapped, unable to make a decision and holding off my final signature on the sale.

As if that isn't enough to contend with, I've just discovered that my two business partners, my ex-wife and my best friend, are sleeping together.

Monroe continues to stare, calmly sipping her tea. I expel a restorative breath. That unexpected news might have poleaxed me, but all I think about is Ava. How cold I acted when she told me about her feelings. And how nothing has been right since I watched her run away.

The emotions that blaze through my chest like forked lightning are so painful, it's easier to focus on Monroe. 'Why don't you tell me all about you and Hudson?'

'I will if you will.' Her reply is typically forthright and insightful. We know each other too well to hide anything. 'You go first.' She sweeps her long dark hair over her shoulder.

I flick her a reluctant smile, recalling all the times over the years that she seemed to know me better than I know myself.

Just like Ava does.

Ava… So strong. So brave. So perfect.

Why is it so hard to dismiss the way I feel about her? Why can't I simply stick to my guns and walk away, the way I have time and time again in business?

Because this is personal. I care about her more than I want to admit.

Perhaps you even love her…

No. I can't go there. I've already let her down because I can't seem to chase Marcus from my mind. I've already ruined one relationship while under his influence. Until I'm free of him, I've nothing to offer Ava.

I refuse to hurt her, although the memory of the disappointment I saw in her eyes reminds me that I already have.

I clear my throat, aware that Monroe is silently watching me. The real issue is too painful to admit, so I hedge. 'I'm about to close a deal for Brent's, which has, of course, been rebranded as Lombard Logistics. What do you think?'

My smile feels like a grotesque mask.

Why aren't I more elated? Why am I holding off from signing over to the buyer who won the bidding war yesterday during our Bold meeting at Monroe's London office?

Because Ava is right. It won't make me happy. It won't erase the past. I'm proving nothing except that Marcus still features in my thoughts. In my decisions. Even in my relationships.

Fuck. Why else would I have behaved so ruthlessly brutal with Ava and watched her disappear into the night?

Oh, I followed her home from a distance, tracking her with the app her assistant uses, just to ensure she was safe. I even sat outside her apartment for an hour, debating where I'd gone so wrong and what I could do to repair it. But I couldn't face her. Seeing how let-down she felt when I stuck to my plan for Brent's all but demolished me.

Rather than congratulate me on the deal as I expect, Monroe levels a similar look on me now.

'I don't know why you bought Brent's in the first place. Why would you keep hold of bad memories? *Is* it even profitable?'

'It will be. I've amalgamated a couple of other companies. I have a buyer desperate to snatch up the lot and make a very nice return indeed.' My voice sounds smug, but urgency beats at the base of my neck until my collar feels like a torture device.

Monroe's intelligent eyes narrow with speculation. 'So what are you waiting for? And why else are you discombobulated if it's not business?'

I drum my fingers on the table, stalling.

Light sparkles in her stare as she figures me out. 'You've met someone, haven't you?'

I smooth my tie and then wince at the nervous gesture she's bound to spot.

I tell myself it's awkwardness that makes me hesitant. Monroe and I have dated intermittently in the years post-divorce, but we rarely talk specifics. 'I have been seeing someone, yes. But it's not meant to be.'

Because you messed up again.

'Why not?'

She's not going to let this go. Perhaps confiding in her will help me get things straight in my head. 'Because I let her down.' I offer a tight smile. 'I have a habit of that, as you know.'

I need to get the focus of discussion away from me and onto her and Hudson and the sexual relationship they started while I was detained in New York for Dale's funeral. 'So, over to you and Hudson.'

Monroe completely ignores my attempt at deflection. 'You didn't let me down. We let ourselves down.' Her voice is full of compassion and understanding. 'We both bungled our marriage. Perhaps we were too young or immature or eager.'

I tilt my head in acknowledgement. We were all of those things.

'Tell me about this woman who has clearly burrowed under your skin—I'm sure she's fascinating.' Monroe's smile glitters. She's enjoying grilling me, but my turn is to come.

With a sigh I relent, spilling mine and Ava's story the way I wanted to the minute I arrived in London. But for Monroe's mother's memorial and the obvious tensions between her and Hudson, I might have unloaded my biggest fear—that I've lost something rare and precious out of a foolish obsession with the past.

When I've finished talking, relief rushes through my body, swiftly followed by sickening dread. Ava and I had a good thing. She said she was falling for me and I ignored that in order to keep my guard up. Without that shield, I wouldn't care about Marcus's stupid company. Josh could have it with my blessing…

Damn…that's the answer. I haven't signed the deal, because I want Ava more than I want my revenge. I don't need the professional success, because I have it all anyway. What I can't tolerate is not having her.

Desperately trying to change the subject until I can think straight, I say, 'So, it seems we've both mixed business and pleasure with disastrous results.'

Monroe holds up her hand. 'Hold on—we'll get to me in a second. Are you seriously telling me that you're damaging your chances with this amazing woman in order to prove you're nothing like your stepfather suggested? Because you already know that. You've already proved that over and over again. You didn't fail at our marriage or let me down. We just didn't work out for many reasons.'

'I know, but—'

'No buts,' she interrupts. 'It's that overprotective side of you, isn't it?'

'I'm not overprotective.'

'Yes, you are. You inherited your father's compassion. You protected your mother. You protected me. Now you're protecting yourself so hard, you're pushing away the chance of love. That's insane.'

I can barely choke out my next words, so violent is my state of dread. 'Ava doesn't love me, not anymore anyway.' I wince, hating my stupidity. 'I ruthlessly sold her family's business when it's all she has left of them.'

Monroe softens her tone. 'I don't know if she loves you or not, but I think you love her. Otherwise that sale would have gone through first thing this morning. I know you—there's no stopping any of us once we get the whiff of a good deal. There's only one reason you haven't signed that contract, and that's because you care more about Ava than you do about revenge, or the past, or probably even yourself.'

I'm nodding even before she's stopped speaking, because it's the same conclusion I've just arrived at. Only it's too late.

As if she can read my mind, she says, 'It's not too late. Go back to New York, tell her how you really feel underneath all that bravado and fear, and do whatever you can to win her back.'

I stare for a handful of frantic heartbeats, praying that she's right and what I've done to Ava is redeemable.

'Is that what Hudson needs to do with you?' I take her hand, because she's smart, and so right about me I want to kick my own ass.

Her mouth tightens into a stubborn pout. 'That's a different story.'

I nod, pouring her a second cup of tea from an elegant floral teapot. 'Well, tell me, but tell me quickly,' I say. 'I have a flight to New York to catch.'

And a wrong to right.

It's late at night by the time I knock on Ava's shiny red door. It's taken me nine hours to get here, every minute of which I've replayed our entire relationship over in my head.

How can I have been so blind? How can I have given my bully so much power? How can I have failed to see the wonder right in front of my face?

Ava.

The door swings inwards and she's there, looking beautiful—her hair caught up in a relaxed topknot, tendrils escaping to caress her cheeks; her soft blue T-shirt cupping her breasts; her feet bare and her long legs encased in skinny jeans.

'Hi. Can I come in?' Fear snatches at my voice. 'I have things I need to say.'

She's wary but shrugs. 'Sure.' Her tone is flat, hurt lingering in her eyes as she turns away and I follow her into the living room.

The sight that awaits me momentarily tilts the floor beneath my feet. Packing boxes sit everywhere. Some sealed, labelled and neatly stacked by the door. Some half-full of books and records and Ava's beloved, well-used pots and pans.

'Where are you going?' I ask, my breath strangled by panic.

She keeps her eyes averted, wrapping photo frames in newspaper before placing them into an empty box. 'I'm letting out my apartment. I'm going to Italy.'

She shoots me a look filled with sadness, so my knees almost give way.

'I see…' She's leaving. I'm too late. I've ruined something wonderful and perfect out of fear and stubbornness. I have only myself to blame.

She packs in silence while I stand there like a statue. Inside my heart races, my mouth is too dry to speak and my mind has stopped working anyway.

The envelope in the inside pocket of my jacket crinkles as I move to retrieve a stack of photos from the table. I hand them to her, our fingertips brushing. Aches rack my body from head to toe.

I want to drag her into my arms and kiss her until she forgets about the pain I caused. Until she forgets about leaving me and stops long enough to hear me out.

I can't let her go like this. It's all kinds of wrong.

I take the envelope from my pocket, the memory of her birthday slashing fresh self-loathing through me. 'I want you to have this. It's not a consolation prize.'

She looks at the envelope but doesn't take it from me. I place it gingerly on the table as if its contents are powerful enough to grant my deepest desires.

'What is it? A cheque?' she asks, barely glancing at my offering. 'Have you sold Lombard Logistics already? I heard from the lawyers that you had lots of interest.'

'No… Yes…it's nothing to do with the deal. It's…' I swallow hard. 'Something I want you to have.' Why can't I verbalise how grave my mistakes have been?

Because I love her. And I've lost her.

'Thanks,' she says, 'but as you can see, I'm packing up all my possessions and those belonging to my family that I couldn't bear to part with. It's time for a fresh start. I've hoarded things from the past for too long.' She levels her brave stare on me until I'm crushed by her strength and her self-awareness. 'It's people that matter.' She reaches for a stack of old vinyl records and slots them into the box. 'I'm taking your advice and going to Italy in order to remember and reconnect with my people.'

My smile feels like blown glass. I'm elated and devastated in the same lancing breath. 'I'm so glad. I'm so happy for you.'

And I don't want you to go.

'Thanks.' She tapes the box closed and stacks it near the door, as if I'm not even there.

I should go. I don't deserve her, but I can't allow her to leave the country without knowing how right she was about me. About us. About everything.

I suck in a breath and close the fraught distance between us. Before she can react, I take her hand, my grip as firm as my resolve.

'There's something I need you to know. I gave Brent's to Josh.' The words spill from me in a cathartic rush. 'You were right—my revenge wouldn't make me happy. It wouldn't bring me peace. All along I've had the power to take back control. You helped me to see that, Ava. I owe you everything, so…thank you.'

Her eyes are huge pools of emotion. I can't see what I want to see there yet, so I push on. 'Hamilton's is yours if you want it. Without you, I have no use for it. While I was in London I dreamed… I hoped we could do something creative with it together, but then I realised I'd let you down too badly, and for that I'll always be sorry.'

She shakes her head, tears shining on her lashes. 'I don't want it any more. I'm moving on. I'll be in Italy for six months…'

I nod, forcing my expression into a reassuring smile, when all I want to do is drop to my knees and beg. 'It's okay—I'll help you to put a management team in until you return, or decide what you want to do. There's one other thing… Before you go, I want you to know that I… I love you.'

'Sterling…please don't…' she says in warning, her exquisite eyes brimming with anguish.

'I know it's too late, but I don't want you to leave without knowing that if you ever need it, there's a place right here,' I rest my hand on my chest, over my thudding heart, 'where you'll always belong. For ever.'

She stares up at me, but I have no idea what she's thinking. Maybe I don't deserve to know.

I press a kiss to her forehead, while my breath slashes my chest to ribbons.

'Goodbye, Ava. Have a wonderful trip.'

I don't know how I make it outside. The cool night air burns my lungs. I stumble to my SUV, my heart in tatters. My hand actually trembles as I reach for the door handle, so profound is my devastation that I had it all and lost it. I pause, rest my head against the cool metal roof and try to make my heart beat once more.

It's no good. Without her I'm a shell. A robot in a suit. Money, success, everything is meaningless.

She'll flourish in Italy and I won't be there to see it. All that passion in her will bloom. She may never come back. She could meet some food-loving Italian and be blissful for the rest of her life. And I'll have to live with my regret.

But as long as she's happy I'll try to bear it.

I can't move from the kerb. I'm stuck. Locked in place by the wrongness of how this has unfolded.

For a man who plans and strategises everything, how can I have messed this up so monumentally?

'Sterling.'

At the sound of my name, I spin to see Ava bounding down the steps from her front door. My heart climbs into my throat. Before I have time to move a muscle, she launches herself into my arms.

I catch her and haul her from her feet, stumbling back against the car with the force of my relief.

She kisses me. I groan into her mouth, kissing her back with everything I've got. I taste salt and realise her cheeks are wet.

'Don't cry,' I beg as I pull back to wipe at her face with my thumbs.

'I can't help it.' She laughs, pressing her mouth to mine once more. 'This is too much.' She waves the envelope in my face, laughter and tears mingling in her beautiful, expressive eyes.

'I love you.' I grip her cheeks and lock eyes with her. 'Nothing will ever be too much, ever again. I'll give you the world. I'll protect you and be there for you so you'll never be alone again. Say you'll give me another chance.'

'I love you, too,' she cries, wrapping her arms around my neck.

I spin her around, press her up against my car and kiss her the way I should have done when she confessed her feelings under the Brooklyn Bridge. Kiss her until the world starts spinning again.

When I tear my mouth from hers to lay kiss after kiss after kiss over her tear-stained face—her closed eyelids, the end of her nose—her soft laughter restarts my heart like a jolt of electricity.

'How did you do this?' she asks, shoving the deeds for the building that once housed Girasole, her parents' restaurant, at me.

'I offered the dry cleaners a price they couldn't refuse.' I shrug. 'It's only money. I'd do it a million times over for one of your smiles.'

Fresh tears glisten on her eyelashes. 'But I'm going to Italy…' Her voice is a choked whisper. 'Why couldn't you have loved me last week, before I booked the flight?' She shoves playfully at my chest, laughing through her tears in a way that tells me we're going to be okay. With her love, I can do anything. And starting today, I'll try to give her the same security.

I grin, picking her up in my arms and striding back towards her apartment. 'I *did* love you last week… I was just a distracted asshole back then.' I carry her inside, kicking the door closed behind me.

'Nothing is more important to me than you.' I press my mouth to hers. 'I'm going to stay awake all night proving that to you.' I head for her bedroom and place her on the bed. 'And then in the morning,' I cup her cheeks, 'I'm going to drive you to the airport and kiss you farewell.'

I lovingly strip her naked, quickly losing my own clothes so we're skin to skin when I cover her body with mine and push inside her.

'I'll miss you,' she whispers, her astounding eyes and the love I see reflected in their depths holding mine captive. 'I've only just found you and now I'm leaving.'

'We'll have our whole lives together,' I promise. 'You're going to teach me how to cook and I'm going to help you start a restaurant. I'll even ship your grandmother's piano to my Park Avenue apartment, where it can stay for ever, along with you, if you want. Or we can put it in the home we buy together. We'll get married and have children and work alongside each other for all of our lives.' I kiss her, pouring all of my feelings into the love we make, knowing that as much as she belongs with me, I belong with her.

EPILOGUE

Two years later
Ava

'I'M BURNING IT...' he says, stirring for all he's worth.

I laugh and lean over the stove. I'm wafted with fragrant steam from the pan of risotto—thyme, mushrooms and white wine—but more delicious than that is the gorgeous scent of my man.

My fiancé.

'You're not burning it. Smells delicious.' I stifle a yawn behind my hand. It's been a long day. The restaurant I named Hamilton's is closed but for Monroe and Hudson, who are in New York on Bold business and have come for a late supper, which Sterling is helping me to prepare.

'I think it's ready,' he says, a nervous grin stretching his mouth.

'I think you're right.' I watch in admiration as

he spoons the creamy risotto, which he learned to perfect in northern Italy last year when he visited for a few weeks of my six-month cooking odyssey, into four white bowls. With a flourish of grated parmesan and a sprig of fresh thyme, he holds his arms out wide at his achievement.

'Ta-da!' Before I can clap, he scoops me up in his arms and swirls me around in a circle. We laugh and kiss and he finally puts my feet back on the ground—although I've pretty much floated through the last two years of living my dream.

Because he's been there, too.

I press my face to his chest, above his apron, and breathe him in. He smells of bread dough and thyme. My heart clenches at how blessed I am to have found a new place to belong: running my own Brooklyn Italian restaurant and living with Sterling, my one-in-a-million man.

'You okay?' he murmurs into my hair.

I nod, looking up at him with so much happiness I could burst. 'I have something to tell you.'

He presses his mouth to mine once more and then backs me up against the scrubbed clean stainless-steel workbench. 'You do?' His mouth trails down my neck, tickling and teasing. He hoists me onto the bench and slots his hips between my thighs.

'Yes…' I drop my head back, exposing my

neck to his kisses as his hand caresses my sensitive breast through my shirt. 'There's no time for this,' I pant. 'Your risotto is getting cold.' But I grip his belt loops anyway, shunting his hips closer and grinding against him.

'They won't mind waiting,' he says about his friends, who have also become *my* friends. Who knew that it was possible to belong to multiple families? I now have three—my restaurant family, Bold and Sterling's family.

And soon there'll be a fourth.

I undo the apron strings at his back and slide my hands under his shirt to his warm skin. He's nibbling the spot on my neck that makes my toes curl and makes me gasp. It's wonderfully distracting.

'I'm pregnant,' I say as my eyes roll back in my head.

He freezes. The sublime torture of his mouth on me, the scrape of his facial hair and his hardness just where I want him between my legs stops abruptly.

'You are?' His green eyes beam. His smile is so delighted I chuckle and kiss him while nodding in confirmation.

We kiss and laugh and kiss some more until the chef in me really can't ignore the cooling risotto a moment longer.

We share goofy grins as we carry two bowls each out to the restaurant. The lights are off bar one spotlight over the window table, where Monroe and Hudson wait.

'Sterling's specialty,' I say. 'He made this all by himself.' I place a bowl in front of Monroe and Hudson then take the seat Sterling holds out for me.

'A man of many talents,' scoffs Hudson. 'Don't show up the rest of us, mate.'

Sterling kisses me and takes his seat, his smile so big I know exactly what's coming.

'I am talented.' He stares at me, his grin wide as he positively vibrates with excitement.

I chuckle and hold his eye contact, silent communication passing between us.

'So talented, in fact,' I say as Sterling lifts my hand to his lips and presses a kiss across my knuckles, 'that I'm pregnant.'

We kiss again. I can't keep my hands off him or my delight inside.

'Congratulations!' Monroe and Hudson say in unison. The four of us postpone dinner a little while longer to share hugs and handshakes.

'Of course,' pipes up Monroe, sharing an indulgent look with Hudson, 'It's women who have the real talent when it comes to procreation.' She winks at me. 'We can show them, right? Because I'm pregnant, too.'

After more laughter and hugs, we swap the wine for sparkling water and raise a toast.

'To Hamilton's, Bold and babies,' says Sterling with eyes only for me.

'To belonging,' I add, and kiss my fiancé.

*   *   *   *   *

MILLS & BOON

THE HEART OF ROMANCE

A ROMANCE FOR EVERY READER

MODERN

Prepare to be swept off your feet by sophisticated, sexy and seductive heroes, in some of the world's most glamourous and romantic locations, where power and passion collide.

HISTORICAL

Escape with historical heroes from time gone by. Whether your passion is for wicked Regency Rakes, muscled Vikings or rugged Highlanders, awak the romance of the past.

MEDICAL

Set your pulse racing with dedicated, delectable doctors in the high-pressure world of medicine, where emotions run high and passion, comfort a love are the best medicine.

True Love

Celebrate true love with tender stories of heartfelt romance, from the rush of falling in love to the joy a new baby can bring, and a focus on the emotional heart of a relationship.

Desire

Indulge in secrets and scandal, intense drama and plenty of sizzling hot action with powerful and passionate heroes who have it all: wealth, status good looks…everything but the right woman.

HEROES

Experience all the excitement of a gripping thriller, with an intense romance at its heart. Resourceful, true-to-life women and strong, fearless r face danger and desire - a killer combination!

To see which titles are coming soon, please visit

millsandboon.co.uk/nextmonth